IN EVERY
GENERATION

BUFFY FOREVER!

IN EVERY
GENERATION

KENDARE BLAKE

HYPERION

Los Angeles   New York

First Edition, January 2022
10 9 8 7 6 5 4 3 2 1
FAC-021131-21323
Printed in the United States of America

This book is set in Minion Pro, Bourbon/Fontspring; Aurelia Pro/Monotype
Designed by Tyler Nevins

Library of Congress Cataloging-in-Publication Data
Names: Blake, Kendare, author.
Title: In every generation / by Kendare Blake.
Description: First edition. • Los Angeles : Hyperion, 2022. • Audience: Ages
    14-18 • Audience: Grades 10-12 • Summary: "Follow the next generation of
    Scoobies and slayers who must defeat a powerful new evil"— Provided by
    publisher.
Identifiers: LCCN 2021027088 • ISBN 9781368075022 (hardcover) •
    ISBN 9781368075152 (ebook)
Subjects: CYAC: Fantasy. • Vampires—Fiction. • Magic—Fiction. •
    LCGFT: Vampire fiction. • Novels.
Classification: LCC PZ7.B5566 I5 2022 • DDC [Fic]—dc23
LC record available at https://lccn.loc.gov/2021027088

Reinforced binding
Visit www.hyperionteens.com

IN EVERY GENERATION

VI AND HAILEY

"Think you bought enough cereal?"

Hailey stood in the kitchen of their small apartment, unloading brown bag after brown bag of the groceries her sister had brought home that morning: three boxes of cereal—two sugary, one healthy—three loaves of bread (pop two in the freezer), three gallons of milk, which apparently she would have to drink until she died . . .

"You love cereal," Vi responded. "You can eat it for every meal." But she wasn't really paying attention. Her domestic duties fulfilled, she had already turned her attention to the more important matters at hand: loading weapons into a gray duffel.

Hailey reached into another grocery bag and pulled out handfuls and handfuls of wieners.

"Four packs of hot dogs, Vi? Seriously?"

"You love hot dogs," Vi replied. "You can eat them for every meal."

"Maybe I can dip them in milk," Hailey muttered. It was like this every three months. Before every Slayerfest (that was their name for the regular gatherings of all the remaining slayers—which usually included the legendary Buffy Summers), Vi would go into hyper-overdrive-abandonment-mom mode. She'd load Hailey down with food both healthy and junk, and triple-check all the locks on the windows and door of their cramped two-bedroom apartment on the outskirts of The Dalles, Oregon. Even though nothing—*absolutely* nothing—ever went down in The Dalles, Oregon. Vi had to drive all the way to Portland to do any decent slaying, and even then she said the vamps were weird: They took their dogs everywhere and chased victims down on pedal bikes, and half of them would only eat vegans.

Hailey sighed. Pacific Northwest vamps were one of a kind.

She turned and watched her older sister stuff the duffel with stakes, knives, crosses, and plastic bottles full of holy water. It was mostly a waste. The meetings were for training and shoptalk. The who-died-this-quarter roll call and the candlelight vigil circle for whoever did, or whatever. Hailey didn't know for certain. She'd never been allowed to go, even though she'd asked to constantly in the beginning, when she first came to live with Vi after their parents died six years ago. Well . . . *her* parents. She and Vi were half sisters. Hailey was their dad's from his second marriage. There wasn't much of a family resemblance—Vi was slim-hipped and narrow-chested, Hailey happily curvaceous. Vi had a thin, frowning mouth, while Hailey's lips were made for deep reds and sarcastic curling. She'd never really known Vi before the car accident, and when Vi came to pick Hailey up after the accident, Hailey'd thought there'd been a mistake. Until Vi had bent down and looked her in the eyes. Both girls had their father's eyes.

So off they went, two sisters against the world. Always on their own, and that had always been enough. Vi's mom was still around somewhere, but Vi kept her hidden, for her own safety. Vi liked to hide things for their own safety.

"Don't you think you should pack other things?" Hailey asked. "Like underwear and socks?"

Vi stopped and put her hands on her hips. Already she looked less like Vi and more like Vi the Slayer. Vi was lanky and pale. She walked with a slight hunch and had guarded eyes and a kind smile. Vi the Slayer was lithe as a cat. She didn't walk—she ran. She leapt. Her eyes were hard and focused.

She cocked her head at her much younger sister and smiled. "Clothes and stuff are in my backpack." She circled the room and surveyed the whole apartment—final mental checks before she'd dash out the door. "Are you all set? Food? Beverages? The internet's paid up for the next month, so I don't want to hear any excuses about falling behind like last time—"

"Last time was summer vacation." Hailey went to high school online. Which was a weird way of putting it. She didn't "go" to high school anywhere. She *did* high school from the middle cushion of their couch.

"Either way, I don't want you sitting around doing nothing but reading your comics the whole time, or traipsing around with those delinquent friends of yours. . . ." Her voice trailed off. Before the Slayerfests, she couldn't even focus long enough to nag properly.

"Comics are a valid form of literature with highly developed themes, characterization, and story arcs," Hailey said. "And those delinquents have names."

"Huh?"

"Never mind. Where is this quarter's fest anyway?"

"Halifax."

"Halifax?"

"Well, we fly into Halifax. The actual meeting is at this remote resort. Cabins in trees or something."

Hailey cocked an eyebrow. The meetings were starting to sound less like training and more like retreats. Every slayer in the world hanging out in a tree house wearing a flannel robe and a mud mask. But her only comment was:

"Long flight."

"Some of us are portaling in," said Vi. "Most of the internationals. With Andrew and the other Witchers."

"You know, he can't just call them that because they're Watchers with magic. They lack the abs. And the white hair."

Vi snorted. "I'll tell him you said so." She held her arm out. "Come here, kid."

Hailey groaned—she was sixteen, not a kid—but she went and hugged her sister tight. It hadn't been easy between them at first; Hailey'd been an angry ten-year-old, and scared. And Vi—Vi had been a young slayer, not even thirty yet, with enough on her hands trying to keep herself alive. It had taken time to figure things out. To become a real family, and a team.

"Don't answer the door without looking to see who it is first."

"Duh, I never do."

"Don't go anywhere after dark."

"Nothing ever happens here after dark."

"Don't spend all our money at the bookstore."

Hailey grinned. "Okay, I promise."

Vi let go of her and stared at her for so long that it started to get weird.

"What?" Hailey asked, and went back to the couch. "You're only going to be gone for a few days. I don't know why you think you have to feed me for two months." Except she did know why. Vi always stocked her up. Just in case she didn't make it back.

"Well," Vi said. "The way you eat . . ." She slung her backpack over her shoulders and reached down for her duffel bag. When she bent, the red roots of her hair stood out in a bright line, growing out under the dark brown dye. Hailey laughed.

"We should have dyed our hair again before you left."

"Oh yeah?" Vi touched her head.

"Yeah. You look like a rooster or something." Hailey's own hair was black naturally, inherited from her mom, who'd been Canadian and mixed-race Saulteaux First Nations. Hailey considered it a gift—it made her Goth aesthetic one step easier.

Vi put her hand on the doorknob.

"I don't know why you have to go to these anymore anyway," Hailey said. "Haven't slayers ever heard of teleconferencing?"

"Too easy to hack," Vi said quietly. "Don't you watch the news?"

"I read the news, Luddite. But even I know that demons can't hack." What had Vi told her? Most demons and vamps were terrible with gadgets. Need to figure out if your new boyfriend is a demon? FaceTime him. If all you get is thirty seconds of his forehead and a lot of saying *What?* then call your big sister to take him out.

"You're a smart kid, Hailey."

"I'm not a kid. But yeah, I know."

"I'll see you Monday."

$$\text{))} \bigcirc \text{((}$$

Except that Monday came and went.

Slayerfests had always come and gone, so often and so routinely that Hailey didn't bother keeping track of them anymore. She should have paid more attention.

On Tuesday morning, she ignored it and told herself Vi was fine. By noon, she was pacing and messaging Vi every two minutes like a desperate ex. But there was no response. There'd been no activity on Vi's accounts for days, not since a few photos she posted of her and a few other slayers hanging out in the city after their plane landed.

"It's because there's no service in a tree house," Hailey muttered. The stupid Slayerfests were always held someplace so remote.

She checked her phone again. In her gut, she knew it wasn't just a lack of service. Something was wrong.

"Screw it."

She pulled her backpack out from under her bed and dumped out the junk she usually kept in it: a small stack of graphic novels and manga, a couple of makeup bags, three studded leather bracelets, and a pair of comfy shoes. Also a notebook and some pens. Then she put back the makeup bag with the best eye-shadow palettes and all the leather bracelets and the shoes. And after a moment of consideration, her dog-eared lucky copy of *Amulet: The Stonekeeper* and the volume of My Hero Academia she hadn't finished reading yet. The rest of the space she filled with clothes: T-shirts and rolled-up jeans. Black leggings. She winced at her eyeliner in the mirror as she twisted her long black hair into a ragged ponytail—the liner was messy and smudged from worry, but she didn't care. She'd layered up in a hooded sweatshirt and was lacing her boots when someone knocked at the door.

Vi was her first thought. But that was stupid. Vi had a key.

Whoever it was knocked again, and Hailey tensed. No one in their apartment complex ever came calling.

She reached for her backpack and looked out her window. She'd never had a need to sneak out of it before, since Vi was gone so much at night anyway. But she could. Their unit was only on the second floor. She could hang and drop.

"Hailey Larsson. You in there?"

"Yeah . . ." Hailey answered hesitantly. She walked slowly to the door. It was a man's voice, and he knew her name. And she could guess who he was, by his British accent.

"It's . . . Spike," he called through the wood.

Spike. Vi's Watcher. She'd rather it was someone else. Anyone else. An intruder. A lost delivery boy. Because if Spike was there without Vi, it meant that . . .

She unlocked the door and swung it open and saw him standing there. Platinum hair. Black leather duster. A heavy blanket to shield him from the sun. And a look of grim relief to see her.

"Hailey," he said. "We have to talk."

PART ONE

WELCOME TO NEW SUNNYDALE HIGH

CHAPTER ONE
IN EVERY GENERATION

S unnydale High. It had been rebuilt so many times that it was known among the students as The Thing That Wouldn't Die. Unlike many of their classmates. But this iteration of the school had fared pretty well. Following the town's complete destruction in that freak sinkhole incident in the early 2000s, it had remained in mostly good shape. Sure, there had been some flooding in the basement when the foundation proved less than stable, but after the sinkhole, that was almost expected. And then there was that time the sewer main broke and "mudded" out the quad, but no one was hurt, and after a short symposium titled "Everybody Poops," life went on. Quietly. Serenely.

As quietly and serenely as life had ever gone on in Sunnydale, California, former home of Buffy the Vampire Slayer and her Scooby Gang, and proud former owner of its very own hellmouth. But that had been a long time ago. The Hellmouth had been destroyed, and the town rebuilt. And Sunnydale residents were of the hardy sort. The blissfully ignorant sort.

The willfully ignorant sort, Frankie Rosenberg thought as she sat in the middle of the quad watching her fellow students chew through their lunch period. The vast majority of them had no idea of their school's (and their town's) storied history. They didn't know about slayers and demons and vampires and that one time the whole town lost the ability to speak for a weekend. They didn't know, and when confronted with even a tidbit of it, they didn't seem interested in the slightest. It was the damnedest thing.

But Frankie knew. You didn't get to be the daughter of the strongest witch in a generation and walk around not knowing. So she always kept one eye on the school, just in case. She stared at it, all its fancy new marble and shiny windows and plaques commemorating civil rights leaders, looking all solid and strong and permanent.

"Don't bet on it," she whispered, and bit into her plant-based-meat sandwich.

On the other side of the quad, Jake Osbourne, the youngest werewolf of the Osbourne werewolf clan, gave a shout and tried to wave her over to where he was eating with his friends, most of them on either the boys' or the girls' lacrosse team. He had his lacrosse stick, and it looked like he and a few of his teammates were using them to pass the remains of half a sandwich back and forth.

"Frankie!" He waved his arms. But none of his friends joined in the waving; they didn't even look up.

"No," she shouted. Then she made miming motions to him that amounted to: *Why do you have your lacrosse stick at lunch? Is it attached to you?* And he mimed back what amounted to: *Huh?*

Frankie rolled her eyes. She and Jake traveled in different circles in public, but at home they'd been hanging out since they were kids and Jake's werewolf parents decided that the best play-date for a young werewolf was a young witch. And who better to chaperone that playdate than Willow Rosenberg, whose experience with werewolves went all the way back to high school and Jake's cousin, Oz.

Frankie turned around and kept eating her sandwich, just in time to see two freshman girls throwing away the trash from their lunch and completely bungling the recycling.

"Whoa, whoa!" Frankie jumped up and went over. "You can't recycle dirty plastic wrap," she explained. "You really can't recycle plastic wrap at all. This stuff is the worst. . . ."

"Sorry," said one of the girls.

"What are you, the recycling police?" asked the other.

"Yeah, kind of," Frankie said. She snatched away their soiled cardboard sandwich boxes and placed them into the compostables bin. As the girls shrugged and walked back into the school, Frankie lifted the lids of the recycling bins and sighed. A third of the contents was too dirty and greasy to salvage, and another third should have been sorted into another container.

"Need some help?" Jake asked.

"Nope," Frankie said as he poked the tip of his lacrosse stick through the refuse. "And I'd get your stick out of there if you don't want it magicked."

"Magicked?"

Frankie took a deep breath. She pulled a bundle of herbs and a lighter out of her pocket and whispered, *"Consilium depurgo."*

Then she lit the herbs and dropped them with a bright orange *poof* onto the bin of mixed recycling. A little smoke and some coughing later, and the items inside were cleaned. After that, it was just a matter of sorting them by hand.

"Frankie," Jake hissed, and blocked the smoking bin with his body. "A little discretion, maybe?"

"Calm down, nobody was looking."

15

"Did you even check? And does your mom know you're doing spells at school?"

"Yes," Frankie said, even though her mom most certainly did not. "Does Oz know you're playing with your stick at lunch?"

Jake made a face. He was a junior, and an athlete, and popular, yet somehow he still had enough time to constantly be on her case. He'd been that way since they were kids, when she was a tiny, budding witch and he was a less tiny werewolf following her around like she held an invisible leash.

"Did your mom teach you that spell?"

"Sort of." Her mom had taught her, but teaching only went so far when she refused to demonstrate anything. Willow Rosenberg had been powerful once. More powerful even than the slayer. But she'd stopped doing magic after Frankie was born, and when Frankie asked why, she would only say, "Because I don't need it anymore." Secretly, Frankie thought her mom hid her magic so Frankie would feel less pressure. And even so it still wasn't easy, taking her magical baby steps and stumbles with THE Willow Rosenberg watching.

"You're getting pretty good," said Jake.

"After many failures and herb burns," said Frankie, and rubbed at the memories of scorches on her hands. "So you can go back to your friends. It was just a little eco-witching, which my mom totally allows."

"Eco-witching?" Jake asked.

"Magic-tivism?" Frankie suggested. She squinted up at him in the sun of the quad, a pen and two pencils sticking out of the red bun on the back of her head. Jake smiled a little. He looked good. Better, these days, than he had in a long time. It had only been a year since his parents had moved to the New Zealand werewolf commune. They'd had to go, after his older brother, Jordy, had an incident with Sunnydale Animal Control. Luckily, Oz moved back to Sunnydale, so Jake didn't have to move with them.

"Are you and Oz coming over for dinner tonight?" Frankie asked.

"Are you cooking?"

"Not if you want it to be edible."

Jake snorted and stretched his broad shoulders.

"Okay," he said. "I'll make a stir-fry. Or Uncle Oz can grab veggie burgers?"

"Stop calling him your uncle. He's your cousin."

"He's too old to be my cousin."

Frankie clenched her teeth on the retort *That's not how it works, Jake* because there was a lot of math involved: Jake's brother, Jordy, who bit Oz with his first grown-up teeth and turned him into a werewolf, was ten years older than Jake. Oz was already seventeen when Jordy bit him, so that made Oz . . .

Frankie squinted. Old. That made Oz old. He was, like, a year older than her mom.

"You've got a point," she said. "There's got to be a cutoff age for cousins, and it's probably somewhere around . . . forty. Anyway, let's do burgers. Now, get out of here."

"Don't you still need help sorting?"

"I'll get my own help."

"How? You don't even know anyone in this lunch period." He looked around. That was an exaggeration. She knew lots of them. Or their names, anyway.

"Jake, go back to your friends. I'll see you after school." With an impish grin, she grabbed his lacrosse stick and held it up in the air. Jake's body tensed immediately and he half crouched, wolflike and ready to fetch. He was even more wolflike than Oz, who embraced

17

his werewolf spirit and could control it, calling it forth on command, full moon or no full moon.

Frankie waved the lacrosse stick back and forth. Every time it moved, Jake twitched.

"Okay, knock it off," he said, and she handed it over. "Have I mentioned your werewolf humor never gets old?"

"Hi, Jake!"

Frankie looked over her shoulder. Jasmine Finnegan and another pretty junior girl waved to Jake, and he nodded and said, "Hey."

"Hey, Jake," Frankie whispered. "There's one kind of magic that's always come naturally to me."

"Huh?" Jake said. "Frankie, don't—"

She fixed her eyes on the recycling bin and flicked her fingers, and the bin went sailing, spilling the contents all over the ground, right at Jasmine's and the junior girl's feet.

"Jake," Frankie fake-scolded. "You are so clumsy!"

"Oh my gosh, let us help you." Jasmine bent and immediately began picking up plastic bottles and empty cans of soda.

Frankie looked at Jake smugly. But before she could say that now she had plenty of help, what felt like a ball of cold water exploded in her gut. It hit so hard she staggered back.

"Frankie?" Jake asked.

She shivered violently as the cold spread from her stomach into her chest and down into her legs, and Jake reached out just as her world tilted and she hit the ground, jaw clenched and limbs seizing.

"Frankie, are you okay?"

"No, s-something's wrong," she stammered as he hovered over her. She heard him call for help, and his face, handsome and annoying, flickered as her vision swam. The last thing she heard was herself saying, "Remember to sort . . . properly. . . ."

And then she passed out.

CHAPTER TWO
THE LIFE, THE LEGEND, THE SLAYER

The next morning, Frankie woke up in her own bed. She lay there a minute, feeling her forehead and stretching her limbs, wiggling her toes and fingers—but all was normal. All was good. She was alive, breathing, had a pulse. She vaguely remembered Jake Osbourne drag-walking her up the front steps, and then a hazy, panicky exchange with her mom (or at least it was panicky on her mom's part). Then she remembered her bed. Cozy. Soft. She'd been out in under a minute and had slept straight through to the next day.

Whatever that unpleasant seizure had been, it had taken a lot out of her.

"Mom?" She sat up and braced for an attack of vertigo. But she felt fine. It was a little weird that her mom wasn't there, that she wasn't sitting on the edge of the bed or curled up in the chair after passing out keeping vigil. That was how it usually was, when Frankie was sick. Her mom was always on it, with a cool, wet cloth, or a hot, wet cloth, whatever kind of cloth the situation called for. She was very, very chicken-soup-to-the-rescue.

Frankie got out of bed. She tried to tie her hair back with an elastic, but the cheap thing snapped—and so did the other two she tried, fresh out of the package. So she left it down and went to brush her teeth—a little loudly to give her mom a chance to catch up on the proper sick-daughter protocol. But when she'd finished (and even finished washing her face and moisturizing), there was still no mom hovering at the door. Weird.

It was when she went back into her room to get dressed that she realized her error: The light streaming in through the windows was late-morning light—maybe even early-afternoon light. Of course her mom wasn't there. She was at work, at the lab, fussing over some new compound they were developing to increase carbon capture in depleted topsoil. Always eco-conscious. Like mother, like daughter. Or in their case, like daughter, like mother, since the planet had been Frankie's cause first.

Frankie slipped on a long-sleeved T-shirt and grabbed her favorite pair of jeans, but when she stuck her leg into them, they promptly ripped down the seam.

"How—" She stared helplessly at the torn fabric flapping against her calf. First the elastics, and now her pants? "Is everything brittle for some reason?"

After carefully putting on a looser, comfier pair of pants, she walked down their carpeted stairs, which already creaked despite being relatively new construction, and heard voices coming from the kitchen. Her mom was home after all. And she was talking to Oz. Frankie poked her head in and saw them seated around the kitchen table. And frickin' Jake was there, too.

"Uh . . ." she said, looking at Jake. "What are you still doing here? It is tomorrow, isn't it? It's not, like, still yesterday?"

"It's tomorrow," Jake said softly, and Frankie heard her mom sniffle.

In her surprise at seeing Jake right after waking up, she hadn't even noticed that her mom was crying. She was surrounded by wadded-up tissues and her nose and eyes were red, and Oz had his hand on her back. There was a phone sitting faceup in the middle of the table, and the name on the screen read "Xander."

"Mom, what's wrong?"

"It's . . ." her mom started, and her face crumpled. Frankie's started to crumple, too, even without knowing why. "It's . . . Something's happened. . . . It's your aunt Buffy. . . . She's dead."

$$\text{☽ ☽ ○ ☾ ☾}$$

Frankie's head swam. Those words . . . just didn't make sense.

Aunt Buffy couldn't die. Sure, she'd died before, a few times, but that was a really, really long time ago. Before Frankie had even been born. Ever since Frankie HAD been born, Buffy had been alive. And she'd been amazing.

"What happened?" she asked. "How? When?"

Willow stood and hugged her tight.

"It's okay," she said. She smoothed Frankie's hair. "It was a—" She took a deep breath but couldn't quite manage the words.

"It was an explosion. At the slayers meeting," said Oz gently.

"At the slayers meeting?" Frankie looked at Jake and at her mom in panic. "Who else was there? Uncle Xander? Dawn? Mom, what's going on?"

"We'll figure it out, sweetie. We've been waiting for you; we've got Xander on the line."

Frankie looked at the phone in the middle of the table. She and her mom sank down into two chairs.

"Xander, you still there?"

Muffled noises on the line, like he was picking the phone back up or pulling it out of his pocket.

"Yeah, sorry," he said. "There's a lot going on here. I put you down for a minute."

The moment she heard Xander's familiar voice, Frankie felt calm. Xander was her mom's and Buffy's best friend. He resisted the official title of Watcher (to get out of the meetings), but everyone knew that's what he really was. He would know the truth. That none of this was real. It was all a mistake. Everything was going to be okay.

"We've got Frankie now," said Willow. "She's awake."

"She's awake? And she's okay? She's not . . . She doesn't seem . . . ?"

Her mom glanced at her uncomfortably. "Not now, Xander, okay? Just tell us what's happening there."

Xander hesitated on the other end of the line. Frankie didn't understand why he'd be asking about her. Because she'd passed out at school? That wasn't important. In the last thirty seconds, she'd forgotten it had even happened.

"Uncle Xander, where are you?"

"We're a little ways outside of Halifax. It's where Slayerfest was being held, at a kind of wilderness tree-house resort or something that Andrew found. Because of the location, we're having a hard time getting access. It's nothing but tiny roads and trees up here." Another pause, and the tone of his voice no longer gave Frankie any comfort. Through the phone they could hear the sounds of sirens and movement. "It took emergency response almost an hour just to get to them."

"You haven't heard from anyone? How's Dawnie doing?" Willow asked, referring to Buffy's little sister.

"Dawn's with him?" Frankie asked, and her mom shushed her. They'd been talking to Xander while she was asleep; they knew things already. Frankie pressed her lips together, frustrated that she had to catch up. They should have woken her. They should have shaken her awake the moment they knew.

On the phone, Xander paused, like Dawn was close by and he didn't want to talk about her when she was right there. When he spoke again, Frankie could hear his sad smile. "You know Dawn. I think she's going to hijack a fire truck pretty soon if they don't let us through."

"Do you need us to come?" Oz asked. "We can get on a plane—"

"They shut down the airport. I think they'll reopen it in a few hours. But no. Don't come. If someone attacked the slayers, then they'll have no problem attacking slayer allies. Why put us all in one basket? Giles is okay. I spoke to him. He's taking what's left of the Watchers down deep."

What's left of the Watchers, Frankie thought. There were already too few of them. Gone were the days of one slayer, one Watcher. Now Watchers were stretched thin, each one doing their best to advise and assist their regiments of the slayer army. She thought of all the Watchers she had met over the years: kind, clever Mr. Giles, who'd been Buffy's Watcher and was now the head of the Watchers Council, the very Australian Mrs. Brown, and Andrew, ridiculous Andrew, who took his Watcher status far too seriously and not seriously at all. He'd been her mother's adversary once. Willow had even tried to kill him, or so he liked to tell Frankie when he was spinning tales about his days as a demon summoner.

"Giles is okay?" Her mom let out a shaky breath, and Frankie took her hand.

"Yeah," said Xander. "He said to tell you . . . He said to say he'd see you soon."

"Soon," Willow said, but it didn't sound like soon to Frankie.

"Listen, Will, I've got to go. It's going to be a while before we know anything, but I'll call as soon as we do. Just stay put. Hey, Frankie?"

"Yeah?"

"You okay, kiddo?"

Frankie opened her mouth, but she couldn't speak.

"I mean, you don't feel weird, or woozy? Or . . . freakishly strong?"

"She'll be okay, Xander," her mom said quickly.

"Okay. Will . . . I'm glad you're not alone."

"I'm glad you're there. Xander . . . be careful."

They heard him breathe, and then the line went quiet and the call ended. Just like that, they were cut off from the sounds, from the knowing, from the one place where it felt like they needed to be.

"Can we . . . do anything?" Frankie asked. She looked at her mother. "Can you?"

Her mom shook her head, the corners of her mouth pulled down. Willow Rosenberg had not done magic in years. But even had she been at the height of her powers, it wouldn't have helped. Frankie knew the rules. The rules of mystical death could sometimes be bent. But mortal, human death was law.

"Well, we need to do something," said Frankie. "Like start finding our friends."

"We're doing that," said Oz. "We already heard from Spike. He's on his way here. Said he needed to pick up a girl first."

"Another slayer?" Frankie asked. "Who wasn't at the meeting?"

"He didn't say."

Frankie looked around the room. There was so much urgency running through her, a refusal to give in to the panic and dread. She couldn't believe they were all just standing in the kitchen. She couldn't believe there was nothing to do but wait.

It had to be a mistake. Buffy scared demons away just by staring them down. She blew them apart with bazookas.

"She can't be dead."

Jake lifted his forefinger and said, "Seconded."

Frankie smiled weakly. She was glad he was there. Aside from her mom, and Oz, Jake was the only person in Sunnydale who knew who Buffy was, and what the loss of her meant.

"Okay." Jake pushed his chair away from the table. Jake was always restless, full of boundless, canine energy. "I've got to do something. Anybody want some tea?" Someone must have nodded, because he got up to make it while Frankie stared at her phone. She thumbed through the last text string she had with Buffy—just a bunch of dumb memes—and willed it to chime with something new. After a while, she didn't know how long, she heard Jake say, "I'm going to do the dishes." That boy couldn't sit still for two minutes, even at a time like this.

Frankie looked at her mom's phone, waiting for Xander to call back. How long had it been since she'd spoken to him? Months? Had it really been since the start of summer? She hadn't spoken to Buffy either, in at least that long. They were all so busy, managing their slayers all over the world.

"Mom," Frankie said. "What did Xander mean on the phone?"

Willow stiffened.

"What do you mean, sweetie?"

"I mean that weird stuff he was saying. Asking me if I was woozy. Or strong."

"I don't know," her mom said, but Oz cast her a look from the kitchen.

"Will," he said. "Maybe you should consider it."

"Consider what?" her mom asked innocently.

"I'm just saying. After what happened to her yesterday."

25

"What are you guys talking about?" Frankie asked.

"Yeah," Jake said. He walked over to Frankie, drying his hands on a kitchen towel.

"It's nothing." Willow stood up. "Frankie is a normal kid. She's always been a normal kid."

"With witch powers," said Oz.

"*Some* witch powers. But not like—"

"Not like you had," he finished.

Frankie wanted to say, *Gee, thanks, guys*, but wisely held her tongue. If she spoke now, her mom would remember she was there and Oz would never get her to fess up to whatever she was clearly trying to avoid saying.

"She was sick all the time in elementary school." Willow crossed her arms and paced a little. "And she was . . . clumsy even. Not like the Potentials, who were never sick and pretty athletic."

"Potentials?" Jake asked. "Like, Potential Slayers? The girls mystically chosen at birth to be the next slayer if the one in line before her dies?" He and Frankie looked at each other. The existence of Potentials was just an idea to them—by the time they'd been born, there were no "Potentials." There were just slayers. Willow had activated every single one when she'd channeled the source of the slayer's power through the Scythe to create the slayer army.

"Look, I'm no scholar . . ." Jake went on.

"That's an understatement," said Frankie.

"But I've always been under the impression that Buffy and the slayer army were it. Like the Scythe said, 'Yahtzee! You get them all! But use them wisely, because that's all there is.'"

Willow pulled her hands into her sleeves, which caught Frankie's eye. It was never a good sign when her mom reverted to nerdy awkwardness.

"That's not exactly true," Willow said. "Or at least we were never sure. We had all these theories . . ."

Frankie knew the theories. That the slayer line was finished, like Jake said. The power exhausted. Or that somewhere in the army of slayers was the last Potential to be called, and when she died, the line would continue and a new slayer would rise. That's the one that Frankie believed. And others did, too: Mr. Giles cast a locator spell every time they lost a slayer. But so far, no new slayer had been found.

"But now," said Oz, "after the explosion . . ."

The explosion, and all the slayers dead. That was her least favorite theory. That the slayer line was dormant. That it would remain dormant until every slayer had died. And then, and only then, would the line begin again.

Jake leaned back and ran his hands through his messy red-gold hair.

"So you think," he said, "that might really be it? That the slayer line might have woken up? And now—" He frowned. Beside him, Oz frowned. Oz's hair was its natural red these days, but the Osbourne family resemblance was never more clear than when they were side by side, eyes half-squinted and shifty.

"A new Potential," Jake whispered.

Something nudged at the back of Frankie's brain, something about snapped hair elastics and torn jeans.

"Why?" Frankie said loudly, over her mom's protests. "Why would you think that I, of all people, would be a Potential Slayer?"

"Not 'potential,'" said Oz. "Just slayer. *The* slayer now."

The slayer, as in, the one girl in all the world. Like Buffy had been.

"Why," Frankie said again, looking at her mother, "would you think it would be me?"

Willow visibly shrank, and her red hair fell across her face in a partial curtain. But Frankie only leaned in closer. That cute nerdy crap might work on Oz, but it wouldn't fly with her own kid, who knew exactly what her mom was capable of.

"Will," said Oz gently. "I think you have to tell her."

"I think all werewolves should go home now," Willow said, and arched her brow. But then she sighed. She looked at Frankie. "Okay. Sit down."

"I am sitting."

"Sit down harder?" her mom offered, and gingerly took a seat across the table. She slid her hand over Frankie's. "This is going to sound strange, but when I did the spell with the slayer Scythe, I channeled the energy of the slayer through it. And through me." She made a face between a grimace and a smile. "And into me?"

"Whoa," said Jake.

"Wait, Mom. What does that mean?" But Willow was rattled, and starting to ramble.

"It wasn't until months after the Scythe spell that I even realized I was pregnant, and even then I didn't put it together right away, because it just didn't seem possible—I thought, 'Maybe it was someone else,' even though I hadn't been with anyone but Kennedy and she—"

"Hang on," said Frankie. "What are you saying? Who is my dad?"

"You know once upon a time, I could have been your dad," said Oz.

"Dude," Jake whispered. "Not now. And also: ew. Please never speak of your sex life. With Frankie's mom." But they all knew the story: How Oz had been Willow's first boyfriend. How the werewolf thing had eventually come between them (though neither would say in exactly what way). And then, after Oz left to try to tame the beast inside, Willow met Tara, another witch, and they fell in love.

And then when Tara was killed, Willow turned to dark magic and became the ultimate evil. You know, very typical first-love stuff.

"And it took a long time for you to be born—I mean, a long time—" Willow continued, and Oz leaned in.

"Fourteen months, according to a calendar Xander kept."

"—and we weren't sure what you would be when you came out, if you would even be human—"

"What?" asked Frankie. Fourteen months of pregnancy? Not human? "How is this all news to me right now?" But her mom just plowed ahead.

"Buffy and Xander and I baby-proofed the entire house. Even the mobile. And I got super strong right before you were born. One time, Xander was late with the Chinese takeout, and when he pulled into the driveway, I tore the door off his car."

Frankie looked at Jake with wide eyes and he mouthed, "Bad. Ass."

Then Willow smiled, apparently at the end of her story.

"But then you were born. And you were just you. Just Frankie."

Just Frankie. Frankie, who had been conceived during a huge, mystical slayer spell and might or might not be human.

"Mom," Frankie said again. She was losing her patience. "Who is my dad?"

"The original slayer," her mom blurted finally. "The essence of the original slayer, Sineya, is your . . . other parent."

Frankie sat back.

"Whoa," Jake said.

"So now you see," said Oz. "You might be it now. You might be a slayer. The only slayer."

CHAPTER THREE

SO IT WASN'T AN ASTRONAUT

Frankie sat at the table, numb. Willow, Oz, and Jake stared at her in silence. Frankie, a slayer. It was a ridiculous idea. And the original slayer, the mythical original slayer, was her other parent? Frankie stood and shoved her chair back so hard it flew into the wall and cracked the plaster.

"Well, that seems to answer the question," said Oz.

But Frankie refused to look at the crack. "Mom, you always told me you were artificially inseminated! By a donor who was an astronaut! The astro-donor! We made up stories about him, that he was going to be looking down from orbit someday, watching me save the world!"

"Well, you still will be doing that," said Jake.

"Saving the world through green energy innovation, Jake," Frankie snapped. "Not by slaying demons!" She slammed her hands down on the table and felt it quake. Everyone in the room froze at the impact, like they expected the table to break in two.

"It's not for sure," Willow said.

"Looks for sure." Oz cocked an eyebrow.

"You should have told me," said Frankie. "Why didn't you tell me?"

"I hoped I wouldn't have to."

"Mom, that is so stupid!" Frankie said. "Before you were this great witch, weren't you like a total genius or something?"

"I was smart, but I wasn't a genius. . . . And hey, language, missy!"

"You weren't a genius," Oz interjected. "But you were basically a brainiac."

"That's what I said," said her mom.

"No, you said smart. And there's smart, brainiac, and genius. There are levels."

"Hello?" Frankie waved her hands in front of their faces. Her head spun. She tried to remember what it had felt like when she collapsed in the quad, if she had heard a voice or seen a flash that would support their wild theory. She wanted to call Buffy and ask her if that's what it had felt like when she became a slayer. She even reached for her phone before she realized there was no one on the other end to call.

"This isn't happening." She tried to imagine the original slayer, that long-ago girl who had been bound by men and infused with the essence of demons in order to gain the power to fight them. She tried to think of her as a parent. But the original slayer was African. And Frankie didn't look like she was biracial; she looked . . . well, she looked very much like Willow's daughter: small-boned, red hair, big eyes.

Frankie slid down onto her chair again, forgetting she had thrown it into the wall. But Jake was paying attention and deftly placed another one under her butt.

From somewhere in the distance, they heard a car pull into their driveway, but Frankie barely noticed. Her mom didn't seem

31

to either. She nudged Frankie gently aside and perched on the same chair.

"Uh, someone's here," said Jake.

Frankie was vaguely aware of him going to the door, and of Oz going with him. In the corner of her eye, she saw them stand up straighter and tense, sniffing the air as they looked out the window.

"They're very wolfy," Willow said quietly, half watching them, too. "It's going to be okay, sweetie."

"It's Spike," Oz said.

"He's got the girl with him," said Jake, and sniffed the window.

"You can smell that through the window?" Frankie asked numbly.

"No, but I can see it through the window."

Oz opened the door, and Spike ran inside, just a pair of slightly steaming legs under a blanket. Not that much steam, though, as it was almost sunset. He threw the blanket off onto the floor and looked at Willow.

"How you doing, Red?"

Her mom shrugged. "How are you?"

"I'm right as the mail. Because she's not dead. She can't be."

"She can't be?" Frankie asked hopefully, and Spike looked immediately regretful that he'd said so.

"Barely saw you there, Mini Red. Sunk down in that chair like you are." He gave her a smile. "I meant she can't be dead to me. Because to me, she's immortal." He looked back at Frankie's mom. "But now that you mention it, no, I don't think she's dead. Every slayer, killed in an explosion, like a bunch of bloody Watchers? It seems . . . downright disrespectful."

"Haven't you been a Watcher for like ten years now?" Oz asked.

"Not like they were. Tweed and books and no calf muscles. Hey, Oz." They shook hands, and he nodded to Jake. It had been a long time since they'd seen Spike—he was Watcher to several slayers and split time between LA and New York and even Baton Rouge, Louisiana—but he was always the same. Platinum-blond hair, leather duster, his clothes black, black, and more black. "Have you heard from Xander or Dawn? Any of the others?"

"Xander and Dawn are in Halifax now," Frankie's mom said. "They won't leave without answers. And if anyone got out, they'll find them."

"Did anyone get out?"

Frankie craned her neck. The girl Spike had needed to pick up on the way was standing behind him. She was wearing an unseasonably warm hoodie pulled up over straight black hair, and she was very pretty. Frankie didn't recognize her, but something about the cagey, quiet way she surveyed the entryway to their house felt familiar, and without asking, Frankie knew that the girl had grown up knowing about vampires and slayers just like she had.

"Who's this?" her mom asked.

"This is Hailey Larsson," Spike said. "Vi Larsson's little sister."

"I didn't know Vi had a little sister."

"She didn't like to tell people about me." The girl crossed her arms. The thick rubber soles of her combat boots squeaked against the floor.

"She barely told me," said Spike. "Vi kept her two lives separate. And remote. You should've seen the tiny town I had to scoop this niblet out of in-the-middle-of-nowhere Oregon."

"I'm no niblet," the girl said quietly. She looked at Willow. "And my sister just wanted to keep me safe."

"Well, sure," said Willow. "That's . . . what a responsible sister would do." She stood up and started to gesture around the room to introduce them. "We're—"

"I know who you are." The girl looked at each of them in turn, starting with Oz. "Daniel 'Oz' Osbourne. Werewolf."

"Uh, yeah," said Oz. "Also youth counselor, and player of guitars?"

The girl ignored him and looked at Frankie's mom.

"Willow Rosenberg. Witch who activated my sister and nearly ended the world. Though that's harder to believe now, since you're so . . ." She gestured to Willow's clothes, a dark green cardigan over a long, dark blue dress embroidered with lighter blue flowers, and Willow tugged awkwardly at the collar. Then the girl looked at Frankie.

"I don't know who you are," she said. "But you look like a little one of her." She pointed to Frankie's mom again. "So you must be . . . ?"

"Her daughter," said Frankie. "I'm Frankie Rosenberg."

The girl raised her chin. But then she nodded.

"I'm Hailey. Hi."

"Hi."

"Who's the jock?" Hailey motioned toward Jake, and he gave a small salute.

"Jake Osbourne. Also werewolf," he said. "And, erm, player of lacrosse."

"Cool." Hailey jerked a thumb in the direction of Spike. "So, this guy says you can help me find my sister."

Spike rubbed his forehead. "Yeah, sorry about that, everyone. She's a real delight. The drive down here was . . . Let's just say I nearly stuck my hand out into the sun just for a refreshing change of pace."

"Spike," Willow scolded. "She's just upset. Like we all are." She got up and went to rub Hailey's shoulder as Spike muttered, "No, I think she's just like this. . . ."

"Can we get you anything?" Willow said, changing the subject.

"Jake can make more tea, or he can make you something to eat? He's good with the cooking-type things. Or we have sodas?"

"No, thanks." Hailey stuffed her hands into the pockets of her sweatshirt, and Willow stopped rubbing her shoulder. "I just want to find my sister."

"Okay. Are you sure? We have sparkling water . . . kombucha . . ."

"Got any cocoa?" Spike asked. "With the tiny marshmallows?"

"Of course," said Willow.

"And I went out and got some blood, too," said Oz.

"Oooh, blood, too." Spike slipped out of his jacket as he followed them to the kitchen. "So you two shacking up these days, mate?" he asked, eyes darting between Oz and Willow.

Willow caught the look.

"What? No!"

"No," said Oz.

"No, no," added Willow, for emphasis. "Also, hi, I'm gay?"

"I meant shacking up non-sexually," said Spike. "Since Oz is fresh back in Sunnydale and you both have the kiddos."

"Jake and I have our own place a few streets down," said Oz. "And I guess we are here a lot, now that I think about it."

In the entryway, Jake held out his arm to invite Hailey farther inside.

"So, this must be pretty strange," he said. "I'm sorry about your sister."

"We don't know that there's anything to be sorry about," Hailey said, her voice low. Then she looked at Frankie, and her expression softened. "But I'm sorry about your . . . Buffy."

"Like you said, we don't know. We're not giving up." Frankie nodded to her, and Hailey nodded back and came into the kitchen, boots clomping. It didn't take long for Jake to get the hot water going, fix Spike's cocoa, and sprinkle it with marshmallows. Frankie watched Hailey quietly as Hailey watched Jake move around the kitchen. It had to be a lot for her, dragged out of her home by a vampire and brought into a house full of people she didn't know. And all of them a little supernatural.

Or a lot supernatural, Frankie thought. She allowed herself a glance at the wall behind her and the crack from when she'd shoved her chair into it. But no. That couldn't be. It was a mistake. It was her witch magic—she'd thrown the chair telekinetically; she was always doing that. Except she had never thrown anything that size. And never that hard.

The stove turned off, and a moment later, Oz came to the table stirring a mug of warmed blood. He set it down before Spike, and to Frankie's horror, the vampire happily added it to his cocoa.

"I'm gonna barf," said Hailey.

"Don't knock it till you've tried it," said Spike, and drank.

They sat in the quiet. Long beats of time, searching for the right thing to say. Waiting for a phone to buzz.

"So how's your cocoa?" Willow finally asked.

"How's my bloody cocoa?" Spike pushed it away. "Honestly, Red, now's not the time for small talk. Where's bloody Giles and little Andrew? Have you heard from Kennedy or Faith? I'd even take a check-in from bloody Angel about now."

"That's a lot of 'bloody's,'" said Oz.

"We've only heard from Giles and Xander," Willow said. "We don't know any more than you do. Just that it was an explosion."

"A bomb? Like a regular, disgusting man-made bomb, or like a psychic, mystical bomb?"

"Would one be better than the other?" asked Willow.

"Well, yeah, actually," said Spike. "If something's going to take out slayers, it should be from their own bloody wheelhouse. They've got enough to deal with, without worrying about bombs . . . or guns. . . ."

"We don't know yet," said Willow. "We just . . . don't know yet."

Across the table, Hailey looked from Spike to Willow and back again.

"I thought you said they'd know what to do."

"There's nothing to do," he said, "but wait."

Hailey shook her head and shrugged. "No way."

"I kind of agree," said Oz, and looked at Willow in that way he had, like he was waiting for her to say something.

"What?" Spike asked. "Is something else going on?" And then he looked right at Frankie.

"What, so you know, too?" she asked. "Have you known this whole time?"

"Known what?" Hailey asked. She turned toward Frankie. "I'm sorry, is it private? Only they're talking about it right in front of me, so I guess I don't care. . . . Known what?"

"That Frankie was conceived when I channeled the energy of the slayer through the Scythe," Willow explained, eyes downcast. "That she might be involved in the line of slayers."

"Involved?" Hailey asked.

"Yeah. More like I *am* the line of slayers. The next one. The only one."

"Well, is she or isn't she?" Spike looked at Frankie. "Not to be in a hurry, but the calling of a new slayer would be a pretty decent source of comfort. Do you feel any different, Mini Red?"

"No," Frankie said, and made a noise between a snort and a guffaw.

"She collapsed yesterday," said Jake.

"Jake!" Frankie snapped.

"What? He's going to find out anyway."

"That could've just been from the spell. I've never cleaned that much recycling at once before!"

"Spell?" her mom asked. "What spell?"

Before Frankie could explain, Hailey shoved herself away from the table and stood.

"I don't know what you're all talking about, but I'm done listening."

"Hailey—" Spike got up to follow her as she headed for the door. "Wait."

She spun.

"Back off, Beatlemania! Vi hasn't been missing for a day and already you're searching around for her replacement." Frankie stood, and Hailey pointed an accusing finger at Spike. "You are the WORST Watcher!"

"Hey!" Spike pointed a finger back. "*Wesley* was the worst Watcher."

Hailey made a disgusted face.

"You're all worthless. And I'm not staying. If none of you are going to help me find Vi, I'm going to find her myself."

"I'm going, too," Frankie said. She went to Hailey and stood beside her, much to the girl's surprise. "You keep talking about your wild theories, and it isn't true! Because if a new slayer is called, it means the old ones are—" She swallowed. "And they're *not*."

"That's not what it means," said her mom. "That might not be what it means."

"And even if it is," said Oz, "it's not your fault."

Frankie wiped at her cheeks.

"Let's get out of here," she said to Hailey. "I'll show you the fastest way to the bus station."

CHAPTER FOUR

NEW SUNNYDALE, LIKE THE OLD SUNNYDALE

Frankie and Hailey hurried through the front door and slammed it behind them. As they walked quickly down the street, Frankie tried to ignore the feeling of adrenaline in her body. She felt lighter, and faster, and healthier than she ever had, like she could jump a mile. Instead, she focused on the upset girl beside her. They'd barely made it down the driveway when she heard the door open and shut again, and Jake reached them in a few fast strides.

"You're not leaving me back there with the parents."

"Are they following us?" Frankie asked. She couldn't believe the adults had just let them go. Especially Spike.

"Well . . ." Jake glanced toward Hailey, who had gotten several steps ahead on her longer legs. "You're not really going to take her out of town, are you?"

"I don't know," Frankie muttered. Hailey had a right to want to find her sister. And she looked like she could take care of herself. She was taller than Frankie and walked with an easy confidence. Her scowl alone was enough to put off most of the weaker demons.

"Hey," Hailey called over her shoulder. "I might not have were-wolf hearing, but I am only ten feet away."

Frankie narrowed her eyes at Jake, and he mouthed, "Sorry," and she tightened her lips and mouthed other words back at him that included "idiot" and "you" as they jogged to catch up.

"But what *are* they doing back there?" Hailey asked. "Are they following us?"

"Nah," said Jake. "Spike wanted to, but Oz assured him that the Hellmouth was closed and there was nothing to worry about. Then he said that the three of them were the baddest things left in Sunnydale, and they started arguing over which one was the baddest. 'I could dust you, full moon or no full moon,' 'I'd have you on a leash in ten minutes.' They're just trying to cheer each other up. They don't know . . . anything."

"You'd better hope you're not the new slayer," Hailey said to Frankie. "Or good luck staying alive with *that* crack team looking out for you."

"Please," said Frankie. "I'm not the new slayer. Do I look like the new slayer?" The question was mostly rhetorical, but Frankie had to admit she was curious. What *did* she look like to an outsider? People at New Sunnydale High had gotten used to her eco-conscious, slightly-bossy-about-her-point-of-view demeanor; they knew not to mess with her when it came to celebrating Earth Day or starting the school composting project. But no one ever thought of her as physically tough or gifted; she didn't get picked first for teams in gym. For the most part Frankie was overlooked, except when Jake drew eyes to her by his mere proximity—and to be honest, that was just the way she liked it.

"Not exactly." Hailey made as if to hit Frankie, and Frankie flinched hard. "You ever even been in a fight?"

Frankie shook her head.

"Well, I guess that doesn't mean anything. My sister, Vi, doesn't look like much either, until there's a demon in her face. Then it's awkward nerd to iron ballerina in the space of a kick. I think that's just how it works. Not every slayer has to be a superbabe from the get-go."

"Lucky for you, eh, Frankie?" said Jake, and Frankie punched him in the arm. It nearly doubled him over.

"Crap." She grabbed him and rubbed the sore spot. "Sorry." But he'd deserved it, saying Frankie was no superbabe. . . . Fine, maybe that was true, but she was no *un*superbabe—she'd always thought of herself as perfectly presentable. Cute even, in the right lighting.

"Don't worry about it," Jake said, wincing. "You always hit that hard; it doesn't mean anything."

"Right," said Hailey, and rolled her eyes at them both. "So you've never known," she said to Frankie, "that you could be next in line?"

"No. No way. I've just been . . . nothing."

"But you are a witch," Hailey said. "He said you collapsed after doing a spell."

"Yeah, just an eco-spell. Which is barely a spell. Magic to help the planet, not to help myself."

"An eco-witch." Hailey gave Frankie an up-and-down assessment, eyes lingering on her loose-fitting, dye-free hemp pants. "Yeah, that tracks. So what's the fastest way out of town? You said something about a bus station?"

"Yeah, it's this way." They walked down the block, but Frankie tried to slow their pace. Now that her head had stopped spinning, she could think again, and Jake was right; it probably wasn't a great idea to let Hailey go off on her own. But they couldn't make her stay if she didn't want to. "You could always hang around, you know. We really won't stop until we figure out what happened to the slayers."

"Listen," Hailey said. "You guys seem really nice and everything. But I've never been the type to stand by."

"Have you trained a lot with your sister?" Jake asked.

"Vi would never let me. She was a slayer by the book. I got into my own trouble." Hailey gave Jake a wink, and to Frankie's surprise, he kind of blushed. All the way up to the roots of his reddish-gold hair. "Vi is all I have, okay? We're all we have. I'm her half sister through our shared dad, and he and my mom died in a car accident when I was ten. We've been together ever since."

"Whoa," said Jake. "I'm really sorry."

"Yeah," said Frankie. "That's awful."

They walked in the quiet dark for a few moments, through the new development of houses that Frankie and Willow lived in. New Sunnydale Heights. One of many new developments in town, along with the new shopping center, the new arts district, the new farmers markets . . . everything new, since everything old had collapsed into the Hellmouth in the great Spikesplosion of 2003.

"So, do you know much about Sunnydale?" Frankie asked.

"Not much," said Hailey. "Vi said she came here to train before she was activated. She said your mom and Buffy took good care of them. That it was kind of like summer camp, just with a slightly higher chance of death."

Frankie snorted. That sounded about right, from the stories she'd heard.

"And she said the whole thing was destroyed in the fight with the First Evil. And the . . ." She made fang gestures with her fingers. "Über vamps, or super vamps, or whatever." She looked around at the development. "Yet here it is, all not destroyed and everything."

"Welcome to New Sunnydale," said Jake, and stretched his arms out to the houses around them. "Everything shiny and modern and bright, to make everyone forget about the old Sunnydale that New

Sunnydale is built on top of. My parents used to say the mayor back then was really 'captains of industry' about it. Saw it as a chance to build something fresh and futuristic, that would stand the test of time. But all these houses were built like crap. Practically made of paper, like no one expected them to last at all."

"Makes sense," said Hailey glumly. "After a town sinks into a hole once, you're naturally going to be a little pessimistic. And why do they call this development Sunnydale Heights? Shouldn't it really be called Sunnydale Slope? Shouldn't the whole town be called New Sunnydale Valley?"

"A few years ago, someone went out to the interstate and spray-painted the welcome sign to read 'Welcome to Sunnyhole' and I thought that was pretty accurate," Jake said. "What about where you're from? Spike said he picked you up in Oregon?"

"Yeah," said Hailey. "The Dalles. There's less there than there is here. But I liked it. We liked it." She smiled a little, which Frankie took as a good sign. "Until that pale limey jackass dragged me out of there and brought me here."

"You know," Frankie said, searching for ways to make Hailey feel better, "Spike died here once."

"What do you mean?"

"She means the Spikesplosion," Jake supplied. "The collapse of the Hellmouth. He did that. He had this wicked, big, mystical amulet and it burned up all the uber vamps, and him, and BOOM! Spikesplosion. Hellmouth closed. Spike reduced to particles."

"Hang on, then who was that guy who just drove me to your house?"

"That was Spike," said Frankie. "He was resurrected not long after the explosion by the Powers That Be, and now he's back. He's been back, like, the whole time I've been alive. So I guess it's not weird to me?"

"Well, it is weird," said Hailey. "Just so you know."

They walked on, and with every step, Frankie felt worse as Hailey's frown deepened.

"I never met Vi," Frankie said quietly. "At least, not that I remember. Some of the Potentials have come to check in on their way to this place or that . . ." Or just to relax. With the Hellmouth shut down, and the great Willow Rosenberg in residence, Sunnydale had become sort of a slayer haven. Her mom used to joke about starting SlayAirbnb, for when a slayer needed a vacation. "What was she like?"

"What she IS like," Hailey said, and Frankie winced, "is a great slayer. And a great sister."

This wasn't going well. Frankie looked at Jake for help, but he only frowned and shook his head to reiterate how well she was not doing.

"Look," she said. "I know it's not the same thing, you losing your parents and having just Vi, and now not knowing where Vi is—but we've all kind of had weird families—"

"My parents left me to live with my screw-up older brother in a werewolf commune," said Jake.

"And I only had my mom," Frankie said.

"You're right." Hailey stopped and looked at her. "It's not the same thing."

"I'm just saying that we kind of know how it would feel . . . to . . ." Frankie sputtered out. She shouldn't have tried to say anything. Hailey was too hurt, too tough, and she'd been on her own with her sister too long—she looked like she was the same age as Frankie and Jake, but she acted a lot older.

"Hey," Jake said. "She's just trying to—"

"I know what she's trying to." Hailey sighed and pressed a gentle fist against Frankie's shoulder. "And I appreciate it. I'm just not in a place to really appreciate it right now."

"Okay," said Frankie. "I'm sorry."

"Don't be sorry. I'm sorry. Look, let's just settle on 'all our lives are screwed up and today was a really crap day' and try to get through the night, all right?"

Frankie and Jake agreed. They left New Sunnydale Heights behind and skirted the edge of the arts district, past the public library all fitted out in sandstone and silver accents. It was nice, but it felt so . . . clean. Soulless. Just like the school felt. At least the old Sunnydale had character. History. Pizzazz.

Of course, it also had the dead rising every Tuesday.

The bus station wasn't far ahead, and Frankie was beginning to despair of convincing Hailey to stay with them and figure things out. And maybe she was wrong to do that. Maybe she and Jake should just get on a bus with her and go. Head to Halifax and find Xander and Dawn and get some answers. Or there were other places they might try, slayer safehouses all over the country: one on Benefit Street, in Providence. Or closer, in Frogtown in LA. But when they got to the station and the ticket machines, Frankie looked at Jake and shook her head. Frankie couldn't leave her mom. Jake couldn't leave Oz. And Sunnydale . . . she didn't feel like she could leave Sunnydale either.

"Hailey, wait," Frankie said. But it was too late. The ticket to LA was already out of the machine and in her hand.

So they wandered around to wait. It was going to be a while before Hailey's bus showed up.

"Hey," Jake said quietly while they walked. "You doing okay?"

"I guess," said Frankie. "What about you? Buffy was your aunt as much as she was mine." How many times had Buffy practiced front kicks and punches with the little werewolf in the Rosenberg backyard? How many stories had Jake listened to her tell around the dinner table whenever she came home to visit?

A lot. Jake's parents were honestly kind of negligent, Frankie realized. But they had always had their hands more than full with Jordy.

"No, she wasn't," Jake said. "Not quite. But yeah, I'm doing okay. I'm glad Oz is here for your mom."

"You guys seem to be getting along better," Frankie said.

Jake shrugged. "I love Oz. It's just taken a while to get used to not having my parents around."

"But now you guys are a thing. The were-bachelors. Cooking and cleaning and bro-ing out—locking yourselves in cages once a month . . ."

Jake grinned, even though Oz didn't need a cage anymore. He'd mastered his werewolf spirit through herbs and chanting. After Jake's own werewolf spirit matured, Oz would teach him how to do it, too. But they'd never been able to teach Jake's older brother, Jordy. That guy just liked to bite. Which is why Jake's parents had to move with him to the werewolf commune.

"Do you . . . miss your parents?" she asked.

"What's to miss?" he said, but she could tell by the look on his face that he did. "They were so caught up in what Jordy was up to they were practically never around anyway. Maybe if I'd refused the cage, gone feral, they'd have—" He shook his head.

"But you're not like that," said Frankie. "You're like Oz."

"Yeah. Sure am. And I guess I do miss them. I guess I even miss Jordy. So maybe I do know a little bit about what Hailey's going through."

Frankie glanced at Hailey, who had moved away to give them a little privacy, or possibly just to kick at the soda machine like she was trying to get a Coke to come out even though Frankie hadn't seen her put in any money. In ripped jeans and boots, Hailey looked like someone who had learned how to keep her own secrets. Frankie, too, had learned early on to bite her tongue when it came to magic and demons, things that other people ignored. But she could still see that Hailey was scared. Not even heavy black eyeliner could disguise that much worry.

"Hailey," she said. "Are you sure you're going to be okay? It might not be safe, traveling alone right now."

"The world's never safe." She shrugged and cocked half a smile in Frankie's direction. The smile didn't light up her face exactly. It didn't even really make her look less mad. But it still made Frankie smile back.

They left the small bus depot and wove through the parked silver buses. There were a surprising number of them, sitting empty or idling, waiting to take off for their next stop. Jake sniffed the air and crinkled his nose. He probably didn't care for the smells of gasoline and grease.

"If you decide to stay in LA, let us know, okay?" Frankie asked. "My mom still has some friends in the area, and they can help you out if you need it."

"Okay."

"Head to the main office of Angel Investigations," she said, and gave Hailey the address. "I don't know who's running it these days, but they'll give you a place to crash, especially if you act really helpless—they live for that."

"Okay."

"You'll probably run into a ton of demons down there. I hear LA is pretty wild, but if you throw my mom's name around, maybe they won't bother you."

"Okay."

Frankie pursed her lips. Hailey wasn't going to be deterred.

"All right, then. At least at this hour, the bus should be pretty roomy," Frankie went on, figuring she might as well switch to small talk. "Would you rather we'd gone to the airport? I'm sorry; we didn't even ask."

"It's fine." Hailey shrugged. "The bus is cheaper."

"I like buses," said Jake, trying to be helpful.

"Statistically speaking, planes are safer," Frankie pointed out.

"Yeah, but I feel like if the bus driver dies, I could probably guide the bus off the highway. Whereas if a pilot died, I could only scream and aim for an unpopulated area."

Jake sniffed the air. This time, Frankie couldn't help but comment.

"Is the bus stop offending your delicate olfactory sensibilities?"

"No," he said. "I smell something." He sniffed again. "I smell blood."

"He can smell that well even when he's not in wolf form?" Hailey asked as Jake took off toward it.

"Yeah, his senses are way good," Frankie replied. "Because he was born a werewolf instead of being turned into one. . . . It's a long story."

They jogged all the way past the last of the buses, around the side of the maintenance garage and the stacks of bus tires and pallet wood. What they saw around the back of it stopped them cold.

Three vampires were feeding on the night station clerk. They had him pressed up against the chain-link fence and drank from three bites: one in his neck, and one on each arm.

"Oh, shoot," said Hailey. "Is that . . . ?"

"Yeah," said Jake.

The vampires turned. They let the dead clerk drop to the dirt and smiled and wiped their mouths. Frankie could practically read their minds: three kids for three vamps, no sharing required.

"Out a little late, aren't you?" the leader asked. Or at least Frankie assumed she was the leader, since she'd been the one feeding at the neck.

"It's, like, nine thirty," Jake said. "What are you doing here? You're not supposed to be here—the Hellmouth is closed."

"Closed," the vampire said. "Not gone. Not gone like the slayers are gone."

Frankie's mouth dropped open; in the corner of her eye, she saw Hailey clench her fists.

"How did they find out so fast?" Jake asked Frankie. "Is there a vampire Twitter?"

"Vamps don't like technology," Hailey said. "But if they did, they should call it Vampchat. Like Snapchat." She started backing up. "Is now not the time to be joking? Because with you people it's hard to tell. . . ."

"You shouldn't be here," Frankie shouted, and hoped her voice sounded angry instead of scared. "Sunnydale belongs to Buffy Summers! Sunnydale is off-limits!"

"Buffy Summers is dead." The vampire smiled, and a lump of mad hurt rose in Frankie's throat. "And Sunnydale is open for business."

CHAPTER FIVE

SLAYER POWERS, ACTIVATE!

"Run," Frankie said, and Jake and Hailey didn't need to be told twice. The three of them raced back the way they came, none daring a look over their shoulders. They didn't need to—the vampires' pounding footsteps behind them, and increasingly loud snarls, told them everything they needed to know. They weren't going to make it.

"Jake, you're faster than this!" Frankie shouted. He was staying with them, holding his werewolf legs back. "Go get help!"

"I'm not leaving you, Frankie. No way—"

"Get her out of here, Jake!"

Frankie sprinted around the side of a bus and hoped the vampires would follow her, and that her new path didn't lead toward a dead end. She chanced a glance over her shoulder, but Jake and Hailey were gone. She could hear Hailey's voice in the distance, objecting to being dragged off, but he was doing it, pulling Hailey along with his werewolf strides, getting them to safety much faster than if she'd run on her own, maybe even fast enough to get help before the three vampires tore Frankie's arms and legs from her body.

"This was . . . maybe stupid," she breathed. Now that she was alone, she realized *she was alone*. And what had made her think that was a good idea?

Some stupid slayer instinct, said a voice in her head. *Save the others, stay and fight.*

Except I'm not a slayer, she thought back. *I tore my pants and pushed a chair.*

"And now I'm arguing with myself."

She swerved around the tail of another bus and felt the adrenaline surge in her muscles. It was there again, that feeling that she could leap tall buildings and run until dawn. *That's all I need to do*, she thought. *Just keep running. Just keep running, just keep running—*

And then the vampire who had skirted around to cut her off jumped out and grabbed her and threw her into the very shiny and very metal side of the bus.

"Ow!" Frankie squeaked. But her cry was just a reflex. It didn't actually hurt that bad.

Huh, she thought, just before the vampire grabbed her.

As she was hauled up, Frankie frantically searched the ground for something to defend herself with—a rock, a stick, a handy discarded tire iron—and found a broken piece of pallet wood. She brandished it in her hand, and the vampire let go and backed off. So did her friend. But they backed off laughing. They looked not the least bit frightened. They looked delighted, like she was an automated meal-delivery service.

"Two," she said. "Where's the other one?"

"Probably eating your friends by now," said the leader. She snapped her fingers at her lackey, who Frankie noted looked like Kiefer Sutherland from that vampire movie *The Lost Boys*. "Hold her."

He growled and grabbed her by the shoulders.

"Oh my god, I'm going to be killed by Kiefer Sutherland," she whispered.

"Hey, you noticed," the vamp holding her said. He turned. "I told you someone would get the reference."

"I know my vampire movies," Frankie said, wriggling. "*The Lost Boys, Fright Night,* even *Twilight* is required viewing in my house. But my favorite vamp cosplay is *Interview with the Vampire.*"

"Too frilly," said the leader, and shrugged.

"But you're the Lost Boys, so I guess that must mean you're . . . about fifty years old?"

The vampire holding her dug his fingers into her arms.

"No, we're not fifty," the leader said, offended. "We're just retro." She lunged for Frankie's throat, and Frankie screamed.

Instinctively, she shoved herself backward, bracing herself against the vampire behind her as she drove her feet into the lead vampire's chest and sent her flying. Frankie's next scream was more of a growl as she dragged the other vampire over her shoulder and slammed him into the dirt and used the scrap of broken pallet wood to stake him through the heart.

"Whoa," Frankie breathed.

The lead vampire got to her feet just in time to see Frankie's look of surprise as the lackey turned to dust.

"What are you?" she asked.

"I don't know!" Frankie shouted. She turned and ran, not sure exactly what she was doing. Buying time? Waiting for help? Leading the vampire farther away from Hailey and Jake? What she did know was that she'd just staked a vampire and kicked another so hard she flew ten feet. And she also knew that afterward, she'd stupidly dropped her improvised stake.

She rounded a tall stack of tires with the lead vampire right on her tail.

Find a stake and stake her, a voice in her head whispered. A voice that sounded a lot like Buffy. Buffy would have stayed and fought all three. She'd have slayed all three. But Buffy was a slayer. Frankie was an eco-witch, and she didn't think the vampire behind her was remotely interested in reducing her carbon footprint.

She passed another stack of tires and pulled it down as she went, burying the vampire under a pile of heavy, bouncing rubber. Then she slowed and tried to take stock: She was still in the yard of the bus garage. There were piles of discarded parts and garbage everywhere. Plenty of weapons, and places to hide.

Fight or hide. Her breath was light, and she felt more bewildered than terrified. But she still couldn't decide what to do. She was frozen.

"Crap," Frankie said as the vamp blew out from under the pile of tires.

"Naughty, naughty." She pushed wavy blond hair away from yellow eyes.

"What?" Frankie asked. "Don't you like a good chase?"

"If I wanted to hunt, I'd go to Montana."

The vampire hissed and sprang, and Frankie went down under her weight. She'd meant to bring her legs up and throw the vamp off over her head, but she'd timed it wrong, and her knee had wedged between their chests, keeping her just a few inches short of biting distance. The vampire was snapping at her neck like some kind of deranged turtle. She could smell the blood on the vampire's breath, and she imagined the feel of fangs in her neck. . . .

Frankie reared her head back and slammed her forehead into the vamp's. The vampire went rolling, and so did she.

"You little brat! I think I'm concussed," the vampire said.

"Good!" Frankie shouted. She ran in and started punching, waiting for the pain in her knuckles and wrists, but there was none.

So she kept on hitting, afraid to let up. If she stopped, the vampire would go on the attack again, and she clearly had no idea what to do about that. But she couldn't hit forever.

At the first lag between punches, the vampire struck, and her closed fist landed square on Frankie's jaw. It hurt and sent her half spinning, half stumbling away. But it didn't drop her.

"What *are* you?" the vampire asked again.

"I'm . . . I'm a . . ."

The vampire didn't wait for her to figure it out. She leapt, and just like before, Frankie went down.

"Not again," Frankie moaned.

"Frankie!"

That was Spike's voice. He was close. He'd found them, or Jake had gotten him and brought him back. But he was still too far away. The vampire was going to bite her.

"Frankie! Fight!"

"I can't!" she cried. "I don't know how!" She screamed as the vampire went for her throat. She couldn't believe she was going to die, in the middle of a garage yard, staring into a pile of shiny silver hubcaps with Spike and Jake watching.

"Use your magic!" Jake yelled.

Just as she felt the tips of the vampire's teeth, Frankie thrust her hand out toward the pile of hubcaps and then pulled her fingers into a fist. A silver disc flew from the pile and spun toward her. It sliced between her and the vampire and decapitated the vamp, the edge barely grazing Frankie's shoulder. Before she even felt the cut, she was coughing on vamp dust.

Spike got to her before Jake and Hailey. He pulled her to her feet and helped her clap the dust off.

"You all right?" he asked.

"What just happened?" She wavered on her legs. Ten seconds

ago, she'd been inches from having the blood sucked out of her. Now she was up and breathing and still surprisingly full of energy.

"You used your mojo." Spike wiggled his fingers at her. "Last time I was here, you were still working on floating pencils. You sure you're all right?"

"Yeah, are you?" she asked stupidly. Of course he was fine. He was Spike. And Jake was fine, too, and Hailey—all they looked was a little winded. "Did Jake find you?"

"He found us," said Jake. "Also, Frankie, that decapitation . . . was wicked."

Frankie grinned. It was, she supposed. She still didn't quite know how she'd managed it, but it was.

"Spike was following us after all," Hailey said. She'd crossed her arms. And her scowl was back in full force.

"Of course I was," said Spike. "I'm your sister's Watcher. I wasn't going to just let you run off to god knows where. This is not *The Journey of Natty Gann.*"

"The journey of what now?" Hailey asked, but Spike just rolled his eyes. "You're hurt," she said, and nodded at Frankie's shoulder.

"Oh." A thin line of blood had soaked through Frankie's T-shirt. It was just a scratch, but the sight of it made her a little dizzy. That, and the fact that she'd just killed two vampires.

No, said Buffy's voice in her head. *Not killed. Slayed.*

"Crap," said Frankie quietly. She looked at Jake, and Hailey. "I am a fricking, fracking vampire slayer."

CHAPTER SIX

THE GUARDIAN OF THE HELLMOUTH . . . RESIDUE

When they returned from the misadventure at the bus station, Frankie sat as still as she could while Willow tended to the shallow cut on her shoulder, managing to be simultaneously far too worried over a little cut and detachedly precise as she washed and disinfected the wound. It always amazed Frankie how many things managed to coexist within her mother: science and magic. Fluttery panic side by side with a steel spine. Fuzzy sweaters in interesting colors and stark white lab coats. And just then, Willow somehow managed to remind Frankie of two people: herself and also Buffy, as she gently gathered Frankie's hair and moved it behind her shoulder, like Buffy often used to do to Dawn.

"All done."

"Thanks, Mom."

"I'm always happy to patch up my kid. Let's not make it a habit now," she said, her voice light and her meaning dead serious.

They were back in the kitchen, which was the most spacious room in the house and the one with the most seats. The actual living room was kind of crowded, full of spider plants and other animal-friendly fauna that was good for air purification (Oz loved it; said it reminded him of the wild), and the seating layout was eclectic: Both Frankie and Willow had a proclivity for curling up in cozy armchairs, so there were three, and one small sofa tucked in beside the piano that Frankie had always meant to learn to play.

Oz set a sandwich down in front of Jake.

"Werewolf metabolism," Jake explained when Hailey gave him an odd look for eating at a time like this. "Needs replenishing after carrying you around."

"You were dragging me. Not carrying me."

"Leaping with you is more like," Spike said. "Tailing you was like watching a production of bloody *Swan Lake*. Speaking of blood, you got any more?"

"In the fridge," said Oz and Willow at the same time, and the vampire went to fetch it.

Frankie fidgeted with the torn sleeve of her T-shirt. She might be able to get the stain out, but the fabric was flimsy and not worth stitching. She hated to waste things, but it was destined for the rag bin. Or maybe she should keep it as a memento: She could hand it down to her own kid, or the next slayer. *This is what I wore the first time I decapitated a vampire with a hubcap.* She blinked. The next slayer. Was that what would happen? And if it was, she could never hand it down. Because it wouldn't be like it was now, with slayers and slayers for days. It would be like it was in the beginning: One slayer calls the next. And if the next had been called, that meant she was dead.

"Holy crap."

"You okay?" asked Hailey.

"Yeah. It's just . . . a lot."

"Yeah. I suppose it's not every day you find out you're a frickin',

57

frackin' vampire slayer." She smiled at Frankie weakly, and Frankie snorted.

"Did I really say that?"

"You did," Hailey said. "And I was impressed by your commitment to clean language even under those circumstances."

The two girls sat together quietly while the werewolves ate, and the vampire sipped blood from a teacup, and the witch-scientist crumpled up bandage wrappers and put the antiseptic away.

"This must all seem pretty strange to you," Frankie said.

Hailey shrugged.

"Less than you'd think. I grew up around slayers and demons, too, remember? Though"—she peered around the crowded kitchen—"never with so much of it in the same room."

"Are you okay?" Frankie asked. "I mean, are you okay with staying for the night? I think we've missed the last bus by now."

"Then I guess there's no choice."

"And maybe you should stay awhile longer." Frankie's eyes lost focus as she remembered what it felt like to discover those vampires feeding on the station clerk. "They knew too soon."

"Who knew what too soon?" Willow asked as she came back from the hall closet.

"Those vampires. They knew the slayers were gone. They'll all be coming back to Sunnydale now. The vampires, the demons . . . None of us should be going anywhere." She looked up, surprised by the tone of her voice. It hadn't sounded like an observation. More like an order. "Sunnydale is where we need to be."

"Well, that's not ominous," said Oz.

"Why would you say that, sweetie?" Willow asked. "Are you getting a feeling? Like, a slayery feeling?"

Spike's ears perked up as he suddenly remembered he was supposed to be a Watcher. "Yeah, like a slayery feeling?"

"What's a slayery feeling?" Frankie turned to Hailey, who shrugged again.

"Vi wasn't big on talking about feelings. Slayery or otherwise."

Frankie looked back at her mom as Willow tugged on her arms, straightening Frankie's shoulders. She had an odd expression on her face, and looking into her eyes, Frankie felt like she could see her mom's pupils contracting and expanding.

"Slayers are naturally drawn to the hellmouths," said Willow. "They are their natural guardians."

Frankie pulled out of her mom's grip, which was a little too tight. The springy feeling in her body was still there, and her cut shoulder didn't hurt in the slightest. Not even a throb. *Is this how Buffy felt all the time?* she wondered. What a rush.

"I don't want anything to do with the Hellmouth," she said. "And even if I did, it's closed. The mouth is shut."

"Maybe it's not as shut as we thought," said Oz. "Three vampires in Sunnydale used to be par for the course, but this town's been quiet for years."

"They knew about the explosion," Spike said glumly. "They were here to celebrate."

But Oz seemed unconvinced. He raised his nose and sniffed. Frankie could swear she saw a few of the short-trimmed red hairs on the back of his head stand up straighter.

"There's still something," he said, "that feels off. Willow, you have to sense that."

He and Frankie looked at her mom, but Willow blinked and dipped her chin, like she didn't want to try.

"The Hellmouth is closed," Spike said. "And I should know, as I was in it when the ceiling came down."

"Well," said Oz, "maybe it's leaking."

"Leaking?" Hailey asked skeptically. "Leaking what?"

"Yeah," Frankie said. "Like, hellmouth pheromones? And I'm, like, attracted to it?"

"Frankie and the Hellmouth, sitting in a tree," Jake sang. "K-I-S-S-I-N— Ow!" he finished when Frankie slugged him in the arm.

"I'm sorry," she said quickly, and rubbed the second growing bruise she'd given him in one night.

She slumped. Slayers, vampires, and the Hellmouth. And all without Buffy to fight it. It was overwhelming. Surreal. A nightmare of catastrophic proportions. Her lip trembled. "This is, like, the worst thing."

Jake took her hand.

"No, it's not. You'll figure it out. Buffy did."

Except Buffy was Buffy. Frankie was a mess. But she tried to smile.

"No, I mean I won't be able to hit you anymore," she teased. "My life is over."

Oz had gone to the window and stood looking out. Willow watched him with eyes full of dread.

"Maybe we were naive to think that something as evil as the Hellmouth would stay dormant forever. Maybe it's been waiting all this time, for its chance to make a comeback."

"Well, it's not going to bloody manage it. Not when I'm standing right here," Spike shouted at the floor. "And I'm the one who died to shut it in the first place!"

"Okay, you died for like five months," Willow said. "Let's not get too precious about it." She looked at Oz. "Maybe Oz is right."

But Frankie didn't want Oz to be right. She'd heard the stories about Sunnydale when the Hellmouth was open. She knew that Buffy was responsible for her class at Sunnydale High having the lowest mortality rate. And Frankie did *not* feel ready for a similar responsibility.

"Could it be the First?" she asked. "Come back for another round?"

"No," said Willow. "Or I don't think so. The First was weakened when Buffy defeated it. I mean, it will always be there, evil doesn't just go away, but the First as a personification was basically obliterated—"

"But so was Spike," Jake said, "in the Spikesplosion. And he's back, obviously."

"Is that what you're calling it?" Spike asked. "I don't think that's what we should be calling it." He prodded Oz. "Is everyone calling it that?"

Willow shook her head. "Whatever force brought Spike back . . . the amulet, the Powers That Be, they didn't resurrect the First alongside him. I haven't caught a whiff of the First since the battle, and believe me, those first years, I was really sniffing."

"Maybe you should use your magic to be sure," said Hailey. She'd stood up, and was leaning against the kitchen wall with the heel of one of her boots against a mural of flowers Frankie painted. "Maybe you should grab that Scythe you've got secreted away some-where and magic all the slayers right back into one piece."

"That's not . . ." Willow said, and looked sadly at Frankie. ". . . exactly how it works."

"Sure it is." Hailey pointed to Spike. "There's the evidence, right there. He was exploded, now he's not. You get the right magic, it can be undone. And since everyone says you're the strongest witch the world has ever seen—you should be able to get the right magic."

"I can't. I haven't done magic since Frankie was born. I don't even know if it's in me anymore."

"Wait." Frankie looked at her mom. She knew that sometimes

Willow's magic had been dark. Addictive. But she had never considered that there might be another reason her mother had stopped doing any kind of magic. "Do you think I stole your powers when I was born?" Her mom opened her mouth. "Because I can tell you right now that I didn't," Frankie went on. "I haven't even figured out how to grow the bamboo."

"Grow the bamboo?" Hailey asked.

"An eco-spell I've been working on," Frankie explained. "The point is, Mom, I don't have the magic in my whole body that you have in one dark root of your hair."

Willow touched her head. "I don't have dark roots."

"Or any gray, Ms. R," said Jake, and winked.

"Willow," Oz said. "Why did you stop?"

Willow went to the kitchen counter and tapped her fingers against it. And when she did, something shifted in the air. Everyone felt it, not just witchy Frankie and the werewolves and vampire Spike, but Hailey, too—the girl pushed off the wall with a gasp and edged away from Willow cautiously.

"I stopped because I didn't need to do it anymore. Because I'd done everything I could think of. Achieved things no witch had ever achieved. Pushed boundaries that weren't supposed to be pushed. When Frankie was born, it felt like time. A reason to retire."

"Well, I think you're coming out of retirement," said Spike, nodding at her fingers. "Unless there's another reason all my body hair is standing on end."

"You have body hair?" Oz asked, and Jake laughed, a short bark.

Frankie looked at Willow, and mother and daughter traded steely, encouraging nods.

"My daughter is a slayer," Willow said. "My daughter is *the* slayer, and she needs me. So yeah. I guess I'm back."

CHAPTER SEVEN

BILLY IDOL, BUT MAKE IT LIBRARIAN

Her mom was back. The famous Willow Rosenberg was a witch again. Frankie didn't know how to feel about that. Relieved, for a start. And a little afraid. And more than a little curious to see what her mom could really do. Were the stories true? Of course culturally they'd always been witches. But seeing her mom's powers in action—Frankie was on the balls of her feet. Even knowing what she knew about Willow's history, it was impossible to imagine her mother doing anything like what she'd heard in stories: Conjuring force fields. Levitating. Bringing people back from the dead. She wanted to ask her to float the fruit in the bowl. She wanted to see her teleport something.

"Come on, Ms. R," Jake said. "Let's see you test out those powers!"

"I don't know what I should do," Willow said awkwardly. "Doing a spell now, without a reason, after so long . . . just feels like juggling for the sake of juggling."

"Is there ever another reason for juggling?" Oz asked.

"I have an idea," said Jake. Then he squinted at Frankie for looking so surprised.

"What's the idea?" asked Oz.

"Well, Frankie's a new slayer, right? New slayer, guarding the Hellmouth—"

"Hellmouth residue," Frankie corrected.

"Hellmouth residue or whatever. She needs a new Watcher." He pointed at Spike, and Spike straightened.

"Yeah. Well, of course I'll be Mini Red's Watcher."

"But the Watcher of the Sunnydale slayer clearly needs to be at the school," said Jake.

"At the school?" Hailey asked. "Why?"

"Because they rebuilt the school on top of the Hellmouth," Frankie explained. "Just like the old school that collapsed in the Spikesplosion. And the one before that—that my mom helped blow up to kill the evil mayor snake-demon."

"And they rebuilt it . . . again right in the same spot?"

"Yeah, the city planners are . . . very optimistic."

"Well, that's one word for it," said Hailey.

"The point is," said Jake, getting up from the table, "that the new Watcher should work at the school." He looked at Frankie. "Isn't Ms. Parker looking to transfer into a public library system?"

Spike stood. He shook his head and paced the length of the kitchen. "No. No, no, no. You want this"—he gestured to all of himself—"to be the new librarian? No. No, no, no."

"I mean, it's not a bad idea," said Oz. "And, Willow, it's a good way into your magic. A glamour. Make him all in tweed."

Spike pointed at the werewolves. "No." He pointed at Willow. "Red, no."

Frankie turned to her mom. She looked so unsure. But glamours were no big deal; Frankie did them all the time, to cover zits or that time her plant-based shampoo gave her a bald patch. She could even help. "You can do this, Mom. A glamour is nothing. Don't even think about it." She went to the counter and took Willow's hand. "Feel that?" she asked, and flinched a little at the current of magic that ran between them. Her mom's magic was not gone. It had been sleeping, and now that it was awake, it wanted to run. It was a little scary. "You okay?"

"Like riding a bike," her mom said. "But with training wheels again. Don't let go." She squeezed Frankie's fingers, a tad too tightly.

Willow closed her eyes. "What are you doing—what are you doing?" Spike stammered. The air around Spike rippled, and when Willow opened her eyes, his black clothes were gone, replaced—at least, they appeared to be—by three pieces of gray tweed.

"Not bad," said Oz.

"What'd you do?" Spike felt himself up and down. "I don't feel any different. But I look . . . bloody awful."

"It's just a glamour," Frankie explained. "Your clothes are still there; they just look different."

"Well, how do I get them back? I love this jacket. And these boots. And my black fingern—" He looked at his hands. "Oh, you missed my black fingernails."

"Oops," said Willow. "I was just focusing on the clothes."

"Well, take it off. You know I can just buy tweed, right? No reason to ruin a perfectly good pair of pants."

"But it's not quite right," said Jake. He walked around the vampire and appraised him from every angle. He flipped a finger into Spike's platinum-blond hair. "Nobody's going to buy this ageless-rock-star shtick."

"Don't touch the hair," Spike said.

"You're right," Willow said. "He looks . . . well, he looks too young and hot."

Frankie wrinkled her nose. She'd known Spike since she was a kid, so to her, he could be neither young nor hot. "That's a bigger glamour, Mom. Are you sure?"

"The more difficult spell is going to be making him safe from the daylight so he can walk around campus," she said. "Giles could never have been Buffy's Watcher if he'd been stuck in the basement. It's too evil down there, among other reasons."

"Red, I don't much fancy being your magical guinea pig."

"We would never experiment on guinea pigs," Frankie said, aghast. "And of course, if you really don't want to do this, we'll stop. If you really don't want to be my Watcher."

Spike cocked his head and sucked his cheeks in. It was a weak guilt trip, really. He could have totally said no.

"Of course I want to be your Watcher," he said, in a grumble. "I could never bite your mum, and I can never say no to you."

"Bite my mum?" Frankie asked, but Willow squeezed her fingers again. This time, she took both of Frankie's hands, and the current of magic left her like a jolt. Willow opened her eyes and looked at Spike.

"There," she said.

"Whoa," said Jake. Oz got up and circled the vampire slowly.

"That is . . . nice work. Bizarre. But nice."

"What?" Spike asked. "What'd you do?" He put his hands to his face, and his eyes widened. "You made me old!"

"I did not make you old; I made you my age," Willow said, and smacked him lightly on the elbow.

"I can feel it! The sagging skin, the creases like plow lines!"

"I'm not even forty," said Willow. "And you still look very handsome."

"You made me like Giles!" He pulled and prodded at his new face. Which honestly was very much like his old face. Just slightly more distinguished. And Frankie didn't know what the big deal was, when it wasn't like Spike could ever see his own reflection. "Take it off!"

"But, Spike—"

"Take it off!"

"Fine." Willow waved a hand in his direction. "Uh-oh."

"Is it off?" the vampire asked.

It wasn't off. Willow grabbed Frankie's hand and tried again. Then she took both her hands, and Frankie felt the magic jolt, but the vampire's face remained the same: glamoured and aged, for all to see. And her mom was starting to panic. If they weren't careful, she would be too afraid to try anything else.

"Mom, it's okay. Spike, you look great. Doesn't he, Hailey?"

But Hailey just made a face.

"Look, it's not real," Frankie said. "And it didn't go wrong. It's just . . . sticky because your magic is so strong and it's been asleep for so long. Your magic is . . . overenthusiastic."

"Overenthusiastic," her mom said, and exhaled.

"Yeah," said Jake. "And, Spike, you don't even look old. You do NOT look like Giles. You look like . . . Giles Jr."

"You're not helping," said Spike.

"The important thing is, it worked," said Frankie. "And now we can work the spell to let Spike walk on campus and get him a job as the new librarian, and he can be"—she took a deep breath and looked at the vampire, decked out in tweed, the one who would teach her how to fight and how to be a slayer—"and he can be my Watcher."

☽ ☽ ○ ☾ ☾

After Frankie had gone up to bed and Jake had headed home on foot, and Hailey was set up in the upstairs guest room, and Spike was cozily ensconced in the basement, probably still pulling at his new old face, Willow and Oz lingered on the front steps.

"Are you okay?" Oz asked. When she didn't answer, he looked up at the house. It was new, and beige, and though the Rosenbergs had made the inside their own, the outside looked like the rest of the houses in the development: very fresh and a little bland, the flat green yard dotted with tulip borders and young trees barely thicker than saplings. "It's starting to feel like old times."

"I hope not," said Willow, following his gaze. "I don't think this place can withstand the damage that the Summerses' house did. And we don't have Xander to rebuild the walls."

"Well, I can . . ." Oz peered around dubiously. ". . . hire someone."

"I don't know if I can do this. Be the new Joyce?"

"You're not the new Joyce, Willow."

Willow crossed her arms. "Oz, Frankie is a slayer." And they knew better than anyone exactly what that meant. What she would have to face. The things she would have to give up. It was all fun and games and superpowers. Until it was all battles, and loss, and death. "I don't want my daughter to have to avert Armageddons."

"But look how many Armageddons we averted. And we're still here. And Buffy, she—" He paused. "She survived a lot. Being a slayer doesn't mean what it used to. It doesn't mean Frankie will die before she gets to live her life. Especially not with you around."

"I'm not around." Willow's lips twisted. "That magic in there, my powers? They're not what they used to be."

"You're rusty. You'll get it back."

"I don't think so. When I reached out, it felt like I was searching for a missing limb. Like part of it was just . . . gone. And even if I could get it back, I don't want it. You weren't here when it went bad."

"Willow, you'd just lost the love of your life," he said quietly.

"No. It was even before Tara. Even in spite of Tara. It took away so much time I could have spent with her."

Oz put his hands in his pockets. "I'm glad I got to meet her. Though I wish I hadn't turned into a werewolf and tried to maim her. . . ."

"Well, you always were kind of a raging, jealous maniac."

Oz snorted. Willow was glad he was there. When he came back to town, she hadn't been sure how it would work. But Jake was clearly having a hard time with his parents leaving, and almost without thinking, she and Oz had both just leaned into it. Figured it out as they went. And before they realized it, it was like Oz had never been gone—they simply become coparents, without taking a moment to address the complicated feelings that arose for the two of them now that they were suddenly back in each others' lives full-time.

"Can you believe Spike made that crack about us shacking up?" she asked, and shook her head.

"I don't think he meant it that way," said Oz. "It just sounded strange because of our history. Our ancient history."

"I just don't want him to be confused."

"All that matters is that we're not confused. And we're not confused." Oz smiled softly, and Willow nodded.

She took a slow breath and cast her mind out into the Sunnydale night. Her senses swept through the city on the breeze, simultaneously winding down alleys and slipping into the last of the old forests that remained in the hills. And as she feared it would, eventually she felt it like a pulse: the remains of the Hellmouth, a black spot beneath the high school, twisting through the bedrock, darkness snaking into every corner of Sunnydale like vines. She snapped back into herself.

The Hellmouth had never really been dormant. It had always been calling, whispering to the demons, the vampires, the malevolent forces that occupied Sunnydale apparently down to the bedrock.

The force of the slayers had held those things at bay. But now that force had disappeared.

Willow hugged herself. Her red hair fluttered behind her shoulders; Frankie had convinced her to ditch her sensible cut and grow it out. She looked almost like she did way back when she had fought the Hellmouth.

So did Oz. She studied him a moment, his familiar profile, his hair that was always red these days and never black or blond, like he used to dye it in high school. He'd gotten broader in the shoulders. And after so long at the werewolf commune, he was much more wolflike. And part of him still loved her.

She knew that, even if she pretended she didn't. Part of him would always, and that made part of her worry—that he secretly hoped someday she would return those feelings, and when she didn't, he would draw away.

"So many thoughts inside that head," she said, and reached out to tap his temple.

"You know you only need to ask," he said, and smiled. "But I think it's your head that's full of thoughts tonight. What's on your mind, Willow?"

She fidgeted. Everything was on her mind. The destiny of her daughter. The fate of the world. And her past. Always her past. But what hurt more than anything was the empty space on the steps where Buffy should be. There was never another leader like Buffy Summers. They needed her. But this time they were on their own.

"Did we depend on Buffy too much?" she asked Oz. "Do we not know what to do without her?"

"Do you really think that's what Frankie being called means? Do you really think Buffy and the other slayers are dead?"

"I don't know. I don't want to believe it, but . . . I thought Xander would have called back by now."

"It's only been a day," said Oz. "A little more than a day. Some of them could still be alive."

But Frankie was the slayer *now*. Not in a few days, or a few weeks, when they would know for certain. Oz was right when he said things were starting to feel like old times. For so long, it had felt like they were living in the After: after the war with the First, after the activation of the slayer army, after magic. But now that tingle was starting in the back of her mind. That familiar tingle of things beginning.

"Oz, I need you to do something for me."

"Sure."

"I need you to take me to the high school."

"What, now?" He looked around at the dark, sleeping neighborhood.

"I want to put up the barrier spell so Spike will be protected at school tomorrow."

"Can you do that?"

"Sure," she said, her voice high and unconvincing. "It's just a modified Saepio impedimentum force field to keep him from burning up on school grounds. He can test it out early tomorrow, use the new sewers to get into the school basement."

"He might become known as the sewer-smelly librarian. . . ."

"So he'll change his shoes. I can do this, Oz."

He looked at her a moment, his expression inscrutable as always.

"Well, that is your resolve face," he said. "Let's go get the van."

They stepped off the stoop together, but as they walked down the driveway, she tugged his sleeve.

"Oz? When Spike tests it tomorrow, tell him to bring a fire blanket?"

Oz smiled. "I will. And, Willow, don't worry so much. I'm sure the Hellmouth is sealed up tight."

71

"Demon taverns are never posh outside of Europe, but this one's a real dive."

Milt looked up from behind the bar, where he was stocking bottles—lots of mundane stuff: whiskey and vodka, absinthe and O neg for the tourists, but plenty of decent stuff, too. He had vials of sickle cell plasma, jars of pickled tongues pulled fresh from the mouths of young Catholic nuns, and a whole bottle of vervain-infused liquor distilled from the blood of a cherub. Or so the label read. None of his clientele had ever been brave enough to try it.

The two vampires who sat at the end of his bar were new. Young, no more than a decade old. They still wore black lipstick and lots of garnet jewelry. They had bland Midwestern accents, and he doubted they'd ever been anywhere farther than to see the St. Louis arch, let alone Europe.

"Where's the blood fountain?" asked the girl, wistfully touching the garnet choker at her throat. "Where's the table-side plasma service?"

"Hey," called her friend, a guy in a black turtleneck with frosted tips. "Don't you have anything that doesn't taste like it was cut with goat's blood?"

Milt smiled at them and pulled a bottle off the top shelf. It was old-looking, but it wasn't old; a demon had actually gotten it for him as a gag gift. It was a prop off an old vampire movie starring Jack Bauer. He kept it half-full of a mixture of gin and pig's blood and a few drops of Drakkar Noir.

"Double the price," he said, and poured them two shots.

They sniffed at it and flashed fangy smiles. Then they handed over the money. They drank it down and licked their lips and declared it worth every penny, and Milt had to turn around to keep from laughing himself silly.

"That's more like it," the girl said. "I mean, we are here for a celebration."

"Celebration?" asked Milt, feigning interest like any good barkeep should.

"Haven't you heard? The slayers are dead. It's time to converge on the Hellmouth."

"The one in Cleveland?" he asked, playing dumb.

"No. The one in Sunnydale. We were born from the one in Cleveland."

Midwesterners. Bingo.

"It's going to be quite a party," said the girl. "You should come."

"Oh, I don't know about that," said Milt. "You really think that all the slayers are dead?"

"Yeah. They were blown to bits," the girl said meanly, showing teeth.

"Well," said Milt. "Should be an exciting time." He pulled out a stone cutting board and reached into his refrigerator for the cooler marked "Human Organs," which he placed on the shelf behind the bar. The two young vampires craned their necks as he opened it up and took out the fresh human heart.

"What is that?" the vampire asked.

"That is the heart of one twenty-two-year-old Rebecca Granger." *Strong and healthy and transplantable. Or edible, depending on your predilection.*

"I want one," she said.

"Well, I only have the one. And it's reserved."

"How about just a sliver?" The guy in the turtleneck got out his wallet. "For garnish?"

"Afraid not. And if you'll excuse me, I need to go serve this table-side." He set his two sharpest knives onto the cutting block. Then he picked up the entire thing and carried it through the tavern all the way to the booths at the back, the ones with no lighting above them. They were so dark he wouldn't have even been sure that the demon was seated there had he not seen him come sliding down from the room he'd rented upstairs. He'd ordered one bottle of whiskey and one of sheep's blood, and Milt hadn't heard a peep out of him since.

But as he approached the table with the heart, two bright orbs of blue lit up in the darkness. It was kind of cute, actually. Reminded Milt of a husky he'd had when he was a boy.

"Got in something special this afternoon," Milt said.

He set the heart on the edge of the table, half expecting that it would be snatched away into the shadows followed by a lot of chewing and smacking sounds. Instead, the blue eyes blinked and then went out. Milt grabbed a candle from another table. He set it down and slid it toward the booth, revealing someone who was obviously drunk: tan skin ruddy from the alcohol, shaggy dark hair a mess. In the candlelight, his eyes were a plain, dark brown. Anyone who didn't know who he was would think he was only a man.

"Some celebration," Milt said. "But don't you think it's time you put something in your stomach that's not liquid?" He picked up the knives and gave the heart a nice, slow slice; the demon's expression perked up. His eyes glowed blue again, and he licked his lips over a set of wolflike fangs. But he didn't reach for it. Tartare style, then, Milt thought, and carved it up, chopping and chopping, sneaking a peek now and then to make sure the demon was watching and interested. He hoped he had enough to pay. But he had when he rented the room yesterday—he'd flashed a wad of cash that had to be ten thousand thick. Which was about what Milt would ask for, for the heart. Human organs weren't easy to come by, at least, not through moral means. And by "moral," he meant not through murder. He realized there were complicated morals at play when it came to stealing organs that were meant to be implanted in other humans.

The heart prepared, Milt took away his knives and slipped them into his leather butcher's apron. (When you were a bartender at a demon tavern, it wasn't worth bothering with the white cloth kind.) Then he watched as the demon reached out, the tip of a finger sharpening to a claw before Milt's very eyes. He took a small fingerful and slipped it into his mouth. He closed his eyes.

Milt produced a small, speckled brown egg.

"Want me to add a quail yolk?"

The demon waved it away. He placed cash—a LOT of cash—down on the table and pulled the cutting board to him to finish his meal. He ate kind of like a cat, licking his lips and then cleaning his fingers first on one hand and then the other.

"Well, it's no slayer heart," Milt said. "But I imagine those will be hard to come by from now on."

The demon froze.

"What did you say?"

"I've been in this business a long time." Milt shrugged. "You think I don't notice when the Hunter of Thrace walks into my bar? I figured you'd heard the news and were drowning your sorrows. All those slayer hearts just blasted to smithereens." He clucked. "Must seem such a waste."

"Yes," the demon said. "Such a waste."

Milt looked at him sympathetically. No more slayers, the poor fellow. It must have been like finding out that his favorite chips had been discontinued, and the last batch destroyed before he could get to the store to buy any. But the Hunter of Thrace would survive. He had since . . . well, no one knew, but he'd been around before there were slayers and he'd be around long after. He'd just have to find a new favorite snack. Eating slayer hearts must have been a luxury anyway, a real special occasion. There'd only been one alive at a time, before Buffy Summers, and they were usually killed by vamps before the Hunter could track them down.

"Listen," Milt said. "I wasn't going to tell you this because it wasn't for sure. But there's a rumor going around that the slayer line isn't gone. That it's been restarted."

The demon's blue eyes flashed.

"Where did you hear that?"

"From my crystal ball," said Milt. "No, really. I got it from a prophecy demon . . . one of those fellows with three eyes. Seems to be there's a fluttering."

"A fluttering?"

"A muttering, then," Milt said. He didn't always know how to decipher the visions that came through the ball. He was no sorcerer himself, no mage, and he had no psychic gifts. He was just a very good barkeep, with a variety of powerful friends. "Just a muttering that a new slayer will rise."

"Where?" the demon asked.

"Where else? The old Hellmouth. Sunnydale, California."

PART TWO

THE NEW SCOOBIES

CHAPTER EIGHT

SPELLS AND STAKES
AND PROTEIN SHAKES

The Sunnydale High School Library (well, technically it was called the Sunnydale High School Media Center) sat at the heart of the campus, an enormous room beneath enormous skylights and a ceiling hung with modern art—silver metal mobiles that reflected beams of sun in every direction. In short, it was the perfect room for a vampire if that vampire wanted to be fried crispy.

"Welcome to the media center," said Frankie, hands on her backpack straps as she walked Hailey through the large open double doors.

Hailey whistled.

"For a town that is constantly getting destroyed, Sunnydale sure has a hell of a budget."

"Government funding," Frankie said, and shrugged. She watched from the corner of her eye as Hailey surveyed the space. So far, her impression of the school seemed to be disdainful, begrudging approval. She hadn't wanted to come at all; when Willow told her she'd gotten her enrolled, she'd balked and said she wasn't going to be there long enough. But the prospect of sitting around and waiting for more news about Vi and the slayers proved worse than any threat Sunnydale High could pose. So she'd tagged along.

And she made a splash. In head-to-toe black, she stuck out like a sore thumb amid all the bare legs and pastel dresses. Beside Hailey, Frankie felt even more invisible than usual, and for the first time maybe a little uncool—Hailey was tough and worldly, her broad hips swung when she walked, and she exuded that kind of confidence that felt less like aloofness and more like a dare. Frankie had always thought she radiated an air of breezy, busy loner's confidence, but next to Hailey's, it felt more like an air of obliviousness. As if she were a happy, tiny dog yapping at this person's heels or that person's heels and not realizing they weren't listening.

"So where's Jake?" Hailey asked. "We haven't seen him at all during this massive school tour you've led me on."

"Jake and I don't really hang out at school," Frankie said. "Different crowds."

"You don't seem to have a crowd." Hailey raised her eyebrows at the graphic novels and manga section.

"Yeah. And Jake has a big one. So . . . different."

She was about to explain about how she and Jake became friends by growing up with their mutual weirdness when Spike jostled them from behind.

"What is this?" Spike hissed. "This isn't a library." He pointed at the screens and charging stations. "It's all computers. Where are the books?"

"On all those shelves," Frankie said, confused. The library had a really good physical collection, and a great occult section, like it was a Sunnydale requirement. "Spike. You look so . . . different." Standing there in a rather tight brown suit, all lit up by the sun and not on fire, he was hardly recognizable.

"This isn't a library," he said again. "There are people in here!"

"Yeah, kids hang out here a lot during their free periods. And clubs run meetings sometimes."

"Well," said Spike. He stared at the clean metal shelving and all the screens. "Giles would faint dead away if he saw this. He would faint. Dead. Away."

Frankie followed Hailey where she had wandered to peruse the manga section while Spike hung back, trying to hide from students. Hailey already had three volumes stuck in the crook of her arm.

"What are you finding?" Frankie asked.

"Everything," Hailey said. "This collection is wild." Then she looked up and said, "Hel-lo. Is every guy in your school gorgeous?"

Frankie followed her gaze to a tall, athletic, and very good-looking boy headed toward them, his eyes already fixed on Hailey. "That's Sam Han," Frankie said. "He's one of Jake's friends from lacrosse. What do you mean 'every guy'?"

"Maybe you don't notice anymore, or— I'm sorry." Hailey looked at Frankie apologetically. "Maybe guys aren't your thing? I didn't mean to assume. . . ."

"It's okay. I don't think I'm queer."

"Okay. But then seriously? Even Jake is hot if you go for that dumb, sweet jock type. And this Sam Han could be in a K-pop group."

"Jake isn't really dumb," Frankie grumbled. "Or sweet."

"Hi, Frankie," Sam said, though he was still looking at Hailey. "Who's your friend?" He glanced at Hailey's chest. "Cool T-shirt. Vintage *Masters of the Universe*."

"Thanks," said Hailey.

"This is Hailey Larsson," Frankie supplied. "She just transferred in from Oregon."

"Oregon. Cool." He checked out the books in her arm. "So

you're into manga? We're always getting new stock. Some stuff that's not even translated."

"Cool," Hailey said. "My online school offers Japanese classes. I can't speak it, but I'm getting better at reading. Which seems weird because that seems harder?"

"Yeah," Sam said, and laughed. Frankie looked back and forth between them, fascinated as they casually flirted. "I'm Korean, so I can't do either. Maybe one of these days you can show me."

"Sam!" Jake blew into the library with his usual not-in-a-library voice and came over. "I see you've met Hailey."

"Yeah. Though that wasn't why I came. . . . Mrs. Nusenheim wanted me to grab a few extra copies of the geography text. Frankie, have you seen Ms. Parker?"

"She's . . . not here anymore." Frankie waved for Spike. "This is the new librarian, Mr. Spike."

"Mr. Pratt," he corrected her, and coughed into his hand.

"Cool," said Sam. "Could you tell me where to find *World Geography and Cultures, Second Edition*?"

"No," Spike scoffed, and then caught himself. "I mean, why don't you use the system? The . . . Dewey decimal system."

"O-kay . . ." Sam said. "I guess I'll just look it up. They probably have ecopies anyway. . . . I don't know why Mrs. Nusenheim wants the real ones. They're so heavy." Sam looked at their little group, gathered around awkwardly. "What are you guys doing here anyway?"

"We're . . . starting a club," Frankie suggested.

"Yeah," said Spike. "A *Dungeons and Dragons* club. Nothing you would be—"

"Cool!" Sam exclaimed. "Can I join? This summer, me and the midfielders had the raddest campaign—"

"Uh, sorry," Jake interrupted. "It's already full."

"Oh, okay," Sam said, and turned away, looking a little dejected.

Spike threw up his hands. "What the bloody hell is going on with kids today? A bloke like that playing *Dungeons and Dragons*? Have I been deader than usual for the last twenty years? And I don't know how we're going to manage this charade if I'm supposed to actually help with the computer thingies and the pad things and with everybody constantly in here—"

"Spike," Jake said. "It'll be fine. Nobody goes behind the desk and in the librarian's office. We'll just run our little Slay and D club from in there. And no matter how cool the library is, it's cleared out by two thirty-five. Nobody wants to hang around after the final bell."

Jake was right. By 2:35, the whole school was practically empty, and Spike shut the doors to the media center and cleared space in the middle of the floor so Frankie could train. Hailey and Jake sat down at a table to watch. And to reorganize the occult books into something resembling a logical order.

Spike tossed Frankie a long wooden pole, blunted on both ends. She held it in her hands and felt its weight as she turned it back and forth.

"Isn't this the thing the nerdy Ninja Turtle uses? Can't I start with nunchuks?"

"No," said Spike. "No swords, no bazookas, no turtle weapons. You start with the basics. Sparring sticks." He twirled it in his hand. He made it look cool. Then he hit her in the shoulder with it. Hard.

"Ow!" Frankie scowled. "Not ready."

"Then get ready, Red Jr."

She took a stance that felt right, and then relaxed with a groan as Red Sr. and Oz came through the double doors, her mom smiling a very determined smile and carrying a drink holder.

"Protein shakes," Willow said. "For training."

"Oz," said Jake. "What are you doing here?"

"I thought I'd come by to watch the first session. Is that okay?"

"Sure. Just not used to seeing you around school," Jake said, in a tone that suggested he'd rather not *get* used to it.

"Spike," Willow exclaimed as she passed out the shakes: chocolate mocha for Frankie and Hailey and strawberry for Jake. "You're not a pile of ash!"

"You sound more surprised than I'd like you to sound," said Spike. He swatted at Frankie with his stick again, but this time, she blocked it. Almost reflexively. "That's better."

Frankie smiled cautiously. Was that all it took, then? All she had to do was relax and sit back, and her slayer reflexes would take over—

Spike bonked her in the chest with the pole and twisted it around to whack against her ribs. Frankie pursed her lips.

I guess not.

She glanced at her mom and at Oz, both trying to observe with the appropriate amount of interest and yet a total lack of judgment. Oz was better at it. Frankie cleared her throat.

"I don't know how I feel about the audience."

"Fights will take place audience or no audience," Spike said. "And besides, your mum's here to help. We may as well use your witch powers to aid in your slaying."

"Can I do that?"

"Let's find out." Spike nodded to her mom. "Willow?"

Willow's face turned serious. She dipped her chin, and though the rest of her didn't move—her drapey-sleeved forearms remained on the table—various objects from around the library began to float: several small, heavy-looking books, a globe the size of a basketball, three paperweights off the librarian's desk, and a lacrosse ball lifted right out of Jake's backpack. As Frankie watched, her mom set the items in motion, until they orbited her like strange, potentially threatening planets.

"Mom?" she asked. But Willow was concentrating, a little nervous sweat beading on her forehead.

"Block the objects and me." Spike advanced on her, his attacks slow at first but getting faster. Frankie used her stick to block and swat. She was almost too late ducking the globe and felt it graze the top of her loose red bun.

"Hold your ground," said Spike.

"I'm trying!" She blocked and blocked. But the items were flying faster. So fast they were a little blurry. "Mom! Take it easy!"

"Do you want to learn to fight, or don't you?" Willow asked, her tone low and a little sharp.

"Use your magic to redirect the paperweights," Spike ordered. "Use them to try and hit me."

Frankie tried to focus on one of the moving glass ovals. One of Spike's attacks got through and knocked her to one side.

"Come on, telekinesis has always come naturally to you," Spike said, as if remembering that would help.

"It's . . . hard." She swung at one of the books and missed. She tried to control one of the paperweights and failed. "I can't!" Frankie took a wrong step, and the lacrosse ball caught her in the back of the head. She fell to her knees.

"Frankie!" Willow jumped toward her, and the items dropped to the floor. "Sweetie, I'm so sorry!"

Frankie blinked up at the ceiling as the faces of her mom and Jake and Oz loomed over her. Spike meanwhile, leaned on his stick, unimpressed.

"Oh, come on. She's a slayer now; she can take a ball to the head. Get up, Mini Red. Let's do it again."

Frankie got up slowly, head down. The echo of her voice—"I

can't! I can't!"—whiny and scared, like a little kid, rang in her ears. She gripped her sparring stick tight. A slayer's hands didn't shake.

"Don't you think you're starting her a little fast?"

Everyone turned to look at Hailey, still seated at the table behind a pile of books and paging through *Abrams's Demon Taxonomy*. "Don't you think it might be a little much to ask her to do magic and combat training at the same time? She is the first-ever witch-slayer, isn't she?"

"We should probably go with slayer-witch," said Jake. "The other way sounds like she only slays witches."

"Fine. Slayer-witch. Slayer who can use magic. There's never been one of those, has there?" She shrugged. "I know Vi can't. And none of the other slayerettes could either; that's why they needed Andrew and the witcher-Watchers."

"That . . . can't be true," Willow said. "Can it?" She looked at Spike.

"Why are you looking at me?" the vampire asked. "I don't read the books. I'm not that kind of a Watcher."

.   "I thought you liked books. Didn't they call you 'William the Bloody' because you were William the bloody bad poet?" asked Jake.

"Yeah. I like poetry. Keats, Tennyson. Real thin volumes. Not the"—he waved his hand in the direction of the occult pile—"gigantic *Watchers Codex*. Why don't you call Giles or . . ." He took a breath. They couldn't call Giles. Giles was in hiding. "Yeah, all right, I'll look into it. I just can't believe there's never been one before."

"Balance," said Willow. "The universe doesn't like to put too much power in one place."

"But the universe didn't do this, Will," said Oz. "You did."

Willow looked at Frankie. Then they all looked at Frankie. And Frankie had had enough of being looked at.

"People!" Hailey exclaimed, and Frankie slumped with relief when they turned away. But the relief lasted only a second. "Phone. Willow's phone. It's Xander."

Hailey got up and leaned over the screen as the rest of them hurried to the table and Willow put the call on speaker.

"Willow?"

"It's me. You're on speaker with Frankie and Jake and Oz and Spike and Hailey Larsson."

"Who's Hailey Larsson?"

"She's Vi Larsson's little sister."

"I didn't know Vi had a little sister."

Frankie glanced at Hailey. Hailey's expression was growing less and less patient.

"Yep, hi, no one knows about me; it's a whole Vi thing. But here I am. What's going on? They said you were going to call back yesterday."

"Yeah, I'm sorry about that. We got down to the blast site, and we . . ." He trailed off. Frankie heard things moving around, clothes scraping against the phone.

"There was no cell service out there," he finished finally.

"So you and Dawn are back in Halifax?" asked Willow.

"Yeah, we . . ." He hesitated again, and Frankie's stomach tumbled. They'd found something awful. Something he wished Willow hadn't put him on speaker for. "It's bad, Will. The whole place . . ." There was another scraping sound against the phone, and his voice went from disbelief to anger in the space of a sentence. "I wanna say it's like a bomb went off, but it's not *like*. That's *exactly* what it is."

"Xander."

"I'm sorry. But you should've seen it. How much wreckage there was. How far it flew. You couldn't even tell what some of it used to be."

"How's Dawn? Is she okay?"

"She's sleeping. They've been . . . They've found some bodies, and we're the best ones to identify them."

"Bodies?" Hailey leaned closer, so far that her long, dark hair fell onto the screen. "How many? Was one of them Vi?"

"No. None of them were Vi."

Frankie looked at Hailey and tried to put on an encouraging face.

"They recovered four, and another one overnight. Maybe more now, but we had to come back and get some rest. Call you. Eat something." Frankie made a choked sound, and Xander must have heard it because he said, "Hey, Frankie, I don't want you to give up, okay? They said because of the access, and the terrain, searching is slow. And it's raining, which makes things muddy and slick—" He took a breath, and his tone changed again. "And we all know Buffy. And Faith. Slayers are notoriously hard to kill, and even when you manage it, it doesn't always stick. There's always a chance."

"I just somehow thought they'd be okay." He sighed. "All of them. I don't know why I expected a miracle. Maybe because slayers perform miracles."

Frankie squeezed the sparring stick hard between her hands, glad she could lean on it because she felt like she could sink down to the floor.

"Hey, speaking of miracles," her mom said, brightening her tone. "Frankie and I have some news."

"Mom, no!" Frankie hissed. She grabbed the phone and muted their speaker.

"Why not? He'll want to know. And Dawn—"

"It'll make them think she's really dead," Frankie said, still hissing and whispering despite the mute. "They'll think I was called because they're dead and there's no hope. And they'll stop searching and—"

"She's right; don't tell them," said Hailey.

"What's going on?" Xander asked. "What's the news?"

"Nothing," Willow said after unmuting. "I guess Frankie wants to save it for later."

"But it's good?"

"Absolutely."

"Okay, then," he said. "Something to look forward to." There was another long pause. "I'm going to go for now. We're going back in a few hours, and we'll be there at least until dark. I'll call you as soon as we know anything." He ended the call, and the screen went momentarily bright, then back to black.

"Who were they?" Frankie asked. "The slayers who died?"

"I don't know, sweetie."

"We must not have known them," said Oz, "or he would have said."

"We have to do something." Hailey shoved away from the table. "We're vampires, and werewolves, and witches in a pear tree. We have to do something."

"There's no sense going there," Spike said. "Xander's right. Too many eggs in one place."

"So we help with the search from here," said Hailey.

"How do we do that?" Frankie asked hopefully.

"Astral projection! Witches can do that, right? Well, why don't you whoosh yourself over there and help with the search? The disembodied essence of a witch has got to be safer and faster than a . . . backhoe or whatever they're using, yes? Right?"

"I can't astral project that far," Willow said quietly, and walked away.

Frankie could tell that Hailey wanted to press her. Part of Frankie wanted to as well. She looked at Jake and Oz—they looked back at her with cautious, wolfish eyes. Jake gave a small frown. *Don't push*, those looks said. And she knew that was always the rule. Never push your mother when it comes to magic.

Still, astral projection . . . it wasn't a bad idea.

"Hailey," she said. "Let's take a walk. I think training is done for the day."

Hailey nodded and slumped her way out of the library. Jake, also depressed, gave a little wave from where he leaned against the table, rolling the lacrosse ball her mom had beaned her with between his long-fingered hands. They were all distracted and sad—Willow didn't even turn around when Frankie and Hailey left. She certainly didn't notice when Frankie took a detour through the librarian's office and grabbed an armful of supplies off a shelf.

CHAPTER NINE
LIGHTS, CAMERA, ASTRAL PROJECTION

The things Frankie grabbed from the library—or more accurately, from the Watcher-librarian's office—were candles to cast a circle (and to see by, since the basement lighting at the high school was flickery and dim), a bundle of herbs for focus, and a thick old book that she'd been nosing through since she was a kid. In its pages was a spell for remote viewing. It wasn't exactly astral projection, but close enough, and without the pesky risk of losing track of one's body, or not being able to get back into it.

Frankie led Hailey through the labyrinthine paths of the basement, through shelves stacked with janitorial supplies and uncommon amounts of first aid equipment, and rows of cage-style dividing walls. She didn't stop until they reached a relatively open space, not far from the thick red door that Spike used to travel up from the sewers.

"Why is that door there, anyway?" Hailey asked, holding the book to her chest as Frankie struck matches and lit candles and the room took on a yellow glow.

"Passages from all over Sunnydale lead right back into this

basement," said Frankie. "I don't know why. I mean, I know why it was that way when the Hellmouth was right over there—" She jerked her head over her shoulder.

"The Hellmouth is right over there?"

"Yep. Well, what's left of it anyway." She set down the final candle and put her hands on her hips. "Why are you looking at me like that?"

"Just making sure you're not evil." Hailey squinted one eye. "You're not becoming the servant of the leaking Hellmouth or anything, are you?"

"Leaking Hellmouth," Frankie said. "There's a menstruation joke in there somewhere if we just look hard enough." Her lip twisted, and Hailey chuckled. She cocked an ear in the direction of the Hellmouth and quieted her breathing a moment to see if she could hear anything, feel any sense that it was waking, or watching, or emanating. But if the Hellmouth called to the slayer, it was less a physical call than a spiritual one. She didn't feel a thing.

"Nope, nothing," she assured Hailey. "I'm not evil. I just wanted somewhere quiet and away from all the parental figures lurking upstairs." She remembered that Hailey's parents had died, and winced. "Sorry, I didn't mean that parental figures—to take them for granted, or—"

"Don't worry about it."

"Okay." She gestured to the candles, laid out in a ring. "Uh, let's sit in the candle circle."

They sat, and Frankie opened the book to the proper page. Then she took up a thick piece of chalk and hovered over the concrete floor.

"How are your art skills?" she asked. Hers were shaky to begin with, and the way her hand was shaking literally would only make it worse.

"My art skills are excellent," Hailey said. "You going to tell me what we're up to anytime soon?"

"We're doing what you suggested. We're going to take a look around that blast site."

Hailey's eyes widened.

"It's not astral projection," Frankie explained. "I can't do that. It's something called remote viewing, which is pretty much what it sounds like. We won't be able to touch anything or interact with anything. We won't be able to dig or help. It's basically—"

"An observe-and-report mall-cop spell?" Hailey asked. Then she shrugged. "Better than nothing."

Hailey took the chalk and the book and carefully copied the symbol from the open page onto the floor, her arm moving in a wide arc. It came out perfect on her first try.

"Your art skills *are* excellent," Frankie said. "Okay, stay across from me. Do you want to see, too?"

"I can do that?" Hailey asked. She didn't seem afraid or nervous. Frankie supposed she'd been around plenty of magic, growing up with Vi. Maybe even around bigger spells than Frankie had.

"Sure," Frankie said. "But—I don't know what we're going to see. Some of it might be bad, and we can't just break the spell in the middle. So are you sure you want to do this?"

"Are you sure *you* want to do this? Are you sure you *can*? You haven't seemed very practiced in this stuff, and this isn't exactly . . . growing bamboo."

"I have to do this. For Buffy. Like you have to do it for Vi."

"Well, not *exactly* like I have to for Vi." Hailey cocked her head. "You've got the guilt thing, too."

"Because they died, and I was called."

"And because, deep down, you always wanted to be called."

Frankie looked at Hailey, surprised. "I haven't told anyone that."

"Relax, I'm not psychic. I'm just . . . human. You can't grow up around that kind of power and not dream of it for yourself. Believe me, I know."

"But when I dreamed of it," Frankie said, "I dreamed of Buffy. Of Buffy training me. Buffy introducing me at my first slayer meeting. And then Faith giving me my first beer. I never imagined it like this." And she would give it back. Trade it for them, right then, if she could.

"You've never had a beer?" Hailey grinned. "Never mind, let's remote view. You need to rebel."

They sat down and joined hands over the chalk symbol. Already the low hum of magic had changed the air. It felt thicker. Charged.

"Will we be able to talk to each other during this?" Hailey asked.

"I don't know. I've never done it."

"Is it dangerous?"

"If it is, we're going to do it anyway, aren't we?" Frankie swallowed. Hailey squeezed her fingers. "Close your eyes, and keep them closed." She waited for Hailey to close hers, then shut her own. She could still sense the light from the candles, could still "see" them growing brighter as her focus increased. "*Tantum oculi,*" she whispered.

After a moment, Hailey started to squirm.

"Don't let go of my hands," Frankie cautioned.

"Okay, but now what?"

Frankie homed in on the slayers. On their essence. On the power they shared. "Open your eyes."

They opened them. But what they saw was no longer the basement of New Sunnydale High School. It was a disaster.

The resort had been obliterated. Frankie had expected to see shells of buildings, with walls still standing. Instead it was as if they stood in a crater of cracked wood and metal pipes, cement slabs and crumbling brick. She hadn't seen what the buildings had looked like before the explosion, and the wreckage before them didn't help her to complete the image. It was only piles. Silent, wet piles beneath a cloudy sky, the sun already almost down.

"Vi!" Hailey shouted. "Can they hear us?"

"I don't think so," Frankie replied. But Hailey kept on shouting, "Vi! Vi!" just in case.

Together their disembodied eyes hovered over the destroyed buildings. Where had the blast come from? Because it wasn't just one structure gone. It was the entire resort. What had used to be tree houses were now piles of glass and split cedar. The old-growth trees that had held them lay splintered on the ground. Toward the center of the area were slabs of what looked like white granite and piles of pretty, speckled bricks. It must have been the communal resort center: a spa and a restaurant, and Frankie thought she saw the remains of a garden, dark soil and tattered bits of green.

She held tight to Hailey with her mind as they stumbled through the spell, hoping to see movement. But there wasn't any. Nor was there any blood. The amount of wreckage simply dwarfed the people hidden inside it.

"What's that?" Frankie asked. Hailey would know what she meant—their remote point of view was the same. She stared down over the remains of what looked like a central building in the complex, one that had been larger and separated from the rest. It was hard to see in the fading light and the rain, but on a slab of concrete that might have been flooring or a section of wall was a burn mark in a particular shape. It was only part of it; the rest had cracked away. But the part that remained was the clear arc of a circle, blackened and seared at the edges, right into the stone. "What does that look like to you?" Frankie asked.

"I don't know," said Hailey. The scorch marks along the edge of the circle were swirling drops of black, almost like a pattern.

"Well, to me it looks like the mark from a portal."

"A portal?" Hailey's voice rose. "You mean one of Andrew's portals? You mean . . . some of them might have escaped?"

Frankie couldn't say for sure. It could just be a scorch mark from the blast, easily explained away by an expert—a firefighter or a police investigator. But it could have been left by a portal. It definitely could have.

She winced as something stung her eyes. "Hailey, I don't think I can hold this much longer."

But Hailey didn't seem to hear. Their shared eyes stared down at the mark, trying to force it into clearer view even as the setting sun cast darker and darker shadows.

"Hailey . . . ow . . . we have to go."

"What? Are you okay?"

"Yeah, but I have to let go. Let go!" She felt her fingers slip loose and thought she heard Hailey call her name. Then everything went dark.

☽ ☽ ◯ ☾ ☾

"We shouldn't have done this," Hailey said as she helped Frankie up out of the basement.

"Why?" Frankie asked, clutching her arm.

"Why? Because—Frankie, because you're blind!"

"I'm only a little blind," she said, and felt Hailey catch her when she stumbled on a stair. She was actually completely blind. But that was temporary, or at least, she hoped so. "The important thing is that we saw what we saw. Andrew or one of the other Wicca Watchers might have been able to portal out of the blast." Maybe they'd even portaled all the slayers out of the blast. Well, except for the four who had already been recovered.

Frankie tried to keep pace with Hailey as they went down what she thought was a hall. Her vision was already beginning to recover; hazy light peeked at the edges.

"Ms. Rosenberg! Willow!"

Frankie heard feet stomping toward her. Lots of feet, each one like a charging buffalo, except for Oz, who had soft, quiet steps, like a wolf in the woods.

"What happened?"

"We . . ." Hailey stammered. "We, uh . . ."

"Remote viewing spell." Frankie held up the spellbook and brandished it in what she hoped was the air in front of everyone's faces. "We did it in the basement."

"The basement?" her mom exclaimed. "Don't do magic so close to the Hellmouth!"

"Why not?" Jake asked.

"I don't know. It just feels wrong. It's like . . . dangling a turkey leg over the tiger fence at the zoo. If they can reach it, they'll take your arm off. And if they can't reach it . . . then . . . well, then it's just rude."

"Helpful to know that *now*," said Hailey. "Anyway, we did it. And now she can't see anything."

"I can see some things. And I can sense that someone is waving their hands in front of my face. So stop that . . . Jake and Spike," she guessed, and they muttered, "Sorry."

"My sight will come back. I thought something like this might happen, trying out a new spell. But the important thing is what we saw. When we were remote viewing the blast site, we saw a mark in the rubble. A scorched black circle. Like from one of the Wicca Watcher portals. Don't you see? Some of them might have made it out!" She blinked a little as her eyes watered. Having her vision return sure did sting a lot.

"A scorch mark could've been made from the explosion," said Spike.

"But maybe not," said Frankie. "Hailey, can you draw it for them?"

"Yeah."

Hailey let go of her arm, and Frankie heard her opening a notebook and drawing, scribbling a little, probably to darken and thicken the lines. It was a good thing Hailey was a good artist. It wasn't like they could screenshot a remote view.

"There," Hailey said. There was a pause, and Frankie listened intently while the drawing was passed around. She heard a few "maybe"s and "could be"s and saw a lot of shrugs.

"Well, someone has to be able to tell us what it is," she said.

"We can hit the books," said Oz. "Like in the old days."

"Except you can do it at home, right?" Jake asked. "Not hanging around at my school?"

"Of course," said Oz.

"We can try," said Willow. "But I think I know someone who can help. I have a friend who's a Sage demon—kind of a warrior scholar. She's well versed in nearly all magics. I'll make a call."

Frankie grinned, and through her blurry, still mostly dark vision, she thought she saw Hailey almost smile, too. They'd found the first real scrap of hope.

You're not dead, Frankie thought fiercely. *I know you're not dead.*

The demon watched the group of them make their way through the dark parking lot. The vampire and the great witch he knew on sight. Two werewolves were easy enough to identify by smell. But it was the two girls, walking arm in arm in the center of them, who had his attention. They looked normal enough—one of them tall and lovely, with long black hair and leather bracelets; the other smaller, and with impaired vision, sipping on what smelled like a mocha protein shake. But in one of their chests beat the heart of a slayer. The beat of that heart pulled the demon's pulse in time with it, the rhythm resonating like a struck drum. He tried to determine which was which, but he couldn't. The presence of her heart was affecting him. He'd thought them all dead after an explosion like that, and the heat of the fire afterward . . . his palms were still scarred from it. And his chest. And his knees, the skin tight and painful and cracked.

He licked his lips but wasn't sure whether it was the slayer heart that called to him or the coffee. The heart of the girl that he'd eaten at the tavern still sang in his blood, and she'd been rather a caffeine addict. Ever since he'd eaten the organ, he'd been drinking two pots a day. It was a wonder that her heart had been suitable for donation.

Across the dark parking lot, the group stopped at a small car and a van parked side by side. The great witch took a blanket from the backseat and wrapped the smaller girl in it. Then both girls climbed inside. Before the werewolves got into the van, they turned their heads, watching and listening. Even the vampire sniffed the air. But the demon was downwind and far away. Unable to be tracked.

Part of him wanted them to see him. For one of the two girls to sit up, and turn, and find him with her eyes.

Those two girls. One of them was like her. *But she wasn't her, and the demon's heart pounded in his chest. She was gone, and he would have blood for that. But not tonight.*

Tonight he would stay hidden and let the new slayer drive away.

CHAPTER TEN

AIN'T NO PARTY LIKE A HELLMOUTH PARTY

rankie's vision returned while she slept. And she slept a long time. Right through Friday's classes. But she woke late that afternoon, feeling fine, and still wrapped in her "yummy sushi"–print blanket that her mom had taken out of their car. She got up and ate, and showered, and read a very poorly punctuated text from Spike. He wanted her to do her first patrol of the grave-yard that night. Alone. Well, with Jake and Hailey. She cringed thinking about all the ways she could mess that up, and then called her mom at the lab to see if there was any news from Xander.

"Nothing yet," her mom said. "But I did talk to my Sage demon friend, and she's sending an expert to Sunnydale to help with iden-tifying the portal scorch mark."

"Well, at least that's something. And . . . I guess I got my sight back."

Willow exhaled so hard that Frankie took the phone away from her ear.

"Good."

"And Spike wants me to patrol the cemetery with Jake and Hailey."

There was a short pause, and then her mom said with forced cheerfulness, "Your first patrol! You'll do great. But no magic this time, okay? Just . . . focus on the slaying."

If there was anything to slay. The three vampires at the bus station were the first demons they'd seen in months. These days, Sunnydale was more of a pass-through town for the undead than a permanent residence. It had been under the protection of the slayers, and even if it hadn't been, why should they stay? All the good crypts and mausoleums had been obliterated in the Spikesplosion. Now it was all mod furniture and skylights.

"No magic. I promise. Don't worry, Mom."

"Okay. I'm at the lab late tonight, so call Oz or Spike if you need anything."

They hung up, and Frankie trudged to her closet.

What exactly was one supposed to wear on their first night of patrolling a graveyard?

She looked through jackets and tank tops, jeans and sneakers. Yoga gear? That was nice and stretchy. Her mom said Buffy used to patrol in miniskirts and high-heeled boots, but that felt like a level up. In the end, she settled for a sweatshirt that had a decent-sized front pocket where she could keep a stake, and a loose-fitting pair of athletic pants. She took a breath and stepped in front of the mirror, hoping to see a hot chick with superpowers, and was disappointed when she only saw herself. Frankie Rosenberg. And she had a zit coming in on her chin.

Downstairs, the front door opened, and Hailey called up, "Frankie, are you alive?"

"Yeah."

"Are you blind? Do you need help?"

Frankie snorted. "No. Come on up."

Hailey bounded up the stairs and leaned into Frankie's room. She looked pretty—almost happy even. But that could have just been the effects of her hairdo: the sides of her black hair were twisted into two space buns on the top of her head. "Hey." She tossed a spiral-bound notebook onto the bed. "I went to all our classes today and took all our notes. So you won't fall behind."

"Thanks." It was a good thing her mom was able to get Hailey registered for Frankie's exact same schedule. Willow had really good, as Spike called it, "computer-beep-boop skills." "Did you hear about our upcoming patrol?"

"Yeah. Spike told me." Hailey twisted and dug around in her backpack, then pulled out a large piece of folded paper. "We did some research on recent burials, and he and Jake drew us a map of the cemetery." She unfurled it: a treasure map to possible vamps. There was a waxing moon drawn on top, and the paths through the cemetery were marked. And there were three different graves circled, each with a little fangy face drawn next to it along with a bunch of question marks.

"Nice."

"Yeah. Spike was very into it. I think the sun makes him giddy. Plus, Jake said that now he was a daywalker like Blade, which Spike loved, so that was annoying." Hailey refolded the map and bit her lip. "Hey, can I ask you something?"

"Sure."

"Did you do that risky spell just to make me feel better?"

"Huh?"

"Because I get that overly helpful vibe off you," she went on, "and I don't want you thinking I pressured you into anything."

"I don't think that."

"Well, Jake does. He was not too pleased with me when I showed up half carrying you from the school basement."

"I didn't get that feeling."

"Yeah, well, you were kind of blind. You didn't see the daggers he was shooting at me with his werewolf eyes."

Frankie waved her hand. "Jake's protective." Her brows knit. "Jake's annoying. Don't pay any attention."

"If you say so. Any word from Xander?"

"No. I just called my mom, though, and she says there's a portal-mark expert on their way to Sunnydale."

"That Sage demon thing? Good."

They smiled at each other and fidgeted in the quiet. Frankie wasn't used to having another girl in the house. She wasn't used to having another girl for a friend. Just Jake. Everyone else was too hard, too impossible to get close to. The secret she walked around with—*Magic is real! Demons will kill you!*—was just too big. But Hailey walked around with that secret, too.

"Is this okay to wear?" Frankie asked. "Should I have picked a sweatshirt without a hood? I mean"—she reached back and tugged on it—"a vamp could grab it? And drag me around by it?"

"And that would be embarrassing," said Hailey. "But you could probably get away."

"Is this kind of like what your sister would wear?"

"Yeah," Hailey said. "I mean, mostly. Vi was a very jeans-and-long-sleeved-T-shirts kind of girl. I mean, Vi *is*."

Frankie looked down.

"My sister would not be happy about you bringing me out on patrol, though," Hailey said.

"Why not?"

Hailey had the tall person's habit of keeping her shoulders loose and her head cocked to seem shorter, but when she stood straight, her feet were solid and well set. At the bus station, she'd been fast, and she didn't seem scared of much. She looked like she could fight.

"I don't know," Hailey said. "I don't think Vi thought I was careful with myself. After my parents died, I went through this daredevil phase, jumping off things to see how high I could jump from before I got hurt, running off to rough places to see what I could handle. You know. Kid stuff. I don't think she ever believed I got over it."

"Did you?" Frankie asked.

Hailey paused. "Does it matter? We're never safe, right? Look at you, all dressed up and ready to kill a demon. So what if I didn't care much about what happened to me? I cared what happened to her. She should have let me help. And I learned to fight anyway all on my own, just by shooting my mouth off and getting punched."

Frankie could believe that.

"My mom's kind of been the same way with magic," she said. "She never wanted me to spend too much time on it. Studies first, eco-witching second. It's probably why I'm only really good at floating things."

"Show me," Hailey said, and crossed her arms.

Frankie pulled up the sleeves of her sweatshirt and looked around her room. If she chose something too heavy, she would only succeed in shaking it. Not terribly impressive. She could make her old stuffed dog dance, but that was clearly babyish. In the end, she decided on the vegan makeup kit sitting out on her vanity table. It didn't take more than a second for her to float them. Every item hung suspended in the air like pieces of an odd, invisible mobile.

"It'll be cool when you can use that to fight. You could have, like, a floating sword fighting on either side of yourself. Like three slayers in one."

"Yeah," Frankie said, though she couldn't even imagine the focus that would take. A spell maybe, enchanting the swords. But if she tried to control two swords at the same time as she was throwing punches . . . She let the makeup kit clatter back to the table.

"Hey, Frankie, I didn't mean to stress you out. Nobody expects you to be able to do it right away."

But didn't they? She could see it on their faces: on Oz and her mom, and especially Spike. They were without Buffy, and they were scared. They wanted Frankie to be just like her. Just as good.

"Okay," Hailey said, and turned to go. "I'm gonna change and gather some weapons and get ready to meet Jake at the graveyard. Do you need the bathroom?"

"Nope." Or should she have said yes? Hailey had on a full face of makeup: killer winged eyeliner, full, red lips. Frankie had . . . just that zit on her chin and some ChapStick.

"I'm not cramping your style, am I?" Hailey asked. "Or are we? Me in the guest room and Spike in the basement?"

"No, it's nice to have the company."

"Well, let me know. I'm used to it just being me and Vi, so I know . . ." She paused when her phone vibrated and quickly read a text.

"Everything okay?" Frankie asked.

"Fine. Just my friend Mols, from The Dalles. Being dumb." She fired off a quick text back and stuffed the phone into her back pocket. "So anyway, I understand. The cramping."

"Everyone who menstruates understands the cramping," said Frankie.

"You and that menstruation humor," Hailey said, and walked down the hall.

106

Sunnydale Cemetery, which was actually called Silent Hills (the owners obviously had no video game knowledge), was green and partially wooded with young trees and shrubbery. There were a few trellises full of creeping, flowering vines and grapes, and a pavilion-style gazebo. And there was a fountain. It felt more like a park than a graveyard, especially considering how expansive and empty it was. The smattering of graves was mostly in the east end, near the border of the woods. There just weren't that many people who'd died there yet. Or maybe they'd just wanted to be buried in another town. One that wasn't quite so prone to collapsing, or reanimating the dead.

"It's so big," Hailey said as they strolled through the entry, keeping to the groomed gravel pathways. "And so not crowded. Which makes it worse that it's so big. How many dead people are they expecting, exactly?"

"I think they thought more bodies would be recovered from the old cemetery," Frankie said. But they hadn't been able to find many. Most of those coffins had sunk down deep and disappeared, almost like the earth had reclaimed them. "A few of them made it over." She pointed to the Rimbauer mausoleum, a stately, Greco-Roman-style mausoleum that held several generations of Rimbauers. "I don't know how many actual bodies are in there, though. I know there are at least two. But the rest might be . . . placeholders? Or partials, like if they only found a few bones."

"Frankie! Hailey!"

Jake jogged up to them, invisible tail practically wagging. "Wow, look at you guys."

"What?" Frankie reached self-consciously for the hood of her sweatshirt. She knew it was a stupid choice. Hailey had picked a tight T-shirt over equally tight jeans—the only change she'd made from her school clothes was to remove her jangly bracelets and trade her leather choker for a crucifix on a string. Jake hadn't changed at all. He was still in his letterman jacket.

"No, I mean your Flavor Flav–sized crucifix necklaces." Jake picked hers up and let it thump back against her chest. Hard.

"Just shut up and take a stake." Frankie shoved one into his hand, freshly sharpened by Hailey, who was very good with a knife.

"Hey, Jake," Hailey said. She held up a neon-green plastic gun. "Check out this Super Soaker full of holy water." She pointed it at him. "Does holy water work on werewolves?"

"No," said Jake, and pushed the tip away with his index finger.

"So," said Hailey. "When is someone going to explain this whole 'born a werewolf' thing to me?"

"Um . . ." Frankie looked at Jake for permission. He shrugged, so she said, "Jake was a Whoops Werewolf Baby."

"A what now?"

"Well, after his parents had his brother, Jordy, and Jordy got bit by a werewolf when he was a little kid, and proceeded to bite everyone else in the family—"

"Including Oz," Jake interjected.

"They didn't really want any more kids," Frankie said.

"Raising a werewolf kid while being new werewolves themselves was a lot to handle," said Jake.

Hailey nodded. "Understandable."

"Yeah, but one full moon his parents—in werewolf form—got out of their cages and kind of got busy—again, in werewolf form—and then Jake was born. A Whoops Werewolf Baby."

"Okay, I get it," said Hailey. "And a baby conceived by two werewolves in werewolf form is automatically born a werewolf."

"Exactly."

"So they were lucky you weren't a litter." Hailey grinned. "Were you born with fur?" Her eyes brightened. "Were you born on the full moon? Oh my god, newborn werewolf baby must be so cute!"

Frankie laughed, imagining Jake's mom carrying him around by his baby werewolf scruff.

"Okay, anyway," Jake said, and Frankie thought she heard a little snarl. "You got the map?"

"Yeah." Hailey pulled it out. She turned it upside down and then right side up, trying to read it.

"Here." Jake grabbed it. "Let me try."

"What's your hurry?" Hailey asked. "It's barely dark out."

"We're a week out from the full moon." Frankie nodded to the large pale orb rising in the sky. "He always gets a little high-strung this time of the month. Like werewolf PMS."

"More menstruation humor," said Hailey, and high-fived her.

Jake gave up on the map and looked toward one row of graves, then another.

"Too bad we can't do a locator spell for this kind of thing," said Hailey.

"Buffy did it without locator spells in the old days," Frankie said. "We can, too."

"You guys are really magic shy," Hailey said. "Why did your mom go dark back then anyway?"

"The woman she loved was killed," said Frankie. "But it was more complicated than that. I don't think even she understands completely. But the lesson is, magic is nothing to fool around with. My mom almost ended life on this planet. *My* mom."

"No arguments here," said Jake. "If too much magic can turn that ball of sunshine evil, then I never want to know what it could do to someone like you."

Hailey snorted. "Here, let me look at the map again." Jake

handed it to her. "The fresh burials are spread out; two should be visible to each other, but the third one is way over there." She pointed. "Over that hill."

"I'm thinking we stake out these two." Jake tapped the map. "The other one is a grave belonging to Mrs. Eleanor Olsen, and we're pretty sure she died of natural causes."

"Why's that?" asked Frankie. She tightened her red ponytail. Gently, so as not to snap another elastic.

"She was a hundred and four."

"Oh. Too bad. Granny vampire would have been good to practice on."

Hailey made a disgusted face. "Sick. Granny vampire would have been terrifying." She folded the map and led the way to the graves.

"Here we go," she said, and used her phone screen to illuminate a headstone. "The first one. Robert Palmer."

"Like the guy who sings 'Simply Irresistible'?" Frankie asked.

"Probably not. This Robert Palmer was only twenty-four. And I think that other Robert Palmer is already way dead."

"Oh. Sad."

The three of them bent down and examined the ground around the grave. The dirt was fresh and soft-packed. Easy for any new vampire to claw up and out of. The dark rectangle of soil had been covered over with a patch of fresh, wet green sod, and Jake grabbed the end of it and carefully rolled it back.

"It's good grass," he explained. "No reason it should get torn up."

"You guys are very eco-conscious," Hailey said. "No big gas-guzzling cars, veggie-heavy diets . . . no single-use plastic containers for your holy water . . ."

"Where's the next grave?" Frankie asked, and Jake pointed.

"Eric Sullivan. Student at UC Sunnydale. Disappeared after track practice and later found dead with a wound to the neck and arm. ME ruled it a suicide." Jake frowned. "Poor guy. His poor family. Stupid ME."

"Can't blame them," Frankie said. "Sunnydale just doesn't see the amount of neck wounds that it used to." And either way, Eric Sullivan was gone. But she was the slayer now. And if he had been killed by a vampire, she was there to stop it from happening to anyone else.

"I guess I'll go keep an eye on UC Sunnydale," said Jake. "You guys want to hang here with Mr. Palmer?"

"Might as well," said Hailey. "That song is already on repeat in my head."

"How does it go again?" Frankie asked, and Hailey shrugged.

"I just know the part that goes, 'Simply irresistible.'"

Jake bounded off for the other grave, and Frankie and Hailey got comfortable. At first, Frankie wasn't sure where to wait—she thought about perching on the headstone like a bird—but then she saw a stone bench near the pathway and she and Hailey sat down on that. Minutes ticked by. Then an hour. At least the near-full moon gave off plenty of light; she wouldn't struggle to see while slaying. If either one of the dead was actually a vampire.

"How's Jake doing?" she asked Hailey. "*What's* Jake doing?"

Hailey craned her neck back to check. "Looks like he's perched on the headstone like a bird."

Frankie checked her phone. It was almost midnight. Buffy always said that new vamps were so eager for their first night, they liked to bust out of the ground an hour after sundown.

Frankie reached into the pocket of her sweatshirt and squeezed her stake. She was eager to use it, and she even had a plan: She would catch the vampire half-in and half-out of the grave. How much of a fight could they put up with their feet still stuck in their coffins?

"Hey." Hailey grabbed her arm. "Do you hear that?"

They stared at the grave. The dirt wasn't moving, but they definitely heard something. Like a knocking. And a scratching. And then a sharp crack. Robert Palmer was indeed no '80s singer. He was a vampire, and he was on his way up.

"Okay, okay, game face." Frankie stood, her legs bouncy with adrenaline, and went to the edge of the grave. "What side do I wait on? The left? By the feet? Can you stake them through the back?"

"I think any side is fine," said Hailey.

The dirt was moving now. Sinking down as it filled the hole of the hollow coffin. It almost churned as the vampire dug his way out of it.

"Hey!" Jake shouted. "UC Sunnydale is coming out!"

"What?" Frankie blurted. "At the same time? Did they count down and go on three?" She pulled the stake out of her sweatshirt. This Palmer guy was taking forever. What if UC Sunnydale made it out first? It would ruin her plan. She jumped up onto the headstone to get a better view of Jake and the other grave. Maybe she should go over there? Or maybe Jake could stamp down the dirt and buy her some time?

"Frankie!"

When Hailey shouted, Frankie turned and saw the vampire burst to the surface. Formerly Robert Palmer's mouth was full of fangs and grave dirt. His eyes glowed sickly yellow in the silver light. And if she didn't move fast, he'd be all the way out.

Frankie sprang and shoved the pointy end of the stake toward the vamp's chest. The next thing she knew, she was flying backward through the air and landing on her butt. She scrambled forward again and stabbed from her hands and knees, to get a better angle, and the vampire hit her across the face and sent her rolling.

"Frankie! He's up!"

She jumped to her feet. Formerly Robert Palmer was standing over Hailey, but instead of running, she grabbed the XL cross around her neck and slammed it into the vampire's face.

"Get him, Frankie! Get him!"

"Hey," Jake called from across the cemetery, "this guy's up, too!"

Frankie growled. Her plans were shot; she was completely flustered. So flustered that when Formerly Robert Palmer turned to attack her, she flipped a panicked kick right up high, under his chin. It landed so hard that it sent him over backward.

"Frankie!" Jake shouted. "He's a runner!"

She turned to see a vampire sprinting through the cemetery and Jake sprinting after him. Of course. UC Sunnydale went missing from track practice. He was literally a runner. Luckily, Jake was a Whoops Werewolf Baby and could leap twice his body length. With an animal roar, he brought the vampire down, his arms locked around the vamp at the waist.

"Jake!"

"Keep going, Frankie." Hailey shouldered the Super Soaker full of holy water. "I'll help Jake."

"Right." In front of her, Formerly Robert Palmer shook off her kick to his chin and pushed off the grass.

"I thought I'd have to hunt for my first meal," he said. "I didn't think it'd be served like breakfast in bed."

"No banter!" Frankie set her feet under her and took a breath. "I need to focus."

"No bant—"

113

She moved forward, shutting him up with another kick and a backhand strike to the nose. Good. Yay. She blocked a wide, slow punch and shoved her palm forward into his chin, opening him up.

"Open," she whispered, and jumped close to drive her stake into his undead demon heart. She pulled the stake out, and he exploded in a cloud of ash.

"I did it!" she shouted, and held up her arms. She also may have jumped up and down a little.

"Great!" Jake called. "Now come do this one!"

"Oh!" She ran to them. UC Sunnydale had made it a quarter of the way through the cemetery before Jake had been able to take him down. But now he was just lying there squirming and steaming with Jake around his knees and Hailey Super-Soaking him with holy water.

"Okay, get back," Frankie said, but she was too late. The vampire kicked loose from Jake's grip and shoved Hailey to the ground. Then he took off again.

Frankie darted after him, astonished by the slayer speed in her legs. She wasn't even winded. But she wasn't gaining either. University of California, Sunnydale, must have an absolutely killer track team.

"Hey," she called. "Don't you want to bite me? I'm all healthy and full of blood!" But the vamp didn't even look back. And then she tripped over a root, or the corner of a grave marker, or maybe her own shoelaces. She went down hard, face-first, with her stake in her hand, and felt the pointy end sink into her leg.

"Frankie! Frankie are you okay?"

Jake and Hailey bent over her, their faces first worried and then a little embarrassed.

Her first patrol, and Frankie had managed to stake herself.

UC Sunnydale, aka the vampire formerly known as Eric Sullivan, raced through the outskirts of the cemetery in the bright moonlight. He didn't know who that girl and her friends were, the ones who'd tried to jump him. He only knew they were slow. Much slower than he was—in life, he'd been able to run the 100 meter in 10.43 seconds. He'd been the best sprinter on the track team. A sprinter. *So it was a little confusing even for him that he could run all the way across the cemetery and most of the way to the west side of town without slowing. His legs felt amazing. Like he could run forever. Or at least until dawn.*

He probably could have eaten those three kids, too. His arms were springy with energy, and with the urge to tear limbs from bodies. But Eric had other places to be.

The mansion on the west end was old—one of the relics that still stood from Old Sunnydale, far enough from the epicenter of the sinkhole, or earthquake or whatever it had been, to survive the cave-in. It had structural damage: cracks in the foundation, shattered windows, and a partially collapsed wall on the eastern side. The garden with its paving stones and low stucco fence had been affected by the upheaval and looked like it was inhabited by a colony of giant moles. But the tall trees had survived—nice thick trees that would cast a lot of shade during the day. Since the collapse, no one trusted these old properties. The city had hemmed and hawed about condemning this one before forgetting about it completely. So it had kept on, lying in wait and growing vines, vacant despite having good bones and a great view of New Sunnydale.

Well, vacant until now.

Eric Sullivan went inside, sniffing. The place smelled of dust and old plaster, of small and not-so-small furry creatures. And fresh paint.

As he walked down the long hall that ran parallel to the exterior portico and colonnade, he passed two other vampires, who nodded to him. They must have been the painters. They had it splattered on their clothes and hands and looked a little tired and cranky.

"Where?" he asked.

They pointed down the hall and to the left.

He hadn't made it to the door yet when she called him.

"What took you so long?" she asked. "I heard you were fast."

"I was attacked."

"A vampire attacked fresh out of his grave?" She clucked. "Barbaric." She extended her hand and beckoned him closer.

There were no candles in the room. No light other than moonlight, and it made her look as though her skin were made of silver. She reclined in a bathtub of dark liquid, exposed only from the shoulders. Except it wasn't liquid, he realized when he drew nearer. It was dirt.

"Who attacked you, child?"

"Three," said Eric. "They had crosses and holy water."

"I thought the slayers were dead," said a vampire from the shadows whom Eric hadn't realized was there.

"They are dead," she said. "I felt it in Jalisco, passing through the air in a great red breeze." She turned her head. She wasn't beautiful exactly, but she was striking. Sharp eyes. A mouth with a clever twist in one corner. She was a woman who preferred thinking to speaking, but when she spoke, it was clear she was used to being listened to. She reminded him a little of his civics professor.

"Then who were they?" the other vampire asked, and Eric bared his fangs at him so he would just shut up and pay attention.

"There is a witch here. A great one. She probably sensed my coming. Don't worry." She plunged her hands down into the dirt. It smelled . . . old, though if you'd have asked him ten minutes ago he'd have said he didn't know that dirt aged. "I've burned and eaten many witches. And when I am strong, I'll burn and eat her, too."

"Burn?" the other vampire asked. "Or eat?"

"Burn AND eat," she said. "Pay attention."

Yeah, doofus, Eric thought, and cast the other vampire a look.

"Come here."

Eric went. She was strong, this one. He could sense it. When she reached out with dirt-dusted fingers to touch his head, he knew that she could twist it clean off with a flick of her wrist, and it filled him with macabre glee.

"Who are you?" he asked softly.

"I am the Countess," she said. "And I have come from far away to wake this place, this destroyed seat of former glory." She took him by the chin. "But first I need to feed. And that is why I need handsome faces, like yours."

CHAPTER ELEVEN

HE GOES NICE WITH POULTRY

"Nobody said I'd have to do training through lunch," Frankie growled. Her stomach growled, too, as she eyed Jake and Hailey, sitting on a bench in the sun in a quiet, shrub-shrouded corner of the campus while Spike continuously attacked her. Since their outing in the graveyard on Friday, when she'd staked herself, Spike had doubled her training. Even over the weekend. The injury had scared him, and it had scared her mom; Willow had threatened to take down the sun barrier and find Frankie a real Watcher if Spike didn't shape up.

"Block this combo, and you can have a cookie," said Spike, and promptly punched her in the nose. He had his tweed jacket off and his white shirt rolled to the elbows. It was still so odd seeing him in the daylight. And older. And dressed up like Giles.

"Ow," Frankie said. "You know this isn't fair. Buffy never had to train with a glamoured-old, librarian-cosplaying vampire."

"That's true," said Jake. "She had to train with an actually-old, librarian-dressing librarian. Who can't beat that?" He stabbed a cube of raw tuna with a chopstick and popped it into his mouth. It was poke day, and both he and Hailey were shoveling down large bowls of rice with vinegar-marinated cucumbers and onions, and generous scoops of tuna. Frankie's mouth watered. For the rice and cucumbers. Not the fish.

"I love poke days," Jake said to Hailey. "I wish we had them more than twice a month."

"It's more responsible this way," said Frankie, trying again to block every punch in Spike's six-punch combination. "Tuna is a dwindling resource and needs careful management. Though it would give you more practice with your chopsticks. They're not for stabbing, you know."

"Maybe you should swap a pair out for your stakes," Jake teased. "It would be harder for you to gore yourself in the leg." He waved a chopstick in the air.

"I could still manage it," Frankie grumbled. She blocked high, then low, then twice on the left, then interrupted the vampire's assault with a kick to the chest. "Ha! And now, cookies."

"Nice work," Hailey said, and high-fived her as she passed by, texting with her other hand. Frankie caught a glimpse of the screen.

Hey hey

Hey Mols, what's up?

School is BORING I want your computer school

Another buzz and a new text came through.

Can we hang at your place tonight? Me and Justin and Erica

No sorry, Hailey texted back. *I'm out of town for a while. My sister's work thing went long so I'm in California.*

"Do they know?" Frankie asked, and when Hailey looked surprised, she apologized. "Sorry. I didn't mean to snoop. I just saw . . . Is that your friend . . . Mols? From The Dalles?"

"Yeah. Mols. Mollie. No, of course they don't know. About slayers and vampires and hellmouths? No way."

"They must miss you."

"Miss my empty apartment, more like." Hailey smirked. She looked Goth-chic as usual in Wednesday Addams braids strung through with crimson ribbon and a pair of silver aviators to guard against the sun. "But yeah. I don't know what I'm going to tell them if the search takes much longer." Her face fell. "Or if I never go back. Ghost them, I guess."

"Ghost them?"

"No, not really. I'll make up something."

Frankie tried to look concerned. She was concerned. But she was also warming up to the idea of Hailey sticking around. She reached for her caprese panini—their fancy new school had an equally fancy new lunch program—and took a bite, but Spike removed the plate of cookies.

"No cookies. You're pulling your punches. That kick barely moved me a foot."

"Well, forgive me if I don't want to hurt my uncle Spike," Frankie said, staring longingly at the plate.

"I'm not your uncle, Mini Red."

"Sorry. Forgive me if I don't want to hurt my great-great-great-great-GREAT-uncle Spike."

Hailey snorted. Jake leaned forward over the screen of his phone. He looked less like a jock today and was wearing one of Oz's old Dingoes Ate My Baby band T-shirts, which Frankie thought was sweet.

"Hey," he said. "There's an article about the cemetery."

They leaned in. Their cemetery escapade had made the news but only as a footnote. And of course it had been called grave robbing. An incident of peculiar grave robbing. And then there were profiles of the two graves robbed, and the victims of said robbing:

Mr. Robert Palmer (not the previously deceased singer, the article noted) and Eric Sullivan.

"Check it out," Hailey said, and pushed up her sunglasses. "It's UC Sunnydale." The article featured a close-up photo of him in his track jacket.

"He was so good-looking," said Frankie.

Jake whistled. "Ladykiller," he said. "Except probably literally now, so I should pick a different descriptor."

"Eric Sullivan," Hailey said, breezing through the text. "His family doesn't know why his grave would have been targeted. They said he wasn't buried with anything of value. The only jewelry or anything he had on him was a promise ring. A promise ring? Oh. Like he was saving himself for marriage."

"They printed that?" Jake asked. "Seems like a personal choice. That, you know, should have been kept personal."

Frankie frowned, suddenly not hungry. Eric Sullivan. She'd failed him. He'd risen. And with the legs on him, he was probably halfway to Canada.

"Wish he hadn't gotten away," Spike said quietly. "Now he'll go shooting his mouth off about a new slayer in Sunnydale, and who knows what will come knocking at our door."

"You think?" asked Jake.

"Sure. Every big bad wants to make a name for themselves. And nothing makes a name like opening a hellmouth or killing a slayer. One by one they came after Buffy: the Master. Me. Angelus. The bleeding government."

"Maybe he won't know Frankie was a slayer," Hailey said helpfully. "I mean, she didn't announce it or anything. And it wasn't *completely* obvious."

"Good," said Spike. "Better to keep a low profile, early on. But don't get down on yourself, all right?" he said to Frankie. "You're not going to get them all." He shoved a cookie into her mouth and walked away.

Frankie chewed solemnly. She knew she couldn't slay every vamp, couldn't save every person. But it still sucked. And she still didn't feel like a real slayer. She'd always imagined that if she was called she would immediately feel different. This felt more like being notified by text. *Hello, FRANKIE ROSENBERG! Welcome to the Instant Badass Club. To opt out, well, you can't. But to stop receiving text messages, reply STOP.* She looked down at her slightly skinny arms, poking out of the sleeves of her T-shirt. All the training should eventually give her biceps, right? Except that wouldn't necessarily be the case. Slayer strength came from the slayer magic, the supernatural force. Not from muscles. She frowned and blew some dangling strands of red hair out of her face. Then she dabbed at a bit of blood coming through the fabric of her jeans. That kick must have tugged at her stake wound.

"Hailey," Spike said. "You're up."

"Huh?" Frankie and Hailey said together.

"She's going to patrol with you; she's going to train. Nobody close to the slayer stays a civilian for long. Now come on, learn to take a vampire punch to the face."

Hailey removed her sunglasses, set down her lunch, and joined Spike in the grass. "You're going to enjoy this, aren't you, old man?"

Spike gasped and touched his cheeks.

"Well, he is now," said Jake.

They started at half speed. But it wasn't long before they were going full tilt. Hailey meant it when she said she'd been in scraps before. And she had no qualms about fighting dirty. At one point, she kneed the vampire in the crotch and pulled his hair.

"Your balance is good," Spike said. "Maybe you won't get killed right away. You sure you never trained with your sister?"

"No, she—" Hailey began, and then she and Spike jumped back as a burning circle opened in the air at the edge of their training clearing.

Frankie and Jake leapt up, ready to . . . they didn't know what. The circle was made of bright gold sparks, no bigger than a basketball, but as they watched, it elongated until it was the size of a person. And then the most handsome boy Frankie had ever seen stepped through it.

He was Black, tall but not too tall, with a soft yet sculpted jawline and the coolest slim gray eyeglasses. When he smiled, Frankie smiled right along with him, like she had no choice. So did Hailey.

"This one's even hotter than Sam Han," Hailey murmured.

"Hello," said the boy. "I'm Sigmund DeWitt."

"Sigmund DeWitt?" Spike said.

"Well, not really," the boy replied. "Actually it's—" He proceeded to say a name that clearly required a nonhuman tongue to say properly. "But 'Sigmund DeWitt' is the closest thing most people can manage." He stuck his hand out for Spike to shake.

"Oh, right. The Sage demon. The . . . warrior poets, or what have you."

"Warrior scholars." He smiled. "Or in my case, just scholars. I'm only half-demon. Human on my father's side." He looked at Frankie and waved shyly, and her knees knocked together. He looked at Hailey and said, "Hi."

"Earth to Hailey," said Jake. "Want some of my protein shake? Because you still look thirsty."

"Shut up, Jake," she said. To Sigmund, she blurted, "I'm searching for my sister," and then ducked behind Frankie. Strange, when she'd had no trouble flirting with Sam. But this Sigmund was no Sam. This Sigmund was . . . Frankie licked her lips. Dinner.

"Oh god, I'm doing it, aren't I?" Sigmund said.

"Doing what?" Frankie grinned.

"My apologies. Sage demons have the ability to charm, and when I'm nervous or meeting new people, it comes on a little strong. How's this?" He took a breath, and the air around him changed. Suddenly, Frankie could see the rest of the world again, and he no longer glowed like a piece of gold or a carousel she wanted to leap onto.

"You did know I was coming, didn't you?" he asked. "My mother is a friend of Willow Rosenberg. . . . She sent me. . . . I'm the portal-mark expert?" He gestured to the now-closed portal behind him. "So I thought I should make a proper entrance? Like through a . . . portal?"

"You're my mom's friend?" Frankie asked, still slightly dazzled.

"I'm your mom's friend's son, actually," Sigmund replied. "So, you're the new slayer. How fascinating."

"It is?" Frankie cleared her throat. "I mean, it is. I am a fascinating specimen. One that should be carefully studied. Perhaps in private?" She caught herself and blinked. "Uh, that charm really packs a wallop." Even without it, he was gorgeous. Hailey had sat down on the bench again, and Frankie didn't think she'd blinked once.

"What the hell is going on?" Jake demanded. He looked from Frankie, to Hailey, to Sigmund and sniffed the air.

"The charm thing, Jake," Hailey said, and snapped her fingers at him. "He just explained it."

"Well, I don't like it. And I didn't feel anything."

"I'm not surprised, werewolf," said Sigmund. "Fellow demons are immune." Sigmund tried to adopt a friendly expression, but

Jake's wolfish side had taken over and he circled the boy with suspicion, sniffing and sniffing, red-gold hackles raised on the back of his head.

"Jake, stop it," Frankie growled. She looked to Spike for adult help, but Spike was never an adult and was instead watching like he was taking mental bets on werewolf vs. Sage demon.

"Are werewolves always like this around new people?" Sigmund asked.

"Only around ones who show up and instantly pull mind-control tricks on girls," said Jake, and Sigmund looked immediately contrite.

"I totally get that, and Frankie, Hailey—I am so sorry. Sincerely, I apologize."

"It's fine," said Frankie.

"I was just very, very nervous about meeting you all. I'm still very, very nervous."

"You're fine. You're better than fine; you're—"

"Awkwardly adorable," said Hailey, and then she pressed her lips firmly shut and put her sunglasses back on.

"Right," Spike said. He crossed his arms. "Well, welcome. So you're our portal expert."

"Yes, and I'm here as long as you need me. My mother made an arrangement with the dean of my academy to transition into their online component. And I think Ms. Rosenberg has already arranged for me to become your librarian's assistant, Mr. Pratt."

"Just call him Spike," said Hailey. "Everyone does." She seemed more normal. Jake, on the other hand, was still sniffing.

"Sage demon," he said. "Like the herb?"

"Sage as in wisdom," Sigmund said. "Knowledge?"

"I prefer it in stuffing," said Jake, and Frankie winced. But after a moment, Jake gave up the wolf routine and sat on the table—still protectively between Frankie and Sigmund, Frankie noticed, and despite his bad behavior, she kind of wanted to scratch him behind his ears.

"So you're going to be spending a lot of time in the library," said Hailey. "Looking for my sister," she added, almost to herself.

"Yes," said Sigmund. "And tutoring. But mostly aiding you in research."

"Well, let's get started." Spike nodded to Hailey, and she took out the drawing she'd made of the possible portal mark. Sigmund took it and studied it carefully.

"You saw this while remote viewing?" he asked. "And this is a perfectly rendered copy?"

"Yes," Frankie and Hailey said together, and nodded to each other to reconfirm.

"What were the dimensions?"

"Uh . . ." Frankie looked at Hailey. That was harder to say. They hadn't measured, and things skewed different when you were a floating, disembodied eye.

"Maybe fifteen feet across," Hailey guessed. She got up onto one knee as Sigmund continued his study, and Frankie could read her body language like a book: *Say it's a portal mark, say it's a portal mark.*

Say it's a portal mark, Frankie thought. *Say they're not dead.*

"It could be," Sigmund said, and Frankie and Hailey deflated.

"Could be? I thought you were an expert," said Spike.

"Yes, but what I'm not is a blast site expert. I'll have to research to eliminate the possibility this mark was created by some secondary explosion or the primary explosive component. See here." He held out the drawing and traced his fingers along the edge of the scorches. "The curves like a pattern? That could indicate a transportation portal. Some demonic magics, like the Kashmas'nik magics, leave similar traces behind."

"Vi said Andrew and the witcher-Watchers were portaling slayers in from the airport. Could it have been that? Like, marks from when they arrived and not even related to the blast?"

"I wouldn't think so," said Spike. "The Watchers Council has money, but they still wouldn't fancy losing a security deposit. If the portals were going to get all scorchy, they'd have arranged to do it somewhere remote. Not in one of the main buildings."

"That's probably right," said Sigmund.

"How do you know?" Jake asked, and raised his chin. "Can you really tell one portal mark from another?"

"Absolutely. Different magics leave different marks. Some leave no trace. Others leave rings of blood or cracked surfaces. Some come through trees and split them down the middle. Certain Mok'tagar magics leave slime trails or scents that you just can't get out of your clothes no matter how many times you wash them. And if you get teleported by a unicorn, you basically explode in a ball of glitter."

"You're making that up," said Jake, and Sigmund narrowed his eyes.

"But what can you tell us about the mark?" Frankie asked. "If you do determine it IS a mark? Can you tell who went through it? Can you tell where they went?"

"Perhaps," said Sigmund. "With the proper spells. It'll just take some time."

CHAPTER TWELVE

KILLER SELFIES

The next morning, Frankie sat on her bed and pulled up the edge of her pajama shorts. Not even two days since she'd staked herself in the cemetery, and the wound above her knee had almost entirely healed. All that remained was some bruising, and a fine red line that would soon fade to nothing. No scars, unless you counted the mortifying memories.

"Gotta love those new slayer healing powers."

Frankie looked up. Her mom had poked her head in.

"Mom. You're supposed to knock."

"I thought I was only supposed to knock when the door was closed?"

"Yeah, technically. But still, a little knock never hurt anyone."

"Sorry, sweetie." She knocked belatedly on the open door. "Can I come in?"

Frankie shrugged, and her mom came and sat down on the bed. "So it's all better?"

"Yeah." Frankie rubbed at the wound. "It itches a little."

"At least you can wear your nice, tight pants again."

"Mom, please don't talk about my nice, tight pants."

"Well, you know. Leggings or jeggings or whatever. To me they just look like tight pants. May I interest you in a broomstick skirt? Or a weird sweater whose colors don't match with anything else that you're wearing?"

"Mom," Frankie groaned. "Have you heard anything from Uncle Xander?"

"Only that the searching is slow. They had to stop for a few hours last night when the rain got bad. I haven't wanted to tell Hailey. It's been hard enough on her."

"It is hard," said Frankie. "But don't keep secrets."

"No," her mom said, but she glanced away for just a second, and her brow wrinkled. "Never important secrets."

Frankie eyed her mom seriously for a moment and then got up to get dressed. Everyone, even Buffy and Uncle Xander, had occasionally implied that her mom had a devious streak. And they'd always, *always* warned her to watch Willow close if she ever did magic. But those were just words. And all those old stories were just stories to Frankie. Her mom was her mom. "Your Sage demon expert got here yesterday."

"They did? I didn't feel them hit town. . . ."

"You've been putting feelers out?"

Her mom pressed her lips together. "Very small, weak feelers. Not even feelers. Whiskers. I've been putting whiskers out. But for something as strong as a Sage demon I thought I would feel at least a little pop. Maybe my whiskers are broken."

"Or maybe it's because he's a half demon."

"Half?"

Frankie tugged a light cardigan off a hanger and threw it over the top of her gray tank top. "Half Sage demon, half oddly attractive human. He said he was your friend's son."

"Sigmund?" Willow brightened, her expression finally matching the exuberance of her dress, which was a pretty pastel rainbow tulle that Frankie couldn't believe she wore to the lab. "She sent Sigmund? I can't wait to see him! I haven't seen him since he was a baby and Sarafina wasn't even sure if his horns would come in. Did his horns come in?"

"Not unless they came in somewhere his clothes can hide them," said Frankie. She cleared her throat. "How do you know his mom, anyway?"

"Well, she works in government, but we met when we were both attending a symposium in Boston on ancient relics of war. We hit it off right away, and I had such a crush. So I gave her my shy, socially awkward move—"

"So you gave her your only move."

"Right. And it worked like a charm. But it was nothing serious. Sarafina DeWitt only seriously dates other demons." She sighed wistfully.

"Then how do you explain Sigmund's human dad?"

Her mom blinked. "Well . . . they aren't together anymore, are they? When are you going out on patrol again?"

"After the full moon's over. Spike wants us to wait for Jake. No idea why."

"The stake in the leg is probably why."

"MOM," Frankie moaned. "I staked myself *one time*."

"I'm sure it was a one-time thing," her mom said. "But never turn down a bonus werewolf. Listen to your Watcher. Wait for Jake."

Frankie walked to school alone—she'd wanted to sleep in a little, so Jake had given Hailey a lift earlier on the back of his moped—but when she got there, Hailey was waiting on the steps of the quad.

"Check it out." Hailey opened the flap of her bag and revealed no less than a dozen freshly sharpened stakes. "Not bad, right?"

Frankie raised her eyebrows. They were pretty good. Way better than Jake's anyway. By the time he got the points sharp, he'd carved them down to nubs. Jake's shorties would barely puncture past the rib cage.

"Hailey, you are sleeping, aren't you?" Frankie peered down at the pile. "You're not just sitting wide-eyed on the other side of the wall, creepily whittling?"

Hailey shrugged. "Any word from Xander?"

"Nothing new," Frankie said. "The search continues." She felt bad, leaving out the details. But her mom was right; Hailey would only be upset.

They turned to head inside, and Hailey accidentally bumped into a group of three girls on the steps. They were posing for a photo and turned on Hailey angrily.

"Hey! Why don't you watch where you're going?"

Hailey stopped short. "Sorry." The girl near the top of the stairs glared at her. So did her two friends, their hands on their hips on the steps below—well, at least their hands that weren't holding their phones.

"Just shut up and get out of my shot!"

For a minute, Frankie thought Hailey was going to lay them flat. Hailey squared her shoulders and lifted her chin—the tan skin of her cheeks even sucked in a little, which made her look sort of like Spike. But when Frankie cleared her throat, she said, "Whatever," and let the rude girls live.

"Jeez," Hailey said as she and Frankie walked the rest of the way up. "You'd think it was the end of the world."

Back on the stairs, the girls had returned to posing. The one who'd snapped at them had her hair thrown back and her hand near her throat to show off her manicure.

"Who is she, anyway?"

"Jane Montclair."

"Is she always such a jerk?"

"Mostly," Frankie said.

"Okay, okay, get in the next one with me!" Jane exclaimed, and her friends raced up the stairs for a group selfie. Then they huddled together while Jane edited and posted it.

"Oh my god, do you see her skin?" Jane asked, scrolling through photos on her screen. "I have to have that product. Buying it now."

"Is this a California thing?" Hailey asked.

She peered around as they walked farther into the quad, heading for their first-period class. The quad was strangely crowded that morning, especially so close to the bell. And there seemed to be a lot of girls taking selfies and posing for photos with the hedges.

"I was already here!"

Frankie and Hailey turned at the shout, just in time to see a girl scream and go flying down the stairs.

"Oh my god!"

They ran back and hurried to the bottom, where the girl lay. One of her legs was twisted in the wrong direction.

"Get the nurse!" Frankie shouted. "Nobody move her!" She knelt at the girl's side. "Stay still. Someone's coming to help. Just don't move your head."

The girl struggled up onto her elbows. Frankie didn't recognize her. She looked young, probably a freshman.

"Where's my phone?"

"Here." Hailey searched the sidewalk and found it. "It's okay, see? It's not even cracked."

"I need to get the shot."

The girl started to get to her feet.

"No, hey, just stay still. You're hurt—"

She wobbled up onto her knee and then onto her wrong-bent leg, and it snapped.

"Stop! You're hurting yourself!"

"Get out of my shot!" the girl screeched, and seeing no other alternative, Frankie grabbed her and pinned her by the shoulders.

"Just lie still!" she said, rearing back and trying to keep from getting concussed as the girl thrashed and screeched. "The ambulance will be here soon!"

"What's wrong with her?" Hailey asked as the girl lunged for Frankie and tried to bite. It was a good thing she'd put her hair up in a tight braided bun today.

"I. Have. No. Idea!" Frankie said as she dodged the lunges. The girl didn't even seem to realize what had happened—like she couldn't feel the bone jutting out of her calf. All Frankie could do was pin her with slayer strength and wait until the paramedics arrived to load her onto a stretcher. When they wheeled her away, she was still screeching about getting her shot.

"What. Was that?" Hailey asked, watching them go.

Frankie frowned. She looked around the quad and realized that most of the people there had barely noticed the accident, or the ambulance. They were all still too busy snapping pictures of themselves.

"Something weird is going on. I think we'd better find Spike."

☽ ☽ ○ ☾ ☾

"Someone shoved a girl down the stairs over a bloody photo?" Spike asked.

"Yes," Frankie said as she and Hailey followed him around the library, where he was placing books back on the shelf. "But that's not the weirdest part."

"Yeah," said Hailey. "Like, everyone was doing it. Well, all the girls, and a good number of guys."

"Yeah, and right there in the quad. Who takes selfies in the quad? It's just . . . the quad."

Spike's mouth crooked, and his eye squinted into a dubious expression. Maybe she'd said "quad" too much. "Well, it could have been a challenge, right?" he suggested. "One of those . . . photo challenge thingmabobs. Or maybe a teacher has an assignment." He finished with the books and moved through the rows of computers and tablets, restarting a few and closing out programs and apps.

"You're really getting into this librarian gig," Hailey noted.

"Sigmund was in early to show me a few things. And he got me this pointer gadget so I can interact with the screens." He held it up and waved it around before bending and continuing with the tablets. "Look, maybe the girl just really wanted the photo. I've seen how you lot get: the forced smiles, the head tilting."

"We don't want the shot so bad we snap our calves until the bone pops out."

"Right." Spike sighed. "That is a bit odd." He looked around the library, but there weren't many students there, just a small study group in one corner, quietly sharing notes and munching on carrot sticks. "Let's go into my office. Anyone seen Jake this morning?"

"I texted him," said Hailey. She pointed to the doors. "Here he comes."

"Got your text. What's up?"

"*D and D*, obviously," said Frankie.

They filed into the librarian's office and closed the door. Jake sat down and put his feet up on the desk. He still looked half-asleep; his reddish-blond hair stuck up on one side, and his usually quick eyes were slow and puffy. The first days after wolfing out were always a little rough. He'd told her once that it felt a little like a weak hangover, and when she'd asked him how he knew what a hangover felt like, he'd said, "How? I don't. What's that?" and disappeared.

"So it was Jane Montclair and she was mean, and you thought that was weird?" he asked after they told him what they'd seen.

"She wasn't *mean* mean. Like Jane mean. She was *weird* mean."

"Oh," he said sarcastically. "Like weird mean. Of course. Well, let's see what she was posting at least." He pulled out his phone and opened an app, then scrolled through photos.

"You follow Jane Montclair?" Frankie asked with a raised eyebrow.

Jake shrugged. "I follow everybody. Here. Looks normalllll . . ." His eyes widened as he checked her feed.

"What?" Spike asked. "Is something out of the ordinary?"

"Not really . . . just that she's been posting constantly for the last twelve hours. Like, constantly. Like, every few minutes all night long."

"Maybe she . . . scheduled the posts wrong?" Hailey suggested. "Or there's a bug?"

"Hang on." Jake leaned forward. "Let me check her cronies."

They waited as he scrolled and scrolled, his screen reflected in his increasingly awake eyes.

"This is annoying," Spike said. "I never thought I'd say this, but I miss books."

"Whoa." Jake thrust his phone into Spike's face. "Does that look out of the ordinary to you?"

Frankie leaned in to see. It was a selfie of a very pretty biracial girl in full makeup.

"What am I looking at?" Spike asked.

"That's Jasmine Finnegan," Frankie explained to Spike and to Hailey, who seemed equally confused. "Check the rest of her feed. It's activism and animals and natural soap products. She is vehemently anti–lip gloss."

"Well, she's not anymore," said Jake. "I can't even find a koala in here. She's been constantly posting, too. But just since this morning."

"So maybe she decided to change up her look," Hailey said. "People do that. Up until fourth grade, I wore pigtails."

"Yeah, but—" Frankie couldn't explain it. It just felt wrong. The girls in the quad, the look in that freshman's eyes as she reached for her phone and stood on a broken leg . . . it was all wrong. "This feels very slayery to me."

"Slayery?" Jake asked. "Like, demony?"

"Maybe? Hailey, does it feel that way to you?"

"No, but I don't have the slayer sense. And I hope it's not." She leaned back and ran her fingers through her hair—loose today and combed soft—with a sigh. "I mean, we've got enough going on already without a fricking . . . Insta-demon."

Frankie turned to Spike. "So what do we do?"

"You get back to class. That's what you do," said Spike. "You haven't shown me anything with fangs. Not even compelling evidence of a witch, just girls being pretty. Which, if I'm not mistaken, girls have been doing since girls were girls."

"But, Spike—"

"Go on."

With a roll of her eyes, Frankie grabbed her backpack and led Hailey and Jake out of the library.

"Jake, you need a pass to get back into class?" Spike asked.

"Nope. I just told my teacher I was going to need a looong bathroom break. She won't ask questions."

"Gross," said Frankie.

Jake shrugged. "Everybody poops. Remember the symposium?"

As soon as they cleared the library doors, Frankie pulled them to the side of the hall. Something strange was going on. It was a tingle in her gut. Her slaydar, or whatever, was definitely going off.

"We have to watch these girls," she said. "Especially in places they gather and there might be . . . I don't know, pushing and shoving."

Hailey and Jake looked at each other.

"What?" Frankie asked. "Did you not see that girl's leg? Did that not seem odd to you?"

"Yeah," said Hailey. "It seemed odd. It's just . . . we kind of have a lot of missing slayers, and now we're supposed to be worried about . . . social media?"

"You guys. We live above an old hellmouth, okay? Sometimes that's going to mean multitasking." She put her hands on her hips. "Am I the slayer, or am I the slayer? You'd believe me if I was Buffy."

After a beat, they both slumped, giving in, and Frankie mentally high-fived herself and started issuing orders.

"Jake, you keep digging through photos."

"What am I looking for?"

"I don't know. See if you can find anything weird in the backgrounds. Or in the poses. Check the hashtags and even the people liking them. Maybe something will jump out." She put her hand to her forehead. She felt warm, and her body was tense and springy. She knew those girls were in danger. She just knew it. "Hailey, we have next period with Jane, so we can keep an eye on her there. Let's go."

All through English class, they parked behind Jane Montclair and stared into the back of her head as Mr. Murphy went on and on about themes of revenge and the cycle of violence in *Hamlet*. They waited for Jane to take a selfie in the middle of his lecture. They waited for her to take out her phone and obsessively scroll her feed. They watched with such rapt attention that when Mr. Murphy asked Hailey a question about the ways in which the character of Hamlet was conflicted she had no idea what he'd said and just blurted, "I don't know, Ophelia's pretty tragic." But just when Frankie was sure she'd been wrong and had caused Hailey to flunk English for no reason, Jane raised her hand and asked to go to the restroom.

Hailey and Frankie traded a panicked glance.

"I need to go, too!" Frankie half shouted, and bolted for the door after her, causing the rest of the class to laugh. She frowned. They wouldn't have laughed if she'd been Jake. Or, they would have, but it would have been a different kind of laughing. "Everybody poops," she muttered, and headed for the swinging door of the girls' restroom.

Jane was inside, but she wasn't taking a photo. She didn't even have her phone out. She stood in front of the mirror, scrutinizing her flawless face. Frankie stopped short and tried to seem casual, like she was just *casually* going to the bathroom, not like she needed to go super bad, or like she was following Jane—it was a difficult tightrope to walk. She stopped first at the sink and pretended to check her eye for an eyelash as Jane touched her cheeks and adjusted the straps of her dress. She had a new black tattoo on her shoulder. It struck Frankie as very un-Jane.

"Hey, you got ink," Frankie said. "That's cool."

"What?" Jane asked. Her reflection squinted at Frankie in the mirror like she was a rodent. A rodent she'd just realized was in the same room with her.

"Your tattoo. It's cool." It wasn't cool, actually. It was sort of creepy—an all-black symbol that looked kind of like a snake with beetle legs.

"What are you talking about? Why are you always so weird?" Jane looked back into the mirror. "I need to fix my makeup."

"Your makeup looks fine." Jane was a golden California tan with peach lips and lush dark eyelashes that were probably all her own. There was not a smudge or a smear in sight. Still, she opened her bag and pulled out a clean sponge and started wiping.

At first, Frankie didn't understand what she was looking at. She thought the makeup was blending together to make a shade of muddy gray. And then she realized that the makeup was covering the muddy gray. The muddy gray was Jane's skin.

"Jane, are you okay?"

"Of course I'm okay. I'm just a little stressed. There are midterms coming up, and I did NOT get the volunteer gig I wanted at the hospital. . . ."

She kept on wiping, and more of the pretty girl wiped away. Underneath was dry gray skin, and as Jane wiped harder, that skin peeled away to expose wet pinkish flesh that began to ooze.

"Oh my god, Jane."

"What?" She kept wiping and stripping more skin. Until one side of her mouth drooped, partially torn away from her teeth.

The door to the bathroom swung open, and someone else came in. When they saw Jane, they understandably screamed and ran.

"Get a nurse!" Frankie shouted. "Get help!"

"What is wrong with this school?" Jane yelled. "Does everyone constantly have to go to the bathroom?" She reached hurriedly into her bag for more foundation and powder. But foundation and powder weren't going to cut it anymore.

CHAPTER THIRTEEN

THERE'S ALWAYS SOMETHING IN THE BUSHES

They had to put Jane Montclair in restraints to get her to the hospital. She wouldn't stop trying to remake her face.

"And she didn't even seem aware of it," Frankie said. "What she was doing, what she looked like." She leaned back over her knees and took deep breaths. Jake and Hailey had brought her outside to a bench to calm down and try to keep from throwing up her breakfast. Jane's face . . . watching it peel apart like that . . . if she never saw it again, it would be too soon.

"Here, drink this." Spike handed her a cup.

"What is it? Slayerade?"

"It's water. What the bloody hell is Slayerade?"

"I don't know," said Frankie. "But somebody should make it. For when a slayer sees something that is so gross they can practically taste it."

Jake patted her on the back, a little too hard.

"Now do you believe me that something's going on?"

Grimly, Spike surveyed the scene. Classes had been halted in the main building after what happened to Jane and the freshman girl that morning. They weren't expected to recommence until the afternoon. Other schools might have declared a half day, but in Sunnydale, as long as the body count was in the single digits, a brief pause would do.

Dotted across the campus, students gathered in small groups to gossip about the "accidents" or just to enjoy the break. A suspicious number also seemed to be taking selfies.

"This is a problem," Spike confirmed. "If what happened to . . . what's her name?"

"Jane."

"If what happened to Jane started happening just last night and the rest of these girls are also involved, we don't have much time to keep their faces from falling off, too. You three should keep tailing them. Especially close friends of . . . what's her bloody name?"

"JANE."

"Right. Would be easier if her name was Esmeralda. Keep tabs on Jane's nearest and dearest. Until we know how students are being targeted, it makes sense to assume her friends could be next. I'm going to go meet Sigmund in the library and see what we can dig up."

"Yes, sir, Giles Jr," said Jake, and gave a salute.

"Shut up and do your job." Spike went back inside, and Frankie, Hailey, and Jake stood up to track Jane's friends.

"A freaking Insta-demon," Hailey said, and shook her head.

"Hey, I didn't want to say anything before because you guys were all gaga over him and would think I was just being jealous." Jake cocked an eyebrow. "But I'm pretty sure I saw Sigmund tutoring Jane yesterday after school. Right before all this started."

"Sigmund?" Frankie asked. "As in, our new ally Sigmund? My mom's friend's son, Sigmund?" She looked at Jake carefully. "Is this an alpha-wolf thing?"

"Another wolf shows up and you've got to challenge him for leader of the pack?" Hailey added.

Frankie grinned at Hailey.

"Jake, if you start marking territory, I won't hesitate to spray you with a bottle of water."

Jake bared his teeth. Then he realized he was baring his teeth and promptly pulled his lips down.

"Bottles of water are for cats! And that Sage Sigmund is not a wolf. And I just thought I'd mention that he was tutoring Jane, since we don't know him, and he is a DEMON—"

"Half demon," said Frankie.

Jake snarled. He looked almost frustrated enough to bite, so she tugged on his sleeve and said, "Look, we get it. He's someone we barely know, and he just happened to be tutoring the girl whose face just peeled off."

"Yeah," Hailey agreed, looking regretful. "I mean, other than he's ridiculously good-looking, what do we know? What does he feed on?"

Jake looked from Frankie to Hailey and back again, his invisible wolf tail stuck straight out exasperatedly waiting for them to put it together until the words just burst out of him. "Perhaps could the super-hot demon feed on beauty?"

Frankie sighed. She didn't like that, but she had to admit, it sort of fit.

"Okay," she said. "So maybe we also keep an eye on Sigmund. Between him and Jane's friends, we're going to be stretched thin. And we still don't know how this demon works. Why posting makes your face fall off."

"I've been all over the posts," said Jake. "The only hashtags all the selfies had in common were 'SunnydaleHS' and something called 'GlowChallengeSuccoro.'"

"'Glow Challenge Succoro'? And you didn't think that was odd enough to mention?"

"I thought it was a makeup brand or something."

Frankie put her head in her hands. "Okay. So how do we figure out how the posts work? There aren't a lot of spellbooks that are going to reference social media accounts. Can you trace them back to an original poster?"

"Already did it." He showed them his phone screen. On it was a selfie of a gorgeous brunette girl with freshly blown-out hair and teeth like porcelain.

"I don't know her," said Frankie.

"Me neither. The only followers she has are here at school. Mostly girls. And the account is new."

Hailey turned his screen to look closer.

"Are you sure this is something? Vi always said demons were crap with technology."

"Well, half demons like, say, Sigmund sure seem to be tech savvy." Jake crossed his arms.

"We have to figure this out," Frankie groaned.

"Yeah, and fast, so we can get back to more important things." Hailey craned her neck. "Hey, isn't Sigmund supposed to be in the library with Spike?"

Sigmund was walking across the quad. It looked like he was headed off campus. And walking rather briskly, with his hands stuck in the pockets of his very-well-fitting pants.

"Leaving school grounds just as things heat up," said Jake. "That's not at all suspicious."

"Don't jump to conclusions." Hailey put on her backpack and tapped Frankie on the shoulder. "But Jake's right. He is our number one suspect. So let's tail him."

$$\supset \;\; \supset \;\; \bigcirc \;\; \subset \;\; \subset$$

Frankie had serious doubts about tailing Sigmund. She'd never tailed anyone before, and she'd never snuck off school grounds in the middle of the day. And—she glanced at Hailey as they hurried down the sidewalk approximately half a block behind Sigmund—Hailey wasn't exactly easy to hide. Tall and dressed as she was in a lot of black and particularly stompy boots—if he turned around, they'd have no choice but to dive into the middle of a shrub or a clothes rack.

"Do we really need to be doing this?" Frankie asked. "How likely is it that my mom would send us an ally who would feed on our classmates?"

"Maybe she doesn't know. You said it's been a while since she'd been in touch with them, right?"

"I guess." They walked quickly, keeping close to the open doors of the shops that lined the sidewalk in case they had to dart inside. Ahead, Sigmund's pace did seem to be quickening. And then he turned in to the coffee shop on the corner. "Caffeine fix," Frankie said. "See? Now can we go back to school?"

"What is it with you and school?" asked Hailey. Her thick-lashed, winged-linered eyes narrowed as she watched Sigmund. "Spike and Jake can handle the research and the following Jane's friends around. I want to know what the hot demon is up to."

"What do you suspect him of? Really? I get the feeling that you're less interested in him as an Insta-demon and more interested in him because of the portals."

"Well, of course I am. What if he's involved? In what happened to Vi and the others? I mean, how many demons travel by portal?"

"A lot, I think," said Frankie. "And it would be a pretty big coincidence if the exact demons my mom reached out to were the ones we were looking for."

Hailey frowned, but she was barely paying attention. She was clinging to any clue, seeing connections where there weren't any. And Frankie couldn't blame her.

"Here he comes." Hailey threw her arm across Frankie's chest and squished her flat against the side of a building as Sigmund came out of the coffee shop holding a cup. He looked both ways—which may have been suspicious, or just traffic-conscious—and crossed the street. "Let's go!"

They followed him down alleys, ducking behind dumpsters, and Frankie wished her striped cardigan had a hood attached for her to pull down over her face. They tailed Sigmund down residential streets and squeezed behind tree trunks. She couldn't feel any more ridiculous than if they'd been wearing camo helmets with ferns stuck to them.

"He's not doing anything weird," Frankie said. "He's touring the town. Getting to know it because he just got here." She watched him drink the last of his coffee. He'd stopped down the street and was window-shopping at a store that sold historical miniatures, little tin soldiers that old men used to re-create the Battle of Gettysburg or whatever. "Look. He's going to build a ship in a bottle."

"Maybe you're right," said Hailey. "For a demon, he's hella boring."

"And if he was behind the faces falling off at school, wouldn't he want to hang around and enjoy it? Or if he's just feeding off them somehow, shouldn't he look . . . I don't know . . . full or something?"

"Okay, okay. Let's go back."

They began to slink backward when Sigmund tossed his coffee cup and peered over his shoulders. Frankie paused. That did seem a little suspicious. And he was rubbing his hands against his pants, like he was nervous.

"Maybe just a little more," she said, and she and Hailey followed as he hurried across the street and ducked into the trees that lined the park. Hailey gave her an *I told you so* nudge as they ran after.

Inside the trees, they caught only a glimpse of his back before he disappeared in a circle of sparks. He'd portaled out.

"We lost him!" Hailey searched the air he'd just vanished into, like she could stick her hand in and hold it open. "Where did he go? Can we follow?"

"Even if I knew how to cast a portal, I don't know how to track him," said Frankie.

"Did he know we were following him?"

"I don't think so. But I don't like this. Let's get back to the school and check in with Spike. Maybe he'll be able to tell us something."

"Like what? Spike's not exactly a fount of knowledge."

Frankie sighed. That was true. But he was a fighter, and they could use his help when Sigmund returned from wherever he went and they had to capture him.

CHAPTER FOURTEEN
ID'ING THE INSTA-DEMON

Frankie and Hailey burst through the library doors, looking for Spike. Instead, they found Spike and Jake . . . and Sigmund. The demon was standing with them in the empty library, and when they came in, he gave a little wave.

"You!" Frankie exclaimed.

"Get him!" Hailey shouted.

They ran at Sigmund and leapt, knocking him backward and pinning him to the ground.

"Who are you?" Frankie demanded.

"Where did you go?" asked Hailey. "We saw your portal, demon. Are you behind what happened to the slayers? Did you portal off to check on the wreckage?"

"No!" Sigmund squeaked. "And yes! I did. I did portal to the explosion!"

"Huh?" Frankie asked. Spike reached down and pulled her off Sigmund. Jake did the same with Hailey and helped her back onto her feet. "What do you mean?"

"I mean I was doing my job! What you asked me here to do!"

Sigmund got up and brushed himself off, though the library floor was hardly dirty. "I wanted to get a direct look at the blast site and the mark you found. I was even going to try and bring it back here for us to study, but . . . the concrete it's scorched into was big and heavy and I'm not"—he made some grr noises and claw gestures—"that kind of demon. So instead I took pictures." He took out his phone and showed them. "Those leaves weren't there originally, I just added them to the shot for scale." He looked at Frankie, bewildered. "Why did you think I was involved? And why were you following me?"

But Frankie could hardly remember. Of course Sigmund wasn't involved. Sigmund was wonderful. Beautiful. The best person she'd ever met.

Beside her, Hailey reached out and lovingly straightened the collar of the demon's button-up.

"Sigmund, lad," said Spike. "I think your charm is on again."

"Yeah, well, this time I'm using it for self-defense."

He took a breath and turned it down. Frankie's eyes uncrossed, and Hailey softly smacked herself across the face. They looked at the photos of the portal mark.

"It's like being back in the remote viewing spell," Hailey whispered. "Shit. Sigmund, I'm sorry."

"Really sorry," said Frankie. "We just thought, with what's going on around here and people's faces falling off—"

"Yes," Sigmund said. "Jake already questioned me about that."

"Yeah." Jake scratched the back of his head, embarrassed. "Good news, it's not him."

"I think we got that, Jake," Hailey grumbled.

"But what about what you saw? Him tutoring Jane yesterday? He wasn't . . . feeding on her then . . . I guess? I'm sorry to ask that, but you were with her, and you're new, and a demon, and now she looks like an extra from *Temple of Doom*."

"So you just suspect any demon? Why not suspect Jake?"

"Well, sure," said Hailey. "If the attacks were a wave of chewed shoes . . ."

"I don't chew shoes," said Jake. But he did sometimes, and Frankie had seen the evidence.

Sigmund crossed his arms over his chest. "I'm not behind this," he said. "But since you asked, and I'm not keeping secrets: I *was* feeding on Jane Montclair yesterday afternoon."

They all blinked.

"Come again?" said Spike.

"I'm a Sage demon. We feed on stupidity. Hence all the tutoring sessions. Listen, I know it sounds strange, but it doesn't hurt them. There are many species of demon who feed on different forms of energy. Most Sage demons like to surround themselves with a constant supply of stupidity and take small sips from here or there. It's why my mom works in government. But I take a more evolved view. So I started tutoring students who were struggling. I feed on them as I'm improving their knowledge base and aptitude. After a while, they're no longer a good source of food, but at least they're better off. It makes the relationship feel more symbiotic."

"That's . . . pretty cool of you actually," said Frankie. "Except it's not nice to call them stupid. Can't you say that you feed on 'ignorance'?"

"Ignorance and stupidity are different, but fine, let's not get bogged down in semantics. I feed on 'ignorance.'" He made air quotes and rolled his eyes. "It's not exactly supposed to be nice. I am still a demon. But Sage demons are not evil. My mom likes a good fight, but so do you, don't you, slayer?"

"I don't know about 'like,'" Frankie muttered. "But I am sorry. About tackling you."

"Yeah." Hailey held up a peace sign and grimaced apologetically. "Times two."

"And now we're back at square one," said Jake. "And while you guys were off belly-crawling after Sigmund, we lost another face. Well, not a face." He showed them his phone. Jasmine's profile was on the screen. She'd been posting madly for the last hour. Nearly twice a minute. "It wasn't as bad as Jane. She wasn't wearing as much makeup, so the effects were visible sooner. But the skin was sloughing and she . . . almost washed her hands off."

Frankie's stomach lurched. Poor Jasmine.

"I need more Slayerade. Spike?"

"Here." He handed her a tumbler of water, and she threw most of it into her face. "We've got to figure out what's going on. And fast."

"So let's figure it out." Hailey slipped out of her zip-up hoodie and tossed her black hair over her shoulder. Then she took out her phone, pursed her lips, snapped a selfie, and posted it.

"Okay," she said. "So now we just wait for my face to turn gray or—"

"Hailey, don't!" Frankie exclaimed. But Hailey just made a skeptical face and kept on taking new selfies, until she stopped and blinked in surprise.

"Hey, I got a new follow. And a DM request."

"Don't read it," Frankie said quickly. "Who's the new follow?"

"Someone called 'CollegeBro21.' Sounds fake. Like a bot."

"Or like a demon who isn't good at coming up with screen names," said Jake. He did a quick search on the app. "No photos, just follows. Looks like he's following everyone at our school."

"Is he following the original poster? The . . . pretty brunette?"

150

"Uh . . ." Jake searched. "No."

Frankie stared helplessly at Hailey's phone. Posting that photo had been so reckless! She was starting to understand Vi's hesitancy to take her on patrols. "Why did you do that?" she asked, but Hailey just shrugged and put her phone away.

"Got an easier way to track this thing? Now we can give my phone to your mom, and she can hack it, or trace it, or do a spell on it. Then you can bag the demon and we can get back to investigating that portal mark."

Frankie pressed her lips together so hard it hurt a little. "Spike! Say something!"

"What?" the vampire asked. "Oh, like you want me to be an adult because you cursed me with old-Giles face." He shook a finger in Hailey's direction and cleaned up his accent. "*That was very irresponsible, Hailey.* Bollocks. Like she doesn't bloody know that already." He sighed. "I'mina call your mum. Get her on the case before Hailey's bits start to fall off." He stalked away into his office.

"Hey!" Hailey shouted after him. "I know dirty British slang when I hear it!" But in response the vampire only gave her a dirty British gesture.

"We have to remember that he only *looks* old," said Jake.

"He's like two hundred!"

"Or eternally twenty-seven," said Frankie, "depending on how you look at it."

"Whoa." Hailey put her hands to her face. She wobbled, and Frankie reached out and caught her by the shoulder.

"Hailey?"

"I'm fine. I just got dizzy for a minute."

Jake narrowed his eyes and pulled out his phone. He opened his app and scrolled through, and his face reddened angrily.

"Hailey! Why are you still posting?"

"I'm not," she said. "It was just the one. You saw. I've been right here and my phone's been in my pocket."

Jake showed them his screen. There wasn't only one post. There were five. Every shot she had taken of herself, somehow pulled off her camera roll.

"How is it doing that?" Frankie asked. Before their eyes, another post went up: the same shot as the first, just with a different filter.

Hailey sank down into a chair, her elbows against the table. "Uh, I don't feel so great."

"Shut her phone off, Jake," Sigmund said.

Jake held the button and waited. Then he frowned. "It won't shut down. It just restarts."

"Spike!" Frankie called, and he came out of his office. "The app's got Hailey. It keeps posting."

Jake showed him the phone.

"Well, how did that bloody happen?" Spike looked around the room, his gaze landing hardest on his slayer.

"Don't blame Frankie," Hailey said. "I did it. It's my fault."

"That's . . . absolutely true," he said.

"Spike!" Frankie hissed.

"All right, all right, let's not panic. I called Willow, and the teachers have been confiscating cell phones since the start of the period. Nobody will be posting again until at least the end of the school day. Should buy us some time."

"I don't think so," Jake said. "Not with it posting on its own. And reposting. The same photos over and over, just slightly edited or with a different filter. Hailey? How do you feel?"

"Like I really want eye shadow. Frankie, do you have any eye shadow in your backpack?"

"I don't even have any at my house," Frankie said unhelpfully.

Sigmund began to pace, his hands first on his hips and then crossed over his chest. "This is bad. Very bad."

"What is?" Jake asked. "I mean, I know this is, but what is?"

"What happened to Jane and Jasmine . . . it sounds like what can happen when a demon overfeeds. You see, by widening the feeding pool—that is, increasing users of the hashtag—the demon may have ultimately gained so many followers that it would have become relatively harmless. Siphoning a small amount of energy from every post. But by confiscating phones and blocking its supply of fresh users, it's being forced to increase the feeding on the existing ones. Like Hailey."

"Great," Hailey said, and glared at Spike.

"What?" he said. "How was I supposed to know?"

She leaned forward and cradled her head. "My skin. It's starting to feel . . . restless. Like I need to put something on it. Foundation, maybe. Or scented lotion?" She looked at Frankie, confused. "What the hell is going on?"

"Uh, Hailey," said Jake. "Do you have any tattoos?"

"Not yet. Why?"

"Because you have one now."

He nodded to her arm, and Frankie folded up the sleeve of her T-shirt. There was a black tattoo emblazoned on her bicep. Black and twisty, like a snake had mated with an insect.

"I know that symbol," said Sigmund.

"What do you mean? What is it?" Frankie rolled up Hailey's hoodie for her to use as a pillow as her head dropped to the table. She was fading fast. And the posts kept going up, again, again, again and every time liked by CollegeBro21.

"I've seen it before." Sigmund got up and jogged to the occult section. He ran his index finger along the rows until he pulled out a small volume with a faded, cracked binding and a cover of dark green buckram. Then he came back, flipping pages. "Here," he said, and set the open book between them on the table.

"What. Is that?" Jake asked.

The ink illustration of the demon was rough, as most of them were. Barely more than an outline. But the shape that was there was terrible: long, gnashing teeth and a pointed chin, appendages affixed to its head that might have been horns or very high, curving ears. The hands ended in sharp, black-tipped claws. And there was no nose.

"Attractive," Hailey murmured, one eye open as she lay against the table. She looked at Sigmund. "Why couldn't you have posted instead of me? The demon could have fed off your pretty backside for years and still had good looks to spare."

Sigmund smiled a little.

"That doesn't look anything like the original poster," said Jake. "Check these out. She's posted new ones." He scrolled through a few shots: the pretty brunette in a cozy off-white sweater, a mug of coffee warm between her hands and aviator sunglasses resting atop her head; another of her smiling at the beach, blue bikini strap visible beneath the cover-up falling off her shoulder. There was even one of her snuggling a fluffy gray kitten.

"Look at her skin," Hailey said, and grabbed Jake's wrist. "It's like glass!"

Frankie had to admit that whatever regime the girl was using she wouldn't mind starting herself. She was so pretty. So healthy. So glowing and happy, and she probably did nothing but cool things with cool people.

"That's not what it really looks like." Sigmund held up the illustration again and tapped it. "That Instagram account is just a glamour. It's curated. Fabricated. That's really a Succoro demon."

"As in, hashtag GlowChallengeSuccoro?" Jake tugged his phone away from Hailey and scrolled through the feed. "Does feeding off Hailey and the other girls help it look like this instead of that?" He pointed to the book. "Because I guess I don't blame it."

"I don't think it is feeding off the girls," Sigmund said. "Succoro demons eat regular human food. They're actually foodies. . . . They glamour themselves and post about the best new restaurants. Succoro demons are energy brokers. They harvest for someone else."

"Yeah, I knew one of those in Belfast," Spike mused. "Good bloke. Made the best blood around with some secret blend of spices. Little bit of nutmeg." He shrugged. "I had him suck energy off a few peasants when Dru needed a boost."

Frankie gave him a look. "You do still have your soul, don't you?"

"I didn't say I would do it *now.*"

"Anyway," Sigmund said. "Succoros aren't usually vicious. But they do need money to fund their gourmet lifestyle, and depending on the size of the energy harvest they're hired for, sometimes their efforts turn dangerous." He reached for one of the school's tablets and did a quick search, then showed them news articles from social media–related deaths: a boy who'd fallen from a viewpoint taking a selfie, a girl who had fractured her skull during a challenge.

"I thought demons were supposed to hate technology," Hailey moaned.

"That's just an old Watchers' tale," said Sigmund. "You know how they cling to their books." He turned the screen back to himself and kept on scrolling. "But these incidents are outliers," he said. "Normally the Succoro's energy haul is modest, and harmless."

"But this one isn't," Frankie said. "So who is it harvesting for?"

"I don't know. But a feed of this magnitude . . . I'd say it was someone who needed to recover their strength in a hurry."

"All right," said Spike. "So how do we stop them? Can we remove the tattoos?"

"The tattoos won't disappear until the contract is complete or the broker dies. Or we get everyone to delete their accounts."

"So there's no choice but to kill," said Jake.

Frankie looked at Hailey. Her tan skin was starting to discolor, turning sallow where it was thin at her temples and the insides of her wrists. The slayer went into the office and reached under Spike's desk, pulled out a chest, then opened it up and started pulling out blades. "What will it take? Beheading? Evisceration? Do I need to aim for the eyes?"

Sigmund picked up the book and read quickly. "Any old death will do. But be careful, Frankie. They're subdued within their glamour, but in their demon state, a Succoro can be very dangerous. The tips of those fingers—" He snuck a peek at her knee, and she knew he was thinking of her stake wound.

"I wish we would stop telling everyone about that," she muttered to herself.

Hailey sat up, staring incredulously at Jake's phone, which she'd stolen back again. "Did you read these posts?" She held the phone up to show Frankie a beauty shot of a jar of moisturizer. "It has affiliate products. Sponsorship. It's taking our energy *and* scamming us on face creams!"

"So where do I find it?" Frankie asked.

"Bet I can find out where this beastie is," Spike said, and threw off his jacket. "I'll trade the tweed for the duster and hit up the demon bars. Someone's bound to know something. Willow is doing what she can on the computer to track the origin, and she said she'd get Oz out sniffing when he's done at the youth center. Between the four of us"—he turned to go but looked at Frankie seriously—"we'll find it. And, Mini Red: If I'm close enough, I'll deal with the demon myself. But we don't have much time. If you're closer, you might be on your own."

"That's fine," she said. But her voice trembled. She hadn't realized she would be alone, since not even Jake could be there; it was still the full moon, and he had to get home soon and lock himself in.

"I can go with you," said Sigmund, but Frankie shook her head.

"No. You stay with Hailey. Let me know if she gets worse, and try to keep her from scratching any of her skin off."

CHAPTER FIFTEEN
THE WOLF IN THE CAGE

"You didn't have to walk me home," Jake said as they walked up the Osbourne driveway after parking his moped. "I am a werewolf, you know. I can take care of myself."

"That's why I came. To make sure you wouldn't go rogue and hunt the Succoro on your own. Then I'd have to bring a knife for it *and* the tranquilizer gun for you." She poked him in the shoulder. "Plus, I thought maybe you'd let me use the moped to hunt for it? So I could cover more ground?"

"Ah." Jake unlocked the front door. "Now I see your ulterior motive."

"Well, it's not like you're going to be using it when you're wolfed out."

"Fine. Just drive careful. You don't have your license."

"Yeah, yeah," she said. Like you needed a license to drive a moped. The thing was basically an ungainly bicycle.

"You coming in?"

"Sure. I can double-check your lock, like in the old days." In the old days, they'd had full-moon sleepovers. She and the Osbournes would play long games of Monopoly and order pizzas, and when the family locked themselves in their cages for the night, six-year-old Frankie would roll out her sleeping bag near Jake's cage. She hadn't slept well at first, with the wolfed-out Osbournes leaping at their cages trying to get at her. But eventually the wolves got used to her presence. Except for Jordy. And when Jordy bent his bars one night and managed to get a claw into the corner of Frankie's sleeping bag, the sleepovers had to stop.

Jake led Frankie into the house, through the living room, and past his bedroom, which smelled very boylike and had walls that were plastered with sports memorabilia and about a hamper's worth of clothes on the floor. The rest of the house was clean, though. Like, sparkling clean. As clean as he'd gotten their kitchen on the day they'd found out about the explosion.

"Why is your room such a dump?"

"Why are you such a dump?" he retorted, and she socked him in the arm. "Sorry. Don't make me think of comebacks this close to the moon. And for your information, my room only gets that way around wolfing times. It kind of turns into a den." She peeked her head in—the blankets from the bed had been dragged onto the floor and made into a kind of nest. She could imagine Jake sleeping there, curled up. He'd done that when he was a kid, too, and they'd used to build pillow dens in Frankie and Willow's living room.

Jake opened the door to the basement—one of the few new houses to boast a basement in New Sunnydale—and flipped on the light. It was just as Frankie expected: a genuine man cave, complete with mini fridge, gaming systems, and foosball table. A completely normal space for a house inhabited by two bachelors. Except of course for the massive cage built into one side, secured by a heavy combination padlock.

"You took out your parents' and Jordan's cages?" she asked.

"I thought I might enjoy the extra room. And they'll be easy enough to put back." He shrugged. "If they ever decide to come home."

"Have you heard from them lately?"

"My mom wrote me a letter. And my dad called . . . maybe a month ago?" He shrugged again, harder. "Sounds like Jordy's really thriving. Finding balance, or whatever. Sounds like they all are. They want me to come, too."

"Are you going to go?"

"What's so great about it?" He shrugged a third time. "Oz doesn't seem to miss it."

"Well, that's because Oz is happy to be here. With you."

"With you and your mom, more like," Jake said. "Mostly with your mom."

But what she said about Oz made Jake happy. He was aggressively fighting a smile.

"Anyway, how am I supposed to leave with the Hellmouth rumbling and you being a slayer?"

"I guess I'd miss you, if you had to go. But I'd understand."

"Yeah, you'd miss me, and you'd die. Besides, I don't need them. Not like the commune's going anywhere."

He made it sound like he was talking about the commune, but Frankie knew that when he said "them," he meant his parents. Willow and Frankie had always tried to be Jake's second family, especially once it became obvious that Ken and Maureen intended to more and more frequently dump him on the Rosenberg doorstep. But it still wasn't the same.

"Jake—"

"Look," he said. "Everything I need to know about being a good werewolf citizen, I can learn from Oz. So stop trying to get rid of me. I'm not going anywhere."

He smiled at her, and she watched as he grabbed cold cuts and hard-boiled eggs out of the mini fridge, and put them in a cooler along with a few juice boxes and several sticks of jerky.

"Jeez, Jake, the kitchen is right upstairs."

"Sometimes I can't wait that long." He grabbed a piece of vegetarian jerky and offered some to her, but she shook her head. Her stomach felt like not so much a stomach as one of those industrial paint shakers they had in hardware stores.

"I hope Spike finds the Succoro demon," she said.

"He will. Hailey will be okay, Frankie. She's too tough not to be."

"Yeah," she said. "Except that's not what I mean. I mean I hope Spike finds it. And Spike kills it. Or Oz finds it and wolfs out on it. Or even my mom. She's rusty, but I bet she can handle one demon. So I don't have to." She crossed her arms. "That's not a very slayery thing to say."

But Jake just sighed. "You're right, though. They could handle it. They're Spike, Willow, and Oz. They've handled this and much worse." He nudged her. "You nervous?"

"Psh." She waved her hand. "Psh."

"It's okay to be. It's your first demon. You going to stay and tuck me in? Tell me stories, like you used to?"

She chuckled. "Which one do you want?" When they were kids, she would whisper stories to his werewolf self from her sleeping bag. "Little Red Riding Hood." "The Three Little Pigs." And she always changed the endings so the wolf won. The next morning, he said he didn't remember, but when she told those stories, the wolf had always crouched down to listen.

Jake patted his stomach. "'The Three Little Pigs.'"

"You got it."

He stepped into his cage and pressed the lock into place. Then he started arranging his blankets on the floor. It was kind of cute, like watching a dog circle before it lay down. Then he started to take off his belt.

"Jake, my eyes!" Frankie exclaimed.

"I'm not taking my pants off. Just the belt. Because it'll hurt when I change."

"Oh, right. I guess I should go. You sort of need to shed clothing." She shifted the straps of her backpack and felt the weapons jostle inside.

"No, stay," said Jake. "I've got a little while before I change, and I don't like this shirt anyway." He sniffed the air. "Almost time. Wish I could be out there with you."

"One day," she said. "When you've tamed your monthly beast."

"Please don't make another menstruation joke."

She grinned. "Do you think he'll know me?" she asked, meaning the wolf. "It's been a while." A decade, almost, since she had actually seen him.

"He is me," Jake said. "And I don't know. But I bet he will."

She pulled her phone out and checked her app. Fresh posts were going up; everyone must have gotten their phones back. She hoped that Sigmund was right and more posters would spread the harvest out and buy Hailey more time.

In his cage, Jake doubled over and groaned. Frankie took an inadvertent step away. She had never liked watching the wolf come out. Even though Jake said it didn't, it always looked like it hurt.

Werewolf Jake got up off the bottom of the cage and shook his fur. He was pretty, as far as werewolves went, with a little golden red in his overall dark coat. If she'd been surrounded by a pack of them, she'd have known which one was Jake. But she'd have also been eaten, because Jake didn't know her anymore.

"Hi there," she said, and the werewolf snarled. "Remember me?" He rammed into the bars of the cage and reached his claws through. Frankie took a deep breath. "Once upon a time, there were three delicious little pigs," she said. "Basted-to-perfection little pigs who lived in totally tear-down-able houses . . ." The Jake wolf sat down on his haunches. By the time she finished the story, he was panting, almost happily. Then her phone buzzed in her lap, and he leapt up, growling.

She picked up the phone and read. Spike had beaten up a bartender and gotten the lead. The Succoro demon had a lair in the woods near Marymore Park. That was less than ten minutes away by foot, no moped required.

Frankie opened her backpack and took out the long-bladed knife. "Can you keep a secret, Jake wolf?" she asked. "I don't know if I'm going to make for a very good slayer." The werewolf snarled, but to Frankie, it sounded like a snarl of encouragement.

"But here goes nothing."

CHAPTER SIXTEEN
A GIRL NEVER FORGETS HER FIRST DEMON

Frankie kept the knife low against her leg as she walked through the residential neighborhood. The darn thing kept flashing in the moonlight. On the upside, the full moon meant that she would have plenty of light to fight by. Of course, on the downside, it had taken her closest and most comforting ally and locked him in a cage in a basement.

She skirted the edge of the playground—playgrounds at night with no children always gave her the creeps, though playgrounds at night WITH children might have been even worse—and plunged into the woods beyond without giving herself a chance to hesitate. No deep breaths allowed. No second thoughts. She was a slayer. She was THE slayer. And Hailey needed her to be as good as Buffy, if only for tonight.

Inside the forest, the trees cut the moonlight, yet she still felt like she could see. Slayer eyes, she supposed. She tested her slayer nose. The only smell was the scent of trees and greenery and cool, dry earth. Nothing rank or demony, though she didn't exactly know what the Succoro demon was supposed to smell like. The book hadn't said. Sigmund had mentioned that they were foodies, so maybe they smelled like garlic and trendy spice blends. It would have long, razor claws, tipped with basil-infused olive oil. When they found her body covered in stab wounds, it would basically be marinated.

Frankie adjusted her grip on the knife and wiped the handle. Her palms hadn't sweated this badly since the time she'd danced with Peter Paulson in seventh grade. But she kept going, deeper and deeper into the trees, hoping to find the demon or its lair before Hailey and the others were permanently scarred or wasted away completely.

She'd gone maybe a hundred yards before she had the feeling that she was being followed. And another fifty yards before she was certain of it.

She glanced up into the trees. The branches were low, and strong. She could climb up there and wait for the demon to pass underneath. But just as she reached a tree and was preparing to scramble up the bark, something stepped out from the bushes ahead.

Ahead. Not behind. Yet she'd been sure she was being followed.

It didn't matter. The demon standing in front of her was definitely the one she'd been looking for. Long, hooked, claw-tipped fingers. Sharp, pointy appendages that were indeed ears and not horns. No nose.

"Nice to meet you, CollegeBro21," she said. "Have to say it's hard to imagine you bent over a tablet posting to an app. Do those claws double as a stylus or something?" She lifted her knife and adjusted her stance, pleased with herself. That quipping was not half bad. And then CollegeBro21 stood up to his full height. Which was over double her own.

"Oh," she said as the demon reached out and slashed.

She ducked just in time. JUST in time. As in, she was fairly sure that later she would discover a new layer cut into her hair. Tucking her knife close, she rolled to one side and popped back up, barely missing another rake of the Succoro's claws. It was a hard rake, too—she blocked it with the edge of the knife and the metal sang with vibration. She dodged and rolled, and dodged and rolled again, like a dance. A dance that occasionally resulted in slices taken out of her clothes.

"Maybe this was a bad decision," she gasped as she blocked again with the knife. But Spike was on his way. Maybe with her mom and Oz. Sigmund had failed to mention how tall the Succoro was going to be. "Stupid hot demon expert," she whispered as the Succoro caught her off guard and its claws cut through the skin of her forearm.

"Ow!"

The demon backed off and licked her blood from its sharp fingertips.

"I haven't seen you, pretty girl," it said, its voice surprisingly cordial. "And I hadn't planned on eating. But since you're here, perhaps a raw preparation . . ."

"What, like slayer carpaccio?" she asked.

A different light came into the demon's eyes, and Frankie realized her mistake. She wasn't supposed to mention that she was a slayer. Spike wanted her to keep that a secret for as long as they could.

The demon's entire demeanor changed. It feared her. It turned to run. And as it did, she saw the tattoo marked on its back: the same as the one on Hailey's arm and Jane's shoulder.

She leapt upon it and drove it to the ground, bringing her knife down hard. But a demon wasn't exactly like a vampire, and she missed the heart. She missed everything good actually—her blade bounced off one of its shoulder blades, and it screamed and threw her off. She rolled onto her feet and darted back in again, ducking claws. It knocked the knife from her hand, but she managed to grab the demon's arm and leveled a kick to its abdomen. And she could swear she heard it say "Oof."

"You're not going to drain my friends," she said as they grappled. The Succoro was strong, though. If she wanted to end it, she wouldn't be able to do it with her bare hands.

Frankie rolled away, then jumped up and drove both heels into the demon's chest, propelling herself back to somersault across the ground. Her knife was easy to find, glinting in the moonlight, and she scooped it up.

The demon took off through the trees.

She gave chase, catching branches to the face that lashed her cheeks. Her legs caught in the undergrowth. She almost lost a shoe. Every one of the Succoro's strides was worth four of hers, and before she knew it, it was out of sight.

She'd lost it.

☽ ☽ ◯ ☾ ☾

Back in the library, Sigmund paced nervously as he awaited updates from the slayer or Mr. Pratt. As he paced, he kept one eye on Hailey where she sat behind the librarian's desk. School was out and the library was completely empty, but Sigmund had shut them inside and locked the door anyway.

"Anything yet?" Hailey asked as he checked his phone for what felt like the hundredth time.

"Nothing," he said, and tried to smile. Then he muttered, "Come on, slayer, hurry up," under his breath. He'd never had to be on guard duty before, and Sigmund DeWitt was not the guarding kind of half demon. When he'd accepted this assignment from his mother, she'd assured him it would be all libraries and earth-loving witches. She said his nose would be ink-stained from being stuck in a book.

Of course his mother would leave out the possibility he would be drafted to fight. She was always on the lookout for ways to make him fight. To become the warrior part of the warrior scholar.

Sigmund glanced at Hailey. When the others had left, she'd seemed quite exhausted. That's why he'd agreed to guard her—it seemed like he'd need do no more than play nursemaid. But since the others had gone, Hailey was less tired and more restless. Every time she moved, he jumped. Maybe she should have been the one to get locked in the cage rather than the werewolf.

You're being a fool, he chastised himself. *The poor girl is ill. She's in danger.*

And she was a human. The only non-powered human in the group. What could go wrong?

Draped across Mr. Pratt's chair, Hailey stretched her arms and neck.

"I don't know what Frankie's so upset about this demon for anyway," she said. "It's just a few pictures! I mean, sure, she's the slayer and has all these slayer senses or whatever, but she doesn't know everything. Trust me, Vi was a slayer for like twenty years and she definitely doesn't know everything."

Sigmund went to the desk and opened his laptop. "Do you want to watch a movie while we wait?" he suggested. "Or . . . listen to some music . . . ?" He didn't know her very well, but Hailey sounded a little drunk.

"It probably isn't even a demon. Just a new influencer. Do you think it could be one of those computer-generated ones?"

"I don't think so—"

168

"I mean, so it advertises face creams. It's not the demon's fault if a few people take it too far and fall down some stairs, or don't wash their makeup brushes enough and give themselves flesh-eating bacterial infections, or . . . wash their hands off. . . ." She paused. "Okay, the last one is a little weird. But I feel fine. I feel better than fine. I feel PRETTY."

"Well, that makes sense at least." Sigmund blushed awkwardly and looked away. "Because you are very pretty."

And he was very pretty, too. And very nervous, so he had to be careful about his charm mojo. But Hailey did not seem charmed. Or docile. Her dark, lined eyes fixed on him, and she licked her lips.

"So can I get my phone back? I feel a serious need to document the moment."

Sigmund jumped up from the table, his hand over the shape of her phone in his pocket.

"I don't think that's a good idea."

"Come on." She held her hand out and wiggled her fingers. "Just one post."

"I'm sorry, Hailey." He tucked her phone deeper into his pocket, and she made a pouty face. But then she sighed, like it was no big deal.

"How are the hashtags looking?" she asked. "Anyone posting anything new?"

"Um . . ." he said, and took out his phone to check. He didn't notice how her eyes lit up at the sight of it.

"There are a lot," he said, scrolling. "I suppose that's good for us."

"Mmm-hmm," she said. She leaned across the librarian's desk. Actually she mounted the desk and began to crawl toward him like a cat.

"Hailey, are you okay?"

"Tired of people asking me that, but yes, I'm fine. Don't I look okay?" She tilted her head and slid her hand innocently toward him. Sigmund jumped away so fast he nearly knocked over his chair. "What's wrong?"

"Nothing," he said. "Just that I know I don't know you very well, but I think it's safe to say that you're not quite yourself."

Hailey sighed and stretched. The twisted, insect-like tattoo flexed on her bicep.

"I'm just bored. Frankie's never going to find this demon that doesn't exist, and I don't know how long you like spending in a librarian's office, but my answer to that is not. This. Long." She rolled over onto her back, again reminding him of a cat in a sunbeam. The way she smiled at him made him feel a little like a mouse.

"Hailey," he said and cleared his throat, "are you feeling all right? You don't seem . . . You seem like you're . . . not in the right frame of mind—"

"Well, duh," she snapped. Then she cocked her head seductively. When she spoke, her voice was slow and sweet. "What do you like to do when you're bored, Sigmund?"

"Read?" His voice sounded ridiculously high and afraid; he gestured to the library shelves. "I could find us some Thomas Paine . . . or even the *Necronomicon* would be better at this point—"

"Give me my phone!" Hailey scrambled over the desk and lunged. He managed to stay out of the way, but not without letting out an embarrassing little *eek*. "Listen, Sigmund. I like you. Really, I do, with your bookish, no-nonsense manners and that modest smile on that perfect face, but I have things to do, okay? Sisters to find. Selfies to post." She scratched a little at her arm, and a thin trail of blood ran down to her elbow.

"Hailey," Sigmund said. "Oh god, Hailey, don't scratch—"

"I can't help it. It feels like my skin is a pair of too-tight wool gloves." She scratched again.

"Hailey—"

"Come over here and stop me," she whispered, in what she clearly thought was an enticing way.

When he didn't, she leapt on him with a roar and brought him to the floor, hooking her feet around his knees.

"Hailey!" He twisted and squirmed. "Let go of me!"

"Stop being so dramatic," she said, grabbing at his pockets. "It's just one picture!"

He twisted hard, broke her hold, and ran to the other side of the desk.

"Hailey, you're not thinking straight. Just stay back." He crouched. She was preparing to jump, straight over the top. "Don't make me use my demon strength," he shouted. "I don't like fighting!" It was a bluff. He didn't have any demon strength. Just like he had no horns to glamour. His physical traits had come mostly from his dad.

"You've got demon strength?" she asked. Then she shrugged. "I'll chance it."

She leapt onto the desk, and Sigmund braced for impact. But instead of jumping at him, she wobbled.

"Sigmund?" she asked just before she collapsed.

☽ ☽ ◯ ☾ ☾

Crap. Crap, crap, crap, Frankie thought as she plunged through the nighttime trees, head on a swivel, searching for any sign of the demon. A moving leaf. A swaying branch. A helpful owl, with a wing pointed west. But there was nothing. The gigantic, panicked, wounded thing had vanished without a trace.

Slow down, she thought, and stood stock-still. *Listen.* She let her eyes lose focus and concentrated on the air. She tried to remember the last moments of her struggle with the Succoro—had she seen it turn or double back? But all she'd seen was that it fled. It only had a second and a half's worth of lead on her. And she'd still managed to lose it.

Okay, she thought calmly. *Try again. Focus.*

She took a deep breath and closed her eyes. Her phone buzzed in her pocket.

"Dammit!"

She took it out. It was a number she didn't know, but the area code showed Washington, DC.

"Sigmund?"

"Yes, it's me. Are you all right?"

"I mean, physically, I guess."

"Did the demon give you any trouble?"

"Well . . ." Frankie looked around hopelessly. "You said the Succoro could glamour, right? Any chance it could glamour into a tree? Because . . ." Sigmund didn't respond. He was probably confused, and she didn't blame him. But he sounded upbeat. Almost giddy. "How's Hailey doing?"

"She's much better. She passed out for a moment and I had to tie her to a chair, but the mark—the tattoo—is gone, and she's up again and requesting something to drink. I think I'm going to raid the vending machine, and then I'll walk her home."

"Walk her home? Wait—tie her to a chair?"

"Yes. And don't worry; I've checked, and all the posts with the Succoro's hashtags are gone. I think it's safe to assume the other posters' tattoos have disappeared as well. Should we meet you at your house? Is Jake coming?"

"Jake's got fangs and fur until seven fifteen," Frankie said, still not sure what was happening.

"Oh," Sigmund said happily.

"Sigmund, let me get this straight—you're saying Hailey is fine? That the posts are gone?"

"Yes, she collapsed, and the mark vanished about two minutes ago. Killing the demon really did the trick. Nice work, slayer."

"Yeah." Frankie peered around suspiciously. "Except . . . I didn't kill it."

"What?"

"I didn't kill it. I found it and we fought, but it got away."

Stunned silence. Then he asked, "Could it have died afterward? Did you badly wound it?"

"I don't think so." One shallow cut across a shoulder blade did not a dead demon make.

"Stay on your guard," said Sigmund. "I'm going to contact Mr. Pratt and your mother and Mr. Osbourne. Where are you?"

She looked up at the full moon.

"Somewhere in the woods behind Marymore Park. They're probably already on their way."

"Actually, some of us are already here."

Frankie turned. Oz was standing two trees behind her.

"Sorry for creeping up. I get real predatory this time of the month. Not, like, *bad* predatory. Or sex predatory. Did I mention your mom's here, too?" He gestured over his shoulder, and Frankie caught sight of her mom, picking her way through the forest. Going on a nighttime hunt, and she still insisted on wearing a long, flowy skirt.

"Sigmund, my mom and Oz are here. I'm sure Spike will be here soon. Are you sure you're good to get Hailey home?"

"I'm sure."

"Okay, we'll meet you there in a little while."

They hung up, and Frankie turned at the sound of footsteps crunching through the woods from the south. Spike's platinum hair was a dead giveaway.

"Cavalry's here," Spike said. "You all right, Mini Red?"

"I'm fine." She held up her phone. "I just talked to Sigmund, and Hailey's fine, too. Like the Succoro's dead, only I didn't kill it. It got away."

"But you're okay?" her mom asked, and felt up and down both of Frankie's arms. "You're bleeding. That demon Iron Chef really sliced and diced this shirt."

The cuts on Frankie's arm weren't bad; they'd almost stopped bleeding on their own. But she stood patiently and let her mom tear strips of bandage out of her already-ruined sleeves.

"If you didn't kill it but the kids are fine," Oz said, "what does that mean? Maybe the demon gave up?"

"It didn't seem to like hearing that I was a slayer."

"I didn't think you were supposed to be telling it," said Spike. "And I don't think it gave up." He raised his nose to the air and sniffed.

"Oh, hey, let me," said Oz, and sniffed as well. "The snout is very at its peak." It only took him a few whiffs before he nodded back the way Frankie had come.

"What do you smell?" she asked. "Blood?"

"Blood, bile, and stomach contents. This way."

"That is so gross," Frankie muttered as they followed Oz through the woods. It wasn't far to the source of the smell, and Frankie tried to pay attention to see whether she'd even come close to finding it. She'd gotten so turned around in the trees. There was no way to tell.

But it was certainly easy to tell that the Succoro was dead. The demon had been left in a clearing, on its back in the moonlight. Something, or someone, had sliced open its torso and cracked open its rib cage like a very red, gory nut. That close, even non-werewolf and vampire noses couldn't miss the smell.

Oz sniffed again. "Last meal was poached salmon," he said, and Frankie turned and threw up into a fern.

"You okay, sweetie?"

"Yep, I'm fine," she said quickly, and turned back, wiping her mouth. "What did this?"

Spike and Oz peered at Willow in the dark.

"It wasn't me!" she exclaimed. "I can't explode demons! I can't even take the glamour off your old face!"

Spike and Oz knelt on either side of the body. They cocked their heads and peered inside the chest cavity. Spike broke off a stick and prodded around in the entrails, conducting a bizarre postmortem. It went on a little too long, in Frankie's opinion.

"The torso's been cut," the vampire said. "But that's not what killed him." He toed the demon's head back and forth. "Neck's been broken. And then, of course, there's that." He pointed to the ground and stepped away so the moonlight could strike the words written out in the dirt and grass and moss, written in the Succoro's entrails and blood.

COUNTESS.

"What the heck does that mean?" Willow asked.

"Nothing good. Demon's laid out like it's on a bloody platter. And I don't fancy a tangle with whatever it was could break the neck of something like this and gut it like so much Thanksgiving turkey."

You stuff a Thanksgiving turkey, Frankie thought, and looking at the dead demon, she was once again relieved to be a vegetarian.

"Well, I almost took it out. I mean, I would have, if it hadn't run."
But her tiny slice on its shoulder paled in comparison to what else
had befallen it, and the adults cast her rather less-than-convinced
glances.

Oz bent toward the Succoro again and looked into the chest
cavity. "Huh."

"What's 'huh'?" asked Willow.

"Well, the 'huh' is the heart, and the fact that there isn't one."
Oz straightened. "Do these things not have hearts? Because otherwise, I think it's safe to assume that this one's been taken."

The energy supply shut off like a cord had been cut. She had been lying quite comfortably, nestled in the dirt from her home country, taking in the healing properties of that good earth—as well as a very pleasant hum of vitality through the black mark on her shoulder— for the better part of a day. And then it was gone. The shock of the sudden absence went straight to her gut, and she erupted out of the dirt and out of the porcelain bathtub, doubling over and frightening her two fledglings. She felt so violently sick that she'd have thrown up blood had she eaten any. But she hadn't needed to. That long-legged demon had been true to his word: The energy he harvested for her was just the kind she liked. Young and pretty and vital. A few tasted less than innocent, but the volume more than made up for that. And then it was gone.

"What happened?"

"I don't know," *one of the fledglings sputtered through his fangs.* "The mark . . . it's gone."

She glanced down at her shoulder. The mark the demon had placed on her had disappeared. But that was fine. It had been an ugly thing: a serpent dancing with a spider or some such. She stretched her neck and legs, all her bare skin streaked with dirt in the candlelight. She still looked good. And she felt better. And at least the energy she'd siphoned from that demon had been enough to get her out of the dirt.

"Box that up," *she said, jerking her head back toward her bath-tub.* "And keep it safe." *The fledgling nearest the door called for help,* and two new vampires hurried to comply. They were very new. She didn't even think she'd met them yet. They were a little thin for her taste; she liked her fledglings bulky and built. The kind of vampire who could lift a stone slab a few inches even before he was dead. But oh well. Soon, she would be able to choose her own. For now, the choice fell to Anton, and she trusted his selections as she trusted him in everything.

"Where is Anton?"

"Right here."

She turned to him and smiled, and he smiled back, happy to see her freed from the dirt, strong enough to walk with him in the moonlight. He wrapped her in a cape and offered his arm.

"Do you wish for a proper bath?" he asked.

"Later. After the tub is cleaned out. But I do wish for something proper to eat," she said, and snapped her fingers at one of the young vampires. "Something fresh and pretty and innocent." Her stomach rumbled. "But if you can't find that, just make it fast."

"What happened to the energy supply?"

"Cut off," she said. "I thought he said that wouldn't happen."

"Something must have stopped him," said Anton. "Or killed him."

"It had best be the latter." She frowned. She still felt so abysmally, frustratingly weak. As if she couldn't crush a skull in the palm of her hand. Perhaps not even with two hands. She looked down at herself and touched the soft waves of her light brown hair. It had been such a long time since she'd seen her own face. It was that sometimes that she missed the most: the sight of her own reflection. She had never been a great beauty, even when she was a young woman, but she'd liked the way she looked. Her cheekbones had been strong, and her expressions full of purpose. Even when she'd been human, men had feared her. There were portraits of her, of course. She'd had several painted—practically one a year up until her death at the age of fifty-four—and that one hung even now, on the wall opposite her tub of dirt. But they weren't the same. Painters had come a long way, though, since then. She should really have a new one commissioned. Perhaps a nude.

"Progress continues on the tunnels," said Anton. "We've managed to clear away much of the cave-in."

"But does it reach the city?"

"It's too soon to say. But it's a very nice space for a catacombs."

It would be a stroke of luck if the tunnels beneath the old mansion reached into the town. Especially considering that the town had dropped fifty feet. An inconvenience, but at least it left the mansion with a lovely view: the lights of New Sunnydale sparkling below like little diamonds, each one marking a human to be tortured and eaten.

"A catacombs," she said. "Like the one I used to have. I want the pillars built from the femurs of young men. I want the doorways arched with the skulls of infants and crowned with the rib cages of virgins." Her face brightened. "I want a mural of my old horse, Lavinia. Wouldn't that be nice?"

"Yes, Countess. Very nice. How are you feeling?"

She exhaled. She felt tired. Angry. Like she needed more blood. But she always felt like she needed more blood. Her ears pricked at the sound of hurried footsteps coming down the corridor, and the vampire she'd sent to find her a meal rushed back into the room. He was back fast. Too fast.

"I suppose this means you couldn't find a virgin," she said. It had been too long since she'd eaten a virgin. It had been since she'd first arrived, when Anton had pulled her out of the dirt and dragged her along at his side, weak as a newborn foal. But the youth they'd *found had been delicious. So strong and so pure, and older than she'd expected. He'd been handsome, too. So handsome that she'd turned him and made him one of her fledglings.*

"I—didn't make it out to hunt," the vampire stammered. "Someone stopped me."

"Who?" Anton snapped. He rose and rolled his broad shoulders back, ready to crack a neck. How she adored him.

"Someone." The vampire shrugged helplessly. Then he scurried out of the way as the someone stepped into view.

He was a young man. Or that's what a human would have taken him for. A young man, with sharp blue eyes and tan skin, a tangle of dark hair that was a tad too long, the kind of hair that would have suited a surfer on his board but looked less at home atop the black shirt and pants that he wore. She of course wasn't fooled for a second. The eyes glowed a little too bright, for a start, and then there were the teeth, curving fangs he tried to hide when he smiled. Also there was the fact that she already knew him.

"Well, well," she said. "The Hunter of Thrace."

"Grimloch," said Anton, using the demon's proper name. "What are you doing here?"

"The same thing you're doing here," the demon said. "I'm viewing the property." He glanced at the ceiling, the faint cracks in the corner molding, the candelabras and defunct electric chandelier. "Very nice, ten thousand square feet, four bedrooms, seven baths plus those recently installed"—he nodded to her tub of dirt—"a wine cellar, a third-story lookout, covered recreation in the courtyard . . ." He cocked a smile. "Hellmouth adjacent."

"I'm afraid we've decided to take it." Anton bared his teeth, the slightest bit. "We're already in escrow."

"Plenty of room, though," the demon said. "You wouldn't mind if

I crashed with you. Just until I find a place of my own. I promise to make myself useful."

The Countess narrowed her eyes. She hadn't seen the Hunter of Thrace in a long time. Not since before his last hibernation. Seeing him in those clothes and hearing him speak like one of the humans, he seemed like a stranger. The first time they'd met he'd been a nobleman. The last time, he'd been the owner of a prominent restaurant in Venice. When had that been? 1850? 1870? Time was so hard to pin down when one had so much of it.

She stepped closer and gave him a sniff. The blood was hard to see, given the blackness of his attire, but it wasn't hard to smell. Neither was the stomach bile. And just a hint of poached salmon.

"You killed my Succoro demon."

Anton growled, but Grimloch held his hands out, empty. Unarmed.

"I ate your Succoro demon. Its heart, to be precise. But I didn't kill it. The slayer did."

"The slayers are dead," said Anton.

"Then whoever killed them all missed one. Because I watched her hunt the demon, and when I found it, its neck had been snapped like a twig." He shrugged. "I sliced him open and ate his heart. Then I came straight here, to you. To offer my services."

"Your services to what?" Anton asked.

"To kill the new slayer."

The Countess and Anton exchanged a look.

"I heard that about you," she mused. "That you'd developed a taste for slayer hearts. They are a rare delicacy, but do they really taste any better?"

Grimloch smiled. But within that smile, she detected the shadow of a frown. "A slayer's heart," he said, "is like no other."

181

"And a slayer must make for a good hunt, even for the Hunter of Thrace," Anton added, and the hunter looked away, annoyed.

"Like you, I thought all the slayers were dead. So when I heard they weren't, I came to see for myself. Now I see that it's true, and she has only the one heart and I do not intend to share it. So—"

"So you want to help me kill her. In exchange for the heart."

"Exactly."

The Countess looked at Anton, who appeared to be attempting to grind his own fangs down to nubs. He didn't like the Hunter of Thrace. Not one little bit. She shrugged.

"I have no problem with that," she said. "Welcome, Grimloch. Feel free to take one of the rooms upstairs. I find they get far too much sun."

PART THREE

YOU KNEW THE BIG BAD WAS COMING

CHAPTER SEVENTEEN

NOBODY REMEMBERS ALL THE DYSENTERY

Frankie sat at the kitchen table tapping her foot and listening to Jake and her mom bustle back and forth before the stove. It was a breakfast Scooby meeting at the Rosenbergs', and everyone was there. Frankie and Oz had already gotten the tea and coffee ready, and Frankie had squeezed orange juice while Oz gently warmed Spike's blood. Sigmund took a seat at the far end and tried to stay out of the way, but he had brought the flowers for the middle of the table, along with a book about ancient herbaries: "A gift for the lovely Willow, from the great Sarafina DeWitt." Frankie liked that. "The great Sarafina DeWitt." She hoped that's how Sigmund's mother always made him introduce her at parties.

The only attendee who hadn't helped with breakfast at all was Spike, who sat sullenly away from the windows. They'd drawn the curtains closed for him, and he looked sour about it. He was getting too used to traipsing around the school in the sunshine. Which was worrisome. He'd just found a new lair to call his own: a basement-level apartment not far from the school. What if he forgot about the spell boundary and bounced out of it one day only to burn into a pile of ash?

Frankie glanced up at the ceiling. Hailey was still in the shower; she could hear the water running. Last night, when Sigmund had half walked, half dragged Hailey home, she'd been washed out and so tired she could barely string two words together.

"Mmm, okay" was all she'd been able to say to Frankie. Which, after a few more tries, Frankie realized was "I'm okay" but the "I" part took too much energy. Hailey had also managed one thumbs-up for a dead Succoro demon and a very poorly aimed high five before Frankie and her mom helped her up the stairs to the guest room. They'd only made it halfway before Willow softly groaned, "Float her," and grabbed Frankie's fingers. Together their magic lifted Hailey's toes an inch off the floor, and the diminutive witches could breathe easy.

Jake set a pitcher of cream in front of her and winked. In the background, she could hear her mom and Oz, softly oooing over the gift from Sarafina DeWitt and also wondering how Hailey liked her bacon, crispy or not so crispy.

They had been part of the original Scoobies. They had made up part of the original team of friends who supported and assisted the slayer and helped her to solve her slayer mysteries. Actually, it could be argued that Oz and his Mystery Machine–style van had been the main inspiration for the term Scooby in the first place. And now they watched over Frankie as she began to form her own team.

Frankie's brow knit. The slayer was probably supposed to be Daphne, but she was clearly a Velma. And Jake probably thought that he was Fred, but clearly he was . . . well, clearly he was Scooby. The dog.

Frankie tapped her nails against the table. Hailey was using so much hot water. Frankie took her showers with a set timer.

But Hailey had nearly scratched her skin off, so Frankie supposed she was entitled to a few long showers. Maybe even some bubble baths.

"What is taking so long?" Jake groaned, tilting his voice toward the stairs. "My frittata is going to turn mushy! Hailey! Eggs! Get 'em while they're hot!"

"Let her take her time," said Spike. When Hailey had fallen asleep, none of them wanted to leave her alone, but Spike said he would stay with her.

"Because I'm nocturnal anyway," he'd said. But Frankie thought it was more than that. And it wasn't just because he owed Vi. Hailey and Spike got on each other's nerves. And they were both starting to like it.

"Probably my fault she's taking more time," Sigmund said. "She might be avoiding me. Unless she doesn't remember throwing herself at me across the desk last night."

"That's giving yourself a lot of credit," Jake said. "She was probably throwing herself at the phone, not you."

"Well, I was the one holding the phone, so she might feel a little awkward about it."

"What's to feel awkward about? Aren't you used to people throwing themselves across tables at you? You're a 'hot'"—Jake made air quotes with two fingers and a spatula—"demon with a charm attack."

"No, he's right." Hailey crept carefully into the kitchen. She was wearing a pair of Frankie's fuzzy orange slippers, and her hair was still dripping. "I owe Sigmund many apologies."

The Sage demon shifted in his seat and shrugged shyly. "It was no big deal."

Frankie and Jake traded suspicious glances. Hailey and Sigmund could barely look at each other.

"Hey," Jake said. "Exactly what happened in the library last night anyway?"

"Nothing," Hailey said. "Nothing bad. Just embarrassing. Sigmund, I'm really sorry I tackled you."

"It's okay."

"And I'm sorry for sticking my hands in your pants."

"The what now?" Frankie and Jake asked together.

"Yeah, the what now?" asked Spike.

"It was only into my pockets," Sigmund said, and grinned. "And I know you weren't really yourself."

"Listen." Hailey came to the table, and Frankie got up and pulled out a chair so she could gingerly sit. "I wasn't really myself, but I still owe you all many apologies. Posting that photo . . . was really stupid." She tugged the sleeve of Frankie's sweater. "Thanks for literally saving my skin."

"No problem," Frankie said.

"We're just glad you weren't hurt," said Willow. She set a hot mug of coffee onto the table in front of Hailey. "Just don't do it again. I have a rule about skin sloughing while under my roof, and the rule is no skin sloughing."

Hailey nodded, and Sigmund slid her a plate.

"Toast?" he offered. "Avocado toast, obviously, since we are in California."

"Thanks. And again, I'm sorry you had to tie me to a chair." She moved to pick up the toast, but Jake leaned over to drizzle it with olive oil and sprinkle on a dash of crunchy salt.

"You're pretty perky for the morning after a full moon," Frankie noticed. Jake was practically floating through the kitchen, wearing her mom's striped apron and carefully plating his mushroom-and-cheese frittata.

"Yeah, the wolf must have been mellow last night. And besides,

188

it's a good morning: Hailey's got all her skin, we've got a dead demon . . ."

"What did happen to the demon?" Hailey asked. "I feel like everybody knows more than me."

Spike stuck a finger into his mug of blood to test the temperature and stuck his lower lip out. "That's what we're here to discuss. How the demon died. Or rather, what killed it and left us a message in its blood."

"You didn't kill it?" Hailey asked Frankie, and Frankie blushed.

"I almost did. But ultimately no. Something else got to it first."

For a second, Hailey's eyes lit up. Then she shook her head and muttered, "Stupid."

"What?"

"Nothing. I just thought . . . it might be Vi. Vi, come to save me again. But that's just"—her lips twisted and she picked a few bits of onion off her toast—"not going to happen."

Oz looked at Hailey sympathetically as he took a large wedge of frittata and half a plate of bacon. "It might happen," he said. "Someday. But this one didn't look like a slayer kill to me. Last time I checked, slayers don't usually leave messages in entrails and remove hearts to take as trophies. Unless something's changed?"

"Nope." Willow shook her head. "Heart collection still frowned upon."

Hailey glanced at Oz's plate. "What's with the piglet's worth of meat products?" she asked. "I thought you didn't turn into a werewolf anymore."

"The wolf spirit still needs to feed," he said. "Plus, bacon is delicious."

"He lets the wolf out sometimes," Jake said, sliding a wedge of eggs and mushrooms onto Frankie's plate. "He used to let it out a lot at the commune."

"The commune where your parents and brother are? Where is that again? Werewolf Mecca? Weremecca?"

"It's called Weretopia. And it's in New Zealand." Jake pointed his fork at Sigmund's plate. "I made you extra eggs. I've heard eggs have a pretty low IQ, so eat up."

"Thanks, Jake," Sigmund said. "But if that was how it worked, I'd be able to eat lots of things. Like wood."

"Right. Sorry. I'm a such a doofus. So I guess you can still eat *me*."

Frankie looked between Sigmund and Jake. That exchange seemed almost jovial. Friendly even. They were both chewing their food to hide their grins.

Boys. One minute it was all growling and puffed-up chests, and the next . . .

"Enough about the food," said Spike, sporting a small blood mustache. "Someone or something, *not* a slayer, carved up that Succoro demon. Broke its neck, removed the heart, and left us a lovely note."

"Countess." Willow set down her fork. "You think it was this countess? She signed the kill like a calling card?"

"Countess," said Sigmund. "You don't mean THE Countess?"

Around the table, everyone looked confused except for Spike, who laughed.

"No, I don't mean THE Countess. That's bloody ridiculous."

"Who's the Countess?" Frankie asked.

"Erzsébet Báthory," said Sigmund. "A Hungarian noblewoman who died in the 1600s. Known to commit atrocities of torture and murder, especially of virgins. In particular, virginal female servants. They say she killed more than six hundred." He looked at Frankie seriously. "When she was alive."

"Elizabeth Bathory," Willow murmured. "I've heard that story. I've never heard that she became a vampire."

"That's because she bloody didn't," said Spike. "Every couple of decades, some vampire comes around self-styling themselves the Blood Countess, and it's all a load of bollocks. Some upstart romantic, fancying a return to the old days of lords and ladies and corsets and those bloody uncomfortable shoes with the top buckles. But they've never actually lived through it. They don't really remember how bad it was back then, how uncomfortable and poorly ventilated, how dark the nights were with no fluorescent lights. Everyone walking around barely knowing how to read, so bored by all the farming that they were starting wars every five minutes." He took out a cigarette, though he thankfully didn't light it, just put it between his teeth. "And nobody remembers the dysentery."

"Thanks, Uncle Spike," said Frankie. "You really know how to paint a picture."

"You're welcome," he said, and then he scoffed. "The Countess. You know that poor woman was probably framed. Probably didn't murder or torture a single person. Back then, a woman showed too much power, or attained too much property, or got her hands on a piece of land that someone else wanted? What better way to get rid of her than accuse her of murder. Or witchcraft. Or even adultery."

"That's terrible," said Frankie, and looked at her mom, who seemed equally disgusted.

"But you're thinking it might be, what," Jake said, "a Countess impersonator? That could be bad enough, couldn't it? If they want to live up to the legend."

"But why are they here?" Frankie asked. Another evil thing had come to Sunnydale? The explosion at Slayerfest seemed like it had set off a chain reaction: Frankie's calling, the first vampires to rise in Sunnydale in years, the first demon attack at the school, and now something even bigger. It was all happening so fast. Couldn't they give her a little while to find her footing? A mini boss, like in the first level of a video game. A weak cream puff of a boss fight just to practice on so she could learn which button did what.

"What if it's all connected?" asked Oz. "You said the Succoro demons are hired guns. Energy brokers. What if the Countess was the one who hired the Succoro demon and brought it to town?"

"But then why kill it?" asked Jake.

"Maybe she wasn't happy about its harvest." Spike looked at Willow. "Were you having any luck shutting it down on the computer?"

"Not really," she said. "I was trying to trace it, and I was also trying to hack it to gain control of the Succoro's account. Which should have been easy. But I couldn't get in. So I tried magic, but magic and computers don't always . . ." Willow reached under the seat cushion of a nearby bench and pulled out her laptop, charred black.

"Maybe we should start spreading the word that Frankie's a slayer," Hailey said.

"Huh?" asked Frankie.

"Well, this is more action than Sunnydale's seen since the Hellmouth, right? Even if the Hellmouth isn't rumbling or leaking hell residue, something is drawing them here. And maybe word of a new slayer would put them off."

"It could keep at least a few from coming," said Willow. "Though I'm a little insulted that they're coming anyway. . . . Has everyone forgotten that I'm here? The witch Willow? Dark Willow?"

"Mom, you haven't been Dark Willow for a really long time."

"Well, they don't know that," Willow said sulkily.

"But what do we do about the Countess?" Sigmund asked.

"The fake countess," said Spike. "And we don't do anything. All this will be is a short fight against someone in one of those big, frilly collars." He grinned at Willow. "Or she'll skip town once she gets wind that you and I are still around."

But Frankie wasn't so sure. The specter of her mom's former badassery didn't seem like it was enough to scare things away anymore. And sure, Spike was in Sunnydale now, but was anyone ever *really* afraid of Spike?

She looked at Jake. She looked at Hailey and Sigmund. She hoped that Spike was right and the fake countess would decide to leave town. But her slaydar was telling her that just wasn't going to happen.

"Who is the vampire she has with her?" The Countess walked back and forth on the third-story lookout, wrapped in a new red satin robe. Or new at least, to her—one of the fledglings had found it in the closet of the master bedroom. It was nice. Soft, and cold, and musty. And the collar was all feathery. Puffed up with real feathers and synthetic fluff. It made her feel like old Hollywood, or like someone's pampered poodle dog. She'd loved her little dogs when she was alive, though she'd never had a poodle; they didn't exist back then. Sometimes she'd let her little puppies take a bite out of a restrained victim, if they were very good.

"The vampire," Anton replied, "is barely a vampire at all. He has a soul."

"Angelus?"

"No. Another one."

Another one? Were souls just finding their way back into vampiric bodies at random these days? Or was it a BOGO?

"He's known as Spike. William the Bloody. He has quite a reputation: killed two slayers, terrorized Europe . . ." Anton made a face. "Saved the world. Turned in the 1800s."

"A young, ambitious upstart," she said.

"Seems so. Nothing for you to worry about."

"What about the witch?"

"Dormant," he said. "Neutered. Or that's the rumor. Apparently she found nearly ending all of existence to be quite traumatizing."

"But she did awaken the entire line of slayers," the Countess said. "And the new slayer is her daughter." They would have to watch her. As for the werewolf, he was barely worth mentioning. How many werewolf pelts did she own? Two hundred? A thousand? They made for very unattractive rugs, but when one removed the fur, the leather could be fashioned into a truly fabulous pair of boots.

"I've never faced a slayer, Anton," she said, and he raised his brows. "I've never fought one. I never liked the idea of it: this poor, put-upon girl having to do everything for the men around her. And then I would go against her, too?" She shook her head. "We ladies must have a code; we must not be pitted against one another."

"So you want to leave her alone?"

"Not exactly. I've been thinking about what Grimloch said: about a slayer heart being like no other. I would like to know what that is. So now I would like to eat her. But just this once, Anton. And after that, the no-slayer policy will go back into effect. Unless she really does taste that much better." She turned away from the twinkling lights of Sunnydale and surveyed the meals her fledglings had brought. Seven of them, pretty maids and lads all in a row. A few were wearing adorable plaid-skirted religious-school uniforms. And they were all innocent. Guileless. She could smell the purity coming off them in waves. She bent down and took the first girl's chin in her hand and inhaled that first big spike of fear. These would not be enough to return her to her full strength. But it was a good start.

"Speaking of Grimloch," she said, "where is he?"

"I sent a few of the larger, older fledglings to test the slayer. He accompanied them to observe."

The Countess smiled. Stalking his prey. Learning its movements, its habits. Identifying the weak spots. She'd never been much of a traditional hunter, but she could certainly see the appeal.

"Please don't hurt me," the girl before her said, shivering.

195

"But hurting you is my favorite part, little darling," she replied.

"Please, don't."

The Countess sighed. "Very well. Mercy for you, since you were brave enough to ask. But none for the others." She reached around the back of the girl's head and tugged, exposing her throat. She bit fast and drank faster, and the girl's frightened little rabbit heart helped her along, kicking, kicking, kicking the blood right into her mouth until the kicks grew fainter, and fainter, and the little rabbit was dead. She'd barely felt a thing. But she had been sweet and awakened such a thirst in the Countess that she tore through the rest of the line, pulling skin like taffy in her teeth, draining two, then three, while the remaining four struggled and wept. The remaining three, actually, as one of them promptly passed out.

After the fourth, a robust young lad in some kind of a fast-food uniform, she took a breath. He'd been very rich-tasting, and she felt full of fresh blood, like a warm, stretched balloon.

"That's enough for now."

"What should we do with the rest?" one of the vampire fledglings asked. "Save them for later? Or can we eat them?"

"No, you can't eat them," Anton snapped, and the Countess went to him and patted his chest like a good guard dog. She reached into his jacket and drew out a sleek, straight razor. She was full, true, but that virginal blood was just too good to waste.

"Has my tub been emptied?" she asked.

"Yes, Countess."

She opened the straight razor and handed it off.

"Then fill it up."

CHAPTER EIGHTEEN

PLAYGROUNDS AT NIGHT ARE EVIL

Frankie meandered around the edge of the playground, twirling a freshly sharpened stake like a baton between her fingers. It was one of Hailey's, so it was a good one, the point just the right combination of sharp and sturdy. She gripped it in her fist and made some practice swipes and stabs, doing the shadow-staking routine she'd worked on with Spike. Shadow staking, like shadowboxing, fast and flawless, ready for anything.

"Come on out, vamps," she whispered. "Tonight's the night. Time to start making my presence known. Frankie"—she slashed the air—"the vampire slayer!" Then she laughed. She could practically hear her mother saying, *Buffy was never this dorky*.

Over her head, the moon was still bright in the sky, though a smaller and more manageable orb now for Jake. The three nights of the full moon had passed, and he would be able to ditch his cage and come out for the patrol. He and Hailey were supposed to be meeting Frankie at the park soon. It would be good to have them back—after all, the Succoro demon might be dead, but whatever killed it was still out there, and who knows how long one heart would tide it over. Sigmund and Spike had been pulling overtime in the library, researching things that were very strong and ate demon hearts, but so far had come up empty. They were probably there right now, bent over a book, late into the night. Or at least Sigmund was.

But where were Hailey and Jake? Frankie put her stake into her pocket and craned her neck to look up the empty street. Still no sign of them. She blew her bangs out of her eyes. It was hot for early October. A breeze would have been nice. Her fingers twitched a little. She knew that spell. Just one little incantation and a whirl of her fingertips and boom, instant cooling. Way more eco-friendly than the freon in AC units.

No magic for personal gain, she heard her mom's voice say. *And what if you conjure up a dust devil in the middle of the playground sandbox?*

Frankie frowned and clenched her fists. But her imaginary mom was right. Mixing magic with slaying was still too hard. Tonight was all about the stakes. And the flip kicks.

She turned around and jumped up onto a park bench, hopping easily over the back of it to land on the balls of her feet. Then she jumped up to do it again, maybe to try a front handspring. But maybe not. Those moves seemed to come naturally to her now, but the last thing she needed was to land on her head and break her neck and for Hailey and Jake to find her dead body and blame the neck-breaking demon and go off on a suicide mission of vengeance when it was really her own stupid fault for experimenting with playground gymnastics.

She glanced over her shoulder at the empty playground. Swings and a jungle gym, monkey bars and two slides: one metal and one of the curly plastic kind. The playground was small and generic, and it was just lingering there behind her, the shadows of all the children who had played on it seething through the empty spaces like . . . like . . . well, like the seething shadows of children. It felt like they were watching her, and the minute she thought that, she couldn't *stop* thinking it, couldn't stop feeling their eyes stuck to her back and tracking her movements.

But that was all in her head. Well, not *all* in her head. Anything in Sunnydale could be evil, if given the opportunity and the right demonic spell.

Still, this playground was just a playground, and Frankie marched up to the monkey bars and jumped, able to easily take them by two. Back and forth, back and forth, legs dangling, and her hands didn't even hurt. She hooked her knees around one bar and let go to hang upside down. Her red hair swung in the air below, and she made a mental note to tie it back when she heard footsteps approaching through the sand. Hailey and Jake. Finally.

Only it wasn't Hailey or Jake. She found herself upside down, staring into the ugly yellow eyes of four vampires. Or more accurately, staring into their belt buckles, since that's what was at upside-down eye level.

"Playgrounds really are evil after dark," she said just before they grabbed on to her shoulders and pulled.

☽ ☽ ○ ☾ ☾

Hailey stood on the edge of Sunnydale Heights, waiting for Jake to show up so they could meet Frankie for another group patrol. He'd texted earlier to say he would meet her on that corner, by the development sign. But he was late. She was about to text him to stuff it when a car rounded the corner too fast and jerked to a stop right in front of her. Jake was in the passenger seat. Sam Han was behind the wheel. Three guys she sort of recognized from school were wedged into the backseat.

When Jake got out, one of the guys from the back moved up to sit shotgun.

"So you're coming tomorrow?" he asked Jake as Jake hopped onto the sidewalk.

"I'll totally try to make it."

"Dude, you haven't made it in like a month."

"It has not been a month. And the last two parties you told us about got busted by the cops anyway. I said I'll try." He waved to them, and the kid in the front seat buckled his seat belt and gave Hailey a wink.

"Hi, Hailey!" called Sam Han, and she waved before they drove off.

"Sorry about that." Jake started toward the playground where Frankie said to meet. He walked fast, and Hailey had to push to keep up. It had been about a week since she'd been energy-sucked by the Succoro demon's demon app, but there was still a left-foot drag in her step, and even her vintage Muppets T-shirt felt heavy.

"What's with those guys and the winking?" she asked.

"I sort of told them I was meeting you for a date. Type. Thing. I hope you don't mind; I had to tell them something to get them to drop me off," he said when she shoved him. "It was lucky I was meeting you and not Frankie. Or they'd never have believed me."

"What's so wrong with Frankie?"

"Nothing's wrong with Frankie. It's just that everyone knows we don't hang out like that. It was easier to say that I was meeting you. Next time I see them I'll tell them I was wrong about the date and we were just hanging out. So there's no confusion, okay?" He shrugged. "It's not always easy to get away for this slaying stuff, you know?"

"Yeah. I guess so." She would have had a hard time, too, she supposed, if she'd had to do it back home and ditch Mols.

He noticed her foot. "You okay to do this? You didn't seem exactly on point training with Spike this afternoon."

Hailey picked up her pace.

"Compared to what? That guy has killed *two* slayers. I'd like to see you or Sigmund go a round with him. Maybe you'd understand how hard his pale fists really are."

"I could do it," said Jake. "I've been training my whole life. Werewolf packs love to scrap."

"I don't think weird family wrestling sessions count," said Hailey, though she had to admit that from what she'd seen, Jake seemed kind of like a natural.

Jake frowned, and his usually open, friendly expression slammed shut.

"Yeah, maybe you're right," he said. "I guess I should ask for some weapons training at least, if I really want to help Frankie."

"Hey, I didn't mean—"

"It's okay," he said coolly.

"No, I mean, I really didn't," she said. "I'm sorry. I have no idea what's going on with your parents and your brother. That was dumb."

Jake looked at her. Then he nodded, fast to forgive. "I guess we all have some messed-up family stuff going on. How are you doing? Being on your own without Vi, I mean? I know what it was like adjusting to living with Oz, and he's family, so I imagine it must be rougher for you, with strangers."

"Yeah," Hailey said. And it was. She missed Vi terribly. So terribly that most times she tried not to think about Vi at all. Not to wonder about the explosion in Halifax, or the search for the slayers. Not to wonder if she was hurt. Not to think about how their lives

201

would never quite be the same, even if Vi did somehow come back.

"But, you know, it's odd," she said. "The Rosenbergs don't really feel like strangers?" And being in Sunnydale, helping the slayer— that didn't feel strange either. Secretly, when she felt brave enough to imagine Vi returning, she'd started wondering how Vi might fit into their new team of Scoobies, instead of Vi coming to take her away.

"Yeah," Jake said, and laughed. "I love the Rosenbergs. Willow basically raised me, you know? My parents tried, but . . . when they saw how safe I would be with two witches and occasional visiting slayers, they kind of . . . checked out to focus on Jordy."

"That's kind of crappy," Hailey said.

"Yeah. But at least I had Frankie and Willow. Like you had Vi."

"Yeah." Hailey smiled and realized it was the first time since the explosion she'd been able to do that while thinking about Vi. "Man, my sister would be so pissed if she knew I was doing this."

"Doing what?"

"Training with the slayer. Messing around with magic. She never wanted me anywhere near the slayer stuff. When I was younger, and she'd come back from a hard slay or a close call, she used to say, 'Don't moon over me, kid. If I disappear one day, don't cry. Don't be sad. Just move on, and forget that any of this is real. Just walk away.'"

"But you couldn't do that," said Jake. "Just walk away."

"Nope. I ran at it instead. Straight to legendary Sunnydale." Hailey kicked at a loose stone with the toe of her boot. "Vi was tough, Jake. She has to be okay." After all, Xander had checked in with Willow every day, and no new bodies had been recovered. That had to mean that the portal mark had really been a portal mark and Andrew and his witcher-Watchers had pulled off a miracle and gotten her out alive.

Jake eyed her cautiously. "Sigmund said that if the mark was really from a portal and it was hastily cast, they might have been pulled into another dimension, and that's why it's taking them so long to get back."

Hailey stopped short, shocked. She stopped Jake, too, with an arm across his chest. "Sigmund said that? Why didn't he say so to me?"

"I don't think he wants to get your hopes up yet."

Well, that was just too damned late. She could not believe that Vi was gone. She refused. And she knew that Frankie didn't believe that Buffy was gone either. The portal meant something. It had to.

"Maybe it's the dimension made up entirely of shrimp," Jake said.

"Huh?"

"Nothing. I just hope our sage-scented portal expert breaks the case soon. So maybe I can meet your sister and watch her yell at you."

Hailey smiled. "Let her yell. Let her ground me; at this point, I don't care."

"Yeah. I just . . . want Buffy back. It doesn't feel right that Frankie has to do this without her."

They walked on in quiet, and Hailey found herself watching Jake from the corner of her eye. He was good-looking. Not like Sigmund-good-looking, but handsome, with watchful eyes and nice, broad shoulders. At least a foot taller than Oz, though they did really look alike when they were thinking hard about something. Hailey wondered why Jake wasn't dating anyone. The whole werewolf thing was bound to be rife with complications, but the people of Sunnydale had to be more open to that than most.

"Jake," she asked, "do you like Frankie?"

"Like Frankie? What, you mean like, *like her* like her?" He snorted. "Yeah. I am very attracted to her brand of overt hostility."

"Well, does she date much?"

"Hardly ever. And not since eighth grade, which, does that even count? But you know, now that she's a slayer, she'll probably take up with some brooding, tortured hero type." He laughed a little, like he couldn't imagine it. Then he frowned hard, like he *really* couldn't imagine it. "Is that who your sister used to date?"

"If she did she never told me. With Vi, it's always slay, slay, slay."

"Maybe Frankie will be like that."

"But my sister did teach me how to put a condom on a stake without damaging it," she said. "So I can pass that essential wisdom on to Frankie."

Jake glowered. "That's not funny. And I don't even think that's a useful skill. I mean how . . . do you do that?"

Hailey laughed. Poor Jake looked so scandalized. She laughed harder and realized how long it had been since she'd really laughed.

Jake put his hand on her shoulder.

"Hey. Do you hear that?"

They stopped. From around the corner up the street in the direction of the playground came the distinct sounds of fighting.

"Sounds like a fight," Hailey said, and pulled out a stake.

"Sounds like Frankie getting her ass kicked," said Jake, and they both started to run.

$$\text{☽ ☽ ◯ ☾ ☾}$$

Frankie ducked and jumped into a flying split kick to knock two of the vampires back. They had her outnumbered four to one, and when they'd ripped her from the monkey bars, one of her shoes had come off, so she was both disoriented and lopsided. Still, she threw punch after punch—and was pleased to find that their punches didn't hurt much—but she just couldn't open up their stances enough to clear a stake to the heart. She clenched her teeth. The four of them were closing in. It wouldn't be long before they were knocking her back and forth like a tetherball.

I'm not going to run away, she thought, but even as she thought it, she knew: She was going to run away.

She bashed the vampire behind her with an elbow and plowed through the one in front, sprinting past the accursed playground for the cover of the woods. If she was fast enough, she could spread them out, take them on one by one, or maybe even lose them. Of course, if she wasn't, they'd only surround her again, after she was tired from running and isolated in the dark trees.

She ran headlong into the low branches, holding her forearms up to block the leaves, and heard the first vampire enter the forest behind her only a few seconds later. She also thought she heard Hailey scream—or, more accurately, heard Hailey bellow with rage—but she couldn't look back to make sure. *Run* was her only thought. *Hide.*

"Slayers don't hide," she growled to herself. She scanned the woods quickly, but she scanned too high. She missed the shadow of the approaching ravine and promptly fell down it, tumbling and eventually rolling until she hit the bottom, right behind a very nice pile of fallen logs. So maybe slayers didn't hide. Maybe they fell and then lay in wait where they landed.

Frankie crouched and listened for the vampires. The first ran right by, apparently able to watch where he was going. But the second fell down the ravine just like she did. She poked her head out and smiled, watching it bounce and screech its way down the incline. She pulled the stake out of her pocket. If she got to the vamp while it was still shaky from the landing, it would be a very quick dusting.

Frankie burst out from behind the logs and landed a solid kick to his chin, then set herself above the vampire and pummeled him with both fists before bringing the stake down right on target. The vampire barely had time to look surprised before disintegrating into a pile of ash.

"One down," she said.

"One right behind you."

She twisted on one knee, and the vampire dove onto her, pinning her leg painfully behind her body. He must have doubled back around.

"Are you sure you're a slayer?" he asked as his fangs snapped perilously close to her collarbone. "I've never heard of one running away."

"Then you've never heard of *me*," Frankie groaned, and threw him off over her head. She rolled to her feet, bringing her stake up to strike, but he kicked it out of her hand. She heard it land somewhere behind her in the leaves and dirt. But she wasn't going to panic, even though she was backed into a narrow ravine with high sides and awful lighting. After all, she was only one-on-one.

Another vampire dropped into the ravine, much more gracefully than she had. Okay, so she was one-on-two. And had no stake. But that was no big deal: She was in the middle of the woods, surrounded by pointy sticks.

The vampires circled, and she briefly noticed how muscular they were and how well-dressed, in matching black T-shirts and silver belt buckles. It was like being attacked by concert security. They jumped at her together, and she spun out of the way, leveling a reverse kick that knocked one into the other and made them both grunt. Then she went in fast, another kick, and another, moving them closer and closer to the pile of fallen logs. The pile had a nice, sharp root protruding at just the right height. If she adjusted the angle, she could skewer them both with it, like a vampire kebab. They snarled and shuffled in the dirt, trying to get their balance back, but Frankie jumped high and drove her feet down onto the nearest vampire's back, impaling them both.

"Nice," she said amid the explosion of dust. She turned and knelt to feel in the dirt where she'd thought she'd heard her stake land, but something out of the darkness hit her hard and she went down, her face pinned to the dirt and dead leaves.

Only one vamp had dusted. She'd missed the first one's heart and hadn't noticed that he didn't disintegrate.

Frankie whipped her head back and forth. She could barely breathe with so much of the forest floor shoved up her nose. But she didn't really start to panic until the vampire's hand wrapped around the back of her skull.

He could break her neck. Snap, and it would be over, just like that. Or he could turn her neck and bite. That would be worse. To be drained. To be eaten. The vampire's cold, putrid breath hit her skin, and Frankie screamed.

Suddenly, the weight on her back disappeared. She pushed to her feet and saw the vampire sailing through the ravine. The person who had thrown it passed by her like a shadow. At first, she thought it was Spike. But it wasn't Spike. In fact, she wasn't even sure it was a person. It jumped upon the vampire, straddling it, and in two fast motions seemed to tear the creature in two. At least that's what it looked like; the vamp dust went up in two separate clouds.

Frankie scrambled backward as an image of the Succoro demon and its cracked-open rib cage flashed in her mind. This had to be the creature that killed it. Was it the demon who called itself the Countess? It wasn't really what she imagined a countess would look like.

The creature turned, and Frankie put up her fists.

"Thank you?" she said uncertainly. Of course, it was probably going to kill her, too. But her mother had raised her to be polite.

It rose to its full height—maybe six foot two, Frankie estimated—and walked slowly toward her.

It was definitely a demon—human eyes didn't glow so brightly blue in the dark—but it was dressed like a human in a man's shirt and dark trousers. The glowing eyes looked her up and down. Frankie tensed and widened her stance, ready to fight.

"Are you hurt?" it asked in a growl.

She hadn't been expecting that. She was still missing her shoe and the sock had been torn (her big toe stuck out of a fresh hole, very becoming) and there was a slight ache in her shoulder from the fall down the ravine. But she was okay.

"Who are you?" she asked. "What . . . are you?" she amended, her voice a little higher.

The creature didn't respond. Slowly, the glow faded from his eyes, and without it, it was hard to keep thinking of him as a "creature" and not a person. He looked . . . very human. Very human, and very tall, and well groomed and handsome, with longish dark hair that hung around his face.

"You're not ready," he said.

"Clearly," she replied, and cocked her eyebrow. Then: "Wait, not ready for what? Are you the one who left me the message about the Countess?" The demon was silent. He just stared at her, and Frankie somehow sensed that he was sad. Sad, and maybe a little disappointed.

But she could do disappointed all by herself, thank you very much.

"Frankie! Frankie, where are you?"

At the sound of Jake's voice, the demon bared his teeth. Then he looked at her one more time and leapt out of the ravine in two strides.

"Wait, who are you?" she shouted, but didn't really expect him to answer.

"Frankie?"

"I'm down here," she called to Jake. "In the ravine. Be careful you don't fall in like I did." She sighed and climbed back the way she'd come, cold dirt getting into the hole in her sock. When she was close enough to the top, Jake and Hailey reached out and pulled her the rest of the way up.

"You're okay," Jake said. He held up her missing shoe.

"Thanks." She took it but didn't bother putting it on. "There's one more vamp out here somewhere."

"No, there isn't," Jake said. "We took it out when we saw them all chasing you. Hailey dove on it like some kind of . . ." He searched for a word and gave up and grinned instead. Frankie looked at Hailey, who shrugged, trying to seem nonchalant but obviously a little proud of herself.

"And then Jake staked it." Hailey frowned. "I kind of wanted to stake it. I always wondered what it was like, and Vi would never have . . ." She trailed off. "Anyway, it felt good having something to pound on. Did you get the other three?"

"I got two," Frankie admitted. "Someone else got the third."

"Someone else? Who else?" asked Jake.

"Let's just go home," said Frankie. "I'll report it all to Spike in the library on Monday."

"On Monday? That's, like, a whole weekend away. You sure you won't forget the details?"

Frankie looked back into the ravine. In her mind, she could still see the demon standing there. Dark, wild hair and broad shoulders. The flash of blue eyes. She could still hear his voice, soft as a whisper, carrying through the quiet. She swallowed.

"Safe to say there's no chance of that."

CHAPTER NINETEEN

NOBODY EATS BUFFY SUMMERS'S HEART AND GETS AWAY WITH IT

"So he helped you?" Spike asked. He, Jake, Hailey, and Sigmund sat around the desk in the librarian's office, listening to Frankie recount the details of the brawl in the ravine.

"He saved me." That vampire had her pinned. He'd had her neck, right there for the biting. "And it wasn't the first time he'd lent a hand."

"You think it was him who killed the Succoro?"

"I can't be sure. But there was something about the way he killed the vampire." His movements had been so fast. So precise. So rib-cage-splitting. "I'm definitely sure that he has the strength. Whatever he is."

Jake leaned back in his chair so far it seemed sure to tip over backward, his hands laced behind his head. He looked tired; he'd been out running before school with his lacrosse team. They did that sometimes, to stay fit during the off-season.

"Whatever he is," he repeated. "Glowing blue eyes, surfer

hair . . . Remember the good old days when demons were full of scales and mucus and they didn't all look like models?" He leaned forward and picked up a pencil eraser to chuck lightly at Sigmund.

"Says the werewolf with two pints of gel in his hair," Sigmund said, and chucked it back. They both sort of smirked at each other, and Sigmund glanced at Hailey. But Hailey wasn't paying the least bit of attention. She was sunk down in her chair with an intense look on her face.

"Hailey?" Frankie asked. "What's on your mind?"

"Your description of the demon," Hailey said. "I think I've seen it before." She pulled out her phone and started scrolling, searching for something. "Vi usually sends pictures from Slayerfest." She glanced up at them. "You know, the slayer meetings."

"Ooh, we're not allowed to call them that," said Jake.

"Apparently my mom has bad memories of something called Slayerfest '98," added Frankie.

"What was Slayerfest '98?" Sigmund asked.

Frankie shrugged. "Concert or something."

"Well, Vi sent me these from Halifax, before they left the city for the tree-house retreat. Here." Hailey zoomed in on her screen and showed it around. "Is this the guy?"

Everyone leaned in. The photo was of Vi and four other slayers. They were huddled close, smiling around an outdoor café table. There were no weapons in the shot, and the day looked bright and warm. They could have been any group of friends. Just young women, talking about movies, or politics, or their terrible bosses. Frankie didn't recognize any of the other slayers in it, but that was to be expected. There were so many she hadn't met. And now she'd never get to meet them.

But it wasn't the slayers that Hailey had zoomed in on. It was the bench across the street. There was a man sitting on it, his face clearly visible between the people walking by on the sidewalk. He was dressed differently than he had been in the woods, in a black button-down shirt, the sleeves rolled above the wrists. His dark hair was partially obscuring his face. And his bright blue eyes were watching the slayers.

"That's him," Frankie said.

"Are you sure?" Spike asked.

"I'm sure. Hailey, how did you even remember that he was in this shot?"

She shrugged. "I have a good memory for images. Plus, I mean, who could forget those eyes?"

Sigmund got up to peer over her shoulder. He seemed a little cross: his brow knit and brown eyes squinty. He'd been taking particular interest in Hailey ever since the fight with the Succoro, and Frankie wondered again just what kind of shenanigans occurred that night in the librarian's office.

"He's more than just hard to forget," Sigmund said. "He's famous."

"Lemme see him again," said Jake, and Hailey held her phone out while Sigmund left the office to disappear into the stacks of the occult section. "Yeah, I think I've seen him before, too," Jake said sarcastically. "In an ad for cologne. Or was it a commercial for men's swimwear?"

Frankie shoved him.

Then Sigmund returned and closed the door. He had a book open and was reading feverishly. "This all fits."

"What fits?" Spike asked. He reached for the book and scanned the pages. "You're not serious." Despite not being much of a researcher, he turned a page. And then another. And then the one after that.

"Hey, library guys," Frankie said. "What's happening?"

Sigmund took a deep breath. "I think your demon is Grimloch. The Hunter of Thrace."

"The Hunter of Thrice?" Jake asked. "Thrice what? Thrice blind mice?"

"Thrace," Sigmund said. "Not 'Thrice.'"

"Thrace," said Hailey. "As in, the region of ancient Greece?"

"Yes, Hailey. Exactly."

She tapped her forehead and winked at him. "You're not going to find a food source in here anytime soon."

"So who is he? Is he linked to the Countess?" Frankie reached for the book, but Spike jerked it away and started to pace, still reading.

"Forget the bloody Countess impersonator," Spike snapped. "If the Hunter of Thrace is in town, then we've got bigger problems."

"Why? What's so bad about him?" She looked from Spike to Sigmund.

"He's a hunter, obviously," Sigmund explained. "Dating back to at least the Macedonian era."

"That would make him pretty old," Jake said.

"Ancient," said Sigmund. "As in, a couple thousand years."

"He should be bloody stone by now," Spike grumbled. "Not running around like an underwear model. Demons this old are supposed to have cloven feet."

"Well, his feet and hands were decidedly not cloven," said Frankie. They were lovely and well proportioned, in fact. "You sure this is the right guy?"

"He hunted with nearly all the tribes of the Thracian region," said Sigmund. "It's where he got his title. But he wasn't exactly a hunter to them. He was a god. The god of their hunts. If Grimloch joined a hunting party, it was considered blessed. Lucky. Tribes would summon him prior to going off to war; they would hunt with him to be imbued with the spirits of the animals they killed."

Frankie didn't like that idea. Killing animals. Borrowing their spirits. But hunting was different than factory farming—hunts were necessary for the health of the herds. They were noble. Responsible. Still, she would have much rather hunted a black-bean burger. She made a face, and Hailey reached out and patted her hand.

"Animal cruelty," she said. "I know."

"It's said that Grimloch would feast on the vital organs of his kills and be enhanced by the essence of his prey," Sigmund went on. "It's not really known when he began to feed on people. Some records seem to reference a sort of ritual sacrifice prior to the hunt, part of the summoning spell. But whether that means he fed on the sacrifice, or if the sacrifice was a human hunter, is unclear."

"If he feeds on humans," said Hailey, "then why did he kill the Succoro demon? Why did he save Frankie?"

"Maybe he wasn't saving her," Spike said, and clapped the book shut. "Maybe he was eliminating another predator. Sigmund, lad, you're burying the lede." He slammed the book down on the desk and grabbed Hailey's phone and slammed it down, too, hard enough to make them all wince and for Hailey to check for a crack in the screen. "The demon Grimloch prefers one organ above all. Hearts. And recently, he's developed a taste for the heart of a slayer."

☽ ☽ ○ ☾ ☾

Frankie didn't know how Spike expected her to concentrate through the rest of the school day. The demon who'd helped her ate slayer hearts. And Frankie had been face-to-face with him, about the same distance as her desk to the whiteboard in Mr. Murphy's

English class. It was a waste of her time and her teachers' time, too—the only notes she took were several doodles of blue eyes and the repeated phrase "not an underwear model" scrawled across the paper. And Hailey wasn't doing any better. She stared out the window, clearly not paying attention, and Frankie couldn't catch her eye. But in the middle of the lecture, Hailey sent her a text:

Was he the one? Did he attack them?

And Frankie sent a fast reply.

If he did, he'll regret it.

They met at the Rosenberg house that evening as soon as the sun went down and Spike could get around without a blanket. Everyone was there except for Oz, who had group counseling at the youth center, which always ran late. Hailey and Sigmund arrived together—she'd stayed behind to help him gather books from the library. He'd wanted to bring every volume he'd found that contained even the shortest reference to Grimloch, the Hunter of Thrace, and it amounted to quite the stack. Willow watched them unload book after book onto the kitchen table with her arms crossed.

"Mom," Frankie said. "I can't believe that he's that old, and you're that old, and you've never even heard of him."

"Hey, smartypants, I'm not two thousand. And I have heard of him. I just thought it was a rumor. Like a slayer bogeyman. Go to sleep, little slayers, or the Hunter of Thrace will eat your hearts!"

"Nice, Mom. Nice."

"It was just a story. We never found any bodies. Are we sure he's real?"

"He's real, but he's hard to track," said Sigmund. "I've been reading since this morning, and it seems that he disappears for decades, even hundreds of years at a time. Only to pop up again somewhere new with the same pattern, the same hunted, sliced-open victims with hearts and other organs removed."

"Which other organs?" Frankie asked.

"Livers. Sometimes kidneys. Never the brain, if that makes you feel any better."

"Why would that make us feel any better?" Hailey asked.

Frankie frowned. She thought back to the night she fought the Succoro demon in the woods. Had the creeping feeling she'd had of being followed actually been him, hunting her while she was hunting the Insta-demon? And in the woods behind the playground, he'd been right there, ready to leap to her rescue. Hunting her. She couldn't say for how long, but she was clearly very good at being the prey. The Hunter of Thrace had been in the same woods with her at least twice, and she never heard so much as a twig snap. She glanced across the table at Spike, but his face was unreadable. He'd traded the tweed for a black T-shirt and was staring at the wall, tapping the surface of the table with his black-painted fingernails—fingernails that some at school had whispered looked weird on a librarian.

"Well," Jake said, and surveyed the table laid out with books. "I'll handle the munchies." He stood up and headed for the stove. In two shakes, he had a pot on for tea and another for coffee and had rummaged through their refrigerator for veggies and cheese to slice up and serve with crackers.

"Um, I'll help you," said Sigmund. He started to get up.

"Sit down, spice rub. My prowess in the kitchen is the only edge I have over you." He arranged the crackers into a circle. "Stupid hot demons, cramping my style. There's only room in Sunnydale for one hot demon, and that hot demon is me."

Sigmund opened his mouth to protest. But then he smiled and sat back down next to Hailey.

"So?" Hailey asked. "When is someone going to say it?"

"Say what, honey?" Willow asked.

217

"That this is the demon who attacked the slayers."

Uncomfortable glances rippled through the kitchen. They didn't know for sure that it was him. But it was on everybody's minds.

"He's a hunter," Hailey said. "And he hunts slayers. And he was in Halifax right before the attack." She stopped short and glanced at Frankie, but Frankie looked down at the table. "So what is the holdup? Let's go get him!"

Frankie grimaced. She knew the facts. She believed Sigmund's research. But in the woods . . . she hadn't felt like she was in any danger. And a big explosion didn't seem to fit—why blow them up and destroy their hearts? A bomb wasn't a hunt. It wasn't stealthy and subtle and oddly graceful. Not that she could say so to Hailey and Spike. Now that something punchable was in their sights, all other thoughts seemed to fade away.

"He was after slayers in Nova Scotia and now he's after Frankie here." Hailey slammed her palm down, hard. "So what are we going to do about it? And if you say wait, I'm going to—"

"We're going to bloody kill him," Spike said quietly. He looked at Willow. "We're going to bloody find him and question him, and then we're going to bloody kill him."

Frankie watched her mom. She expected her to tell them to wait, to slow down. To figure out more first. But she didn't.

"Mom?" Frankie asked.

"He's right," Willow said seriously. Frankie could have sworn her mother's eyes flashed black, just for a second. "Nobody eats Buffy's heart and gets away with it."

CHAPTER TWENTY

AN OLD-FASHIONED DEMON-FINDING SPELL

Willow led Frankie upstairs and into her bedroom, which, while not much bigger than Frankie's, did have a walk-in closet and a private bathroom. As soon as they got there, Willow disappeared into the closet and started rooting around on the shelves.

"Mom? What are we doing?"

"Locator spell." Willow's voice was muffled and a little breathless, like she often got when she was nervous. "Spread out that map I gave you in the middle of the paisley rug."

"Okay." Frankie knelt to do as she was told and heard her mom whisper, "Or maybe not, I like that rug. . . ." The map of Sunnydale was large and rectangular. It was weird that they had it. And actually that they had a pile: Willow had pulled it off the top of a stack. "Is this a big spell? Did you do it a lot?"

"No," Willow said. "I mean, no, it's not big, but yes, we . . . sort of did it quite frequently. Which explains the extra maps."

"What have you got in there?" Frankie asked. She hadn't

ventured into her mom's closet in a while, but she recalled that it was mostly jewelry boxes and drapey clothes in many patterns.

Willow emerged holding a wrinkled, yellowed plastic bag full of what Frankie assumed was a stash of old spell supplies.

"Mom. Plastic?"

Willow frowned. "It's what we had back then. Go light the directional candles."

Her mom kept four large white pillar candles on the window-sill; Frankie brought them back and set them in the north, east, south, and west, lighting them and casting a circle large enough to surround the map and give them room to stand or sit. While she did it, she kept one eye on Willow, who seemed to be sniff-testing the contents of the plastic.

"Are you sure we can do this?"

"Absolutely! This is a very basic spell. It was one of the first ones I ever did with Tara. I'm just worried about the freshness of this conjuring powder."

They took their seats on either side of the map. One little chant and a dusting of charged powder and the map would light up with small orbs, showing the location of every demon in the area. The brighter the light, the stronger the demon, so the Hunter of Thrace should pop like a thousand-watt bulb. But even if he didn't, at least it would give them a good idea of how many demons they were currently cohabitating with. Frankie hoped for less than a dozen. She feared that the map would sparkle like the Milky Way.

"Oh, the crystals." Willow reached into the bag and set them on the rug: four small, jagged crystals in shades ranging from white to pale lavender. When she set the last one, a softness came into her eyes, like she was remembering that first spell.

"Are you thinking of Tara?" Frankie asked. "Do you miss her?"

Willow smiled, lips closed. "Always."

Frankie smiled at her gently. Every relationship her mom had was shadowed by the memory of Tara. As if being a single parent and a witch wasn't already complicated enough. And now she would be raising a slayer. Was her mom going to be single until the end of time?

"Mom, why did you and Kennedy break up?"

"We broke up not long after I found out I was pregnant with you."

"You broke up because of me?"

"No, sweetie," said Willow. "We broke up because she was a new slayer, just figuring things out. She wasn't ready to be a parent, and I—well, I couldn't wait to be one." She touched Frankie's cheek, and then swatted her in the arm. "Now pay attention. This may be just a little spell but I'm still rusty. So you're taking the lead."

"Me?"

"Yep." She handed Frankie a folded piece of paper with the incantation written on it. Frankie frowned. This wasn't eco-magic and it wasn't telekinesis, which were her only areas of expertise. The remote viewing spell had made her temporarily lose her sight. What if this one made her . . . temporarily lost? What if it dropped her into the middle of the desert?

"Can't I just transmogrify that plastic bag into compostable paper?"

"Sweetie, if you could do that, we would be millionaires." Willow dropped a handful of the potion powder into Frankie's palm. It was tinged light pink and smelled like musty flowers. Frankie wondered what it smelled like when it was fresh.

"Okay." Frankie took a deep breath. She grabbed her mom's hand—the one that wasn't also filled with potion powder—and focused on the map. The crystals beside it began to glow, and the flames of the candles perked up like dogs hearing a whistle.

"Thespia," Frankie said. "We walk in shadow, walk in blindness. You are the protector of the night. Thespia, goddess, ruler of all darkness—we implore you . . ." She paused. Nothing was happening. The air above the map didn't waver. "We implore you . . . we implore you . . ." Frankie felt the magic passing between their joined hands. It was growing, but slowly. As she watched, the map seemed to brighten, just a fraction.

"Screw it," Willow said quietly.

Frankie yelped as her mom squeezed her fingers hard.

"Thespia," Willow commanded. "Do not anger me. Show me every demon in this town . . . show me the eater of hearts." She threw her powder into the air without warning, so Frankie had to scramble to add hers to the mix.

It cascaded onto the map and disintegrated into a fog between the candle flames. The fog hovered there, and as they watched, little points of light fell like falling stars. There were not a Milky Way's worth, but there were more than Frankie hoped for. Tiny sparkles gleamed on the outskirts of the cemeteries and a few inside: vamps, making homes of the new crypts. A few winked brightly in the motels out by the highway, and others in homes in town. There was a small, shiny cluster in their development of New Sunnydale Heights: their house, packed full of the demons Spike, Sigmund, and Jake.

"Wait, what's that?" Frankie asked. "In the hills."

As they watched, more and more tiny lights fell into the same small space. At first five, then seven, then a dozen, blinking about on the map like tiny fireflies.

"It's a nest," Willow said, and just as she said it, a sparkle the size of a dime fell from the fog. The moment it hit the surface, the map caught fire and started to burn.

"Crap, the rug!" Her mom clapped her hands and broke the

spell—the fog changed back to powder and fell, snuffing out the tiny flames, but her mom slapped at it anyway with the flat of her palm.

"Was that supposed to happen?" asked Frankie.

"Maybe. This spell has burned up a map before—of course that was when an army of a few thousand demons was waiting right inside the Hellmouth, and I doubt that's happening again—"

Frankie blew out the candles and got up to set them back on the windowsill. Then she turned and watched her mom, still batting at the rug.

"So do you want to explain that?"

"Explain what, sweetie?"

"What just happened. I was doing the spell. It was working. And you just lost your patience and basically bullied Thespia, the goddess of all darkness, into doing our bidding."

"And she did it," Willow said lightly. "Yay!" Her nose wrinkled, ashamed. "I'm sorry, sweetie. I was just . . . mad about Buffy and thinking about Tara and . . . I'll get a better handle on this. I will."

Frankie peered at her mother in the bright light of the bedroom. Her roots were still red. And her eyes were just her normal Mom eyes. Not black or even glassy. She just hadn't done magic in so long. Maybe that was why she was so eager.

"And there was no harm, see?" Willow picked up the map and brushed it off. "Barely scorched. Now there's just a handy mark on it for you to follow. What's wrong?"

"Nothing, just . . . you haven't done magic in sixteen years, and you're still so . . . I'm never going to be as good a witch as you. And I'm never going to be as good a slayer as Buffy." For Pete's sake, she'd staked herself. She tried a spell and went blind. "It should have been Hailey. She knows what she's doing and she doesn't even have powers. Do you think we can work out some kind of

223

a transfer? Maybe if we both hold on to the Scythe and click our heels together?"

Willow brushed Frankie's hair away from her cheek and rubbed at a smudge of pink potion powder.

"Hailey is kind of a natural. Way better at killing vampires than your uncle Xander and I were when we first started." Her brows knit, remembering. "But she's not the slayer. You are."

"Because you made me." Frankie put her hands on her hips. "You and the spirit of the original slayer, who I would someday like to know more about."

Willow snorted a little. She pulled her daughter into a hug. "I know your aunt Buffy casts a long shadow," she said. "But I also know she would be proud of you."

"For staking myself?"

"Buffy missed the heart a lot in the beginning."

"But she's never staked herself."

"No. But she's almost been staked. Being the slayer doesn't mean you're perfect. It just means you're stronger than most people. And you're strong, Frankie. You've always been strong. In here." Willow pointed to her heart.

Frankie made a face. That was all cheese, but she kind of loved it. And knowing that Buffy had almost been staked shouldn't have made her feel better. But it did, a little bit.

"I wish she was here." Frankie squeezed her mom tight. Buffy would have made short work of the Hunter of Thrace, that's for sure.

"You will be as great as she was someday," Willow said. "Just maybe don't die as often as she did. Okay?"

"Okay."

"Good. Because I'm not allowed to bring people back from the dead anymore."

"Mom."

"What? I'm just kidding."

$$) \ ) \ \bigcirc \ (\ ($$

Hailey and Jake cast their eyes to the ceiling as the lights dimmed.

"I wonder if that means the spell is going well or going poorly," Hailey mused.

"At least it's going," said Jake. They were alone, twiddling their thumbs. Sigmund was in the other room, quietly nosing through a book. Spike was downstairs, doing who knows what, probably shadowboxing in his black leather coat. "I'm bored." Jake stood. "Wanna get some weapons?"

Hailey shoved away from the table and followed him into the other room. Ever since Frankie became the new slayer, Spike and Oz had been stocking up on a veritable arsenal, and the Rosenbergs stored most of theirs in a trunk in the living room. Jake (carefully) moved a few potted ferns off the top and popped the lock. The lid opened with a creak, and he dove down inside. When he came up, he had a short throwing ax in one hand and a razor-tipped arrow in the other.

"What's your poison?" he asked. "Skull cleaving or heart piercing?"

"Skull cleaving," Hailey said. He handed it to her, and she twirled it by the handle, then took a few practice swings, nicking the hip of her jeans in the process. "Shit." She touched the torn spot, and her fingertip came away bloody. "It's okay; it's shallow."

Jake held out the arrow. "Change your mind?"

"No way." The ax was nice. A good weight, light enough to maneuver but heavy enough to sink in deep. And it had a nice blunt top, too, for bashing noses. The arrows were of no use to anyone;

Spike hadn't trained them in projectiles yet. No compound bows, no crossbows, not even a dart gun. Projectiles of any kind seemed to make him nervous.

Jake looked over Hailey's shoulder. Sigmund had crept into the living room.

"Arrow for you, Secret Seasoning?" Jake asked, and placed one in the half demon's hands.

"No thank you, Thriller." Sigmund gingerly returned it to the trunk. "I don't fight."

Hailey cocked an eyebrow at him. "I thought you said you had special Sage demon strength."

"An empty threat. I was trying to de-escalate you. I get most of my physical traits from my human father. All that's demon about me is the feeding. And the charm. And the smarts."

Hailey and Jake looked at each other and shrugged. There were lots of demons who appeared mostly human. Even the Hunter of Thrace, as long as he shaded his eyes and didn't smile too wide. Other demons glamoured themselves on a regular basis and lived regular old lives, hiding in plain sight. Jake and Oz did, to some extent.

"You haven't mentioned your dad," Hailey noted, and bent down to the trunk to rearrange bottles of holy water.

"That's because my mom ate him after the mating." Jake's and Hailey's eyes widened, and Sigmund grinned. "That was a joke. He works in government, too."

"Well," said Jake, "even if you're not fighting, if you're coming with us you have to at least have a good, old-fashioned stake." He pushed one into Sigmund's hands. One he'd made himself, so a shorter one, bordering on stubby. "It's classic, it's understated . . ."

Sigmund cleared his throat. "I don't think I am going. I think we should leave the Hunter of Thrace to his business."

"What?" Hailey snatched the stake away. Then she tossed it onto the carpet; it really was no good. "He eats slayer hearts. Weren't you listening?"

"Of course I was listening; I was the one doing the reading. Look, I don't know what the Hunter of Thrace is doing here or what his interest is in Frankie. We certainly shouldn't let him near her, but what you're doing, running in blindly because you think he was behind the attack on the other slayers—"

"He was," Hailey said, her voice low. "He was in Halifax. I showed you."

"Yes, but he was there doing what? We don't know. Nothing about the Hunter of Thrace suggests he kills in a manner like the attack in Nova Scotia. He stalks his prey. He prefers single targets, not groups. And he doesn't use advanced weaponry—most accounts say he likes to use his hands. The technology—or the magic, if it was a mystical weapon—isn't exactly his modus operandi."

"But *could* he do it?" Jake asked. "Does he have the ability to use magic?"

"I suppose so." Sigmund looked down. "It wouldn't be unreasonable to assume that a being that old could be versed in magic. But—"

"So the portal mark could have been his, then!" said Hailey. "He could have secreted the slayers away somewhere and be holding them. He could have used the explosion as a cover to make us think they were all dead!"

Sigmund hesitated. "I just think that he would be the last demon who would want to see the slayers die out. Hailey, I know you want to find your sister alive—"

"Vi," she said. "Her name is Vi."

Sigmund looked at her hands. They were shaking.

"Of course," he said. "Of course. And I just want to help." He reached into the weapons trunk and pulled out a knife, turning it back and forth under the light. "I just hope we're not moving too fast. Frankie's still so new at this. And the Hunter of Thrace is a legendary warrior."

"Frankie does run away," said Jake. "And she winds up on her back a lot. But cut her some slack; she's only been the slayer for a few weeks."

"And you don't know slayers like we do," said Hailey. "They always get the job done."

The stairs creaked at both ends of the house, and Spike emerged from the basement as Frankie and Willow came downstairs. Even Sigmund had to admit that Frankie looked like a slayer that night, in a dark canvas jacket and her hair in a high bun. She had a look of determination in her eyes and a stake squeezed tight in her hand.

"Hey," Jake said, and poked Sigmund in the ribs. "How long have you been waiting to call me 'Thriller'?"

"About a day and a half," the Sage demon replied. Then he stuck out his hand. "Good luck tonight, werewolf."

CHAPTER TWENTY-ONE
NOT SO MUCH WITH THE STEALTHY

Following the map Willow had burned, they took Spike's car to the northwest side of town, driving with the blacked-out windows down to keep from getting carsick. When Frankie pointed her finger, Spike pulled off and parked on the shoulder.

"It's up this road," she said, pointing to a winding strip of tar that disappeared into the trees. "About half a mile."

"You said this was a nest?" Spike ducked under the rearview mirror to get a better look.

"Maybe," Frankie said. "We couldn't be sure. There seemed to be a lot of demon lights, but then the spell freaked out."

"What do you mean, 'freaked out'?"

"Like, laid a big, burning demon egg right on top of it."

"All right, let's go," Jake said, from the backseat. "Weapons, weapons." He handed Frankie another stake and a knife to strap to her belt. In the side mirror, she saw Hailey heft a small ax.

"Nice ax," Frankie said.

"Thanks. If I get to sink it into the demon who attacked Vi, I might even name it." Hailey pointed the handle toward the front seat. "Unless you want it?"

"No, no, keep it. I actually wish we'd brought my sparring stick. It's what I'm best with."

"Little big, though," said Jake. "And not exactly lethal."

They were rambling. Nervous. But not a one of them asked if it was really a good idea. They were, Frankie realized while looking at their determined faces, true Scoobies.

Not that that had stopped Willow from gathering them all into an overly long, tight hug before they left the house. Oz had even given Jake a particularly emotional jut of his chin.

They got out of the car and trudged up the hill. It wasn't easy; it was steep, and the waning moonlight was overcast by clouds.

"Are there rattlesnakes in California?" Hailey asked as she stepped gingerly through the brush on the side of the road.

"They'll be asleep," said Spike. "Just don't stick your foot into any holes."

Hailey stepped even more gingerly.

After what felt like forever of slow going but was probably no more than ten minutes, they came to an offshoot of the road: a long, poorly kept gravel driveway.

"This should be it," Frankie said.

"Then let's go," said Hailey.

But Frankie paused. Hailey hadn't seen how many sparkles had fallen onto that part of the map during the locator spell. If it really was a nest, it was a big one. She craned her neck to peer toward the side of the house, which was not so much a house as a grand old stucco mansion. The grounds that faced Sunnydale were flat, dug out of the hill. But at the rear of the estate, the hill rose steeply and was nicely forested with a lot of tree cover.

"Let's go around the back. Take the high ground and get a better look at what we're dealing with?"

"If you want to be boring about it," Jake said jokingly.

They skirted around the back with Spike in the lead. As they passed the side of the house, Spike suddenly leapt up into a tree and dragged someone down screaming. A quick twist of his neck and the screaming stopped, the body disappearing into dust.

"Lookouts," Spike said. He pointed ahead toward what looked like candlelight emanating from the windows. "Time to get stealthy."

They snuck across the grounds and climbed up a sandy, rocky hill behind the mansion until they found a good vantage point with enough bushes for them to hide behind. The mansion below looked less like a nest and more like a beehive: Vampires came and went in a near-constant stream. And they were carrying tools: pickaxes and shovels, paint cans and brushes, all moving deeper into the house.

"Are they restoring that old condemned mansion?" Jake asked. "Industrious."

"How are there so many?" Hailey asked. "Maybe that's what your spell was trying to say, Frankie. Maybe there were so many demon lights that it got fed up and just plopped down one big one."

"Or maybe not," said Spike. "Look."

From their spot on the hill they had a clear view of a small, walled courtyard, and the second-floor room that looked down upon it. It was brightly lit by candelabras and refurbished chandeliers. Furnishings were sparse but opulent: chairs and chaises of red velvet and gilding, tapestries the size of Rhode Island. Tables that belonged in museums somewhere. And standing around the center table: an imposing woman in a long gold dress.

"The Countess?" Frankie asked.

"The fake countess," Spike corrected. "The Fountess. Keep your mind on our target."

"But even if she is a Fountess—fake countess, she might still be strong enough to have caused the bright egg on the map," she said, and then, as if on cue, the man standing to one side of her turned so they could see his very handsome profile.

"Never mind," Frankie said. "That's the demon who helped me."

"The Hunter of Thrace," Spike said. His eyes narrowed. The demon was dressed in a well-fitting buttoned shirt, rolled to the elbows to show the lean muscle of his forearms. His jawline was sculpted and strong, and his hair—Frankie thought maybe Jake was right, and she had seen him in an ad for men's swimwear.

"He doesn't look so tough," said Spike. "Looks like someone I'll enjoy taking apart."

"Taking apart?"

"None of the readings mentioned how to kill him," the vampire said. "But I find that pulling off arms and legs works more often than not."

"Okay," said Hailey. "So what's the plan?"

"The plan?" Jake croaked. "Are we seeing the same thing? There have to be two dozen vampires down there, along with one possible Countess, and one highly likely hunter god of ancient Greece."

"What's your point?" Spike asked.

"My point is, we should run. Or more specifically we should slink back down the hill quietly and come up with a better plan back at the house." He pointed at the vampires. "Look at how ripped those vamps are! Have they been feeding at Muscle Beach?"

Frankie studied the vampires. Most of them did seem uncommonly burly. And male. And dressed like security guards, just like the ones who attacked her on the playground. Except for the house servants, who were still ripped, but more handsome and dressed like butlers.

"We're not running," said Spike.

"Fine by me," said Hailey.

"Are your vengeful bloodlusts clouding your judgment?" Jake asked. "We're outnumbered. One vampire, one angry girl, one newborn slayer—"

"Hey," said Frankie.

"—and one non-wolfy werewolf between moons." He held up a finger for each of them. "We don't even make a whole hand!"

Spike rolled his eyes. "Look, the numbers won't matter if we can filter them. Draw them out one at a time. Or even in a flood right through that narrow hall, where they won't be able to—" Jake shifted to see better and knocked a large rock loose from the hill. It rolled noisily down to the mansion and struck the side of it with a loud crack. Inside, every head turned and located them at once.

"Or we can run," Spike said lightly. "Because they've seen us."

$$) \,) \, \bigcirc \, (\, ($$

"The jig is up!" Jake shouted as the first of the vampires emerged and ran around the side of the mansion.

"The jig is up?" Hailey asked. She looked at Frankie and shrugged, then leapt down with Jake to meet the vampires head-on.

"Guys! Wait!" Frankie watched as Spike roared and leapt down to join them. They had no choice. The hill was too steep to run up, and they were boxed in by trees on both sides. Below in the courtyard, Jake ducked a punch from one vampire and hit a second with an outstretched arm. It went down like it had been clotheslined. Then two quick strikes of a stake: one into the chest of the vamp on the ground and the other a hit from the rear to the first vampire's back. They were a memory of dust. Jake could fight, and even better than Frankie would have guessed, despite seeing him rough people up on the lacrosse field. But they were only the first two vamps. From the rumble of footsteps inside the mansion, they were the first two in a stampede.

"Back down the way we came," Spike said, and waved to her. "Fight our way back to the car!"

"Okay, I'm coming!" Frankie made it down in two big leaps. But she was flustered. Their plan hadn't been much of a plan to begin with, but it had still fallen apart so quickly. She chanced another look through the mansion window, and there they were—the fake countess, her henchman, and the Hunter of Thrace with his eerie, glowing blue eyes. They didn't seem inclined to join the fray, so at least they only had to worry about the vampire lackeys. She turned away just in time to see a vampire raise his huge biceps over Hailey's head.

"Hailey, duck!"

She did as Frankie said, and Frankie swept in to stake the vamp, dust cascading over Hailey's bent shoulders. They were fighting well, but it was like fighting a swarm: For every vamp they dusted, two more popped out of the mansion. And even though Spike spun and kicked and threw other vampires ten feet, their circle of fighting space was shrinking. They were going to be overrun. They had to do something.

She had to do something. Her eyes scanned the battle, and her slayer instincts clicked into place.

"Frankie?" Hailey asked.

"We've got to splinter them," Frankie whispered.

"What? What are you doing?"

"Some stupid slayer thing!" Frankie replied. She bolted across the ground, punching through vampires. She leapt feetfirst and pinned one of the butler types to the grass, staking it so fast she dropped to the dirt through his vanishing dust. Then she raced across the lawn in the other direction, away from the fight and away from the car, down the hill that led back toward Sunnydale.

"Hey, vampires!" she screamed. "Who wants a bite of fresh slayer?"

"No, Frankie!"

Frankie looked over her shoulder and gave Hailey a confident wink. That confidence hiccuped when she saw no fewer than ten vampires racing down the hill after her, but still, it had worked. Hailey, Spike, and Jake would take care of the remaining vamps and make it back to the car.

"Frankie!" Spike shouted.

"No!" she shouted. "Go! Get the car!" *Get the car and meet me on the road below.* Regroup. Only she didn't have time to say all that. She just hoped that they knew what she was doing.

☽ ☽ ◯ ☾ ☾

"I am once again running away," Frankie said as she raced across the dark estate and through the dark trees in the direction that she hoped was the way back to town. "But this time, I am running with a plan."

She didn't know exactly who she was talking to. Aunt Buffy, she supposed, wherever she was. Behind her, the sound of the pursuing vampires was a steady rush of crashing and stomping feet, snarls and snapped twigs. But at least it didn't sound like they were gaining on her. She ducked a low branch and kept her eyes on the ground. No falling down ravines this time. She was nearly to the bottom of the hill. The road was right below.

"Right behind that enormous stone wall." Her feet thudded to a stop. It wasn't that tall of a wall, really, but it wasn't going to be easy to climb. She hadn't noticed it when they were driving in. She must not have been paying attention. Or maybe she'd mistaken it for a ground-level retaining wall. That's probably what part of it was—only built up higher than the curve of the hill. For aesthetics. Marking the boundary of the very expensive mansion estate.

"Got you!"

She darted to her right as a vampire dove out of the trees and tried to grab her by the shoulders. It missed and tumbled down the last of the hill like a demonic log.

"Time to move." She drove her legs underneath her in long strides toward the stone wall. The higher she jumped, the less there'd be to climb. She heard the rest of the vampires burst through the tree line and she leapt, saying a silent prayer to the lizard gods that she would stick—and she did! Her hands caught and held as she bounced against the rocks. Unfortunately, her surprise made her hesitate, and by the time she started climbing, the rest of the vampires had also reached the wall and leapt up to grab her dangling foot.

Frankie didn't need to look back to know what lay below: a roiling pit of fangs and yellow eyes. If they dragged her down into that, she would never get up again. Using all her strength, she pulled her knee up and drove her foot back down, hitting the vampire in the face until he let go. She finally understood why Buffy used to fight in heels—very handy for kicking a vampire in the face. Maybe she could get Hailey to take her shopping. Triumphant, she reached for the last stone at the top of the wall, and felt it wobble.

"You've got to be kidding me."

The stone came loose, and she fell, landing in the pit of writhing vampires with an audible "Oof." She rolled to her feet and tried to somersault out only to be held back by grasping fingers. They had her. Their weight crushed against her shoulders, and she heard their gnashing fangs. *Mom*, she thought. It was the only word that cut through the panic. *Mom!*

The vampires exploded backward, and for a moment, she thought her mom had heard, and Willow had thrown them with an unseen force. But when Frankie opened her eyes, she saw the Hunter of Thrace. He stood over her, his eyes glowing blue.

Frankie listened for the roar of Spike's approaching car. But no one was coming to divert him this time. He was going to make a snack of her heart.

"She's mine," he said.

"She's a slayer," said one of the vampires. "The Countess will want her alive."

You're the first slayer-witch, an inner voice said, a voice that sounded suspiciously like Hailey. *So use your magic.*

Frankie brought her focus down into her fingertips. She knew the words to conjure fire. She could feel the heat there, starting in her palm.

The Hunter of Thrace lunged for the vampire's throat and tore it out, leaving nothing but a cloud of dust. The other vampires snarled and jumped for him. But not all. A few were smarter and jumped for Frankie.

The fire bloomed in her hands and flared into the first vampire's face like a torch, but there was no time to conjure more. There was no time to think. She fought for her life, stake in one hand and her other a fist, kicking and stabbing and punching until there was so much dust she felt a serious sneeze coming on. When she drove backward with her stake and someone grabbed her wrist, she barely registered that the hand gripping her was warm—not the cold dead hand of a vampire—and just twisted and kicked high, connecting

237

with the Hunter of Thrace's cheekbone and bending him over at the waist. Then she righted herself and spun away, tensed for the next attack.

But there were no more attacks. The vampires were all dead. All that remained were her and the Hunter. Face-to-face. Again.

He's too much for you, an inner voice said. This one sounded like Spike, and she wished that her inner Scoobies would just cool it for the rest of the battle.

Frankie jumped and punched hard. He dodged and blocked and knocked her off-balance. She went in again and landed a flurry of strikes to his chest and head.

"Too bad Hailey's not here. She deserves to sink her ax into you. But I guess a stake will have to do."

"I'm not a vampire," he growled.

"I know. But a stabbing is a stabbing whether it's a stake or a knife. Or an ax. I hear that works for lots of demons." She raised her stake in her fist, and the Hunter lifted his head and stared intently over her shoulder toward the woods. "What?" she asked. "Trying to get me to look over there? That's a pretty weak diversion tactic."

"They're coming. Get up the wall."

"Huh?"

"Get up the wall." He reached out and grabbed the hand that held the stake, clearly not threatened by it in the slightest, which she thought was rude, and pushed her toward the wall. But when he reached around her waist to boost her up, he growled. "There's no time. They'll see you go, and I'll have to pursue. We have to hide." He took her wrist and pulled her along, running so fast her feet barely touched the ground. They made the cover of the trees just as the next wave of vampires ran into the clearing.

"What are you doing?" Frankie asked. "Why are you helping me?"

"I suppose I'll have to tell you," he replied. "But first let's get to someplace safe."

)) ◯ ((

Willow and Sigmund sat together at the kitchen counter, stirring cups of tea.

"How do you think it's going out there?" Willow asked.

Sigmund set down his cup and wiped up a bit of tea that splashed over the edge.

"Oh, very well, I'm sure." He cleared his throat. "I haven't known your daughter long, Ms. Rosenberg, but she seems very capable. And Mr. Pratt is with them."

"Mr. Pratt." Willow smiled. That didn't give her as much confidence as Sigmund implied it should. Before they'd left, she'd asked Spike about their plan, and he'd said they were going to "kill whatever they came across." She was starting to have serious doubts about his Watcheriness.

"I'm surprised you didn't want to go along," she said. "Your mom was always . . . very interested in combat."

"She still is. Takes home a medal every year during the tournaments."

"Tournaments?"

"Yes. Sage demons have annual tournaments. All nonlethal, with various classes and categories, armed and unarmed . . . capped off by a barbecue. It's kind of like our version of a family reunion."

"Sarafina still fights?" Willow looked at her hands. They didn't look so much older. She didn't feel so much older. It was hard to believe that she had a daughter who was old enough to be a slayer. "It's kind of strange to be around unaging immortals," she said. "You'd think with so much magic in me I'd stay younger longer."

But even Buffy was the age she was. Just a very spry, fit age she was.

"You're not old, Ms. Rosenberg."

She drew her hands back. "Of course I'm not. But I'd be even more not old if you'd stop calling me Ms. Rosenberg." She smiled. "How's the portal research going? Can I help?"

"I would welcome your help. It might be useful to re-create a similar portal. For comparison. Are you familiar with demon magics?"

She made a face. "Demon magic was more Andrew's specialty. But I'd be willing to try. So you think it definitely was a portal? Not a burn mark from the explosion?"

"Yes, I think so. But I haven't wanted to tell the others."

"Why not? They would be so happy."

"I'm not entirely sure that they should be." Sigmund leaned over his tea. He really was such a nice-looking boy. He had his mother's same large, alert eyes, even if hers tended to be looking down imperiously while Sigmund's were stuck in a book. "Portal magic is extremely touchy. I've been studying it for years, and I've still only mastered half a dozen methods."

She nodded, but she didn't quite understand. Andrew had managed it. Andrew. And whenever she thought of Andrew, the first two words that came to mind were still "weaselly" and "inept," no matter how much he'd grown within the Watchers Council.

"Think about what we know of portals," Sigmund said. "It's not like teleportation. They take time and intention to cast. The reports have said that the explosion was one large blast, is that right?"

"Yes. One main blast and a few smaller explosions from the resort. Propane tanks, gas lines."

"An explosion is so fast. Instantaneous. A portal is not. It's very unlikely that the slayers were able to use a spontaneous portal to escape from the explosion."

Willow blinked. "So what are you saying? That someone knew?"

"All I'm saying is there's more going on here than it looks like." He stirred another cube of sugar into his tea, even though it was already cold, and set the spoon down with a despairing clatter. "If a portal was used, someone had to have planned it ahead of time. The slayers . . . or someone else."

"But if they did cast it, they could still be alive?" Willow asked.

"Yes, but depending on who cast the portal, it doesn't mean they're safe. Who would want to kidnap all the slayers? That's what we need to be asking."

Willow got up from the counter and refilled the teakettle. They should tell the others. Just . . . not yet.

"Don't say anything about this," she said. "Not until we know more."

"Of course," said Sigmund. "I won't stop researching. That's . . . what I do."

"We have to find out where that portal went. Can you do that?"

"Maybe. Collecting samples of the residue would help to narrow down the possible destinations." He tapped his chin. "Does your lab have equipment to identify radionuclides?"

"Not my department, but I think so."

"Certain dimensions leave certain signatures. That might help."

"No problem," Willow said. "Just get me the samples."

CHAPTER TWENTY-TWO

GRIMLOCH, THE HUNTER OF THRACE

rankie and the Hunter of Thrace stole through the trees, down the hills, and back into Sunnydale. They kept to the ditches and trees and crossed roads like nighttime coyotes, doubling back and turning downwind to throw any pursuing vampires off their scent. Personally, Frankie thought it was a wasted effort—Jake was right about the vamps: They seemed like mostly muscle, partly fang, and an itty-bitty bit of brain. She wondered whether Sigmund could feed on vampires—if so, he could be their secret weapon in eliminating the fake countess's small army. But maybe that was judging them unfairly; surely there were lots of overmuscled scholars out there. Really burly Mensa chapters.

"Where are we?" she asked. They were back at New Sunnydale level, in woods that felt familiar.

"We're in the same forest where we hunted the Succoro demon."

"Where *you* hunted the Succoro demon." She narrowed her eyes at him. "I was there to fight and kill it."

"Your tone implies that to hunt is inferior. But I achieved the same end as you. I just made some use of the flesh that remained."

He glanced at her over his shoulder, and she caught a flash of blue eyes.

"I didn't mean inferior, exactly. But don't go being all *superior* either. It's not like you utilized the entire demon nose to tail. There was plenty of waste for us to bury afterward, believe me."

"Here. This is the Succoro's lair." He pushed aside some leafy boughs to reveal . . . a tent. A large, family-sized tent, but still a tent. Not a deep, cool cave with walls wet from rivulets of groundwater. Not even a dirt burrow, dug out of a hill. Many of the natural cave formations that the demons of Sunnydale used to live in had been destroyed by the collapse of the Hellmouth. It looked like the ones who came after just had to make do.

"Get inside," he said.

"You first." Frankie reached down to her ankle to pull a knife from a hidden sheath.

He frowned at the knife and ducked inside the flap. A moment later, the tent lit up as he turned on a battery-powered camping lantern. She was getting sort of tired of how unimpressed he was by her slayeriness.

She followed him inside. The tent was outfitted nicely with an elevated cot and several tables—one that held a stack of books, another a hot plate and a rack of spices. The Succoro hadn't just been camping; it had been glamping, and the sight of so many human furnishings gave her a funny feeling in her gut. When she looked at the cot, she imagined the Succoro lying there. Dead, and with its chest cracked open.

So what? she reminded herself. So it seemed human. It was trying to kill Hailey. And Jasmine. And even poor, horrid Jane Montclair, who she'd heard was going to need six months of reconstructive procedures on her face. Demons were demons—well, except for Sigmund, and Spike, and Jake. Even the extremely good-looking one who was now bent down over the hot plate trying to brew her a cup of tea.

"Have you been living here since you killed the Succoro?" she asked.

"No," he said. "I've never been here before tonight."

She watched him riffle through tea containers until he found a jar of honey.

"You sure seem to know your way around."

"I do. The same way I knew where this tent was." He glanced up, and for a moment, his eyes flashed bright before settling back to a normal blue. "Because I ate the Succoro's heart."

Sigmund said that the Hunter of Thrace consumed the essence of his kills.

"So you really are the Hunter of Thrace."

"Grimloch," he said. "The Hunter of Thrace is kind of a mouthful."

Frankie cocked her eyebrow. "You don't think 'Grimloch' is a mouthful?"

He didn't reply. He just opened the top of a teapot and dropped in a packet of tea.

"What's with the tea?" she asked. "You eat slayer hearts, right? So do you prefer them chamomile-infused?" Or maybe he was intending to drug her. Gross. She gripped the handle of her knife tighter. She'd rather have her heart ripped still beating from her very conscious body. "What are you doing in Sunnydale? Are you working with the Countess?"

"I'm here because I heard a new slayer had risen," he said. "And I thought all the slayers were dead."

"Because you killed them."

He poured tea into two cups and added liberal amounts of honey to each. "No." He held out a cup. "Here."

"Hmpf." Frankie snorted. "I'm not drinking that. You don't drink things that weird guys make for you, demon or not."

Grimloch shrugged and took a sip. "It's good. The Succoro had good taste."

"He was a foodie."

"What?"

"A foodie. Sigmund—our researcher—said Succoros appreciate novel cuisine." She looked around at the Succoro's home: the piles of quilted blankets, the reading glasses. "Hard to believe it was the one responsible for so much carnage." It was also hard to believe that it fit comfortably in that cot or that its long talons hadn't ripped this standard-issue camping tent to shreds.

"That was the Countess's fault. She demanded a high level of energy—far more than it was accustomed to procuring."

"You mean the Countess was the one who hired the Insta-demon?" Frankie paused. Her slayer sense was tingling again. No, more than tingling—it was ringing like a bell. *THE COUNTESS*, it flashed at her in blinking red lights, despite the other legendary demon standing two feet away.

"She might have demanded it," she said, "but he did the procuring. He could've said no."

"He could not have said no. I take it you and the Countess have not yet met."

"I suppose you guys are old friends?" she asked. "That was her back there, right? In the gaudy gold dress?"

"Yes. The Countess and I have met on occasion. A few different countries. A few different centuries." He sipped his tea, watching her over the rim of the mug, his dark hair wild. "A few different centuries" was a strange thing to hear when he looked so human. Except for the glowing eyes. And the incisors.

"My Watcher says she's not the really real Countess."

"Your Watcher is not a really real Watcher," said Grimloch. "He's a vampire."

"He's a Watcher," Frankie said defensively. "He's been a Watcher for almost as long as I've been alive." Though she supposed for a demon like Grimloch that amounted to about a week and a half.

"She's the real Countess," he said.

Her slayer sense stomped again, spelling out the word like a horse counting with its hoof. Frankie swallowed. *Okay, okay, slaydar,* she thought. *I believe you.* But that didn't mean that the Hunter could be trusted.

She stepped forward and held up the point of her knife. He couldn't be that much faster than she was—there was no demon alive that a slayer couldn't beat one way or another. That was the point of the slayer. Except how could that be true, if he'd eaten so many slayer hearts that he'd developed a taste for them?

"Why are you telling me this?" she snapped. "Why are you helping me? Did you attack the other slayers?"

"Tell me first why you weren't there. A new slayer has not been called since the dark witch ignited the line. Why weren't you called until now?"

"I don't know. My mother—" She paused. He didn't need to know their family secrets. But the look on his face—he wasn't just asking for the sake of asking.

"Please," he said, his eyes downcast and his voice soft. "Tell me."

The same slayer sense that told her the Countess was real now whispered, *Tell him.* Tell him. She wondered if her slaydar could be broken.

"Do you know about how my mother made the slayer army?"

"Of course," he said. "Every demon knows that story. They tell it around fires and bellied up to demon bars. They say your mother's name and spit on the ground."

Frankie made a face. "Well, anyway . . . when she channeled the essence of the slayers through the Scythe"—she pointed to herself— "it made me. The spirit of the original slayer is my dad. Or my other mom. We haven't decided yet what to call them." She swallowed. "I guess I was called because the other slayers, or one of the other slayers who was the last in the line . . ."

Grimloch set his tea on the cot-side table. He came closer until the tip of Frankie's knife was pressed to his chest, and she took a sharp breath. His eyes moved over her hair and down her shoulders. He lifted his hand, and she flinched, ready to drive the blade in deep. But he simply brushed his fingers against her cheek. The way he was looking at her—no one had ever looked at her that way before.

"What?" she asked. "Do I have something on my face?"

"You were made from the essence that entered all the slayers," he said gently. "You are of them. Part of them." He covered her hand that held the knife with his own. "And I am not here to harm you."

Frankie squeezed the knife harder. His fingers were warm, and slow, and before she knew it, the blade was laid flat to his chest, and she could feel his heartbeat. "You haven't really answered the question." She cleared her throat. "About the attack on the slayer meeting."

"Why would you think I killed them?"

"Because you eat slayer hearts. And now because you're being hella evasive about it."

He let go of her hand and walked away across the soft rugs covering the floor of the tent. "If I wanted to eat their hearts, why would I kill them in an explosion?"

"Yes, I thought of that, too," Frankie grumbled. "Though nobody else seemed to." She pointed her knife at him again. "But maybe you needed the bomb to thin the herd. We know you were there. We saw you, hunting them."

"You saw me?"

"In pictures. One of our Scoobies has a near-photographic memory. Bet you weren't counting on that."

Grimloch frowned. "I wasn't counting on a lot of things. What is a 'Scooby'?"

"It's a cartoon dog from the 1970s and a reference to the team of mystery solvers who were his friends. Never mind. You're a demon; you wouldn't get it."

Grimloch went to stand beside the wall of the tent. He just stood there. Doing nothing. Not trying to eat her heart. Not trying to get her to drink any more roofied tea. He just stood there looking like he'd been kicked. Looking like he'd lost something. Or someone.

"I wasn't hunting the slayers," he said. "I was watching her. Guarding her from a distance because I wasn't allowed to be present at the slayer gatherings. Even though they knew me."

"They knew you?"

"Yes." He looked at her. "And they knew what I was."

"They knew you ate slayer hearts and they just let you hang around? No way. Buffy would have cut you down before breakfast."

"I never ate a slayer heart," he said, and bared his fangs a little. "That was only a story. I fought a slayer once, and the legend grew out of that. You know how these things tend to snowball."

"I do?"

"In the old days, there were centuries where it was believed I had a set of ram's horns." He gestured to the space beside his ears. "For almost two hundred years, I had to wear a set whenever I was summoned or the tribes wouldn't believe that I was me. It was . . . annoying."

"So you fought a slayer," Frankie said, to keep him on topic and to keep herself from imagining him with an adorable set of fake horns. "And then you, what? Followed her around to fight her again? Tagged along to slayer meetings to find new slayers to fight?"

He sighed. It seemed like the question almost hurt him, but she didn't care. Whatever role he had played in the attack, he had to pay. It didn't matter if he felt guilty about it now.

"What did you do to them?" Frankie half shouted.

"I fought her," he snarled. "And then I loved her." His eyes flashed hot—Frankie took a step back. "But I couldn't protect her. So now I'm here. To protect you."

The tip of Frankie's blade wavered in the air. There was a lot to unpack in that confession, and a lot that made her heart beat faster. He had loved a slayer. And he had seen her die.

Cautiously, she lowered her knife.

"You saw what happened?"

"Only the aftermath. I don't know who, or what . . ."

"Did you see anything? Did anyone make it out?"

Grimloch looked away. "I saw no one. And I searched."

Frankie wanted to scream. She would have punched the wall except the wall was made of canvas.

"So who was she?" Frankie asked. "Your slayer?"

"I won't speak of her."

"Seems pretty convenient."

"It is not"—he clenched his fist—"convenient. Our time together was ours. I have no wish to share it."

"Was it Buffy Summers?" she blurted. "I have to know that at least. Was the slayer you loved—did you love my aunt Buffy?" A lump rose into her throat. Would that make it better? Would it make it better to know that Grimloch had been there and loved her? That someone had been there who cared.

"No," he said, and his eyes softened. "My slayer wasn't your

249

Buffy. But I did know her. And I admired her. Buffy Summers was a great leader."

"She was," Frankie said, surprised to find tears in her eyes. Grief snuck up at the strangest of times. "And don't talk about her like that. Like she's gone."

"She's not gone," he said. "Not for you. You are a piece of them all. Their legacy. It's why I had to come. To see if you were ready to take up that mantle."

"I can see by the look on your face that you don't think I am," she muttered. "Also because you said so in the woods."

"Well, you *did* stake yourself."

"How many people know that?" She threw up her hands. "Does the Countess know?"

"The Countess knows nothing," he said. "Except for the faces of your allies, thanks to your attack on her mansion tonight."

Frankie grimaced. But at least she wasn't alone in being a screwup. She was just the head screwup in a whole team.

"What are you doing with her?" she asked. "The Countess, I mean."

"I'm buying you time. Until you're ready to confront her."

"Why don't you just kill her yourself?"

"I'm not strong enough," he said. "You really don't know who she is, do you?"

Frankie sighed. He had a real way of making her feel unprepared.

"Don't worry," he said, "she's not at her full strength. She's been dormant for almost a hundred years and slowly regaining her powers for the last decade. She just now got out of her bath of dirt." Bath of dirt? Frankie had no idea what he was talking about but figured it wasn't worth interrupting. "If you can keep her from fully rising, you have a chance. But the Countess is not like other vampires. You can't stake her."

"What do you mean I can't stake her?"

"She's been staked before. And beheaded. And burned. The Countess is a true immortal. Can't be killed. Can't be destroyed. Can only be neutralized."

"That's . . ." Frankie paused. "Totally not fair."

"Fair or not, she's been drawn here to the reawakening Hellmouth." He walked past her and poked his head out of the tent, listening for movement and scenting the air for vampires. It must have been all clear, because he dropped the flap and turned back to her. "So that makes her your problem. I'll run interference for as long as I can. But I can only kill so many of her henchmen and come back empty-handed so many times."

"You shouldn't stay there, then," Frankie said. "You shouldn't put yourself in danger."

"I said I couldn't kill her," he said. "I didn't say she could kill me. You should go. Your allies will be worried."

"Hang on." She raised her knife. "I still don't know if I'm supposed to slay you."

He looked at the knife. Then he looked into her eyes, and it was fairly obvious that she wasn't going to be slaying him tonight. She put the knife back in her boot.

"Fine, then how will I contact you?" she asked. "You know, in case I need to tell you something."

"You won't." He finished his tea and wiped the cup with a towel before walking out and leaving her in the tent alone. "I'll find you. It has been easy enough so far."

CHAPTER TWENTY-THREE
STUPID HOT DEMONS

Frankie waited until they were under the bright lights of the library before reporting her encounter with Grimloch, the ancient Hunter of Thrace. She couldn't think of him as a hunter anymore, since instead of stalking her to rip out her heart, he seemed to be protecting her. And she couldn't really think of him as ancient either, after seeing the modern cut of his clothes and hearing his voice. In her head, she'd even shortened his name from Grimloch to Grim—not that she was going to tell that to anyone else.

But when Spike finished listening to her summary of events, starting with the fight beside the wall and ending with his exit from the Succoro's tent (she left out the part where he'd touched her face), he was none too pleased.

"A brooding demon comes to town with a tortured, romantic sob story, creeping on the new slayer." He tightened his jaw so his cheekbones stood out and narrowed his eyes. "Where have I heard that before?"

"It isn't like that," Frankie said. "He's . . . annoying. And he clearly didn't rip my heart out and eat it, so let's mark it down as a win."

Around the desk, Hailey's and Jake's brows collectively wrinkled. Even Sigmund seemed skeptical.

"Annoying?" asked Jake. "What does that mean? *I'm* annoying."

"Yes, I know." Frankie narrowed her eyes. He was also tired. Jake didn't do well with these early, before-school meetings. He looked like he'd much rather be curled up and napping in a sunbeam.

"Jake is annoying," said Spike. "But he's right. What does that mean? Tell me everything that happened, and don't leave anything out. I'm your Watcher, remember? So they pay me to . . ." He pursed his lips. "Listen."

"Wait, they pay you?" Jake asked. "*And* you get paid by the school?"

"Focus, Jake," said Sigmund, and squeezed a squeak toy, the kind you buy for teething puppies. Hailey hid a chuckle behind her hand, and Sigmund grinned as Jake sat up and snatched it, then softly squeaked it to himself. "Go ahead, Frankie."

"There's not much I haven't told you," she started.

"You said you fought him. How did he fight? Weapons? Fangs?" Spike crossed his arms.

"Bare hands?" she said. "When we fought off the vampires, he used his bare hands to tear their throats out."

"Whoa," said Jake. "He *Road House*d them?"

"I don't know what that is."

"That's when you tear someone's throat out with your bare hand."

"Then yes. There were *Road House*s galore." She looked at Spike. "But he wasn't there to kill me. I think we can trust him. He even said he knew Buffy."

"Funny how she never mentioned him," muttered Spike.

"But why was he there?" asked Hailey. "What could a demon—who still clearly eats hearts even if those hearts aren't slayer hearts—be doing hanging out with the biggest and best demon-fighting force the world has ever seen?"

"Why does any vampire hang around a slayer?" Frankie shot a look at Spike. "He was there because he was in love with one of them. Not with Buffy," she added, and looked at Spike again. His jaw was clenched so tight his cheekbones could cut glass. "But he wouldn't say who. He wouldn't tell me her name."

The office went quiet. They hadn't expected that. Sigmund looked intrigued; Hailey skeptical. Spike took a long swig of blood from his "World's Best Librarian" mug and then stared down into it while Jake absently squeaked his dog toy.

"And you believe him?" Hailey asked, not *not* skeptically.

Frankie recalled Grimloch's expression in the tent, the slump of his shoulders, the bitter clench of his jaw. "You didn't see him. He could have killed me if he wanted to. And not just last night, but in the woods. Or he could have just let me die. Those vampires had me as good as buried."

"That earns him a pass, Mini Red," said Spike. "But just one."

"I don't know. My slaydar is really telling me he's an ally."

"Are you sure it's your slaydar talking?" Hailey scrolled through her phone until she landed on the photo of Vi with Grimloch in the background. "We've all seen him. We all know he's at least as hot as Sigmund. And I bet he's even better up close."

Sigmund cleared his throat, looking like he couldn't decide whether to be pleased Hailey considered him hot or jealous not to be the hottest.

"Assuming it's true," he said, "it would be a good thing to have the Hunter of Thrace as an ally." He paused as his stomach growled audibly. "Sorry—I've got tutoring sessions back-to-back this morning."

"What happens to your tutorees after you're done feeding on them, anyway?" Jake asked. "Does the stupidity grow back?"

"No. They're a little tired afterward. Most of them get sharper. Less able to be fed on. The tutoring works the brain, you know. And the brain is like a muscle. The more you work it, the better it gets: quicker, hardier, more capable."

"The brain is not a muscle." Jake tossed the dog toy into the air and caught it. "Even I know that, smart guy."

"I said 'like a muscle.' And if you want to know what being fed on feels like, I'd be happy to nibble off that morning grogginess."

"You're not nibbling anything," Jake said, and grinned. "But feel free to bite me."

Hailey patted both of their knees. "Down, boys."

"Yes, let's focus, children." Spike set his mug down on the desk. A little bit of blood sloshed over the lip and ran down the side, and Frankie and Hailey gagged. They gagged harder when he wiped it up with his finger and licked it clean. That was never not going to be gross. "Assuming the Hunter of Thrace—"

"Grimloch," Frankie interrupted. "He prefers Grimloch."

"Assuming *Grimloch* really is here with no ill intent toward Frankie's heart . . . then what is he doing here?"

"Protecting me," she said. "He's looking after the slayer line in memory of his dead slayer love. It's—" Sweet. Swoonworthy. Devastatingly romantic. "It's actually not the biggest problem. Remember the fake countess we saw in the mansion, the one with leagues and leagues of vampires restoring it and digging to who knows where?"

"Yes, I think I recall that."

"Well, according to Grimloch, she's no fake countess. She's the real deal. And she can't be killed."

That shut everyone up.

"So," Frankie said, pleased by their lack of questions. "After-school research session?"

No one peeped. But Jake did accidentally squeak his dog toy.

"Oops," he said. "That meant yes."

$$) \,) \, \bigcirc \, (\, ($$

After classes ended for the day, everyone showed up in the library to hit the books. No one even complained about it. Not even Spike. Sigmund had pulled the most pertinent volumes and already done a lot of the reading in between sessions of tutoring, though he'd still only scratched the surface. Countess Báthory was a legend among the living and the undead. So in addition to the stacks from the occult section, they also had to read, like, actual history books.

"You know, when I became a werewolf fighter in the struggle between good and evil, I had no idea there'd be so much extra time spent at school," Jake noted, rubbing his eyes. "We'd better have this lady vanquished before the lacrosse season starts or you guys are going to be down one wolfy ally."

"We'll work around your schedule," said Hailey. "I can get a gig as the new water girl and brief you on the research between scrimmages."

"I can tape spells for you to review on the inside of your jersey," said Frankie.

"No, thank you," the werewolf replied. "I know we have no work-life balance, but I demand to have a work-sports balance."

Sigmund set down a fresh pile of books.

"Jake's priorities may be skewed, but he has a point. Slaying is a calling, but it can't take over everything." He cocked his head at Jake. "Honestly, though, lacrosse? Why don't you play a real sport?"

Jake's eyes nearly jumped out of their sockets, and Frankie and Hailey shrank in their chairs.

"Jake, I'm joking. My dad and I go to the pro games sometimes—I actually play a little."

"Dude!" Jake stood and followed Sigmund back into the occult section. "You should come to tryouts; we could really use you. Some of our second string just started playing, like, last year. . . ."

"Aaand we've lost them," said Hailey. She opened a book and skimmed a few pages. So far, they hadn't had any luck finding ways to kill the Countess. The history books treated her like a serial killer and obviously only chronicled her mortal life. Her immortal life was when the really outlandish stuff had occurred, which was saying something considering that when she was alive she'd tortured and murdered several hundred of her servants. Many of them virginal girls procured from neighboring Hungarian towns.

"I'm starting to get what Grim meant when he said that legends tend to snowball." Frankie flipped her book around to show Hailey an ink engraving of a young woman being overcome by some kind of fog. "According to this one, the Countess can take the form of mist."

"Like Dracula."

"Except that unlike Dracula, the actual mist can feed on a person. Like, the mist can suck the blood right out through your pores, like sweat."

"Gross. So it says she's stronger than Dracula. That does sound like BS."

Half the books read like they were written by Countess groupies. *The Countess can't be killed and can feed in the form of mist, and also she lays golden eggs and on Sundays she goes to the hospitals and cures polio.* The only consistent point was how much she enjoyed feeding on virgins. Frankie sighed.

"No wonder so many vampires have tried to pass themselves off as her. It must be like being a Cher impersonator. If Cher was dead, and no one knew you were an impersonator." Hailey closed her book and opened another. They had come across a few passages suggesting that people had tried to slay the Countess before, including one account in the late 1800s that seemed to be successful. And all it had taken was enough mounted cavalry to stage a crusade, six priests, one burned-down fortress, and a mystical poison known only as "virgin's bane." It wasn't clear on what was done with the Countess's remains, but she hadn't been seen since. Or at least, the real Countess hadn't been seen. The dates of the disappearance would jibe with what Grimloch said about her being recently dormant. Unfortunately, that's when the fake countesses started cropping up, committing atrocities of their own. The wannabes were really complicating the research.

"Did Grimloch say anything other than she can't be killed?" Hailey asked. "Nothing useful about how he's just kidding and he can totally kill her for us?"

"No. But he didn't seem afraid of her. I mean, he seemed respectful? But he didn't seem afraid."

"I guess you wouldn't be afraid of much, after two thousand years. Did you ask him why he doesn't have cloven feet?"

Frankie grinned. "Maybe I'll ask that next time."

"So there's going to be a next time," Hailey said, and Frankie blushed. "I guess so, right? Since he's been stalking you on the regular?"

"He hasn't been stalking me. And stalking is nothing to joke about." But she still had to hide her grin. It hadn't been real stalking, because it hadn't been about her at all, really. It had been about the memory of his slayer. "He just wants answers about what happened to the slayers, like we do. He wants to help us. I know it."

"Oh, don't do that," Spike groaned, and slammed shut the book he'd been flipping through.

"Don't do what?" Frankie asked.

"I've seen that moony look before. You've no idea how many times I saw it on Buffy's face when she was chasing after old Tortured McForehead. And even on your mum's face when she was in the thick of it with Tara."

Frankie picked up another book.

"I have no idea what you're talking about."

"And you should talk," Hailey snorted. "Weren't you pretty moony-eyed over a certain slayer—"

"Enough!" Spike snapped. "I'm telling you right now, Mini Red—stay away from that demon until we know more."

And with that, he pointed a finger at them and walked away.

Hailey moaned and stretched her back. "It's getting late. And we aren't getting anywhere. What is this Countess broad's deal, anyway? Does she have a master plan? Or is she more of a Heath Ledger Joker, chaotic-evil alignment?"

"Hey," Jake said. "Get over here."

He and Sigmund had returned from the stacks and were in front of Sigmund's laptop. The group gathered around the screen as Sigmund scrolled and clicked through missing-persons reports and photos of Sunnydale's recently deceased. There were far too many in the last month alone, and too many were young.

"You think the Countess did all this?" Spike murmured.

"There's more," said Jake, and poked Sigmund in the shoulder. He clicked on to another news site. "That old Benedictine abbey on the edge of town." He pointed to the photo on the screen, a small structure of white brick topped by a thin, simple cross. "A few weeks ago, it was discovered abandoned. All twelve nuns who lived there just gone. Nuns, get it?" Their faces fell. "Nuns are virgins, usually!"

"We get it, Jake," Frankie grumbled. Sigmund clicked again and stopped on the photo of a teenage girl, who'd gone missing the week before. She couldn't have been more than fourteen.

"You guys finish up," Frankie said, her voice stony. "I'm going patrolling."

She'd lost nearly two dozen of her brood in the attack on the mansion. Two dozen young, loyal, handsome—if slightly stupid—vampires, many of whom Anton had painstakingly selected himself. They were all dust, gone too soon for her to even remember them fondly or know most of their names. All because of that little slayer brat. And to think she'd held up this one-sided truce with slayers for all these years.

The Countess smoothed the sleeves of her shirt as she sat and listened to Anton rage and pace. The movement caught his eye, her first movement in hours. Anyone watching would have taken her for a statue or one of those wax figures people were so fond of. She was fond of them, too. On a trip to London in the 1830s, she'd posed as one of the displays for days, and it made for an amusing form of hunting.

"Countess?" Anton asked.

But she didn't reply. She just sat, still as stone, forgoing even the show of breathing. Poor Anton. He was looking pale and sallow. She'd asked him to turn so many fledglings lately; she couldn't possibly ask him to replenish the lost stock. How long had they been together now? Five hundred years? How long had she known him? Since she was seventeen, and alive. Such wild times those had been. No one could convince a peasant girl to come and work in a drafty castle like Anton could. No one could manage a household's accounts and lands like he could. No one could wield a hot poker like he could.

When she died her strange, sad death, I'm cold had been her

last mortal words, and she could hardly imagine being so fragile. Thankfully, her death hadn't stuck. All the blood she'd drunk and all the evil she'd done in life had an unintended side effect and she'd awoken. A vampire. And immediately, she turned Anton into one, too—a fumbling, first-time turning. They'd hardly known what to do with each other.

"Should we continue work on the catacombs?" one of the remaining fledglings asked. "Now that so many are dead, there are a bunch of empty chambers—"

Anton paused. He looked back at her, unsure of what to do, probably worried that the empty chambers would make her sad, like a mother bird crying over the empty shells of broken eggs.

"Keep working," she said suddenly, and the young vampire shuddered and bowed. "But not too hard. We'll fill the chambers back up soon enough. I like a big house. A large hive, full of busy bees."

"We'll need to turn many," said Anton.

"So we'll turn many. Girls, too," she said, and shrugged when his eyes widened. It wasn't her style—girls were for eating, not for companionship, but perhaps that kind of thinking was outdated. This was a new decade, a new millennium, and if she wanted to thrive, some things had to change. Even her own habits. She'd started already, and today had dressed as a man, in trousers and one of Anton's shirts with buttons, which she liked even if she thought them a little ugly. "Where is my hunter?"

"He returned. Unharmed and empty-handed, as usual."

"Send for him."

Grimloch must not have been far; he walked into the room only a few seconds later.

"What happened with the slayer?"

"You were there," he said. "She and her friends dusted your vampires and escaped. I followed her down the east side of the estate and

over the wall, where I tracked her back to her home without being detected. She's impressive. She tore one of their throats out with her bare hands."

"Did she?" Anton asked suspiciously. "I've heard other reports say she's startlingly inept."

"Reports from who?" Grimloch asked. "Baby vampires she's sent running home with their fangs between their legs?"

Anton bared his teeth. It looked rather silly without his vampire face on.

"As far as I know, no vampire who encounters her walks away from that encounter. So who have you been asking?" Grimloch crossed his arms. "I know you haven't dared face her yourself."

"The Countess forbade it," Anton said. "You, on the other hand, have followed her a dozen times now and done nothing. Just how long do you usually stalk your prey?"

"As long as I like."

"Well, hurry up. The poor girl doesn't need a bodyguard so much as a restraining order." The two men snarled at each other, and Anton's demon came to the surface, warping his features and turning his eyes a deep golden yellow. "Or maybe you're not hunting her at all. Maybe you're the one who has been tearing into our fledglings."

"Vampires are of no use to me. Your hearts turn to dust the second I bite into them."

"Are you saying we're dry?"

"I'm saying you're not a food source."

Not a food source, the Countess thought. But the Hunter of Thrace didn't just hunt for food. He hunted because that's what he did. That's who he was.

"Fun as it is to watch you two squabble," she said, "we do have a problem. A small, slayer-shaped problem. I was happy enough to mind my own business, taking a virgin here, a few virgins there, *building up my family until I had a hive with which I can rule over this stupid town. It was the slayer who arrived uninvited. As far as I'm concerned, she picked this fight."*

"What would you have us do, Countess?" Anton asked.

"I want you to do as you promised," she said to Grimloch. "Track her, catch her, bring her to me so we can share in the eating. And you"—she looked at Anton—"I'm tired of waiting. I want to go out. Sipping from the virgin fount is not enough—I want buckets. I want to bathe in it like I used to. I want enough in one night to walk outside again. Dozens. Pure dozens." Her mouth watered, her fangs pressed against her gums, ready to burst through. "I want to have a party. And then I want to torture those party crashers from last night." The vampire with the pale hair, the young werewolf, the angry girl with lovely black hair. "I want them flayed from the legs up. Fangs and fingernails pulled out. Stretched on the rack. Burned and fed pieces of themselves." She clapped her hands and twirled. "Now, send the boys out after my virgins."

"Yes, Countess."

"And, Anton?"

"Yes, Countess?"

"Maybe get some balloons."

CHAPTER TWENTY-FOUR

THE SLAY-LIFE BALANCE

After Frankie left, Jake took off, too, and Spike disappeared into the basement to make his way back to his place before heading over to Willow's to talk about warding spells to protect their dwellings. So Hailey and Sigmund had the library all to themselves.

"We should probably call it a night." Sigmund gathered a pile of books to return to their shelves. "I'm going to bring a few of the codexes home to go through after hours."

"More reading? On top of all of this reading?" Hailey gestured to their table of open pages. "Maybe you should take a break for . . . some quiet reading."

"I'm trying to find a reference to the poison that the priests used on the Countess. This 'virgin's bane.' But I can't find anything." He set down his book: a volume that focused on eaters of virgins.

"It's disturbing that there's a whole book's worth of demons that eat virgins," said Hailey.

"Even more disturbing that this is only volume one," said

Sigmund, reading the spine. He placed it on top of his stack and lifted it; the stack wobbled precariously.

"Here. Let me help you." Hailey stood and took half off the top. Things had been a little uneasy between them after the disagreement about the Hunter of Thrace at the Rosenbergs', and she wanted to show him there were no hard feelings. After all, he'd been right. And he hadn't rubbed it in her or Jake's noses even one little bit.

"Thanks." His brown eyes wrinkled at the corners. They were kind eyes. Comforting eyes. She liked it when she looked up from a book to find them resting on her, and she didn't think it was because of his attraction-charm mojo.

They walked to the occult shelves. When Sigmund stretched to place a book in the top row, a plastic bag fell from his pocket and onto the floor.

"Oh, you dropped this . . ." Hailey picked it up. At first, she thought it was empty. But there were scrapings of thin black material, like flakes of paint, lining the bottom of the bag. Black dust had gathered in both bottom corners. "Your garbage."

He took it from her and stuffed it back into his pocket.

"What is that?" she asked.

"It's—it's a sample I collected from the blast site. Scrapings from the mark that you and Frankie remote viewed. Ms. Rosenberg is going to take it to her lab for analysis."

"Oh." Hailey stared at his pocket. Now that she knew what it was, she wished she'd studied it more closely. "Did you get that when you went to take the photos?"

"No, I portaled back again. Late last night, after we knew that Frankie was safe. I'm sorry I didn't tell you."

"How soon will we have the results? And what are the results, exactly? Can you detect magic in a lab?"

"It might be inconclusive. Another reason to wait to tell you. I was going to drop the sample off now. . . . Can I walk you home?"

Hailey nodded, and they grabbed their bags and left the library. She was a little mad that he hadn't told her he'd portaled back to get the residue, but she was letting it slide since she'd come down on him so hard about the Hunter of Thrace. After all, Sigmund was only trying to help. He hadn't even known the slayers, yet he'd dropped everything to portal across the country and try to find them. Hailey hadn't even thought about that. All she could think of was Vi.

"So, Sigmund, where are you staying, anyway?"

"I have an apartment over the bookstore."

"That makes total sense." They walked on, past a "Sunnydale Razorbacks Pride" banner and the trophy case, past several dozen flyers for a dance on Saturday.

"Hey, think there's a dance coming up?" Sigmund asked sarcastically as they passed another patch of flyers.

"Hmm, I don't know," she replied, and put her finger to her chin. She looked at the flyers. It looked corny. It would be corny, a gymnasium full of balloons and bad punch. "Hey, Sigmund, do you want to go to the dance with me?"

He laughed until he saw her face. "Sorry, I didn't know you were serious. Are you serious? A dance doesn't really seem like your thing."

"It's not," she said, and clomped a black-booted foot. "But it could be a fun, stupid time. And I bet you look great in a suit."

"I look great in most things." He grinned, and she knocked into him with her shoulder. "I'd love to go. If you're serious."

"I said I was."

"Okay."

"Okay." They walked out of the school into the streetlights of the parking lot, trying not to smile like idiots. Hailey chewed the inside of her lip and hoped she hadn't made a mistake. Sigmund wasn't the kind of guy she normally went for. Her type was dyed hair and piercings, or easy smiles and band T-shirts. And not a single one had been a demon.

Vi wouldn't like this, she thought, not that Vi had ever liked her boyfriends, and it had never stopped Hailey before. Besides, as she looked at Sigmund, at his careful, put-together profile and the disarmingly awkward way he shifted the books in his backpack—she thought she might be wrong. Vi might really, really like this one, demon or not.

It was kind of a long, awkward walk to the Rosenberg house, but when they turned into Sunnydale Heights, Sigmund took Hailey's hand and slipped his fingers through hers.

The rest of the walk wasn't bad at all.

$$) \;) \; \bigcirc \; (\; ($$

Frankie walked home through Sunnydale Heights practically dragging her feet. She'd done sweep after sweep of the cemetery and come up with nothing. The image of the missing girl flashed in her mind, along with the photograph of the abandoned abbey. Where were those women now? Where were those innocent people? Lying in shallow graves. Or worse, risen again, with fangs.

She had to do better. The Countess was stealing people away right under the nose of the slayer, so where were the vampires? She clenched her fists, a stake in each hand. Even overmuscular vampires needed to eat.

She stomped across the corner of her yard, cutting through the grass to their front stoop, when Grimloch stepped out of the shadows beside the house.

"Wah!" she said, and flinched backward. "What are you, invisible?"

"No. Just quiet."

"What are you doing here?"

"Looking for you," he said bluntly. He walked farther so she could better see him under the neighborhood lights. He was dressed like he had been in Hailey's picture: a dark shirt rolled to the elbows over gray trousers. If he was a hunter, he really ought to wear camouflage. Or something less modern: lots of leather and a coonskin cap. Antlers or those ram horns he mentioned affixed to his head. A bare chest and a loincloth.

Jeez, snap out of it, Frankie.

"I think we should have a better way of getting in touch," she said. "Do you have a phone, or anything?"

"No."

No phone? That was such a weird idea. Who just bounced around the world with no phone? Disconnected, floating along like a ball full of helium, with no apps.

"Frankie—" he said.

"You know my name."

"Of course. I know your friend Hailey's, too: the slayer Vi Larsson's sister. And Jake Osbourne, the werewolf who is always carrying you around on his motorbike. The other boy has been less easy to track—the half demon."

"Sigmund," she said. "He doesn't get out much. Kind of new to town, too. And Jake is just a friend. I don't know why I'm telling you that."

Grimloch made a face like he didn't know why she was either. But then he almost smiled, the barest hint of a curl in the corner of his mouth.

"So why were you looking for me?" she asked.

"The Countess is planning a massive feeding party. Large enough to return her to her full strength. And when the party is over, she's planning on having you and your friends for dessert."

"She wants to drink us?"

"Only you. The blood of a slayer. The others"—he waved his hand, a little flippantly, in her opinion—"she just wants to torture. Flay, burn, feed pieces of themselves. Her head manservant likes hot pokers."

Frankie swallowed. Hot pokers. Fed bits of themselves. She would never let that happen. Not to Hailey, or Sigmund. Not even to Jake. Or to Spike, who used to enjoy it when he was evil.

"But you said I couldn't kill her. So what am I supposed to do?"

"The Countess cannot be killed. But she can be neutralized. There were a group of priests once who managed to—"

"Virgin's bane," she said, and nodded. "We know. The poison."

"'Virgin's bane' wasn't a poison. It was an actual, poisoned virgin, who volunteered to drink poison and let her feed on them."

"A virgin sacrifice," she said softly. Then she wrinkled her nose. "Why virgins? That's so . . . typical. And gross. That's so typically gross. What's so special about a virgin anyway? It's just an arbitrary status foisted upon young people to turn them into a commodity. Invented and perpetuated by the patriarchy."

"You must be a lot of fun for your teachers," he said. "But while virginity may be no indication of a person's worth, it does impact their blood. Virgins tend to be younger, for a start. And young blood is potent. The blood of infants can—"

"Stop." Frankie held up her hand. "Just, stop talking."

"As you are a witch, I didn't think you would be squeamish about the ways of magic."

"Hey, the practice of magic isn't always ethical," she said. "But I try to be. Like if a spell calls for the use of a mummy hand you can bet I'm finding a vegan alternative!"

Grimloch frowned. "Be that as it may, virgins are a strong food source. And the Countess has been eating them almost exclusively for several hundred years."

Frankie took a deep breath. The Countess wasn't going to get anyone else on her watch. They had to stop the feeding party. They had to get to the Countess while she was still vulnerable, before she regained her full strength.

What would Buffy do? she thought. And then she imagined it: Buffy vs. the Countess, all the sick moves and the smart-assery. And it would end with the Countess good and dead, because pulling off the impossible? Buffy did that all the time.

"Why do you have that look on your face?" Grimloch asked.

"No reason. I was just thinking how much I'd like to see Buffy take on the Countess."

"But Buffy Summers is not here. It has to be you, Frankie."

But before she could say that she knew that, Spike raced across the lawn and threw a hard, flying punch into Grimloch's face.

"Spike!"

Grimloch bent beneath the force of the blow, and the vampire managed to slam down one more before being thrown backward and bouncing off one of their skinny trees.

"Spike, stop! He's not hurting me!"

"'Course he's not." Spike got to his feet. "He's too busy playing the wounded puppy. Fooling her into letting her guard down. Like no one's ever tried that before!" He dove in and grabbed Grimloch by the back of the head, slamming his face into the side of their house.

"Mr. Pratt, do you need help?"

Sigmund and Hailey ran up the driveway.

"Does it look like I need help?" Spike asked, right before Grimloch sent him flying.

"Well, kind of," said Hailey. "Also it seems like you're projecting your own issues onto Frankie and Grimloch's situation."

Grimloch stood and growled, showing his fangs. Spike's demon face came out in response.

The vampire roared and went in again, peppering the Hunter of Thrace with punches and questions. "How'd you know where the slayer meeting was? How'd you prove to them you weren't a threat? Say their names, you sodding—"

"Enough!" Frankie threw herself in between them, ducking punches and landing hard punches of her own, right into each of their guts. When they doubled over to whine about it, she pushed them hard and stood between them with her arms out. This was mortifying. At that moment, she wouldn't have minded if the Hellmouth opened right under her feet and swallowed her up.

"I wasn't going to hurt your Watcher," Grimloch said.

"You *couldn't* hurt her Watcher," Spike said, and sneered. "Frankie, get inside."

"Spike, no, we need his help!"

"I said get inside!"

Grimloch brushed dirt from his sleeves. "I'll go."

"No, wait!" She hurried after him as he strode away through the grass and onto the sidewalk.

"Listen, Spike is just . . . protective. Like you are! He's my Watcher, so he has to be—" She grabbed Grimloch by the elbow. "Slow down!"

"My presence is making things more difficult for you."

"No, it isn't. You're—" She looked him up and down. Then one more time for good measure. "You're this badass hunter god, right? And you're the best in we have to the Countess's mansion. We need your help."

"They don't want my help." He gestured back to the house, where Spike, Sigmund, and Hailey stood, Spike still in vampire face.

"I don't care. *I* do." She touched his wrist; his skin was warm, almost hot, like he had a fever. "Listen, come to training tomorrow. New Sunnydale High School Media Center. Three o'clock. You'll have to answer a bunch of annoying questions and maybe dodge a punch, but they'll have to see that you're here to help. Okay?"

Grimloch glanced from Frankie to Spike. He ground his fangs lightly in his mouth. Finally, he said, "Very well. Should I bring . . . flowers, or a casserole?"

"No." Frankie grinned. Jake would actually love a casserole. "Just come, okay?"

He nodded and walked off into the dark. Frankie took another deep breath and steeled herself to go back and face her Watcher.

Spike's demon face had receded, but he was still spitting mad. When Frankie approached, he pointed his finger and said, "You! You, you, you!"

"You?" Hailey asked.

"He's trying not to swear at me," Frankie explained. The front door opened, and Willow stepped out.

"I heard a scuffle. What's going on?"

"Your daughter," Spike said, and pointed at Frankie again, "is not following orders!"

"Mom!" Frankie sputtered. "Like Buffy never disobeyed Mr. Giles? Tell him!"

Willow looked confusedly between Watcher and slayer.

"Well—sure, Buffy did what her instincts told her to do, and she was the leader—"

"Willow!" Spike shouted.

"But she also respected her Watcher. And trusted him to know things and to have plans—" She looked at Spike. "This would be a lot easier if I knew what order of yours I was supposed to be defending!"

"I told her to stay away from that demon," Spike said. His shoulders slumped as he pointed to the now empty yard. "The same one that was making googly eyes at her right in front of your house."

"Googly eyes?" Willow asked.

"Okay, I'm sorry," said Frankie. "I wasn't looking for him, Spike. Honest. He found me."

Spike turned to Willow. "How did Giles manage to do this for so bloody long?"

"Practically weekly for seven years," Willow said, and crossed her arms. "But Giles was an authority figure. A grown-up grown-up. Whose wild past dealings with the dark arts only almost got us killed five? Or six times."

Spike shook his head. He motioned for Hailey and Sigmund and even Willow to go inside. "I need a moment with my slayer."

Frankie watched them go, creeping up the stoop. Hailey gave her a fist of solidarity before the door closed.

"Listen, Spike, I wasn't in any danger. Grimloch is *helping* us—"

"You don't know that. But you think so, don't you? You think he's been there this whole time . . . like a shadow or some bloody guardian angel—"

"Well, he has been."

"Slayers don't have guardian angels," Spike growled. "No one is always there. Don't you see? You can't depend on me. Or your mum. Or Oz, or Jake, or Hailey, and you certainly can't depend on *a demon who eats hearts.*"

"I know!" Frankie shouted, and Spike stopped short. "Don't you think I know I shouldn't need this much help? Don't you think I'm ashamed?"

"Frankie—"

"But I do, okay? I'm not Buffy!" If not for Grimloch, she would have been dead already. Twice, he'd saved her when she'd gotten in over her head. "And now you want me to go up against some legendary vampire who is so lethal that other vampires *impersonate* her."

"Yeah, I do." Spike stuck out his arms, palms out. "Because you're it. One girl in all the world with the strength to fight the vampires, the demons, and the forces of bloody darkness."

Frankie blinked. She'd expected him to soften, to say that he'd protect her.

"Those phone calls from Xander." He pointed into the house. "All that searching? They're not helping. You keep hoping it'll all go away, and the other slayers will be around to do the hard parts with you. You keep fighting with half your head. You keep waiting to be rescued by Buffy, when Buffy's gone!"

"Don't say that! You don't know that—"

"She's gone." He touched his chest. "I can feel it. I don't want to, but I do. She's not here anymore. None of them are. There's only you."

"That's not true," she whispered.

"It's not fair. But it is true."

The anger left her like water dumped from a bucket. Was he right? Had she only been fighting with half of herself? Holding back like it was only a game, a temporary thing, that it would go away once Buffy and the real slayers were found. Maybe it had been in the back of her mind. But when she fought, she fought hard. She did her best.

"I can't face the Countess," Frankie whispered. She turned and sat down heavily on the stoop. She felt like she weighed a million pounds. Like the step would collapse underneath her. But it didn't, not even when Spike sat down on the other end.

"I used to think I wanted this," she said. "But I don't. I just want my aunt Buffy to come back and slay this virgin-eating piece of crap."

"Yeah," Spike said. "She had a way of taking things in hand. Or making it seem like she had it in hand. But you have that in you, too, Frankie."

"All I want is to be like her."

"Well, you can't," Spike said, and shrugged. "You can't be her, because you aren't her. You can only be you. *Frankie, the vampire slayer.* The first-ever witch-slayer, or slayer-witch, whatever you want to call it."

He put his arm around her and squeezed.

"You just have to learn to fly on your own. Don't make me shove you out of the nest, little bird."

Frankie rested her head on his shoulder.

"Don't make me cling to it and peck you." That made him laugh a little, and she smiled. "Thanks, Uncle Spike."

"Don't worry about it."

She leaned back and looked up at the sky filled with stars. "So what should I do about Grimloch? I invited him to training tomorrow. Should I tell him he can't come? He doesn't have a phone, so I don't know how I'd do that exactly—"

"You invited him to—" Spike's lips formed a thin, angry line. He looked a little like her mom looked sometimes. But then he relaxed. "Let him come," he said.

"Really?"

"Everyone needs some help sometimes. I remember once I was in the battle of my life—it wasn't long before you were born—army of demons, even a dragon. We were cooked." He nudged her. "And then who showed up but your mum. And Buffy. And a legion of slayers. Slayers, just like you."

Frankie reached out and hugged him. Though she hoped he wasn't saying she was going to have to fight a dragon someday.

CHAPTER TWENTY-FIVE

PORTALING WITH PORTAL DUST

"Everything okay?" Willow asked as Frankie and Spike came inside.

"Everything's fine, Mom."

"No worries, Red." Spike touched Frankie's shoulder and headed for the kitchen and the refrigerator for a pint of blood. He didn't bother with a mug or the stove—just stuck a straw into it like it was a juice box. After a few sips, he looked at Hailey and Sigmund.

"What're you two doing here, anyway?"

"I live here," said Hailey.

"And I was delivering this." Sigmund reached into his pocket and produced a plastic bag with a scant amount of dark shavings and dust in the bottom. "Residue scraped from the possible portal mark in Nova Scotia."

Frankie looked at Hailey.

"I just found out about it, too," Hailey said.

"Oh, good, that was fast," said Willow. She went to Sigmund and took the bag. "I'm going to take it to the lab and run it through the spectroscopes."

"What will that do?" Frankie asked.

"Well, for one, it will tell us if it really is a portal. And maybe tell us something about the portal's destination," said Sigmund. "You see—"

He began to rattle off a lot of technical specs about demon magic, occasionally slipping into demon languages. But Frankie was only half listening. Mostly she was watching her mom. Willow had opened the bag and was peering down at the contents. As Frankie watched, she stuck her finger into the black dust like it was sugar and placed it on her tongue.

Willow jolted backward. Her eyes flashed—bright white orbs.

"Mom!"

"Red?" Spike stepped in between Willow and Frankie, holding Frankie gently back. "You all right?"

Her mom's eyes turned back to normal. Then she made a face and stuck her tongue out like it had a bad taste. So bad that she almost reached for Spike's blood bag before hurtling to the sink and sticking her mouth under the faucet.

"Mom, that was dangerous," Frankie snapped.

"Yep," said Willow, touching her nose like she was checking for a nosebleed.

"Does seem a little reckless, Red," Spike said quietly.

"No." Willow waved her hand awkwardly. "I always . . . taste black residue that smells like magic."

"So it is magic," Hailey said excitedly. "It was a portal!"

"What happened?" Frankie asked. "What did you see?"

It took her mom a few moments to catch her breath. She went back under the faucet for another pull of water and spat it down the sink. Then Spike handed her a hip flask of whiskey, and to Frankie's surprise, she drank it.

"Brightness," she said. "And pain. I think I saw the explosion.

And I don't think I need to take this to the lab." She held the bag up to the kitchen light. It didn't look like much more than soot. "It's definitely from a portal. And there's enough of a charge left in this residue to recast it. If you think you can." Willow looked at Sigmund, and the Sage demon took the scrapings back.

"Can you?" Hailey asked. "Can you take us where it went?"

"Not us." Spike threw off his leather jacket. "Me. The rest of you aren't going anywhere. You need to stay here to fight the Countess," he said before Frankie could argue. "We can't risk anything happening to you. Any of you."

Sigmund scrutinized the contents of the bag. There wasn't much left.

"I can do it," he said. "But this will have to be stretched. With blood." He held his hand out, and Spike slapped the half-empty pint into his palm with a hangry frown.

"Why blood?" asked Hailey.

"Blood is an excellent magical conduit. It's also a jack-of-all-trades; if you're not sure about a particular ingredient, try blood, and often it works."

"Well, which one is this?" asked Frankie. "Is this blood a conduit or a magical guess?"

"Both," said Sigmund. "But if the guess is wrong, it won't explode or anything. It just won't work." He stepped into the middle of the kitchen, between the counter island and the table. He moved the closest chairs away against the wall and, after a moment of thought, took a broom to the floor.

"Didn't we just clean?" Willow whispered, and Frankie shrugged.

"May I use this bowl?" Sigmund pointed to a wooden bowl of red and green apples. When Willow and Frankie nodded, he carefully removed the fruit and restacked it on the counter. Then he wiped the bowl clean with a towel and squeezed the last of Spike's dinner blood into it, before adding the contents of the plastic bag.

Frankie and Willow looked at each other. The moment the residue touched the blood, Frankie felt a tilt, like the room had moved without moving. And she felt her mom's magic grab on to her own and draw it up, like protection.

Sigmund returned to the center of the kitchen carrying the bowl. He whispered to it softly in a demon language and swirled it with his finger. The air in the room began to quake. The air itself. Not the walls, or the floor, and the sensation made Frankie sick to her stomach. Fingers dipped in blood, Sigmund bent to the floor and scrawled demonic symbols. Then he dipped his fingers again and traced a doorway through the thickened air, from just to the outside of his left foot, up above his head, and arching down to end at the floor beside his right. The blood and portal ash hung suspended in the middle of nothing, like a door drawn out of milky red chalk.

Sigmund stepped back.

"Now what?" Spike asked.

"Now it opens," he said, and open it did, into a whirling void of blackness. The wind from it knocked them backward and sent the stacked apples rolling across the counter and onto the floor.

"It's really a portal," Hailey cried, and the sound of her voice mirrored what Frankie felt: the sudden hope, the fervent wish to see Buffy, and Vi, emerge from the swirling darkness.

"Where does it go?" Frankie shouted over the deafening noise. "Can you see?"

"We'll know in a minute," Spike said, and made to jump.

"Wait, what if we can't get you back? What if the portal closes?" Willow called out.

"It shouldn't!" Sigmund squinted at them, holding his glasses into place with one hand. "Just pop in and pop out. It should hold, for at least that long!"

But before Spike could jump, Hailey shoved past and threw herself into the portal.

"Hailey, dammit!" Spike yelled. He jumped in after her.

Frankie took her mom's hand as the portal raged in their kitchen, and they waited for Spike to grab Hailey and return. The seconds ticked by. Then a minute. The portal began to waver.

"They're not coming back!" Frankie said, and felt Willow let go of her fingers. "Mom?"

Willow leapt into the portal.

"Mom!" Frankie stepped toward it. "Mom!" She looked at Sigmund. "You're a portal expert, right? So get us all back!" Frankie took a deep breath and dove into the darkness.

It felt like having her tongue sucked out through her ears, but that only lasted a moment. Then her feet hit solid ground. Solid pavement, actually. She emerged into a darkened alley and ran right into Spike. He steadied her, and she saw her mom and Hailey, all there and safe. Behind them, the portal snapped shut.

"No!" Hailey exclaimed. "How do we get back?"

"We don't need to," said Spike. "We never left."

Frankie looked around. The night was quiet with the portal gone, and the air was crisp and familiar.

"I know where we are," said Willow. "We're behind the old Magic Box. Or, at least, where Giles's old Magic Box used to be."

"Did we do something wrong?" asked Frankie. "Did the portal not work?"

"It worked," said Willow.

"I don't understand," Hailey said. "Why would the portal lead to Sunnydale?"

Spike knelt and touched the spot where the portal had closed. A familiar scorched ring blackened the ground, just like it had blackened the slab of pavement at Slayerfest.

"Oh," said Willow. "Well, I guess that's also on our kitchen floor."

Frankie knelt down beside Spike. "If the portal led to Sunnydale, then whoever went through it would be here now."

"But who would run away to Sunnydale?" he asked. "And why wouldn't they reach out when they arrived?"

CHAPTER TWENTY-SIX
MEET THE PARENTS

The puzzle of the portal was no closer to being solved by the following afternoon's training session, despite many wild theories and so much research for Sigmund that his eyes briefly crossed. Who had portaled into Sunnydale? Where were they? At least they knew that the portal mark was in fact from a portal. But it would have been nice had that answer not led to so many more questions.

"Who's . . . this person?" Willow asked warily.

Grimloch stood just inside the door of the library, his blue eyes bright under the skylights. He had come, as promised, dressed casually in denim and a faded T-shirt. It made him seem even more like a model than usual, and he looked at once at ease and unsure what to do with his hands. Maybe Frankie had been wrong to tell him not to bring a casserole.

"This is Grimloch." Frankie jumped down from the long table she was standing on, training with Spike. "From the picture, remember?"

"So he's coming to training now?" Jake asked. He closed the

demon taxonomy book he'd been pretending to read and walked to Grimloch and Frankie, circling and sniffing.

"He knows the Countess," Frankie said. "He can tell us what it takes to beat her."

"An army, a priest, and a poisoned virgin," Grimloch said, and Frankie made a face. Grimloch moved farther into the room and took a place near Sigmund and Hailey, seemingly oblivious to the suspicious looks he received from Willow and Oz, whose face was uncharacteristically expressive.

"All right, Mini Red. Back up on the table."

Frankie climbed back up. The table was sturdy but not meant to be walked on and certainly not fought on. It would be an extra challenge to her balance when Spike attacked. The vampire stood on the other end of the table, holding a sparring stick. Frankie noticed he was wearing his usual black T-shirt and jeans instead of tweed and assumed it was because he knew Grimloch was going to be there and wanted to look especially demony.

Grimloch. She managed to keep her eyes front, but she was very aware of him at the side of her vision. Some might even say distracted.

Spike nodded to Willow, and she opened a kit of lab knives and scalpels, removing them and setting them on the table. They were small, and light, and very, very sharp. "Float those," he said to Frankie. "Don't do anything else. Just float. Keep them hovering."

"Okay." Frankie looked at the blades, and her magic popped them into the air. Since she was nervous, it popped them into the air with great speed, and Hailey and Sigmund stepped back.

"Do we need to be behind something?" Hailey asked.

"She's not going to move them. Just going to float. But just in case." Spike looked at Willow.

"I'm here," the witch said. "I'll play catch if something goes wrong."

"Playing catch with scalpels," Hailey said as she and Sigmund edged behind the nearest bookshelf. "Vi would be thrilled about this."

"It'll be fine, Hailey." Frankie shook her head to loosen her shoulders, and the scalpels wiggled in the air. *Whoops.* She narrowed her eyes at them, and they grew still and steady. How embarrassing would it be if she invited Grimloch to a training session and then stabbed him with a razor? Only moderately embarrassing. Not mortifying at all.

Spike spun his sparring stick and attacked fast—left, right, left—and swept her legs. She jumped, and the table wobbled when she landed. So did the scalpels.

"Keep them up."

"It's hard," Frankie said through her teeth.

"Come on, Frankie, we're starting small." He attacked again, right, right, and spun in close to kick her in the chest. She slid back so far she almost fell off the end, and the scalpels clattered to the floor.

"It's all right, sweetie," her mom said. But Frankie saw the concern on Willow's face. Jake was trying not to frown, and Oz's eyebrows were moving closer and closer together. She couldn't bring herself to look at Grimloch.

"Let's do it again." Spike reset. "Float them. Try attacking this time."

"I thought we were focusing on slayer training and witch training separately." Frankie lifted the scalpels again. It took her a second to get them all hovering straight and facing the right way, with the blades toward Spike.

"We were. But if the fake countess is the real Countess like the demon says, then we speed things up. We work harder." He came at her again, despite saying it was her turn to attack. She blocked him angrily. Splitting her focus between magic and the fight was too difficult. It sapped her; made both of her abilities flicker.

She swapped effort from one to the other—her slayer gift pushed against her magic, and her magic knocked against her slayer gift. They were two separate things, and they liked it that way.

"Let's go," Spike ordered, and Frankie leapt across the table, keeping a part of her mind on the scalpels as she slashed and spun with her stick. Her attacks were slower than usual, and less crisp. Spike looked almost bored when he blocked them. She wondered if Grimloch was looking bored, too.

"We shouldn't have brought him here," Spike said. "You're distracted."

"I'm distracted because everyone is watching me. And because I haven't done this before!" Frankie attacked again, sharper this time, with more ferocity. Instead of trying not to mess up, she tried to hit.

"Good," Spike said. "More."

So she gave more. And faster. The sounds of their sticks striking rang through the library, as did the rattling of the table as they jumped and stomped and landed. Beside them the hovering scalpels vibrated with each impact like they were suspended from wires.

"Again," Spike ordered.

Frankie jumped and spun through the air, kicking him to his end of the table. She swept the sparring stick up under his chin and twisted it back to crack across his cheek. Her breath felt light in her chest. The two powers within her softly clicked, and her mind cleared. She twirled her stick for her final move: the fake stake to the vampire's chest. When she struck, Spike flew backward, and the hovering scalpels flew forward. All six sank deep into his torso.

"Spike!" Frankie dropped her stick and rushed to him. He lay on his back, stunned, the handles of the scalpels sticking out of him like he was a pincushion. "I didn't mean to," she said as her mom hurried over and assessed his injuries.

"It's okay; they're nowhere near the heart."

"But they still bloody hurt." He plucked one out like a big splinter and looked at the blood on the tip before dropping it onto the table.

"I'm sorry," Frankie said.

"But this is good, right?" Hailey asked from behind the shelf. "She attacked with slayer strength *and* with magic. Yay for goals."

"It is," Spike said, and Frankie brightened. "I'd like to see more control, and less stabbing of your Watcher. But it's good."

"You're not training her correctly."

Everyone turned to look at Grimloch.

"Oh? What are you, some kind of expert?" Spike removed another scalpel from his chest and rolled off the table. "Did you gain some special slayer insight when you ate their hearts?"

"I—told them you didn't do that," Frankie murmured.

Grimloch uncrossed his arms and met Spike face-to-face, or face-to-neck, since Grimloch was taller. "William the Bloody," he said, "didn't you kill two slayers?"

"That was before I had a soul."

"And now your soul absolves you?"

Spike frowned. Nobody talked about the old Spike anymore. Frankie had never even known him. Spike shrugged hard and walked away as Grimloch continued to press.

"One soul wipes your slate clean?" he asked.

"Worked for bloody Angel," Spike muttered. "But no. Of course it doesn't." He narrowed his eyes. "So what do you suggest? What are your notes? You want to take over?"

"I want the slayer to survive the fight."

"Yeah? Well, so do I. I'm the one who's been around since she was this tall." Spike put his hand near his knees. "But you think you know best. How long have you been watching her? Since the night you killed that Succoro demon in the woods—"

"I was here before that. I was here, right here, the night you allowed her to lose her sight."

Frankie blinked. Grimloch had been watching the night she and Hailey had done the remote viewing spell? She remembered very clearly the sensation of being led through the parking lot to her mom's car and being wrapped up like a child.

"You saw me in my yummy sushi blanket?" She looked at Hailey, and Hailey winced.

Oz pushed off the shelves he'd been leaning against and came to stand beside Willow. "This guy reminds me of someone," he said. "About six foot two, billowy coat. Used to hang around Buffy a lot. Tried to kill us on occasion."

Willow looked at Grimloch, and her eyes went wide. "Oh no. No, no, no. No way, young lady!" She held up a finger to give the most horrifying speech of Frankie's lifetime, but just as Frankie was sliding away across the library floor, Willow's phone buzzed and she took it out and looked.

"Xander."

"Pick it up!" Hailey exclaimed, and came around from the stacks with Sigmund.

Willow shot Frankie a *This isn't over* look and picked up. Frankie slid back to the group.

"Xander?"

"Hey, Will. Is everyone there?"

"Everyone," her mom said, "plus some surprising extras."

"Okay. Hey, guys."

"Hey," said Oz and Jake.

"They found a survivor this morning."

"Where?" her mom asked. "Who?"

"It's Sadie. You remember, Will? She was part of our escort when we went to see Oz in Weretopia."

"Sadie. I remember. She was one of Kennedy's Potentials."

"I remember, too," said Oz. "Dark hair, good appetite. Nice girl. Is she okay?"

"She's pretty banged up. We're at the hospital, and the doctors don't seem optimistic. But it takes a lot to kill a slayer." They heard people in the background, calls over an intercom. "Just by being found she might've saved a few of the others—"

"Others?" Hailey asked.

"I don't know yet. I don't want to raise your hopes. But these last two days, Dawn and I have had to beg the rescue teams to stay out. They want to shift the protocol from rescue to recovery."

"They can't do that," Willow objected. "Xander, you have to convince them! Slayers can survive for a lot longer than regular people; they're strong, and there's been rain—"

"I know, Will. That's what we've been telling them. That these women were survivalists and extremely fit. It helps that the meeting was registered at the resort as 'Yoga for Self-Defense.'"

Spike snorted fondly. "That sounds like an Andrew idea."

"Yeah. And now that Sadie's been found, the rescue teams know there's still a chance."

"Xander?" Frankie asked.

"Yeah, kiddo?"

"Was she—was Sadie rescued from the same building that Hailey and I saw the portal mark on?"

"Not exactly," he said. "But she was found not far away. The crews are still out there, searching for anyone who might have been with her.

"Dawn and I are going to take shifts—one of us here, one at the blast site. If Sadie pulls through . . . if she wakes up . . . I want her to see a friendly face. And I want her to be able to tell us anything she remembers about what happened." Xander took a deep breath, and Frankie wished she was there to hug him.

"How are you guys holding up?" he asked. "Everything status quo in good old Sunnydale?"

Willow's brows knit, but she said, "Nothing we can't handle."

"Don't I know it," said Xander. "I love you guys. Except for Spike."

"We love you, too," said Oz.

"Except for Spike," said Spike.

Xander hung up, and Oz raised his eyebrows. "This is good news," he said. "Before we get depressed that it wasn't Buffy or Vi, let's remember—this is good news."

"It's really good news," said Hailey, and there were tears in her eyes. Sigmund put his arm around her and squeezed. "It's not over."

Frankie turned to Grimloch. The demon hadn't spoken, hadn't so much as frowned.

"Sadie," she said. "Is she your . . . ?"

"No," he said, and walked out of the library.

"Some help he was," Spike said, and snorted. "The bloody Countess is gearing up for the feed of the century, and he doesn't last even one training session."

"Cut him some slack." Frankie watched him go. "This hasn't been easy for any of us."

With the training session derailed, Frankie told Spike she was heading home for dinner and that she'd do a few sweeps of the cemetery before she went to bed.

"Take Jake," he said.

"Hey, I'm not a dog," said Jake. "You can't just say 'Take Jake' and expect me to bound right after. What if I'm busy?"

Spike raised an eyebrow.

"Come on, Jake," said Frankie. "We'll stop for pizza."

"Okay," Jake said, and jogged behind her down the hall.

When they got to his moped, she snapped the chin strap of her helmet and frowned. She thought of Sadie, the surviving slayer she had never met. She thought of her lying in a hospital bed far away from wherever she called home.

"You okay?" Jake asked. "You thinking about the slayers?"

"I was thinking about her. Wishing she would be all right."

"Wondering what it means, for you?"

She looked at Jake a little guiltily. She was glad that a slayer had been found alive. She was thrilled. Relieved. And it seemed to support the theory about the slayer line that she liked best: that one of the slayers was the last in the line, and when she died, another would be called. So not all the slayers had to die for Frankie to be there. Just . . . the right one.

The right one. What a terrible thought.

"I'm thinking about the four they found before," Frankie said. "I almost said 'the four bodies,' but they weren't bodies—they were slayers. They were girls. Well, young women. What if one of them had to die so that I could be—"

"That's not how it works," Jake said. "That's never how it

worked. The slayer before Buffy, she didn't die so Buffy could be the slayer. She was killed. So Buffy had to be the slayer. It's a calling. It's a responsibility. You didn't wish some girl dead so you could get something out of it. This power chose you."

Frankie shrugged. "With a little help from my mom," she said doubtfully.

"Come on." He bopped her on the helmet. "Pizza." He grinned his easy Jake grin. "It's gonna be okay, Frankie."

As she climbed on the back of the bike, she gave him a brief hug.

"You know, Jake, you're going to make a pretty decent Watcher someday."

He straightened like he'd never thought of that before. Maybe he hadn't.

"Yeah," he said. "If Spike can do it, then I can." He revved the moped. "Jake Osbourne, Were-Watcher."

PART FOUR

FRANKIE THE VAMPIRE SLAYER

CHAPTER TWENTY-SEVEN

LIKE A VIRGIN. ACTUALLY, LIKE A LOT OF THEM.

With the dance at the high school only a few days away, Frankie found herself being dragged to Sunnydale Mall to help Hailey find a dress.

"Isn't there something less terrifying we could be doing?" Frankie asked. "Like hunting down the immortal serial killer who wants to drink my blood and flay your skin?"

"Later," said Hailey. "Listen, you have clearly devoted much of your life to being on the lookout for slayers and demons even before slayers and demons found you. I've been with Vi since I was ten. And what I have learned is that you need balance."

"But I hate shopping," Frankie groaned.

"Really? I love it. Mols and I used to rideshare into Portland all the time. But those stores are different. More indie boutique and less big-box monstrosity." Hailey's eye began to twitch as they passed by a glass window front of wall-to-wall mannequins in khaki pants.

Unlike Old Sunnydale's indoor mall of arcades and escalators,

New Sunnydale Mall was a pod of buildings grouped together and connected by landscaped sidewalks. It was surrounded by an enormous and mostly empty parking lot on all sides, and several of the retail spaces stood noticeably vacant.

"Have you . . . heard from Mols lately?"

"No," Hailey said, like she'd just realized it. She checked her phone. "I guess she got fed up with my non-responses."

"Sorry."

Hailey shrugged. "Not your fault. And it sounds mean, but I don't really mind? It's nice having friends like you and Jake. I've never been able to talk about the vampire stuff with anyone but Vi, and she never really wanted to."

"Friends like me and Jake . . ." Frankie smiled. "And Sigmund?"

"Ugh." Hailey rolled her eyes. "I can't believe I asked him to a dance. Let's try in here."

Hailey pulled Frankie through a door. They weren't two feet into the store before Hailey pulled a shirt off a rack and held it up to her chest.

"What do you think?" she asked.

"I think you just picked that up at random and it would still look good on you. Everything looks weird on me. My arms are too long."

"Your arms are fine. Very normal arm length." Hailey reached into the rack and flipped through hangers. "But I can't comment on your style." She gestured to Frankie's loose pants and stretchy long-sleeved T-shirt. "What is that, combat chic?"

"It's easier if I don't have to change for patrol. Saves on laundry tablets and water." She followed Hailey into the jeans section. "Shouldn't we focus on dresses? If we don't find you something today, you're going to be stuck in something of my mom's from the nineties." The irony, Frankie realized as she looked around, was that's what seemed to be trendy. She shuddered at the idea of her mom being . . . cool?

"Do they even have Goth-style dresses in this store?" Frankie asked.

"Every dress is a Goth dress with the right eyeliner and boots," said Hailey. "We'll get to the dresses. I just need to pick up a little of everything. My one bag of clothes has seriously worn out its welcome." She grabbed two pairs of jeans and added them to the stack in her arms.

"Hey," Frankie said, "I hope you don't mind me asking, but how are you going to pay for all this? Do you have savings from a job in Oregon or something?"

"Vi set me up with credit cards. Balance is paid automatically by the Watchers Council every month."

"They do that?"

"Yeah. After the previous council went kaboom the assets eventually found their way to Buffy and the other slayers." She paused. "I shouldn't have said that. 'Kaboom.' So casually."

Frankie's brow creased. "My mom does say the old council was surprisingly well funded. Good with their investments."

"Yeah. And then some of the new Watchers got us some swanky new silent investors."

"Silent investors? Please don't tell me the slayers are funded by big pharma."

"Nothing like that." Hailey wrinkled her nose. "But with all those new slayers to support, the Council needed a lot of cash. I mean, they're a small army with clothes that constantly need replacing. Bloodstains, demon slime, big rips from claws. You just can't fix those."

Frankie looked toward the formal-wear section and the wall of dresses. "There's the formal wear. Hey, how do you feel about blue?"

Hailey shrugged. "I mean, it's a color."

But apparently, blue was more than a color, it was the color of the season; there were no fewer than six different blue or blue-accented dresses to choose from. "Maybe you should get one," Hailey teased. "To match Grimloch's eyes."

Frankie quickly put back the dress she'd been looking at, which happened to be the exact shade of his eyes when they lit up.

"What's going on there, anyway?" Hailey asked. "He's at your house; he comes to training. At one point he was, like, almost smiling."

"Nothing's going on there," Frankie lied. Actually she hadn't been able to stop thinking about the Hunter of Thrace since the moment they met. So he was a demon, and ancient. There was just something about him. "I guess I feel sorry for him."

"Sorry for him?"

"Yeah. I know we're all going through the same thing, but he lost somebody in a different way. It's hard to explain."

"Frankie." Hailey stuck a dress back on the rack. "He's a demon."

"I know."

"He's on the rebound."

"I know."

"He's a demon on the rebound."

"That's what you just said."

"Well, it bears repeating." Hailey held up another dress. It was burgundy, and light and slinky at the same time. "What about this one?"

Frankie nodded. Hailey would look amazing in that dress. "Sigmund would definitely approve."

"Great, then we're done. But one more thing. We're friends, right?"

"Sure." Frankie smiled. She probably seemed like a dork, grinning just because someone called her a friend, but she didn't care.

"Then be careful with the Hunter of Thrace, okay? I know you're a slayer, and he's a demon, and there's a grand tradition of stupid decisions in that department, but if I'm a good friend—and I think I am—I'd have to tell you to veer away sharply. Ahead lies only heartbreak and complications."

"It's not like that," Frankie said.

"It is like that," said Hailey. She looked at Frankie with the steady eyes of someone far wiser about those kinds of things, and Frankie buckled. Hailey had probably had a dozen relationships. Frankie, not even one. She hadn't even known what wanting one would feel like until she met Grim. Now she couldn't stop. She looked for him everywhere, even at the mall, a place he would not be caught dead at. It was like a fixation.

"I just feel bad for him," Frankie said. "And I want to beat the Countess even more than I did before, because if I died, he'd feel like he failed again. Like it was his fault."

Hailey pressed her lips together. "That's not healthy."

"Probably not, but yay for wanting to live?"

"Yay for wanting to live," Hailey said.

They headed for the register, and Frankie wandered outside to wait in the sun while Hailey paid. While she waited, her eye kept catching on the information board across from the fountain. It was tagged with a bunch of light blue flyers, shiny with blue and silver glitter.

"So," said Hailey when she'd joined Frankie beside the fountain, holding a very large plastic garment bag, "Have you thought about going to the dance, too? Maybe with Jake?"

"Why would I go with Jake?" Frankie asked.

"I don't know. I just thought it would be fun if we were all there . . . and Jake is no Grimloch, but they both have big incisors sometimes—"

"Hey, do you see all those flyers?" Frankie walked to the information board and read.

PROMISE DANCE
Saturday Night!
Celebrate your dedication to wait!
BYOB

"That's a purity dance," Frankie said darkly. "Like, a dance for people who have pledged to wait to have sex, i.e., people the Countess would like to eat."

"Don't jump to conclusions," said Hailey. "It's the same night as the dance at the high school, so maybe it's being put on by a church or something as an alternative. Not that the school dance is an all-sex dance or anything. Or is it?" She waggled her eyebrows.

Frankie shook her head. "Grimloch said the Countess was gearing up for a big feeding. Well, what better place to round up virgins than by putting on a dance like this?" She ripped the flyer off the board and then ripped down all the others for good measure. "This is no coincidence."

☽ ☽ ○ ☾ ☾

The next morning in the library, Frankie slammed the flyer down on the desk in front of Spike, Hailey, Sigmund, and Jake. But they'd probably already seen them. On the way to school, she'd passed at least six more, tacked to telephone poles and the message board at the café. They were probably stuck up all over town. All blue and glittery and eye-catching.

"Is this a joke?" Jake asked. "Or do they not know what 'BYOB' means?"

"Maybe it's code," Sigmund suggested. "A code for vampires. Or an in-joke. BYOB—'bring your own blood.'"

"Great." Frankie nodded. "Vampire in-jokes. Perfect to set the mood for a vampire purity dance where all the attendees get to be eaten!"

"But we don't even know if this really is a vampire thing, right?" Hailey asked.

"There are certainly plenty of churches in Sunnydale, plenty of organizations that might put on something like this," said Sigmund.

"And there's certainly nothing wrong with being a virgin," Jake added.

"Of course there isn't," Frankie said. "Tons of people are virgins! It's just that right now, being one puts you at a much higher risk of having your blood drained and possibly turned into one of the evil dead!" She threw up her hands, then looked around the table at their blank faces. "Okay, maybe it just puts *me* at a much higher risk," she said, and lowered her arms.

"Frankie's right," said Spike. Frankie looked at him in surprise. "She's the slayer, and if she thinks it's worth looking into, then we look into it." He leaned over the flyer, careful to avoid the glitter, and Frankie straightened her shoulders. She almost made a joke—that her Watcher was proud of her, and she should get a cookie—but she really was happy that Spike was proud of her and starting to trust her instincts.

"There's no email address or phone number," Spike said. "Just a street address. And I know this address. It's a warehouse just outside of town. Would anyone actually go to this? Seems blatantly suspicious."

"Hold on, guys," Sigmund said. "I bet this isn't even what we think it is. The glitter, the sneaky address, the warehouse, the BYOB—this kind of thing pops up every once in a while around DC. It's not a dance; it's an underground rave."

"Oh." Frankie took the flyer back and sat down, knees pulled up to her chest. She hadn't thought of that. As far as she knew, Sunnydale did not rave. And she'd never noticed these kinds of weird flyers before. Not that she'd been looking. "But what if it isn't?"

"Then maybe the Countess will pull in the underground, twentysomething rave crowd and her purity dance will get really interesting?" Sigmund shrugged.

"I just . . ." Frankie took a deep breath. It was too tempting for the Countess. And too perfectly timed for her planned feeding. "I just have a feeling about this. Grimloch said the Countess wanted to have a party." She tapped the flyer. "A party. I think I should check it out just to be safe."

"I'll go with you," said Jake.

"What if it turns out to be just a rave?" asked Hailey.

"If we get there and everyone outside has glow sticks, we just won't go in."

"Or we'll go in for a little while," said Jake.

"Maybe we should go, too," added Hailey.

"No," Frankie said. "No way. You guys have actual plans at a for-sure dance, and I didn't get dragged around the mall for nothing. Go. Jake and I can handle this. And if we need backup, we'll . . ." She searched around until her eyes settled on Spike. "We'll call in the chaperones."

"What?" the vampire asked. "Me? No, no. Not me. I'm not getting all gussied up to crash a rave. And besides, I already have to get all gussied up to . . . actually chaperone the real dance. Have your mom and Oz on backup. And keep in touch. If you see anything weird, call or text."

"Fine," said Frankie. Of course, it would be easier if she could just go to Grimloch and get confirmation about the dance from him. But she'd looked for him last night and hadn't been able to find him. She glanced at Jake. She guessed Hailey was right. She'd be going to the dance with Jake after all.

CHAPTER TWENTY-EIGHT

RETRO GETUPS

Frankie tore through her closet with a deep scowl on her face, her mood distinctly different from her mother's, who was practically bouncing on the bed.

"This is going to be so fun! Getting all dressed up for a mother-daughter dance—"

"This is not a mother-daughter dance," Frankie groaned. "You're just getting dressed up to stay here on backup in case we need you. And, hey, they don't even have mother-daughter dances."

"Well, they should." Her mom frowned. "They have father-daughter dances."

"They shouldn't have those either." Of course, if it was a father-daughter dance, Frankie could wear anything she wanted and her date would be a shirt on a pillow labeled "Spirit of the Original Slayer." "I don't have anything. My closet is hopeless. Hope-free. Utterly lacking in hope."

"Well . . . does it matter?" her mom asked. "I mean, it's not a real dance, unless you and Jake are on a real date." She laughed, then stopped abruptly at Frankie's horrified expression. "Are you and Jake on a real date?"

"Definitely not."

"Of course not." Willow swung her legs innocently. "Silly to even say such a thing. But he is a very good-looking young man who has a soul and is not a broody, mysterious demon—"

"Mom!"

"Okay, okay." Willow peered into the dark recesses of Frankie's open closet door. "What about the dress you wore to Great-Aunt Nancy's fourth wedding?"

That dress was still in there because they never got rid of any of Frankie's clothes. But the wedding had been four years ago and the dress was far too small and covered in a perky spring flower print.

"Maybe I should go in pants. People do that now."

"They do," her mom agreed. "To hell with gender norms! But they would still need to be kind of fancy pants. I don't think your yoga pants will suffice."

There was a light knock on the wall, and Frankie backed out of the closet to see Hailey, dressed to the nines in the burgundy dress, her black hair swept up with the ends slightly curled.

"Wow," said Willow. "Hailey, you look beautiful."

Hailey blushed. "Uh, thanks. Frankie picked out the dress." She gave a little twirl, and the skirt flared out, a perfect fit even though she hadn't bothered to try it on. If Frankie dared that with a purchase, she'd come home to discover that what looked normal on the hanger looked like a fabric sack on her.

"Sigmund's going to go wild."

"Sigmund going wild," Hailey mused. "That would be something to see. How's it going in here? Any luck?"

"No." Frankie swung her closet door shut. "I'm about to give up."

"But you need a disguise."

Frankie scowled deeper. Maybe she and Jake should just stake out the Promise Dance in a more traditional manner. In all black and stocking caps, crouched behind a pile of wooden crates.

"Hang on," her mom said. Willow's eyes had lit up. "I'll be right back."

"Uh-oh," said Hailey after she hurried excitedly from the room. "Does that mean—"

"Yep. We're resorting to something very retro from my mom's closet."

A half hour later, Frankie stood in front of her mirror while Hailey pulled her hair back into a sophisticated braided ponytail and did her makeup. The result was rather . . . shocking. Frankie looked grown-up. With lips and eyebrows and everything.

"Wow," Frankie said. "You're really good at this."

"This is nothing," said Hailey. "There's a girl on the internet who can turn herself into Robert Downey Jr. with nothing but a contouring stick. Hey, Willow," she called into the hallway. "She's ready!"

Frankie turned to face her mom with an uncertain expression. "Well?"

Her mom nodded. Her eyes teared up. Her mouth puckered and then smiled and then puckered again. She started shaking a little and emitting a high-pitched sort of squeak. She was thrilled.

The dress her mom had pulled out of her closet wasn't too bad either. Floor-length black with a high, wide neckline. Frankie had seen pictures of her mom in it: Willow had worn it to her homecoming dance. But for some reason, she never really wanted to talk about it. Frankie wondered what Jake was going to wear. Probably one of those T-shirts with a tuxedo printed on it. But looking at herself in the mirror, so transformed, she sort of wondered what he was going to say.

"You look almost perfect."

"Almost?" Frankie asked as her mom reached into her pocket and pulled out a silver crucifix on a delicate chain. "Was that . . . ?"

"It was Buffy's. I think she'd want you to wear it."

"Plus, it goes with the whole 'purity' motif," said Hailey.

Frankie fastened it around her neck. It was heavy. It kind of thumped against her sternum. But it looked just right.

Downstairs, the doorbell rang, and Hailey jumped off the floor like a startled cat.

"Oh crap, that's Sigmund," she said, and elbowed Frankie lightly away from the mirror to check her lip gloss and hair.

"I'll go show him in," her mom said, and left.

"It's fine." Frankie patted Hailey's shoulder. "You look incredible."

"Not as incredible as he's going to look. You've seen his head and body, right?"

Frankie grinned and dragged Hailey from the room. They stopped at the end of the hall and peered around the wall of the stairs: Sigmund was chatting with her mom in the entryway. He really did look good, in slim black pants and a well-fitting buttoned shirt. His thin tie was burgundy, to match Hailey's dress.

"What do I do?" Hailey hissed.

"Slide down the banister or walk down the stairs," said Frankie. "But sliding would make more of a statement."

Hailey snorted, and Sigmund looked up at their hiding place. The look on his face as Hailey walked down the stairs was priceless. Like he was watching in slo-mo. Frankie regretted not having a song cued up on her phone.

"Wow" was all he said. "Wow."

"You kids have fun," Frankie called down. "But keep your phones on in case we have to interrupt you to save dozens of lives."

"Will do," Sigmund said. "Hey, Frankie, you look great."

"Yeah, there's just one problem." Frankie came down the stairs and twisted a little in the dress. "Not much freedom of movement. Arms, yes." She punched the air. "But legs?"

"Hang on." Her mom disappeared into the kitchen and reappeared with a paring knife. "Hold still." Before anyone could object she had cut a slit all the way down from Frankie's right thigh.

"Mom!"

"What?" she asked innocently. "I'm a problem solver. Now I need to go get ready."

Frankie stuck her leg out. She could definitely kick now. And run and leap. The cut had just been so sudden. It was a good thing she'd decided to shave above the knee.

"You guys sure you're going to be okay without us?" Hailey asked. "I'm bringing my ax just in case."

"And I've got the address to the warehouse in my phone," added Sigmund. "I've plotted out a few different routes to get there in case of traffic."

"We'll have my mom and Oz on backup. I've got this. You guys have fun."

They turned to go. They seemed uncertain. But Hailey did give her an excited raise of her eyebrows from over Sigmund's shoulder. They were sweet, those two. She really hoped she wouldn't have to interrupt them.

☽ ☽ ○ ☾ ☾

Jake was late. She should have known he was going to be, but it still irritated the living daylights out of her. Did he not comprehend the seriousness? Sure, they were probably only about to crash a rave in semiformal wear but possibly not. Virgins could be dying. And there was Jake, flitting around, probably on his gaming system

308

until the very last minute when he would throw on a moderately clean pair of pants and rub too much gel into his hair.

Frankie paced, the heels of her sensible, well-fitting black shoes clacking across the wood of the entryway, then onto the linoleum of the kitchen, then back onto the wood, until the sound finally disappeared on the hallway rug. She was so preoccupied by the hypnotic, clacking rhythm that she didn't even notice when the front door opened and Jake walked in.

"Frankie."

She turned in surprise. He was gaping at her, but she barely registered that. It paled in comparison to what he was wearing, which was a number so retro, so mauve, and so edged in crushed velvet that it defied explanation.

"Frankie," he said again. "Whoa. You look really . . . Goth."

Her shoulders slumped. "Thanks. You look like the bass player from my bat mitzvah. And you're late."

"Not my fault. It was Oz." He pointed over his shoulder at Oz coming up the steps.

"Hey, Frankie." He arched his brow. "That dress looks familiar."

"It's the one my mom wore to your homecoming."

"Yeah," he said. "I remember." Then he looked up and promptly stopped talking as her mom came down the stairs.

Frankie didn't know what he was staring at. Her mom was in her usual clothes: a long, drapey dress with lots of colors and embroidery. The only difference was the wrap around her shoulders and maybe the way she'd done her hair. She looked nice, but the way Oz was watching she could tell that *he* wished he'd had a song cued up on his phone. "I know we're just hanging out here by our phones," he said when she got to the bottom, "but I brought you a lily corsage."

Willow took it and put it on her wrist. "This is like déjà vu. And we look so nice."

"We do," said Oz. "If we were teenagers, it would be very romantic."

And to Frankie's horror, her mom smiled a little and whispered, "It still kind of is."

"Or it's not," said Frankie. Her mom flirted with guys sometimes. And she'd told Frankie how she had an occasional crush on Mr. Giles, mostly when he sang (which Frankie found absolutely mystifying). They'd had discussions about how sexuality is fluid and the flirting didn't make her any less gay. But saying something like that to Oz, especially when he had that look on his face—it didn't feel right. "It's a stakeout. People in peril. We're not double-dating with our parents, and I don't have time for your reckless flirting." Willow winced. Frankie grabbed Jake by the sleeve and felt velvet, so she let go and instead shoved him through the front door. The Osbourne van was parked in the driveway, oversized, with the ghosts of old murals painted on the side-panels. Not at all conspicuous.

"Actually, Frankie," said Jake, "Oz isn't my dad, so . . ."

"I'm basically your dad," Oz said from the steps.

"No, you're not."

"Sure, I am. Anything else at this point is pure semantics."

"You're my uncle."

"I'm your dad-uncle."

"We're taking the van?" Frankie asked.

"Well, I don't think you can get on the moped in that dress," said Jake. "And Oz and your mom should keep the car in case they need to drive to our rescue. It's faster than the van."

"Let's just go," said Frankie. She hauled Jake down the driveway and scowled at her mom and Oz as they waved from the doorway. Then the van roared to gas-guzzling life, and they pulled out onto the street.

)) ○ ((

"Think they'll be okay?"

Willow watched the van as it hurtled away up the street.

"Sure," said Oz. "They'll probably be back in twenty minutes."

"Maybe in time to go to the real dance with each other," Willow said hopefully.

"And since Frankie thinks of us as her parents, that won't be awkward at all."

"Oz, what Frankie said just now—what I said just now—"

"I know, Willow."

"No, I mean . . . I didn't mean *romantic* romantic. I meant—"

"Nostalgic. I know, Willow." He smiled at her, and she smiled back. But did he know? Did he really know, when she had barely figured it out herself? Oz was family, but not family. Friend, but more than friend. Not romantic. Yet not platonic.

Oz was Oz.

"Okay," she said. "As long as we know."

He went into the kitchen and popped back into the living room with a bottle of red wine and two glasses. "I know I said this was just like old times, but I don't think you have any red cups and beer."

They sat on the couch, and Oz poured while Willow gazed out the front windows. She detected movement in the neighbor's curtains. The Rosenbergs had a corner lot, so they had only one neighbor on the right. But Mr. Erickson across the street was end-lessly nosy. And judgy. He'd given the stink eye to every woman she'd brought home after a date. And he'd given Oz the same look, at least once he saw the van.

"Cheers," Oz said, and clinked her glass.

"You really do look nice," she said. "It's always fun to see you all fancy in formal wear."

"The jacket and tie is hardly a tux. But you look really nice, too, Willow."

She smiled. Then she set her glass onto the side table. "Maybe we shouldn't have gotten all dressed up."

He laughed. "I know you look nice, but I can control myself."

"No, I mean . . ." she started, and chuckled awkwardly. "I mean in case we have to fight."

"Oh." He tugged at the cuffs of his sleeves and loosened his necktie. "Well, I don't think I'll have any trouble shredding out of this. And last I checked, you could do magic in just about anything."

"Yeah." She picked up the glass of wine and drank half of it.

"Willow? Did something happen with your magic?"

"No. Well, not really." She'd just taken over a locator spell that she knew like the back of her hand. But it had bothered her, how impatient she got. How impulsive. And how easy that impulse was to give in to. "I don't think it's important. My magic isn't like it used to be. It's still shaky." But was it shaky like a newborn deer, starting over? Or was it shaky like a skeleton brought back to life, ready to snap back together and go right on flaying people and destroying the planet?

But that was ridiculous. She hadn't been Dark Willow since before Frankie was born. Dark Willow was gone.

"How are you?" she asked. "Things going okay at the youth center?"

"Yeah," he said. "They're good."

"And with you and Jake? You seem to be getting along as dad-uncle and son-nephew. Or son-cousin-nephew."

"That's good, too," said Oz. "He still . . . resents me for being here. But I know that's not about me. It's about his parents and them being *not* here."

Willow nodded. Even though they were older, Oz's aunt and

uncle, Maureen and Ken, had become her friends. Frankie and Jake had played together so often as kids, it was inevitable. But it had always rubbed her the wrong way, how Jake's brother, Jordy, sucked all the air out of the room. Jordy, Jordy, Jordy, every time he did something wrong, or needed more attention. He'd been so wild that Jake had grown up mostly at the Rosenbergs'. And when Jordy had needed to go to Weretopia, Maureen and Ken had gone with him, without a second thought.

"Jake always deserved a little better," Willow said. "He always deserved someone like you."

"Thanks, Will."

"So. Any lovely ladies down at the youth center?" She frowned. "That sounded wrong. I meant any lovely appropriate-age ladies down at the youth center?"

"Why?" His mouth crooked. "Did you want me to set you up with someone? No. There are no lovely, appropriate-age ladies down at the youth center. I'm mostly focused on Jake right now."

Willow took another sip of wine.

"If Maureen and Ken come back, do you think you'll stay in Sunnydale?"

"I don't know," he said.

"Because, I'm getting kind of used to having you here again."

"I'm always around if you need me. Even in Weretopia."

"So if I go bad and try to channel energy through an old satanic temple—"

"I'll be the first one to knock you on the back of the head." He smiled. "Or hug it out of you. Which as I recall worked the last time."

CHAPTER TWENTY-NINE

TAKE THE SHUTTLE TO YOUR DEMISE

I t didn't take long to get to the warehouse, even with the way Jake drove and the van's very limited acceleration. When they reached the address on the flyer, they slowed, creeping through the alleyways in search of the best vantage point to observe the entrance before going inside. Jake managed to angle them snugly behind a high stack of crates and a pile of tires. The van probably looked like a large bulldog crouched behind a sapling, but Frankie had to admit that his parking job was on point. They had a perfect view of the front of the warehouse.

It didn't look like a rave. The people gathered outside were paired in distinct couples, holding hands and chatting in small groups. They were also dressed in formal wear, so she and Jake should fit right in. She glanced at Jake's mauve and velvet. At least *she* would fit right in.

"Okay, let's go."

"Hang on," Jake said. "According to the flyer, the dance should have started already. So why isn't anyone going inside?"

He was right. They were all just standing around in the lot.

Like they were waiting for something. But there was only one way to find out what they were waiting for.

"Come on," Frankie said, and opened the door. "We didn't get all dressed up for nothing."

They walked across the pavement and joined the nearest group. Frankie swatted Jake's hand away when he tried to take hers.

"What?" he asked. "They're all doing it. Worried you won't be able to think pure thoughts?"

"With you in that outfit? I'm not worried in the slightest. Why do you have that outfit, anyway?"

He tugged on his lapels. "It's what I was going to wear to the actual dance. You know, the one everyone else is at."

"Oh," she said. "Um . . . I'm sorry to ruin your night."

"Don't be. I hate dances." He grinned at her, and she grinned back.

They approached the nearest group, and Frankie nudged her way to the middle and craned her neck toward the warehouse doors. "Is this where the Promise Dance is being held?"

"Yeah," said a girl in a floor-length blue dress. "Well, not exactly. There's nothing in the warehouse. The real dance is being held someplace else."

"Supposed to be a really swanky mansion estate," her date added. "In the hills."

"A swanky mansion in the hills," Frankie repeated, and she and Jake exchanged a look. "How do you know? Do you know who's hosting it?"

"Not really. We heard about it from our pastor . . . figured one of the big churches was behind it. They put on parties like this a few times a year. If you've never been, it's really fun. And the food is great."

"There's food? Cool," Jake said, and Frankie elbowed him lightly.

"Yeah," another girl said. "It's really good. By the way, I love your jacket."

Frankie looked at the girl. Then she looked at Jake. Then she looked at the girl again to make sure they were looking at the same thing. Sure enough, the girl reached out and ran her finger along the velvet trim. Frankie slipped an arm into Jake's elbow and tugged him closer. She hadn't figured on needing to fight over her date at a purity dance.

"So how do we get there?" Frankie asked.

"They've got a shuttle running. The first one's already gone—we're supposed to wait for it to come back and pick the rest of us up. It was a really nice shuttle, too. And the guys running it were, like, security guys. Very strong-looking and all in black. Fancy."

"Fancy," Frankie agreed. Fancy and UNDEAD. She tugged Jake gently back toward the van. "That's cool. We're just going to go tell our parents what's going on. Well, not OUR parents, not like both of our parents, we're not brother and sister or anything, just my mom and his dad-uncle, you understand . . ."

"Very smooth," Jake muttered as they hurried back.

"It was my first time undercover. Just be glad I didn't stake myself." She got back to the van and threw open the door; she and Jake climbed in and they called Oz and Willow and put them on speaker.

"What's the word?" asked Oz.

"Well, it's not a rave," said Jake.

"It's the Countess," said Frankie. "I knew it! We've got to call Spike. And Hailey, and Sigmund. I wish we didn't need them, but there's already a bus full of virgins heading to the Countess's mansion, and I have no idea how to get them back. We could smuggle them out in the same bus, I guess, but I can barely park my mom's Prius let alone a giant party bus. . . ." She looked at Jake.

"Don't look at me, I drive a moped," he said, and shrugged.

"I've driven a bus before," said Oz. "No problem. We can drive up to the mansion and leave the car there."

"That's great, but I kind of need you over here. There are a lot of possible victims meandering around the parking lot." Frankie peered at the crowd of dancers. Then her eyes lit up. "Okay, better! You get here, make sure none of these dancers get on the shuttle when it gets here, and steal it. Then meet us at the mansion to help us get the first load out."

"Steal the party bus?" her mom asked uncertainly.

"Yes. It's going to be guarded and driven by a couple of vampires. Maybe four or five? Can you handle that?"

"No," said her mom.

"Not without definitely possible death," Oz agreed. "If it was three . . . what are the chances it'll be three?"

"It might be three."

"Three I can handle."

"It might be five."

"Five I can't handle."

Frankie frowned. She needed muscle to help them at the mansion. Grimloch would probably be there—and she would need Spike. But Hailey and Sigmund . . .

"Call Hailey and Sigmund," she said. "Get them to meet you here. Sigmund can charm people to safety, and Hailey can help with the vampires. Jake and I are taking the van to the mansion."

☽ ☽ ◯ ☾ ☾

Dancing wasn't so bad when you had a partner like Sigmund. Hailey'd thought it would be awkward—that they would stand at the edge of the floor all night making small talk and critiquing the punch. But instead, Sigmund had swept them out into the thick of it the moment they arrived. And he was such a strong leader that it didn't really matter that her feet didn't know what they were doing. She just swayed and shuffled, and if she leaned on him a little too much, he didn't mention it, and he certainly didn't seem to mind.

"Hey, Hailey," said Jasmine Finnegan. She was wearing a beige dress and seemed to have fully recovered from her encounter with the Succoro's energy-draining app, except for the long gloves she wore to cover the scars on her hands. "You look gorgeous."

"Thanks," Hailey said. "So do you." She didn't know how Jasmine managed to make beige look so glamorous. Or even where she'd managed to find it. Who makes a beige dress?

"I made my dress myself," Jasmine said proudly. "From undyed natural fabrics."

"Cool," said Hailey, and Jasmine danced away.

"Frankie would love that dress," Sigmund said.

"She would. Maybe I should learn to sew . . . make her some natural-fabric, dye-free slayer pants." She rested her chin on his shoulder and felt him chuckle. It was nice. Everyone seemed to be in a much better mood than they usually were on school grounds. A night like this made it hard to believe that there was an old hellmouth opening not a hundred feet away. It made it hard to believe there were hellmouths at all, or slayers, or demons, or evil. Except that at that precise moment, there was a slayer across town, undercover at what might be a harvest dance for vampires.

"I really hope the Promise Dance is just a rave," Sigmund said.

"That's what I was just thinking. Sage demons can't read minds, can they?"

"You mean you don't already know? I figured you'd have profile-stalked my demon side by now."

"Excuse me for trying to respect your demon privacy."

He chuckled. "Well, no, to answer your question. We can't read your thoughts. Which is why I have to ask: Is this a date? Or just a distraction?"

Hailey rested her chin on his shoulder so she wouldn't have to look into his eyes. "Can't it be both?"

"Sure." He spun her out and back, fast, and she laughed.

They kept on dancing and waving to other students. So many of them said hi to Hailey, almost like they were friends. And only a few wore sour expressions when they saw her dancing with Sigmund. Not that she could blame them.

"You know, I think half the people in our grade are pretending to flunk math just so you'll tutor them," Hailey said. "How are you so hot and yet so nerdy?" She drew back and looked into his eyes, calm and perfectly at ease behind his gray-framed glasses.

"Nerdy is hot. Haven't you noticed?"

"And you seem a lot"—she swayed in his arms—"smoother tonight than usual."

"That's because we're on a dance floor." He spun her out and back again. "I'm in my element. Ask me to throw a punch. I'll be pathetic again in no time."

"I didn't mean pathetic," she said. "I meant awkward. But seriously, after you go back to DC, a lot of Sunnydale students are going to be playing some serious catch-up."

Sigmund chuckled.

"Is that your way of asking when I'm going back?" he asked. "Because . . . I was thinking of staying."

"Staying? Like, *staying* staying?"

"I mean, I'll go back to visit. But being here, helping the new slayer . . . that feels like more than just research. It feels like a purpose. I never knew what I wanted to do after graduation. My mom wants me to work in government and take martial arts classes so I can fight with my cousins. But I think I can do more good here in Sunnydale. Do you know what I mean?"

She nodded. There was something about Sunnydale that wanted to keep her, too. That should be its town motto. *Sunnydale: Come for a tragedy, stay forever.*

"I'm sorry; I'm being too serious." Sigmund drew back to smile at her. "This is a dance. It's supposed to be fun. And I must say that the decorations are far better than the streamers and balloons you predicted."

That was true. Not that there weren't streamers and balloons. But there were also LED-lit clouds and stars, and one big, bright, full moon, spinning in the center. It was a good thing Jake was with Frankie, or he would have freaked out.

"I heard that the drama club repurposed some of the scenery from last season's stage production," Sigmund said.

"It is surprisingly not terrible," said Hailey.

Even Spike was having a good time. They turned and waved to the vampire, who looked strange in a buttoned shirt and necktie. He waved back a little too eagerly, and they quickly spun in the opposite direction before he could corner them to talk about killing demons and how dry the cookies were.

Sigmund held her close, and Hailey sighed happily. It was very, very not terrible. The gym was transformed, and the dancers happy. Every face was lit with the slight curl of a smile, including a familiar-looking college-age guy as he chatted up an underclassman in a dark pink dress.

"Oh, dammit," Hailey cursed under her breath.

"What?" Sigmund twisted to see what she was looking at. "Do you know that guy?"

"Unfortunately." It was UC Sunnydale. "He's a vamp who got away from us in the cemetery. He was a track star when he was alive. Turns out they only get faster when they die."

Sigmund took a deep breath. "Guess we'd better get Spike to slay him. I don't suppose you've got a stake tucked in that dress?" He let go of her and started to make his way toward Spike, but Hailey caught him by the arm.

"Hang on. I'm remembering something. When we looked up UC Sunnydale, formerly Eric Sullivan, we noticed that he was wearing a promise ring."

"A promise ring," said Sigmund. "Like the same kind as the party Frankie and Jake are at?"

"Exactly. We didn't think anything of it at the time. We didn't know about the Countess's taste for virgin blood."

"But now we do. So that means"—he studied UC Sunnydale grimly—"he's probably one of hers."

Hailey held her hand up and gestured for Spike, who pushed his way through the crowd.

"Are you sure it's him?" Spike asked after she pointed him out.

"I'm sure. Near-photographic memory, remember?"

He raised his eyebrows. "Well, he might be hunting on his own. Doesn't necessarily mean that Frankie's in any trouble—" But he didn't get the chance to finish that hopeful thought because his phone beeped a moment before Hailey's started to ring.

"Text from Frankie," he said.

"Call from Willow." She held up her phone.

"Right. Take the call—I'll go try to catch Frankie at the mansion."

"The mansion?" Sigmund asked. "What about the warehouse?"

"What about UC Sunnydale?" Hailey called as Spike turned and ran.

"I'll take care of him on my way out."

"Be careful," she shouted. "He's fast!" She answered the phone. "Willow? . . . Got it. We're on our way."

CHAPTER THIRTY

DANCE LIKE YOU'VE NEVER DONE *IT* BEFORE

Frankie and Jake ditched the van on the side of the road just past the mansion's driveway and went in on foot. It wasn't easy creeping onto the dark grounds in dress shoes and formal wear, but at least they weren't going to get lost: The mansion was strung up with lights like it was Christmas, and music from a sound system or maybe even a live band blared through the hills.

"This feels like a bad idea," said Jake. "Moreover, it feels like a bad idea we've done already."

"As long as you don't kick any rocks down onto the place, we should be just fine."

"So we're just going to scope it out? Wait for backup?"

"Yes." Only what better place to scope it out than from inside? They reached the edge of the groomed courtyard and ducked behind a shrub. There were so many people in there. And who knew how many vampires. Spike had better get there soon. And Oz and her mom and Hailey. She didn't know what she could do if the feeding started first.

"Okay, Jake. Take off your jacket."

"Why?"

"It'll attract too much attention."

"We're going in?"

"That's why we're dressed up—so we'll blend. We're just going to check it out until Spike and the others arrive. We need the lay of the land."

"Alone?" he asked. But they wouldn't be alone. Grimloch was bound to be there. She knew Spike was right and she shouldn't depend on him, but she couldn't quite help it. After all, what kind of slayer refused help when it was offered? The dead kind, that's who.

"Take my hand."

"I thought you didn't want me to take your hand," he said as he took it. "What are we going to tell them if we get caught sneaking in? That we were off in the bushes reaffirming our decision to wait until marriage?"

"We'll tell them we got lost." Frankie pulled him close. She counted five, six, seven vampires patrolling the mansion grounds, and that was only the exterior. Many more were sure to be inside with the crowd, ready to grab dancers and throw them to the Countess when the feeding began.

They slipped in through the wide-open front doors, and Frankie noted a small group of attendees who were wandering the halls on the way to the dance, oohing and aahing over the very recently installed finery. She didn't remember seeing half the beautiful furnishings on their last trip here. The vampires must have been working overtime bringing in oil paintings and lacquered armchairs. To say nothing of the streamers and balloons.

They tagged onto the back of the group just as they passed into the ballroom—everything done up in gold, gold, gold, plus blue and silver to match the flyers—and Frankie tucked her chin into Jake as they passed by two vampires in security-guard-style black.

But the vampires' eyes slid onto them and slid right back off. It was only a visual count: two more virgins for the slaughter.

"Good," she said. "They didn't recognize us. Though done up like this, I don't know if I'd recognize myself."

"Don't speak too soon," Jake said. "Someone's recognized you."

He nodded up to the balcony, where Grimloch stared down at them. At her. And he did not seem pleased. He lowered his head to hide the flashing blue of his eyes and jerked his chin to the side. They hadn't known each other long, but Frankie could decipher that easily enough. *Get out of sight.* Also *What are you doing here, you idiot?*

She and Jake slipped discreetly into an alcove behind a large bowl full of glittering gold punch. Jake sniffed at the passing trays of hors d'oeuvres: little finger sandwiches, lots of fancy cheeses to pair with fancy crackers, and these charming little fruit tarts that glistened with glaze.

"Not now, Jake."

"If not now, when? If it's going to be my last meal, it might as well be served to me on a little gold tray."

"It's not going to be your last meal." But he looked surprisingly nervous. And he was right. They were outnumbered. Severely. As she looked around, it suddenly hit home that they were alone in the middle of a feeding ground, fenced in like cattle at the meat factory. But she couldn't think like that. Not when it was her job to protect the entire herd.

"Frankie, are you a virgin?"

"That's none of your business, Jake."

"Because I am," he said. "So . . . protect me."

She looked at him, sort of surprised. "You? Really? I never thought that . . . with all the girls you date . . . And when I brought up the Promise Dance you said you weren't."

"Actually if you recall, I said no such thing. I didn't say any-thing." He shrugged. "It's a personal choice that I kept personal. No big deal, until you bring me to a place where my blood is on the menu."

"Everyone's blood is on the menu," she said. "Once the feeding starts, I don't think the henchmen will be too choosy."

"I wonder how they can tell . . ." Jake mused. "Can you tell? Just by looking at me? Or is it more of a scent thing, do you think?"

Grimloch pulled her to one side. Frankie had no idea how he'd reached them so quickly. The mansion was too big and too full of passageways.

"What are you doing here?" he asked. "Alone?"

"I'm not alone; I have Jake." She pointed to him, and Jake held up a hand in greeting.

"One werewolf won't be enough to get you out of here alive."

"That's what I said," said Jake.

"We have backup coming." Frankie paused as a vamp in black passed by the alcove. "Besides, what choice did I have? You told me there was this big feeding going down and then neglected to tell me when it was. What were you trying to do?"

"I was trying to keep you out of it." He reached into his jacket and produced a vial of pale purple liquid. "I was going to take care of it myself. Virgin's bane."

"Virgin's bane." Jake zeroed in on the vial. "The poison! That's the poison those monks used?"

"Priests," said Frankie. "And no, it's not. Virgin's bane was just a poisoned virgin. So I guess that's poison. Meant for one of these unsuspecting victims. You can't do that, Grimloch. That's not what slayers do. One life in exchange for the rest? That's not how slayers think."

"I know," he said, and lowered his eyes. "That's why I didn't tell you. She never would have—" He broke off. "But there's no other way."

"We'll find one. How would you even choose?" Frankie gestured out to the dance floor. "Him? He seems a little shy—does he look like he'd be willing? Or what about her? That's a terrible dress, so maybe she deserves it?"

Grimloch hid the poison in his fist. "I was going to choose one near the front of the line. To save the others. But if you have a better plan . . ."

"I don't," she said. "I just know I can't do that."

"That's why *I* was going to do it," he said, a little sulkily. But she held her hand out, and he put the poison in it.

"No, no, no." Jake shook his head and grabbed the vial. "I'll hang on to this. I don't need you pulling any desperate, self-sacrificing heroics."

Frankie frowned. "I hadn't thought of that. But it wouldn't have been the worst plan."

"Poisoning yourself, our only slayer, who might be the very last slayer the world has . . . You're right. Not the worst plan. It would have been the second worst, behind poisoning one of these innocent people." He leveled a high-and-mighty gaze at Grimloch. Frankie's stomach tightened. They couldn't bring themselves to use the poison. But before the night was over, they might come to regret that, depending on how many people they lost.

In the ballroom, the music quieted and a rustle of whispers ran through the party. Frankie crept to the wall and peeked out. On the balcony where Grim had stood now stood the Countess.

She wasn't beautiful, exactly. If Frankie had seen a picture of her, she would have said she was a handsome woman in her fifties who spent a lot of money at the salon. But there was something about her. Power. A sharpness. Her eyes weren't empty; they were

327

thoughtful and careful. They were smart. Even though Frankie knew the Countess wasn't at her full strength, she still looked like more than she could handle.

The Countess leaned forward, hands gripping the railing, and looked over the gathering. Occasionally she would whisper to the tall, muscular man beside her and gesture into the crowd. Then she took a deep breath and held her arms out, the fabric of her short gold-embroidered dress sparkling warmly in the light.

"Oh god," Frankie said. "She's going to give a speech."

"Where are your reinforcements?" Grimloch asked. "Because she is not waiting any longer."

$$\mathcal{)} \mathcal{)} \bigcirc \mathcal{(} \mathcal{(}$$

Sigmund and Hailey pulled up to the warehouse in the midst of what appeared to be a standoff. There was a bus—one of those nice party buses that could fit about fifty people—parked and idling, with four burly dudes dressed in black standing outside of it. Gathered around the bus was a crowd wearing dresses and suits. And in between them were Oz and Willow.

"Are you counting four vampires?" Sigmund asked as he turned off the ignition.

"Five," said Hailey. "Don't forget the driver." She picked up her ax and tried to tuck a stake into her pocket until she realized she didn't have any pockets and stuffed the stake down the front of her dress. "Sig, do you think you can get those people out of here?" They didn't look very keen on leaving. Now that the engine was shut off, Hailey could vaguely hear what was being said and heard Oz shout, "I am an adult! And no one is getting on this bus!"

"I'll turn up the ol' charm," Sigmund said, but he sounded uncertain. "They'll be putty in my hands."

They got out of the car and hurried toward the bus. Hailey did her best to keep the ax hidden behind her back, but one of the vamps must have caught a glimpse of it because he shouted, "Grab them!"

And the fight erupted.

"Sigmund, hurry," Hailey yelled. She started to run. The poor Promise Dancers were confused. A few screamed, but most simply stood there with wide eyes as the men dressed in black shed their handsome human faces for their demon ones. Two of them picked Oz up by his nice jacket and threw him twenty feet across the parking lot. But before Hailey could wince, he tucked and rolled and popped back up.

And he popped back up not quite human.

Oz's eyes had gone black as tar, and a large set of fangs protruded from his mouth. His hands were very wolfy and *very* clawed, and his jacket was torn where the sleeve met the shoulder. Hailey thought he might Hulk the rest of the way out and become a full-on werewolf in a necktie. But instead, he spoke. Or rather, he snarled at the kids.

"Get out of here!"

That woke them up. They shrieked and scattered, running in all directions. Some in the wrong direction, making straight for the bus. The vampires scrambled to grab them, and in the heat of the scrabble, they forgot their mission and started to feed. Hailey saw one sink his teeth into the neck of a boy in a gray suit and ran faster, dodging fleeing people, aiming for the feeding vampire. She got to him right as he dropped the dead boy onto the pavement.

"That meal was your last!" She swung the ax, and it cut his arm off above the elbow; the detached limb disintegrated to ash before it hit the ground. She swung again and made ash of his leg. He fell to his knee, and for a split second, she forgot where she'd stashed

329

her stake, but then she fished it out of her bodice and staked him in the back. Dust.

She'd fought a vampire all by herself. And she'd lived.

"Not bad," she whispered, shaky with adrenaline. "Wish Vi was here to see it."

Hailey turned when she heard Sigmund shout, and saw him leading a group of dancers toward his car. He was just so handsome. Who wouldn't follow that? She shook her head and smacked herself lightly. That charm of his was no joke.

She gave her attention back to the lot and the people running everywhere. Oz was near the rear of the bus, grappling with two vampires—he sliced at them with his claws and bit, shaking his head back and forth violently. Willow was at the front, trying to get the people off who had mistakenly boarded. It looked like she was going out of her way not to use magic, ushering the group of teens by hand in a hurry. When her back was turned, the vampire bus driver got out of his seat and dove at her through the open door.

"Willow!" Hailey yelled. "Behind you!" Willow turned and faced the giant vamp flying through the air toward her.

"Oh, screw it," she screamed, and threw her arms out in front of her. *"Incendia!"*

The vampire burst into bright orange flames and ran screaming into the crowd of people who were already running and screaming.

"Oops!" Willow said. "Well, now he's a fire hazard." A few moments later, the vamp went up in a cloud of dust and soot. But fire hazard or not, Hailey couldn't help feeling that they were winning, especially now that Willow was using her magic. The witch turned to where Oz was fending off two more vampires. She gestured to one, and he flew back and was impaled on a handy piece of rebar, leaving Oz free to finish off the other one. The empty lot was starting to look empty again. The last vampire climbed inside the bus.

"Don't lose that bus!" Oz shouted.

Hailey charged onto the idling bus. It wasn't exactly the best decision, which she realized when she tried to swing her ax at the driver and got it caught on the mechanism that opened the door. The vampire drew back and struck her hard across the jaw, so fast she hardly felt it. Or at least felt it no more than she felt herself bounce off a sideways seat and onto the floor, her back striking painfully against one of the upright poles.

"Hailey!" Willow shouted as she came up after her. The witch's eyes had gone a little dark, or maybe the pupils were just a little large from the excitement.

"Don't set him on fire in here," Hailey squeaked, and struggled to her feet. Her dress was a mess. And there was a good-sized tear in it, just below the hip. She glared at the vampire. "Just because I didn't pay for this with my own money doesn't mean I'm not mad about it." She charged him, and Willow threw her wrap around his neck. With teeth clenched, Willow yanked him back into the stairwell, opening his chest up for a perfect hit from Hailey's stake. He was dust.

Willow shook ash off her wrap, and she and Hailey jumped down the steps and surveyed the parking lot. Two people in formal wear lay motionless on the asphalt, and Hailey frowned. She didn't know who they were. But they'd only wanted to dance.

"Okay," Oz said. He was Oz again; no more teeth and claws, but his suit was torn to shreds. "Let's get this bus up to Frankie and Jake at the mansion."

Hailey looked toward where they'd parked, but Sigmund and the car were gone. He probably had his hands full corralling panicked

Promise Dancers, but at least he was safe. Hailey climbed onto the bus with Willow, and Oz got into the driver's seat and threw it into gear.

This was only the first wave of the fight, she realized. There was much more fighting still to do. She hoped Oz was a fast driver, so they got to the mansion before she ran out of adrenaline.

CHAPTER THIRTY-ONE

THE PRICE OF SLAYING

Frankie stared up at the Countess as she spoke to the crowd. Her voice was like the rest of her: full of steel and yet also full of warmth. Frankie could see why so many young people went with her to their deaths, why so many girls went to her when she was alive. She was a leader and she was strong, and if she promised you safety, you would believe her. If she promised you anything, you would believe her.

But she wasn't promising safety to the people gathered in the ballroom. When her speech ended, the screaming would begin. Blood would fly. It would run from throats all the way to the floor; it would paint the walls and stain the silk upholstery. Frankie could picture it in her mind like flashes from a horror movie: the before—dancers laughing, spinning, smiling. And the after—a silent room of gold and red, littered with empty-eyed corpses.

"Frankie." Jake nudged her. "What do we do?"

She didn't know why he was asking her.

"Frankie."

"What?" she snapped. "I don't know what to do, Jake." That's what they would say about her, in the slayer codex. It would be Buffy the Legendary. Faith the Reckless. Kennedy the . . . Overeager. And Frankie the Unprepared. Jake took her hand and squeezed it.

"Yes, you do," he said softly. "You knew at the warehouse. Like you knew that the Promise Dance was no rave. You're the slayer. You can do this."

"Oh, ye of blind faith," she whispered.

"I can stop many," Grimloch said, eyeing several of the Countess's goons. "A few will bring the victims to her; she likes to be served her meals. And others will need to contain the crowd. If I focus on keeping victims away, you'll be able to get to her first."

Frankie frowned. "So we just wait for it to start? How many do we allow her to have as an appetizer before we make our move? No, we need a distraction. A diversion. Chaos."

"Chaos." Jake grinned. "Hang on a minute."

"Wait, where are you going?" she asked when he ducked out of the alcove.

"The front door."

Jake disappeared and Grimloch moved closer, and even in the tense situation, his sudden nearness made Frankie's stomach flutter.

"Do you have any idea what he's up to?" Grimloch asked.

"Not a clue."

"Do you trust him?"

"Yeah, I trust him."

On the balcony, the Countess was still welcoming her meal. "Tonight we celebrate your decision to wait," she said. "To preserve yourselves. And in a world of increasing pressures, of endless temptations, of loosening morals . . . each one of you is precious." She paused, and Frankie caught the shine of fangs just breaking through her gums. "Each one of you is a true jewel."

"Can't they tell what she's thinking?" Frankie whispered. "I've seen dogs look at bacon with more subtlety."

Then, not thirty seconds from the time he'd left them, Jake burst into the ballroom from the direction of the front door.

"Cops!" he screamed. "This party is busted!"

Gasps and shrieks erupted from the crowd, even though by all appearances this group wasn't doing anything illegal. They started to jostle, and the buzz of questions rose quickly to a dull roar.

"Cops everywhere!" Jake continued to scream. "We gotta get out of here! They found something in the punch! Drugs! A hint of booze! Minors for everyone!"

"I'll lose my scholarship," someone cried. "My mom will kill me!" cried someone else. And then the mass panic began in earnest as an exodus of virgins made for the door.

"Nice work, Jake," Frankie said as he gave her the thumbs-up from inside the current of people. She nodded to Grimloch. "Let's do it. You know, I mean, the attacking."

"Your friend is smart," Grimloch said approvingly. "He stirred up a ruckus and set the victims to save themselves."

"They're not victims yet." Frankie emerged from the alcove and leapt over fleeing bodies. She landed on the table with her feet between trays of baklava and parkoured through the ballroom using the backs of chairs, low shelves, and even a hanging tapestry to land on the stairs en route to the Countess, who was calling in vain for someone named Anton.

Frankie reared back and leapt, grabbing a chandelier in midair and flipping onto the balcony right before the Countess, who reeled backward as Frankie straightened into a fighting stance.

"Were you calling for me?" Frankie asked. "Am I Anton?"

"No, you are not," the Countess said, and struck.

Frankie dodged. She cast a glance down into the party and saw

Jake punching a vampire who was trying to prevent a couple from leaving. "They're in on it!" he shouted. "The security guys are in on it with the cops! It's entrapment!" More dancers screamed and fled from the men in black. A few of them actually flailed their arms.

Frankie swerved as the Countess struck again, and swerved back in to land a punch to the Countess's face. It was a test punch mainly, to see what happened. Would her hand break? Would the Countess bite her hand like a snake and rip it off at the wrist? But the Countess's face was just a face. She took a punch like any other vamp.

"Okay," Frankie said, and went to work.

The Countess was fast. Brutally fast, even in her weakened state. The hits that Frankie didn't manage to dodge rattled the teeth in her head. But it wasn't as bad as she'd feared.

"Shame we have to do this in dresses," Frankie said. "But at least you're wearing one, too. Same limited range of motion."

"I'm used to fighting in dresses," said the Countess. "I'm a lady."

"An old lady," said Frankie, and the Countess bared her teeth. Her vampiric face was different from other vampires'. Less forehead and more fang. And her eyes were not yellow but a deep bloodred.

Below in the ballroom, Grimloch tore through so many vampires that the air around him was a constant cloud of dust. The Countess growled.

"You turned my Hunter against me," she said. "That makes me angry." With a vicious twist of her arm, she tore a long piece of the banister free and swung it into Frankie's torso. The impact sent her flying against the wall so hard, she lost her breath and couldn't even make a snappy comeback.

"I didn't turn him," she gasped. "He was— It's a long story."

"You don't have time to tell it."

The Countess used the banister to beat Frankie onto the floor.

She struck again and again, so hard that when Frankie heard a sharp crack she was sure it was one of her bones until half of the banister landed beside her. The Countess reached down and yanked Frankie up by her hair, dangling her like a worm on a hook. Frankie kicked high through the slit in her dress.

"Thanks, Mom," she whispered just as she drove the broken banister she'd grabbed off the floor right through the Countess's heart.

The Countess staggered back. The smaller battles taking place around them paused as her henchmen waited and watched. Once she was dust, they would scatter. That's just the way vampires were. They would find a new leader, someone to provide for them. For a moment, the Countess clawed at the wood in her chest, terrified. Then she sighed.

"I thought you knew who I was," she said, and plucked it out like a splinter.

"I was hoping that was just a rumor," Frankie murmured just before the banister hit her across the jaw and sent her flying.

"Frankie!"

She dragged herself to the edge of the balcony as Jake fought his way to her through a sea of people, unaware of the vampire coming up behind him. When the cold hand wrapped around his mouth, a look of surprise dawned on his face. Like he didn't quite believe it, right until the fangs sank into his neck.

"Jake!"

Frankie sensed more than actually saw the shadow of the Countess raise the banister for one final blow, hard enough this time to crack her skull and put her to sleep forever. Time seemed to pause, the moment stretching out, suspended. And then it disappeared as Grimloch jumped onto the balcony and tore the weapon from the Countess's hand.

"Traitor!" she growled.

"Trait-ee," he said, and knocked her backward. It was horrible to watch the two of them fight, like seeing two wild animals tearing at each other. Frankie had to help him. She had to help Jake. She had to get up.

"Everybody this way!"

She looked down. Spike rushed into the ballroom and took out a vampire in midleap, twisting its head so hard it tore right off its body. Oz and her mom were there, too, guiding people to the exit. And Hailey.

"Hailey!" Frankie shouted desperately. "Jake! Get Jake!"

She pointed. Hailey and Oz jumped over tables and tore the vampire from Jake's neck. Oz picked him up and pulled him away.

"Jake!" She wanted him to open his eyes. Show her he was okay. He was so pale. And limp.

Frankie ducked as Grimloch flew over her head and struck the wall, cracking the plaster. He struggled to his feet, and the Countess was on him in a blink. She punched her hand into Grimloch's chest.

"No!" Frankie shouted.

"You promised me a heart." The Countess dug her fingers deep inside his rib cage. "That was the bargain."

Frankie didn't think. She picked up the broken banister and swung it around into the Countess's head. The Countess fell away from Grimloch, and her hand came out of his chest, red but empty.

"Come on!" Frankie pulled his arm over her shoulder. She walked to the edge of the balcony and jumped off, the landing hard with Grimloch's extra weight. It was a disaster. So many wounded, including her friends. Bodies of people she hadn't saved tangled up in her feet.

"Get to the bus!" Hailey called. "Everybody get to the bus! Frankie! Use your magic!"

But what magic did she mean? What spell? There were too many screams, too much blood. All she could think of was getting out, and getting as many people out with her as she could. She saw two vampires thrown up and back to be impaled on a chandelier and saw Willow, teeth bared and eyes black. That, too, seemed like a failure. Her mother, using too much magic, because Frankie hadn't beaten the Countess.

"Hailey!" Frankie shouted, and pointed to a girl and a boy huddled under a table.

"Got them," Hailey shouted back, and pulled them out. Frankie lingered, blinking against double vision. Her head throbbed, and she felt sick, looking at the bodies of the dancers. But she waited until the last of the people ran out the door before she went after, dragging Grimloch on her back.

☽ ☾ ○ ☾ ☾

Oz gunned it down the hill, heading for the Sunnydale Hospital ER far faster than a party bus was ever intended to go. It was a wonder they didn't flip over each time they went around a bend in the hills, as everyone on one side of the bus fell into everyone on the other.

"Oz," Willow said gently. She had Jake on her lap, her wrap pressed to the wound in his neck. "We can't take all these kids to the ER—there'll be a panic. How will we explain it?"

"I don't know," he said. "But Jake needs to go. So we're going."

"I can jump out with him," said Hailey. "You take the bus, drop the kids off, get Frankie and Willow home, then come back."

"I'm not leaving him." Oz was quiet, but there was no arguing with the tone of his voice.

Hailey glanced at Frankie, and Frankie looked away. She couldn't think.

"What about Sigmund?" Willow asked. "Can he help?"

Frankie sat silently in the front of the bus with Grimloch. Her weight bounced against the hole in his chest, keeping pressure on. His breathing was rough. Ragged. And Jake—Jake wasn't moving, except to bounce limply with the motion of the bus.

Out of the corner of her eye, she saw Hailey pull out her phone and heard it when Sigmund answered.

"We need you to meet us at the hospital. At the ER. Right now. And we need you to drive a bus."

Frankie blinked. Could Sigmund even drive a bus? His car was little, not even a stick shift. But what did it matter?

The people inside the bus looked like it had already crashed. They were cut and bruised, their clothes stained with blood and dirt, their faces stricken. A few were crying or had the dried streaks of tears on their cheeks and chin.

The effects of the battle were wearing off. The adrenaline and the clarity, the reflex to fight and survive, were fading. Without it, everything seemed blurred and dull. Frankie felt every scrape, every hit. Her body throbbed in all the places the Countess had struck her.

The bus pulled into the ER entrance. Oz slammed the brakes hard and threw the bus into park. He picked Jake up off Willow's lap even though Jake was bigger than he was by nearly a foot and a few dozen pounds.

"I'm going with them," her mom said. "I'll be right back." She hurried off the bus and ran ahead inside the hospital for help.

Hailey stood.

"Okay. Anyone whose injuries are bad enough to need a doctor, come with me. The rest of you stay here, and we'll get you home." A few of the injured got up: a girl with a broken arm who was helped by her date, and two boys with blood running down their temples.

Hailey led them from the bus and got them inside. Frankie heard a car pull up and heard Sigmund's voice. Then Hailey was in front of her again, tugging at her arm.

"Frankie? Come on, we have to get you and Grimloch home. Frankie? It's okay, okay? You stopped her. You saved them."

But not all of them. When Frankie looked around, she didn't see a bus full of survivors. She only saw their wounds, and the missing spaces of the ones they'd left behind. This was the thing that slayers never talked about. The weight that descended even after what would be considered a victory. It didn't feel like a victory. It felt like they'd lost.

CHAPTER THIRTY-TWO

WHY WON'T YOU DIE?

F rankie sat at her kitchen table behind an untouched cup of tea while Spike spoke on the phone with her mom, who was still at the hospital with Jake. It sounded like Jake was going to be fine—he was already awake again. The werewolf constitution had helped. So had Oz's recklessly fast driving, which, according to the doctors, had made all the difference.

Grimloch was laid out on the rug in their living room, after refusing to get bloodstains on the couch. He was going to be fine, too, despite having a sucking chest wound. He wouldn't answer Hailey's questions about whether having his heart pulled out would have killed him. So Frankie thought it was safe to assume that it would.

Hailey was . . . well, tough, like Frankie had known she would be. Capable. She'd done what she had to: get them that bus and save those people. But she'd still wound up with a wicked purple bruise across her chin and Sigmund kept bugging her about needing an X-ray to check for jaw fractures.

They were all miserable. Even Sigmund, who had only seen the aftermath. They were miserable, and defeated, and exhausted. But she couldn't let them sleep. They tiptoed and whispered around her because they thought she had lost the ability to form words. They made her tea and used soft gestures because they thought the Countess had broken her. Frankie supposed she nearly had, if one were to judge by the battered sack of skin in which she was currently residing. But what the Countess had really done was wake her up.

Seeing Jake get bit had woken her up. Seeing the Countess's hand in Grimloch's chest. Seeing her friends fight so hard, and watching those kids still die. But those kids weren't Frankie's fault. Their deaths weren't her doing. And they would only weigh on her conscience if she allowed the Countess to live.

"Sigmund," she said, and Sigmund, Hailey, and Spike spun to face her. Their expressions were priceless. Like they'd forgotten she was even there. Or like they thought she'd been turned to stone. "I need you to round up all the books we have on the Countess."

"Okay," he said uncertainly. "What are you hoping to find?"

"Something we missed," said Frankie. "I staked her." Their brows knit, confused. "In the heart. I didn't miss. And she pulled the stake right out again and kept on talking."

"That's not possible," said Spike.

"I told you." Grimloch came into the kitchen and leaned against the entryway wall with a towel pressed to the hole in his chest. "The Countess has been staked many times. And beheaded. And burned."

"That's not possible," Spike said again. "And it's not fair. What makes her so bloody special?"

Bloody special. Inside Frankie's tired brain, something clicked.

"It's the virgins' blood." Frankie stood up. "That's what sets her apart."

343

"The virgins' blood?" Sigmund thought about it, scrolling through his Sage demon mind full of codexes, and inventories, and myths. "No other vampire has fed on it exclusively."

Spike scoffed. "Because it's just not practical. A virgin is nice every now and then, all pure and rich and—" He wiped his mouth, and they all looked at him in disgust. "But virgins only? That's like babies only. Or being pescatarian. Who's got the bloody time?"

"All an immortal has is time. And the Countess has filled hers with a steady diet of virgins for about five hundred years. Not to mention all the virgin blood she bathed in when she was human." That had to be it. All that youthful blood, it gave her gifts—her vampire face didn't even look like other vampires': it was softer and less demonic. And her eyes were bloodred.

"Some say that she wasn't even turned," Grimloch said. "It was rumored that when she died her mortal death, she was mystically reborn a vampire. After all the blood she'd drunk as a mortal." They stared at him.

"In the future," Frankie said, "these are the kinds of things that allies share with each other."

"It was just a rumor." He shrugged, then winced at the pain of shrugging.

"Fine," Frankie said. "Anyway, it doesn't matter what she is or how she got that way. I just need to know how to kill her."

"But what if there is no magic bullet," Sigmund said. "What if she really is . . . unkillable?"

"If we don't find anything, we wait," said Spike. "We'll come up with a solution." He looked at Frankie, and she looked down, afraid he would know what she was thinking if she looked him in the eye.

Because Frankie wasn't waiting for anything. One way or another, the Countess would die at dawn.

The wound in her chest was gone. The jagged piece of banister was certainly gone. But the Countess could still feel it there, stuck in between her ribs, piercing the little bag of ventricles and arteries that she swore she could still occasionally hear beating when she dreamed. That little brat had staked her. And for a second, she'd felt what it would be like to die, again. To know it was the end; no time for disbelief, no time for bargaining, no time to change it. For a split second, she'd known what came next would be dust, and darkness. Oblivion. As if she never was. No more thoughts, no more hopes, no more hunger. No more anything.

Unless there was a hell.

Her lips twitched. Hell didn't seem so bad to a vampire, and especially not to her, since she tried to create one nightly in her drawing room. Hell she could handle. Trouble was, not even she who had lived so long knew for sure which awaited. An eternity of delightful torment? Or nothingness? A flat black ending. She dug her nails into her palms. She hated the uncertainty. Hated the fear. The slayer had made her remember that, like those priests had, and like that strange illness had the last night of her mortal life.

The slayer had ruined everything, that smallish girl with the witch's red hair and the skirt cut so high it might as well have been a cape. She and Grimloch had been in it together, and the Countess wondered what kind of game he was playing at. Did earning her trust make the heart taste better? Or had he really been softened by her charms? The girl didn't have any charms that the Countess could see. No manners, no style. But she did have to admit, she could swing a piece of wood. She rubbed absently at the side of her head. And the girl had staked her. It hadn't really mattered in the end, but she had done it.

Only because I was careless, *the Countess thought. After so many centuries being impervious to harm, what was one supposed to expect? Except that she hadn't been impervious to harm. Not for a long time.*

She wandered through the wreck of her ballroom. Tables and chairs were overturned and split. Crystal glasses shattered. Candles broken and the wax left to drip onto the floor. The place looked like it had been trampled by a herd of elephants. She ran a finger through the glaze of a smashed tart and tasted it, the flavor watery and muted on her vampiric tongue. There were a few bodies lying around that hadn't been drained, and she supposed she ought to eat them. Never let it be said she let a virgin go to waste. But she was just so depressed.

So many of her fledglings were dead, with not even a body to mourn over. Her ballroom was absolutely trashed, blood and food everywhere, when they'd just repainted. So many virgins dancing into the night, and she hadn't been able to drain even one. And to think, poor Anton had gotten all that glitter from the craft store for nothing. Come to think of it—she turned around—where was Anton? She hadn't seen him since before the fight began. But he couldn't be—he couldn't be among the dust. She walked from pile to pile and stared down like she could discern one from the other, like she could detect a hint of his toughness, or his steadiness, or his loyalty, from the way the ash had fallen.

"Anton?" She spun and called. "Anton!" She called again, and

again, and a few fledgling servants came from the interior rooms to see what was the matter. But none knew where he was.

"Maybe he's gone down to the catacombs," said one, a handsome young man with long, fast legs, still in semiformal wear. "Most of us who are left are there already, this close to sunrise."

"Yes, thank you . . . Eric," she said after searching her mind a moment. She was going to do better at remembering their names. Especially those that survived such an attack. "Go down and find him for me, will you?"

"Never a need to search for me," Anton said. He came into the room with his arms spread wide. She could have fallen right into them, were she a weaker sort of person.

"Anton," she said instead. "That little slayer brat spoiled my party."

"Not all of it."

Before she could ask what he meant, he gestured to the doorway, and her servants started shoving them through: virgins. Terrified, confused virgins in their precious little dresses and suits. They shuffled in, hugging themselves and casting about with wide white eyes. Nearly twenty of them.

"I don't understand," the Countess said. "How?"

"I was giving this group a tour of the wine cellar when the trouble began," Anton replied. "We hid down there until we were sure it was safe."

"Are we safe?" one of the boy virgins asked. "Are the cops gone?"

The Countess and Anton smiled at each other. He really was the best of her servants. Someone she could always depend on.

"Of course it's safe," Anton said, and pushed the boy toward her waiting embrace. "I assure you there are no police officers anywhere."

Afterward, when all the screaming had stopped, and the Countess had licked her fingers and let the fledglings have the scraps, she and Anton sat together in chairs he'd righted and set beside the wall. The ballroom seemed a much more comforting place now. It was quiet, and the first beams of sunlight would soon stream through the upper windows to bathe the lower levels with indirect light. And after such a nice kill, she could almost imagine that she'd been the one to do the damage.

"Are you well now, Countess?"

"Yes, Anton. I am well." Twenty virgins was not the hundred she'd hoped for, but it would do, and it was certainly better than nothing. She tapped her fingers against the wooden armrest and thought for the thousandth time how glad she was to have lived into an era with cars and tailored clothing and electricity, when people went out at night and you didn't need to steal them from around campfires or lure them into the woods anymore under the guise of some fraught quest. She felt so good and so sated and so powerful. She could barely remember what had gotten her so down. Barely.

"I need to change my clothes," she said.

"Are we going after the slayer?"

"No. Not now. Right now I just want to punish her."

"How would you like to do that?" Anton asked. "Poison? Beatings? Hot pokers?"

Anton and his hot pokers. But that wasn't what she was after. After the ruckus the slayer had raised at the party, more than pain was in order. Suffering was on the menu. Weakening. She thought back to the attack, her memory touching on each of the girl's allies: the werewolf, who was probably dead; the girl with the cheap black hair. The witch, the old werewolf, and the vampire Watcher. Something told her to lay off the witch. Not to push that, just yet. She was the slayer's mother, and that was a big pain. The kind to save for later.

"I want the vampire," she said. "The Watcher. After all, what is a young slayer without her Watcher?"

"What about Grimloch?" Anton asked.

"He's yours, if you like. Shouldn't even be hard." She remembered the warm wetness of the inside of his chest—the satisfying crunch and crack of his rib cage. "You just have to reach in. Like stealing bread off a windowsill from a window I've already opened."

Anton smiled. "I'll bring the car around."

CHAPTER THIRTY-THREE

A BAD IDEA IS STILL TECHNICALLY AN IDEA

They researched all night, Saturday into Sunday, drinking coffee until Spike took it away to prevent caffeine toxicity. Around five a.m., Spike left them to go back to the library and continue from there. Frankie went through the motions, turning the pages of a book balanced on one knee while she balanced a knife on the other, sharpening it, then the next, and the next after that. She even sharpened their paring knives in the kitchen, since she already had the whetstone out and why not.

In between knives, she checked her phone for texts from her mom or Oz about Jake. And she let her thumb scroll through her old text thread with Buffy. If Buffy had been there, she would have found a way to kill the Countess. If Buffy were alive, the Countess would never have dared to come to Sunnydale.

By five thirty, Hailey was asleep, her chin resting in the spine of an open book with soft, soft pages like parchment.

Frankie crept quietly up to her room and changed out of her pajamas. She pulled a T-shirt over her head and threaded a belt with a knife sheath through the loops of her jeans. Then she put on another. And another on her ankle. Her phone buzzed, and she was surprised to look down and see that it was Xander.

"Xander?"

"Hey, kiddo. I'm sorry to call so early, but I couldn't get your mom."

Frankie rubbed her eyes. "She probably turned her phone on silent in the hospital."

"The hospital? What happened?"

"Nothing," Frankie said. "We're okay. What are you . . . ? Is there more news?"

"Frankie, is your mom okay?"

"My mom's fine," she assured him. "What is it?"

"It's Sadie. She woke up."

Sadie. In the madness of the Countess and the Promise Dance, she'd almost forgotten about the slayer, lying in a Halifax hospital.

"Is she going to be okay? What did she say?"

"We don't know yet. The doctors . . . She had burns, and the doctors say there's some kind of infection." His voice was low. What she wouldn't give to hear him sound like his old self. "But they let us talk to her. Frankie—Faith's dead."

The words hit harder than she'd been ready for. *Faith's dead.* Like bags of cement against her chest. Memories of Faith rose like ghosts, of lopsided smiles, and all that sweetness behind all those defenses.

"Why does— How does she know?" Frankie asked.

"She said . . . Faith saved her. Shoved her out of the way and into a culvert. But she saw the explosion. After Faith pushed her, she ran into a building and it exploded before she opened the door. Sadie said she saw it. She said she saw it all."

"Faith's body," Frankie said numbly. "We have to bring her home."

"There's nothing to bring home. They said with the force of the blast . . . there wouldn't be anything left."

Frankie pulled in a slow breath. No body to find. Nothing to mourn. If not for Sadie, they'd have always wondered—

"Frankie," Xander said. "Faith was going into that building after Buffy."

His words hung in the air, and Frankie waited. She waited, with the phone pressed hard against her numb cheek.

"I'm so sorry," Xander said. "I have to talk to your mom; I have to talk to Willow—"

"I know," Frankie heard herself say. "I'll make sure she calls you. I'm . . . sorry, too." He was quiet on the other end. She couldn't hear him breathing, or any sounds from the hospital, if that was even where he was. "Are you and Dawn—are you okay?"

"It's not sinking in," he said softly. "It's not the answer we wanted. Hey, what time is it there, anyway?"

"Almost six."

"I'm sorry for waking you up."

"You didn't. It's okay."

"You sure your mom's okay?"

"I'm sure."

"Okay," he said. "I'll talk to you soon, kiddo."

"Bye."

Frankie let the phone fall to her side. Then she pulled it back up and found Buffy's text string. She hammered out a text.

Buffy?

She stared at it. Watched it glow. Her thumb hovered over the send icon. Then she put her phone back into her pocket.

On the back of Frankie's door hung a corkboard full of photographs. Buffy and Mr. Giles at her birthday parties. Vacations. A trip to the zoo when her mom made them pose all fierce in front of the hyena enclosure and Xander hadn't wanted to be in it and kept muttering about how bacon came from pigs, and pork chops came from pigs, and there was nothing wrong with it.

Frankie took off her stretchy yoga pants and put on a pair of dark jeans and boots with the highest heels she could find. She looked at herself in the mirror. With the knives in her belt and the jeans and the boots, she looked like a different person. She reached into her closet and pulled out one of Buffy's old leather jackets, which she'd given Frankie for her last birthday. Frankie had never felt cool enough to wear it, but now she slipped it on and crept downstairs, out the back door, and into the last of the night.

She'd spent too much time in the dark lately; she was starting to be able to tell the difference between the hours after sunset and the hours before dawn. She tested her muscles—felt the bruises and the weight of the knives. The long blade strapped to her side. There were a few stakes, too, in the pockets of the jacket, for any young stakable vamps who crossed her path. Buffy's cross hung heavily around her neck.

"Where are you going?"

Grimloch's voice was sudden in the dark. She'd forgotten about him. Forgotten that he was there. She hadn't thought that was possible.

"You look . . ." he said, studying her. "All dressed up in a slayer's clothes."

Frankie snorted and raised her chin.

"I'm going back to the mansion. I'm going to take care of the Countess and the rest of her flunkies."

Grimloch's eyes narrowed, his features shadowed in the low beams of the streetlights.

"I'm going with you."

Frankie turned away. "No, you're not. There's a hole in you. Get back in the house."

"It's not a bad hole." He stepped off the patio and took the towel away from his chest to look at the fabric. The stain seemed mostly dry. Hunter gods healed fast.

"It's through your rib cage and into your chest," Frankie said.

"I'm a two-thousand-year-old immortal hunter demon. I've had worse. I'm coming with you. Either you welcome the company, or you go alone and I wait five minutes and follow right after."

"If you come with me, you'll die."

"Perhaps," he said. "But if I die bravely enough, I might be rewarded and join her, wherever she is. Or if nothing else, maybe she'll see, and find it worthy."

"Her," Frankie said. "You mean your slayer."

"Yes."

Frankie clenched her jaw. She couldn't bring herself to tell him what Xander had said. Like she couldn't bring herself to wake Hailey. Not yet. Not when she had so much work to do.

"You know she probably doesn't want you to die," Frankie said. "She probably wants you to live and not take stupid chances."

Grimloch shrugged and dabbed at the bit of blood produced by the movement. "It's my choice. My choice to take stupid chances, like the one you're taking." Frankie rolled her eyes and started to walk. She couldn't stop him from following. But once they reached the mansion, he was on his own.

"I've been taking these kinds of chances and making these choices since the day I was hatched," Grimloch said.

"Yeah, yeah," Frankie said. "Hang on, you were hatched? Like, from an egg?"

He shrugged again.

"So there are more of you?"

"If there are," he said, "I haven't run across any. And I vaguely remember eating the rest of the eggs in the clutch."

"You *ate* your brothers and sisters?" She drew one of her knives and pointed it at him in the dark. "Did you romance your slayer with stories like these?"

"I suppose so," he said, and chuckled. "When we first met, she saved me, so I owed her and saved her back. Then she saved me again. It became a competition between us, until it became something else. Until we realized that it was all either of us wanted to do."

"Sounds like a pretty sick game, if you ask me."

"Well, I didn't," he said. "And it's over now. I didn't save her from the explosion. So I guess she won."

"I didn't mean that," Frankie said, but Grimloch just kept walking. She needed to focus anyway. More vampires than she'd ever faced lay ahead, including one that wouldn't go down from a staking. She wished Jake and Spike and Hailey were there, and then hated herself for wishing it. She was the slayer. Buffy was gone. And it was time to grow up.

☽ ☽ ○ ☾ ☾

"Hailey! Hailey!"

Hailey woke to her name, shouted repeatedly in her ear, and also to what she thought was a rather violent shaking of her shoulders, considering what she'd just lived through and her many bruises.

"She's gone," Sigmund said, and ran his hands across his face. He'd been asleep, too, from the look of the book-shaped indentation in his cheek.

"Who's gone?" she asked.

"Frankie. She's gone, and so are all her knives." He gestured wildly toward the windows, which glowed with the first light of sunrise. "Along with the Hunter of Thrace. I think they went back to the mansion."

"Hang on." Hailey jumped up from the floor. "She's gone?"

"Gone and for who knows how long."

Hailey blinked. She'd never woken up so fully so quickly. Her eyes moved over the open books, the empty space where Frankie had been sitting. The empty chair where Grimloch had sat at the kitchen table. The slayer and her hole-y boyfriend were trying to ditch them.

"Grab weapons and get in the car," she said.

"Where are we going? To the library? To get Spike?"

"To the hospital to spring Jake." Frankie was trying to ditch him, too, and hell if Hailey was going to do the same. "I'll be down in a minute." She headed up the stairs to the guest room she'd been sleeping in.

"Wait, where are you going?"

She took the stairs by twos. "Honestly, Sigmund, I have to pee. And then I have to grab something I made for Frankie."

Five minutes later, they were on the road to the hospital. Fifteen minutes after that, they were parked illegally in a handicapped space, a fact that appeared to be giving Sigmund some kind of attack.

"Just stay with the car and move it if anyone comes along who *actually* needs it," Hailey ordered, and got out. It didn't take long to find Jake. He was standing outside the ER entrance in his ridiculous velvet-trimmed suit pants and bloodstained white shirt. She'd texted him to be ready; she just hadn't counted on him being ready so immediately.

"How'd you get out?"

"Wolf stealth." He shrugged with the shoulder on the side without the vampire bite. "Oz is passed out on the empty bed next to mine. He sleeps hard. I transferred the pulse-reading thingy and the sensors from me to him and crept out, past Willow draped over a very uncomfortable-looking chair. They're going to freak when they wake up. So? What's happening?"

"Frankie's decided to go it alone."

"Well, it shouldn't be hard to find her, since we know where she's headed." Jake rolled up his sleeves and sniffed the air, presumably searching for the scent of a Sage demon in an idling car. He caught it and started to jog around the side of the hospital to the space where they'd parked.

"Jake, are you sure you're okay?" Hailey asked. "Was I wrong to come and get you?"

"I'm fine," he said. "Many, many blood transfusions later. When it comes to Frankie, don't ever leave me behind."

☽ ☽ ◯ ☾ ☾

Frankie's shoulders scrunched the second she heard the vehicle driving up behind them. At that hour of early morning, on the secluded, winding hill road, it wasn't hard to figure out that she and Grimloch had just been caught. But she was surprised to see Jake hanging out the rear passenger window of Sigmund's car.

"Get in, loser," he said.

"Jake, you're out of the hospital." He had bandages on his neck, but he looked much better than when she'd seen him last. Much more lively. Much more annoying, just the way she liked him.

"Yeah. Jake." He pointed his thumb at his chest. "Remember me?"

Hailey rolled down her window. "And me."

357

"And me," said Sigmund, leaning over from the driver's side.

"Guess we caught you," Jake said. "You should have taken a car."

"I don't know how to drive."

"I know how to drive," Grimloch said unhelpfully.

"Then you should have said something." She narrowed her eyes at him, and he shrugged and dabbed at his wound.

Hailey got out of the car and jogged up beside them. "So what's the plan?"

"The plan is go home." Frankie turned her back and kept walking. "The plan is don't get you killed. Don't get Jake bit. Don't get Sigmund . . ." She wasn't sure what to say after that. She was pretty sure even if he came along, Sigmund would stay in the car.

"You can't just leave us behind!"

A door slammed, and Jake appeared on her other side, shouldering Grimloch out of the way. She heard another door shut softly after Sigmund parked the car. She glanced at Grimloch. "Can't you stop them?" she hissed.

"I could hobble them. Break one ankle apiece. It would slow them down, and they'd eventually heal."

Frankie scowled. "Just go home, you guys. This isn't your job. It's mine."

"You're not going in there alone," said Jake.

"I have to."

"Why? Because Buffy did? Tell that to your mom. Or Xander. Tell that to Oz. I seem to recall that in the stories they were always, you know, *in the stories*."

"Yeah," Hailey said. "You think Buffy could have beaten that government-experiment Frankenstein's-monster demon without your mom's magic? That was one story Vi did tell me."

"Or you think she could have taken out the Mayor Wilkins-snake without . . . the help of her entire graduating class?" Jake asked.

"It seems fairly clear," Sigmund said, "that what made Buffy Summers special wasn't just a superior ability. It was also her allies. Her friends."

"Her Scoobies," said Hailey, and shrugged. "Face it, Frankie. Buffy the Vampire Slayer was never alone, and Frankie the Vampire Slayer isn't going to be either."

Frankie felt a hard lump rise in her throat.

"But we're not Scoobies," she said softly, and swallowed. "We're not even really friends. We didn't choose each other. Jake's parents forced him to play with me. Hailey got dragged here by Spike. And, Sigmund, you're here as a favor to my mom."

"So what?" Jake asked. "So we didn't choose each other. Who really gets to choose their friends? If I could choose my friends I'd pick someone with a theater-grade gaming system and season tickets to the LAFC."

"I'd choose BTS," said Hailey.

"Um, I'd still choose you," Sigmund said. He pointed at Hailey and Jake. "You guys are jerks."

"Maybe," said Hailey. She looked at Frankie and cocked her head, and Frankie didn't know how Hailey's eyeliner still managed to be perfect when she'd just slept facedown in a book. "But we're your Scoobies. We're what you've got."

"I don't need your help," Frankie said gently. "I can do this on my own. I know I can."

"We know you can, too."

Frankie stopped and blinked at Jake. "You do?"

"You're the slayer," said Hailey. "This Countess does not know what she's stepping into."

"We know you can do it," said Jake. "You just . . . aren't going to do it without us."

Frankie shifted her weight. "I don't know what to say."

"Well, don't get too choked up," said Jake. "Because I'm still pissed about you trying to ditch us." He slipped his hand onto the back of Frankie's neck and tugged her close. "So go get in the car."

"Guys, wait." Frankie squirmed loose. "It's still too dangerous. There are way too many vampires in there for you to take on."

Grimloch stepped forward. "The fighting will be in close quarters. I've seen the catacombs and the halls are like tunnels in an ant farm."

"And of course it'll be pitch-dark down there," Hailey added.

"Catacombs," Frankie mused, and remembered what they'd seen during their recon: lots of vampires moving in and out of the mansion with picks and shovels. Is that what they were digging? Catacombs to house a hive of vampires? They really were like fangy little ants. "How many does it accommodate?"

"It was dug to house fifty."

Their eyes collectively widened. Fifty vampires.

"But it's not full. At its height, she had perhaps thirty fledglings, and you've taken out many in your attacks on the mansion and the feeding dance."

"You should start with the lower number next time," said Jake.

"And I don't understand," said Sigmund. "The vampire wants to be an apex predator. To populate to that degree—they would run out of prey in a matter of months. The entire city of Sunnydale would be picked clean to the bones."

"The Countess likes a hive," said Grimloch. "Virgins aren't easy to come by. She sends her workers out to different cities, different towns, to find them and lure them back."

"She's a virgin trafficker," said Frankie. "A trafficker of virgins."

Hailey nodded. "She has to die. Too bad she can't."

Frankie started to pace. The catacombs were a problem. She couldn't drag Jake and Hailey down into a space like that. It was darkness full of teeth, with a nasty, unkillable Countess chewy center. "The Countess will be down there, sleeping?"

"In the Queen's Chamber at the end of the catacombs." Grimloch nodded. "Recognizable by its large size. And the mural of the horse."

"You've seen her bedroom?" Hailey asked, and cocked an eyebrow while Frankie continued to pace.

"Even if we creep by undetected, the fight is going to make noise. The other vamps will wake and box us in. If only we could lure them out, take them out first somehow. And we're going to need light."

Sigmund raised a finger. "Light I could get you. All I need are several cheap bathroom mirrors. Egyptians used reflected sunlight to paint the walls of underground tombs. We could do the same and possibly give you some nice beams to burn a few with at the same time."

"But where are we going to find a bunch of bathroom mirrors?" Jake asked. "The hardware stores aren't even open yet."

"I know where," said Grimloch.

They loaded into the car and drove the rest of the way to the mansion, then parked in the driveway because why not? Grimloch led them around the side of the slope.

"There," he said. At the bottom of the slope was a quarry that looked to be serving as the Countess's personal dump. All manner of things from inside the mansion that she deemed unworthy had been thrown there, including several gaudy printed dresses, beach sandals, and a variety of bags and home decor.

"Is that a Prada backpack?" Hailey asked. "Oh my god, I'm coming back for it. Those things resell for like seven hundred bucks."

"Yeah. After we fight, there will be much looting. But first . . ." Jake pointed to the far end, and a pile of discarded mirrors.

"Why get rid of all of these?" Hailey asked. "Vampires don't even cast a reflection."

"That's exactly why," Grimloch replied. "She finds her lack of reflection depressing."

In the pit were mirrors of all sizes and shapes, from small and handheld to large silver rectangles that fit on the backs of vanities or hung upon walls. Many were broken, but many others were intact, including a swiveling cheval mirror housed in dark-colored wood.

"Perfect," said Sigmund. "I can work with that."

CHAPTER THIRTY-FOUR

A TOMB FULL OF BLOODSUCKERS

I nside, the mansion was deserted. Since it was daylight, the vamps had all bunkered down in the catacombs. It didn't take Sigmund long to set up a short, reflective line of mirrors from an eastward-facing window down to the opening of the catacombs. He would stay at the top and direct the sunlight down.

"Someone else will need to operate the mirror at the bottom. They should be able to reflect it right and left, up and down. But it won't have much range, as far as burning them is concerned. The scattered light should still give you something to go by, though. Maybe not far enough to reach the Queen's Chamber."

"Fighting the Countess in the dark only a few hours after she nearly killed me in a fully lit space?" Frankie nodded once. "Sounds smart." She turned to Jake. "I need you at the mirror."

"What? No way—"

"You're not at a hundred percent. I don't want to worry about you. Just stay at the mirror and use your lacrosse reflexes to burn vampires with reflected sunlight. And back up Sigmund. If any get past us, you need to keep them off him."

He glanced at the half Sage demon and nodded. Then he pushed Frankie affectionately. "But if you need me, shout a code word and I'll come running."

"What's the code word?"

"How about 'Jake, get your dumb ass over here'?"

"Great, that'll be like second nature." She studied his face a moment and was surprised by how well she knew it. The curve of his jaw. The slight crook in the bridge of his nose. The way his eyes wrinkled in the corners when he smiled. "I'm sorry I let you get bit."

"Me too. Don't let it happen again; I just got all this new blood like eight hours ago."

She turned to Hailey, who already had a stake in one hand and an open bottle of holy water in the other. "Oh shoot," Hailey said. "Hang on, I forgot something in the trunk." She turned and ran out of the mansion.

Grimloch stepped up to the ladder leading down. They wouldn't have much time when they hit the bottom. Down the opening, Frankie could see only a five-foot circle of light against the dirt floor.

"Five by five," she murmured. Jake and Sigmund would need to be fast with the mirrors.

"I'll go ahead," Grimloch said. "I can see in the dark." And then the demon dropped down into the hole, ignoring the ladder completely.

"Can that guy get any cooler?" Jake asked.

"Okay, I'm back!" Hailey ran up and held out Frankie's sparring stick. One end had been sharpened to a lethal point. "Nighttime whittling," she said. "Now you have a sparring stake."

Frankie spun it in her hands. She felt the tip. "Perfectly carved."

"Duh," said Hailey.

"Hailey—" Frankie stopped. She felt bad, not telling her about the call from Xander. But it wasn't the kind of news she needed to hear right before descending into a nest. "Thank you for staying in Sunnydale. Let's go kill some vampires."

They climbed down the hole, and when Jake hit the bottom, he called up to Sigmund and they swiveled their mirrors. It took a minute, but they got it in sync and produced a beam of relatively bright sunlight. Just in time to dust the fledgling vampire who'd been waiting in the shadows.

Past the first one, Frankie counted five more vampires clogging the path, fangs bared and vampiric faces on display. Three of them were in semiformal wear. Promise Dancers who'd been turned.

"Oh, damn," she whispered. But there was nothing they could do for them now. After the first vampire caught fire from Jake's sunbeam, the others scattered. Grimloch returned from farther down the tunnel and caught two around the neck. He pulled their heads off, and they collapsed into dust. The other two, both newly turned girls in blue dresses, were so put off by that that they ran back at Frankie and Hailey, who jumped out of the way so Jake could take them out with the light from the mirror.

"Sig, this works pretty sweet," Jake called up.

"But it won't take us far." Frankie peered down the dark corridor. She could just make out burial holes dug into the walls on both sides. A few had feet sticking out of them. Heavy-sleeping vamps? Or corpses that had yet to rise?

"Look at these sleeping conditions," Hailey said. "I'm claustrophobic just looking at them. They remind me of those capsule hotels in Japan." She walked to one that had feet and splashed some holy water onto the legs. They started to smoke, and the vampire started to scream. When he wriggled out of his sleeping hole, Hailey staked him cleanly through the chest. "Takes them some time to get out. That helps."

Farther into the catacombs, the path opened up on larger chambers. Already they were out of range of Jake's sunbeam, and it was harder and harder to see in the light cast from it.

"How long till we find the Countess?"

"Not much farther," said Grimloch. "Just through there . . ."

"You'll never reach the Countess."

Frankie turned just in time to see Grimloch be grabbed from behind by a burly pair of arms and dragged away into the dark.

"Grim!" She jumped forward half a step. Then she stopped as six pairs of yellow eyes emerged from the shadows, led by a tall, handsome vampire in a black suit. "Hey," she said. "Isn't that the vampire formerly known as track star Eric Sullivan?"

He didn't reply. The vampires attacked, and Frankie spun her sparring stick and went to work with the pointy end. She spun and struck with the sparring stick, knocking two vamps back with the blunt end only to twirl it like a baton and stake them with the sharp side half a second later. She used it to trip a third and reverse-kicked a fourth off-balance. She felt fast and focused. But none of these fledglings were the Countess.

Frankie turned as Hailey doused the fifth vampire with holy water; it was easy enough to stake it when it was steaming and clawing at its face. She looked around the chamber. All that remained was the vampire from her first patrol in the graveyard. UC Sunnydale.

"You go," Hailey said. "I've got this one."

"Are you sure?"

"I'm sure. Trust me."

Frankie nodded. "Use Jake's code word if you get into trouble," she said, and ran past the vampire into the darkness.

Hailey repositioned her grip on her stake. "UC Sunnydale," she said. "The one who got away."

"You," he said. "I remember you. From the cemetery. Where's your squirt gun full of holy water?"

Hailey narrowed her eyes. They circled each other and snarled. His snarls were better than hers. But at least the chamber was no open field. Those speedy legs of his would be less of an advantage this time around.

Hailey darted forward, and the vampire grabbed her and threw her against the wall. It hurt—nearly knocked the wind from her lungs, but she forced herself up and went straight back in, slashing with the stake.

She focused on attacking and landed a good kick to his midsection. It didn't move him like a slayer's would, but it wasn't bad. Another kick drove him back farther, and another got him nearly pinned to the wall. Then there'd be nothing left to do but drive the stake home.

"No running this time," she said.

He boosted a foot off the wall and vaulted himself over her head.

"I also used to pole-vault." He hit her in the jaw. She briefly saw stars and felt him lift her over his head. "And shot-put," he said, and threw her across the chamber. She landed hard, rolled, and felt the tip of her stake press dangerously into her own ribs. She grunted as he kicked her in the side, and lay on her stomach, panting. It was too soon to feel it, but her whole body was going to hurt later, if she lived.

"You know, I ought to thank you," he said. "I forgot how much I used to love track practice."

She tried to catch her breath, listening to him pace and crack his knuckles.

"I was never very good at the long jump. But maybe now . . ."

He planted both feet and leapt, readying to land on her back with his whole weight.

Hailey rolled out of the way and grabbed his ankles when they hit the ground. She yanked them out from under him and propelled herself up to drive her stake through his undead heart.

"Will you cool it with the track stuff?" she shouted at his dust. Then she collapsed. "God, I hate sports."

$$\text{☽ ☽ ○ ☾ ☾}$$

Frankie ran long after she had outrun the reach of the light, following the sounds of Grimloch fighting with his unseen assailant, who she suspected was the tall vampire they'd seen the first night at the Countess's side. Her right-hand man, as it were. And probably her strongest soldier. She took a slow breath and tried to calm the beating of her heart. Grimloch was a millennia-old demon. He would be able to handle one vampire. Or he usually could, when he didn't have a door to his beating heart standing wide open in his chest.

She took another step, listening to the scrape of her shoe against the dirt. She needed to be able to see. The dark was too total to fight in, and she and Spike hadn't done any training while blindfolded.

From somewhere ahead, Grimloch bellowed, and Frankie darted forward and ran straight into a wall. This wasn't going to work.

Use your magic! she could almost hear Jake say.

It was probably a dumb idea. Upstairs in the mansion, Sigmund's stomach probably started rumbling the minute she thought of it. Her mom had never told her, and Frankie didn't think she understood the scale anyway, but her witchcraft proficiency level had to be about a two.

"Mom," she whispered. "Lend me a little of your juice."

She concentrated. Breathed slow. When doubt crept in, she forced it out. And soon enough, she felt the magic rising in her blood, bubbling in her chest like a warm cauldron.

"*Fiat lux.*"

The chamber filled with soft, reddish light. An odd, unnatural light, as it seemed to have no source but itself. But at least she could see. And what she saw immediately was that she was standing in the Queen's Chamber. And that it was empty except for the giant horse mural on the wall, which she had to admit was kind of nice.

"Where's the Countess?" she asked.

"Gone."

Grimloch shoved a vampire through the chamber's doorway so hard that he bounced off the crate full of dirt. It was a strange thing to have in a sleeping chamber, but it must have been special dirt, because the crate that held it had been draped with silver silk.

"I know this one," Frankie said, and pointed at it. "This is the way Dracula traveled. All safe and tucked into the dirt of his homeland. I always heard that didn't do any good."

"It does plenty of good." The vampire got up off the floor and brushed daintily at the knees of his pants. Surprisingly daintily, considering his size. He was as tall as Grimloch and more broad-shouldered. Much more muscular. But there he stood with a bloodied lip and blackening eyes, while Grimloch remained alive, heart intact.

"I heard you bellow," said Frankie. "Thought you were in trouble."

"Victory bellow," he said. "I never liked this guy."

Hailey ran into the chamber, stake raised, then quickly lowered it when she saw them. "UC Sunnydale is dust." She looked around the chamber. "Nice light." She nodded to the wall. "Big horse. Where's the Countess?"

"That's what we're about to find out." Frankie struck the vampire hard in the chest with the blunt end of her sparring stick. With one end sharpened to a point, it barely looked like a sparring stick anymore, just a very large, long stake. She aimed the pointy end at the vampire's heart.

"You're too late," he said. "She's already gone up."

"Gone up?" Frankie asked. "Gone up where?"

"To kill your Watcher."

"Spike?"

"He's safe," said Hailey. "He's at the library, which is by now in broad daylight."

The vampire laughed. Grimloch lifted him up and shoved him against the wall.

"What's so funny?" Frankie asked.

"You think the daylight will help your Watcher? You think it will keep him safe?" His icy eyes enjoyed only torment and had seen enough of it over the years to have actually grown bored. But when he looked at Frankie, his eyes twinkled. "Virgins' blood. Drink enough of it, and it instills all sorts of little perks."

Frankie realized what he meant. She turned back the way they'd come.

"Grab him." She ran out of the chamber. "Throw a blanket over him and take him with us in case we need to trade. We have to get to Spike." They had already taken too long. The Countess was going to find him. She was going to get to him.

"Frankie!" Hailey ran after her, and Grimloch, too, dragging the vampire farther behind. "What's going on? Spike's at the library. He's safe."

"No, he's not," Frankie said as she hurried past burial chambers to Jake and Sigmund at the mirrors. "The Countess is a friggin' daywalker."

370

The Countess liked the new car. It was small, and fast, and sporty. Black, like her old horse, Lavinia. And easy to drive in heels. She'd changed out of her gold dress—which was ruined, stained, and ripped, with a nasty hole right over the heart—and into something a little more comfortable: a cream pantsuit over a peach silk blouse. She could have been on her way to a society luncheon in that suit. She could have been a senator. But she was only going to kill a vampire.

Normally she didn't like to kill vampires. They were her kind. Lesser than she was, certainly, but still her kind. She tended to look upon them as her children, even the ones she didn't sire. Every one her watered-down, bloodsucking kin. But this one was different. This one was a Watcher. He had a soul. His very existence made her cold with rage. She would have killed him eventually, anyway. The little slayer had merely moved it up on the calendar.

She parked the car in the lot of New Sunnydale High School and stepped out. The library wouldn't be hard to find—books had a particular smell, and this library was full of old and particularly pungent volumes. She let her nose lead the way, keeping to the outdoor paths for as long as she could before going inside. The day was so fresh and bright. Artificial light was a wonder, but nothing really compared to the sun, and it had been so long since she'd been strong enough to dare it.

When she reached the doors of the library, she almost knocked. The school was so clean and quiet on a Sunday morning that to *do anything else seemed impolite. But then she remembered what awaited her inside, and blew the doors off their hinges instead, with one fierce kick.*

The vampire jumped up from the table where he'd sat surrounded by open books and a computer with a bright white screen. Modern humans. Staring at those things was bound to make them blind.

"William the Bloody."

"Countess."

He looked terrible. Nearly too bleary-eyed to even be surprised. But he still backed up. Smart boy.

"I know I've been away for a while," she said, "but you still don't look like a librarian to me."

He was dressed all in black: black T-shirt, black jeans, big black boots.

"Well, it's a Sunday. Usually I'm in tweed. . . . It just . . . bloody itches. . . ." He backed up again. "How'd you find me? Come up through the tunnels?"

"I came across the front lawn." She leapt to him, up over tables, and grabbed him by the throat. "Why don't you try it?" She held him up a moment, enjoying his feeble kicks and the way he gurgled and flopped like a caught fish, and then she threw him hard, right through the large glass windows and into the sunlight.

It was over too soon. She instantly regretted not torturing him a little—the muscle in her arm was still springy with unused adrenaline. But what was done was done.

She waited for the screaming to start, and the smoke, and the delicious, greasy-smelling flames. That would have to be satisfaction enough. Except the vampire didn't burn.

"Interesting."

She followed him out the window and snagged him by the back of his collar when he tried to run.

"You're not on fire," she said.

"So what? You're not either," he replied.

"Is it the soul?" She sniffed at his skin. He didn't smell of good blood, of good feeding. Who knows how long it had been since he'd had a decent meal from a human source? So he certainly hadn't been drinking virgins.

"Yeah, it's the soul. It protects me. Sucks to be you." He put on a decent show, nostrils flaring, indignant over his obvious fear. But she knew a lie when she heard one.

She turned him right and left, inspecting him for charms or protective marks. She scanned the sky and saw nothing but the bright and normally blistering sun. Except there—she narrowed her eyes as she looked across the grounds of the school. There, at the edge, there was a disturbance in the air. A slight shimmer. As if from a border of magic.

"The witch," she said. "She enchanted the school. Very clever. Lets you have the run of the place to help her slayer child, yet keeps you set in one spot . . . doesn't let you fully off your leash."

"I don't need a leash." The upstart vampire twisted in her grip and drove his elbow into her eye, hard enough to make her drop him. But only for a second. He kicked and punched, and she didn't bother dodging. But she did squeeze his throat when his blows made her dizzy. She wanted to tear his head clean off, but she'd come with a plan and she'd never been one to deviate.

"You're going to burn," she said, and pointed a manicured finger at him. "All your witch friend bought you was a few hundred yards."

CHAPTER THIRTY-FIVE

ALL THE COOLEST VAMPIRES ARE DAYWALKERS

"Sig, drive faster!" Frankie shouted from the passenger seat. "If I drive any faster, we'll flip." Sigmund gritted his teeth as they took another curve, tires squealing. He was probably right. And that would be bad, considering he was the only one currently wearing a seat belt. Hailey was wedged onto the center console between him and Frankie, her hands slapping the dash in agitation and also in an attempt to hold on. As for the rest of them . . . the vampire tied up under the blanket was too big to fit in the trunk, so he was in the backseat with Grimloch and Jake. And Jake had to sit on his lap.

As they neared the school, Frankie tightened her grip on her sparring stick, which hung out the open window. They had to make it in time. She needed her Watcher. But more than that, she needed her uncle Spike.

"When we get there I'm jumping out running. The rest of you stay back and guard the prisoner."

"Frankie, no way," Jake started.

"I mean it, Jake. She's too strong. She'll kill you in one hit."

"She'll kill you, too," said Grimloch. "If you face her alone."

She looked back at him. He wasn't afraid for her. There were no tortured glances or silent pleas for her to stay. He was just stating a fact.

"On any other day," she said, "that would be true."

He blinked slowly. Then he nodded. "If you die, I'll help your friends to escape."

"Thanks," she said. It was what she'd wanted him to say. But it still made her want to throw up a little.

"And then, after I've healed, I'll come back and grind the Countess into paste for you."

"Right, got it." She turned around in her seat. Sigmund hit the brakes hard and Tokyo Drifted around the last turn to the school. She heard him mutter, "Not bad for a hybrid," and wasn't sure if he meant the car or his half-demon self.

"There they are!" Hailey pointed to the sports field. The Countess had Spike by the collar, dragging him behind her across the grass. She had him but he was alive, and Frankie's heart thudded with relief.

"She's taking him to the end." Jake leaned into the crowded front seat. "Frankie, the spell—the school boundary—is it the parking lot or the end of the field?"

"I don't know. Slow down, Sig." She opened her door as he eased his foot onto the brake. "Time to roll."

She had a half second to look at the speed of the pavement going by beneath them, and less than that to consider how many sharp knives she currently had strapped to her person, each one ready to slice an artery if she landed wrong, before she dove and tucked and popped up running. All without letting go of her stick. She leapt onto the sidewalk and over the fence that divided the track from the bleachers, her pace increasing as she closed in on the Countess and

Spike. The Countess had seen them coming—their burning-rubber entrance into the empty parking lot had been hard to miss—but it didn't matter. Frankie was going to make it. She was going to get there in time. And she was going to put a footprint in the ass of that really nice cream-colored suit.

"Little slayer," the Countess called. "Come to say goodbye to your Watcher?"

Frankie didn't reply. There was no time for quipping. There was only the wind in her ears and the pounding of her feet across the ground. In the Countess's grip, Spike saw her coming, and his mouth quirked into a familiar smile. Until the Countess hauled him up over her shoulders.

"I've never been one for long goodbyes." She threw him. Impossibly high. Impossibly far. Frankie heard Hailey scream, "No!" as Spike flew. Or maybe it wasn't Hailey at all. Maybe it was her own voice she heard.

Frankie's knees buckled, and she hit the grass. She could see it even though it hadn't happened yet: his face as he crossed the boundary of the spell, and the explosion of the flames. He would be ash before he hit the ground.

Or he would have been, had someone not leapt up and caught him.

"What?" Frankie and the Countess asked together.

The rescuer landed on the field in a crouch, Spike in her arms only lightly smoking. The vampire seemed dazed—she set him down gently in the grass and stalked toward Frankie and the Countess.

"Who are you?" the Countess demanded. "The witch?"

But while her mom was many things, Frankie had never known her to be able to jump like that. She stared at the figure coming toward them in a black hooded sweatshirt and jeans, hood pulled down to shadow her face, and a scarf hiding her mouth like a mask. Frankie's heart rose into her throat.

"Buffy?"

The figure broke into a run. She headed straight for the Countess and drove into her with leaping punches and spinning kicks. She deftly ducked every counterblow, and her punches spun the Countess like a top, keeping her off-balance. She landed hit after hit, a hook that led into a spinning heel kick, so fast that it was almost as if her feet never touched the ground.

"Aunt Buffy," Frankie whispered, because who else could it be? The fighter she was watching was a real slayer, the kind that Frankie had grown up idolizing, the kind she had watched with stars in her eyes. The slayer she was watching was a hero.

The Countess staggered, and the slayer reared back with a stake. The scarf she wore fell away to reveal her face, and Frankie's heart sank. It wasn't Buffy. This slayer had pale, pale skin and dark hair. Frankie recognized her from the pictures on Hailey's phone. The slayer drove the stake into the Countess's heart, and backed off, waiting for dust.

"No!" Frankie scrambled to her feet. "That doesn't work!"

Vi looked at her, puzzled, just as the Countess struck her across the cheek and sent her flying.

$$\supset \; \supset \; \bigcirc \; \subset \; \subset$$

"Vi!" Hailey screamed. She jerked forward, and Jake and Sigmund held her back. "Let go of me! That's my sister! That's Vi!"

But they didn't let go. They'd all seen the miraculous save she'd pulled, snatching Spike right out of the sky. And then they'd stood dumbfounded as she gave the Countess the beating of her immortal life. Hailey hadn't dared hope, until she saw her face. She hadn't dared, even though the shape and the movements were so familiar. But it was her. Her sister was alive.

"Your sister is alive," Grimloch murmured. He sounded shocked, near to the point of numbness, and Hailey knew how he felt. "But if she is alive . . ."

Hailey glanced at him just in time to see their captive vampire take advantage of Grimloch's distraction and twist free, running toward the bleachers for the protection of the shade. Jake and Sigmund tensed to go after him, then changed their minds. There were more important things going on. They'd get him back later.

"Vi's alive," she said dreamily.

"Yeah," Jake said as they watched the Countess punch Vi across the field and pluck the stake from her own chest. "And hopefully she'll stay that way for more than the next ten minutes."

$$\unicode{x263D}\ \unicode{x263D}\ \unicode{x25CB}\ \unicode{x263E}\ \unicode{x263E}$$

Frankie joined the fray with a leaping kick to the Countess's back, which sent her lurching forward but wasn't quite enough to knock her to her knees. It was enough, however, to allow for a few seconds to run to Vi and help her to her feet.

"I didn't miss the heart," Vi said. "But I'm guessing you already knew that."

"Yeah, I tried the whole staking thing already. Doesn't work with this one."

They righted themselves and took a breath as the Countess approached, a look of less-than-happiness on her face.

"Got any other plans?"

"Just one," said Frankie. "Follow my lead."

They spread out to flank her, with one in front and one behind. But the Countess wouldn't allow it. She was blazingly fast and too strong to dare taking a clean punch from. Somehow she managed to keep them both at bay. Actually she managed more than that, and in less than a minute, both slayers found themselves side by side on their backs.

Vi grunted angrily. "This chick's tough. What was that plan again?"

They flipped back onto their feet, and Frankie tried to slow the Countess's advance with a blow from her sparring stick only to have it knocked out of her hands.

"I wasn't planning on killing you today, little one," the Countess said. "But it was rude of you to hide your friend from me."

"Wasn't intentional; I thought she was dead." With a heave, she kicked the Countess in the chin.

The three fought, blows coming faster and faster, and Frankie began to tire. She'd just had a long battle in the mansion catacombs, and she'd had to do a spell, and she'd had no sleep since being nearly obliterated by the Countess at the Promise Dance the night before. But even if she had been fresh, she would have still been tired. She was new at this, not seasoned enough to fight for hours like Vi. And who knew how long it would be before the Countess's batteries started to flicker, after just drinking all those fresh partygoers. She'd meant to wear the Countess down a little. But that just wasn't in the cards.

Frankie drew the long blade at her side and darted in while the Countess was occupied with Vi. She moved fast but carefully. If the Countess turned the blade around on her, it was over.

The Countess struck Vi in the chest and sent her flying backward. She grabbed Frankie by the wrist and studied her lack of reflection in the shining metal.

"That's a very big knife you have. But an ax would be better if you're aiming to cut my head off."

"I'm not as fast with an ax." Frankie pulled another knife out of the sheath at her belt and tossed it to Vi, who leapt back in and swung it in a sharp arc.

The Countess raised her hand to block it and missed. She looked slightly confused as three of her fingers fell into the grass and bounced lightly. Vi also looked confused. The fingers remained fingers; they didn't turn to ash.

"Gross." Frankie made a face. She tried to pull her knife hand free, but the Countess wrenched the blade loose and knocked her to the grass. Then she threw Frankie's knife across the field. Frankie popped up and drew another, only to have it, too, stripped from her hand and thrown. The sight of her own blood had made the Countess furious—she grabbed Vi by the wrist and held her fast as she punched again and again; it didn't take long for Vi to fall and for Vi's knife to be thrown across the field, too.

"I liked this suit," the Countess said, not at all out of breath. "And my gold dress. And my fingers. But I don't need all of my fingers to beat you to death."

Frankie pushed up onto her knees. Her bones ached. Her gut felt like a swollen bruise. She tasted blood on the back of her tongue. And she had no knives left.

She was the first slayer-witch. She was the daughter of Willow. But she'd never lived up to that, never been anything special. She was only Frankie. Doubt filled her heart with every ragged pant. With every tremble of her hands.

Let it go, she heard Buffy say. *You have to let it all go.*

The Countess raised her hands over her head, and Frankie closed her eyes.

She reached out with her mind and called her knives back.

When the Countess slammed her fists down, Frankie rolled left and sliced the Countess's thumb off below the knuckle.

"You little brat!" the Countess cried, and knocked the knife again from Frankie's hand.

Frankie called it back before it hit the grass. She twisted and cut, twisted and cut, the blades arcing and singing through the air as they were thrown and recalled. She pushed off the ground and threw her knives high out of the Countess's reach only to use her magic to drive them down through the Countess's arms and back into Frankie's grip. For the first time, the two halves of her that had felt like mismatched puzzle pieces clicked into place. Her slayer power and her witch magic danced, as in sync with each other as she was with her own shadow.

"Vi!"

Frankie sent another knife slicing through the air to the other slayer. Vi caught it and both slayers went on the attack. Using her magic to guide them made Frankie's two knives as effective as twenty, and when she bent and called her blade down low, dragging it across the back of the Countess's knee, the vampire buckled.

The Countess was weakening. Vi saw it, too, and together they cut even faster.

Finally, one of the Countess's punches went wide, and Frankie caught hold of her hand. She used her knife to stab through the wrist, splitting the joint, and sliced through the dangling skin until she was holding the Countess's detached hand in her own.

"My hand!" The Countess reached back, but Vi was there to catch her wrist and do the same to the other side.

"Yes!" Jake yelled. "And also, ew!"

Frankie looked toward the bleachers, surprised. She hadn't realized that the fight had taken them so far across the field.

Then the Countess bared her teeth, and the detached hand Frankie was holding sprang loose and went for her throat. She held it off but just barely—it was surprisingly strong for a disembodied hand—and stabbed it into the ground, pinning it there like an insect in a display case.

"Watch yourself," she called to Vi. "Even the pieces fight back."

Vi nodded, and the slayers kept on cutting, dismantling the Countess bit by bit. It was hard, grisly work, especially when they neared the end. By the time they were finished, bits of the Countess lay everywhere: her legs below the knee, her left arm from the elbow, and the right from the shoulder. Her head had been separated from her torso and lay upside down, glaring at them, still alive. But even worse were the smaller pieces. Countess meat squares in the grass. Frankie had never been one to partake in the school cafeteria's poke days, but after seeing that, she doubted that Jake and Hailey would either. Kabobs might have also been off the menu.

The slayers looked at each other and stepped away from the mess, watching their step to keep from getting Countess on the bottoms of their shoes.

"Not bad, little slayer," Vi said. "I guess the rumors are true."

"What rumors?"

"About the first slayer being called in years. About her being . . . more . . . than what we bargained for."

"More?" Frankie asked. "And we? Who is 'we'? Did more slayers survive with you?"

"Vi!" Hailey shouted.

Frankie brightened. She may have been standing in the midst of the grossest still-living carnage she could imagine, but seeing the sisters reunited would make it all worthwhile. Except Vi didn't run into Hailey's waiting arms. Instead, she backed up a step. And then another.

"Vi?" Hailey asked.

"Look after her," Vi said to Frankie.

"Wait—" Frankie blinked. "You're going? But how did you survive? Who else—"

"You'll find out soon enough," Vi said. She turned and ran, even though Hailey yelled, "Stop!" and "Wait!" She tried to catch her, but she couldn't catch a slayer. Vi dove into the trees at the edge of the field, and disappeared.

"Why did she go?" Hailey asked when Frankie, Sigmund, and Jake had caught up. Grimloch had come, too, and seemed almost as bewildered as Hailey. "She didn't even speak to me."

"I don't know," Frankie said. "But we'll figure it out, I promise."

"The important thing is, she's alive," said Sigmund, and touched Hailey's arm gently.

Hailey stared at the place in the trees where her sister had gone, and Frankie reached out and touched her other arm. The brightness in Hailey's eyes at seeing Vi slowly faded and turned hard. Her mouth turned down at the corners. But she didn't cry.

"Yeah," she said in a tough tone that sounded like it had had a lot of practice. "That's the important thing."

"Guys?" Jake turned and jogged back to the remains of the Countess. He jumped back when one of the legs tried to kick. "Guys! Where's the head?"

They ran back to take a quick inventory of the pieces, but it didn't take long to see what he meant. The Countess's head was gone.

"The head is gone." Grimloch looked toward the bleachers. "And so is Anton."

"Who's Anton?" Jake asked.

"What can he do with the head?" asked Frankie. "Can he bring her back? Even without all of this?" She gestured to the legs, the arms, the rest.

"If he can, it will take a long time," said Grimloch. "By the time she regenerates, you'll be too old to fight her. Or long dead. Even if he packs her in Hungarian dirt."

"It'll be another slayer's problem," said Spike. "If there is another slayer."

"Spike." Frankie went to her Watcher as he limped toward her, and threw her arms around his midsection.

"Quite the mess you've made," he said. "Good work, Mini Red."

Frankie looked down upon the pieces of the Countess. She didn't feel elated or energized by the victory. She felt exhausted. And a little weird, as the Countess's right hand had started to make very offensive gestures at them.

"In every generation," she mused. "Maybe we should leave a note with the Watchers Council. About how to beat her if she comes back again." She looked at her friends and sighed. "But for now, I could totally go for some pie."

CHAPTER THIRTY-SIX

CHOSEN ONE. AND CHOSEN TWO. AND CHOSEN THREE, FOUR, FIVE.

The pie was a delight. They got three kinds from the bakery in town: warm apple with a crumble top, blueberry with an almond crust, and chocolate cream, and watching Grimloch prod a fork awkwardly at ribbons of chocolate shavings greatly elevated Frankie's mood. Of course, pie couldn't last all day, and afterward they had to return to the school and gather up every last piece of the Countess, which they all agreed was the worst egg hunt ever.

When they got back to Frankie's house, Willow and Oz were waiting and more than a little pissed about Jake's disappearing act from the hospital. But when they were presented with squirming bags of dismembered vampire, they put their parental rage on hold.

"Also, if you grounded me right now I don't think I'd remember it when I woke up," Frankie said as her mom hugged her. "I haven't slept in dozens and dozens of hours."

"Go," her mom said. She looked at the others. "All of you go. Get some sleep. You all have raccoon eyes."

"Yeah." Oz held up a sack of Countess parts. "And when you

wake up, you can tell us all about these fun, literal grab bags." He poked at the side, and the contents jumped back at him. "Sigmund, you can come crash at our place."

Sigmund nodded and whispered to Hailey, who nodded back. Then he left with the werewolves.

"I'm going to catch a few winks in the basement," Spike said, and went down without another word. Hailey shook her head before anyone could ask a thing about Vi and headed up to her room. That left Grimloch, and Frankie, and her mom.

After a few moments of strange, charged silence, Willow hefted the bags of Countess parts and gestured toward the kitchen. "I'll just—er—go put these in there."

Once Willow was gone, Grimloch took a step closer.

"Frankie—" Grimloch began, but she held up her hands.

"Can we just talk later? I know there are things . . . because of Vi, and what it means. But I'm way too exhausted to even remember anything you say to me right now."

He smiled a little, just enough to show the tips of his fangs. It spoke to just how strange her life was that she found the fangs cute rather than odd in his otherwise all-too-human face.

"All right. Come and find me when you're feeling better. I'll be at the Succoro's tent."

After he was gone, Frankie hauled herself into the kitchen to face her mom.

"Mom," she said quietly. "Xander called. Faith—"

"I know, sweetie. I saw his messages on my phone."

"But now Vi's here—alive. Could he have been wrong?"

"Sadie said she saw Faith die. Saw the explosion. Vi must have been the one to use the portal to Sunnydale."

"But why didn't she tell us? And could anyone else have made it out with her?"

"That's what we have to get to the bottom of," her mom said.

But not now. Now Frankie was nearly out on her feet.

They slept for most of the day and emerged one by one, stretching and yawning, even Spike. Oz, Jake, and Sigmund returned from their place and assembled in the kitchen to help dispose of Countess parts. Frankie grabbed a quick shower and joined them. Her sleep had been deep and dreamless. Yet somehow she was still tired.

She walked into the kitchen and almost immediately walked back out. Willow had taken the Countess out of the bags and spread her across the table and countertops. It looked like the case at the grocery store's meat department except that some of the meat was wearing a really nice pantsuit.

"You're awake," her mom said. "Are you feeling better?"

"Some," said Frankie.

Jake squinted at the carnage. "What do we do with all of this? And what do we do about the slayers? If Hailey's sister is alive, what does that mean for the others? And why didn't she stick around?"

"I guess that solves the mystery of who took a portal to Sunnydale," said Oz.

"But why did she stay hidden?" Spike frowned. "And why didn't she contact me? I'm her Watcher; she's supposed to report!"

"The important thing is, she made it." Frankie looked at her mom. "And if she made it, maybe others made it, too. Maybe Buffy," she said, and Willow and Spike looked at each other.

"They're probably still dealing with whatever caused the blast," said Hailey. "And that's why my sister couldn't stay."

"But why not tell you that?" Jake asked.

Hailey shrugged. Her lips were a firm, grim line. "She must have had her reasons."

"She did," Frankie agreed. "And we know one thing: She was keeping tabs on you. Making sure you were safe."

"That's true," said Sigmund. "Her arrival was more than timely."

But Hailey didn't look convinced, and Frankie couldn't blame her. She knew how she would feel if Buffy had saved them and disappeared with no explanation.

"Look," Spike said. "We will find out what happened and what is happening to the slayers. I for one never thought it could be that easy: one explosion, boom, no slayers? Buffy'd have . . . they'd have all been too sharp for that. Something larger is afoot, and for the time being, we have to trust them to handle it. They're slayers; they're not bloody children. So let's deal with the problem at hand." He snatched up one of the Countess's hands, which was discreetly trying to creep away across the counter.

"Well, I've been tinkering with that problem while you were all sleeping," Willow said.

Frankie looked at her mom. Willow had on her most nerdy-smart face, excited and a little bouncy. Oz was watching, too, and hid his smile as she approached the pieces and picked up two small chunks.

"See, they won't just smoosh back together." She squished the two bits into each other, and everyone winced. "Not unless you find the right two pieces." She searched a moment, and then pushed another two pieces together. They fused like drops of oil.

"Whoa," said Jake.

"Right. So we want to keep them away from their adjacent parts. That's why I arranged them like this. No hands next to wrists, no legs next to feet. Also, I've noticed that while they are still 'alive'"—she made air quotes around "alive"—"they appear to be slowing down. The hands aren't as grabby, and the legs aren't as kicky. Which is nice."

"Do we know why that is?" Oz asked. "Will the pieces eventually die?"

"From what we know of the Countess, I doubt it," said Spike. "But they might go dormant. Or maybe it just means that her head is sleeping, wherever it is."

"They also seem to be decreasing in awareness of each other," Willow went on. "Like, at first if I poked one of the legs, one of the hands would give me the finger. But now . . ." She prodded a leg and waited. Neither hand so much as twitched.

"So what does that mean?" Hailey asked, glumly. "Is that good?"

"It's very good. At least I think so. It means we should be able to hide them, and she shouldn't be able to sense where they are to put herself back together. But just to be safe, we should get all these pieces out of here, pretty quickly."

"Teleportation spell?" Spike asked.

"I was thinking parcel post."

"We could send one of the legs to Weretopia," Oz offered.

"Won't they just eat it?" asked Jake. "Unkillable meat might seem like a delicacy. But I bet it gives wicked stomachaches."

"We'll include a note," said Oz.

"I can send one to my mom for safekeeping," said Sigmund. "She has a vault."

Frankie reached for one of the Countess's hands. It squeezed her back, probably meaning to hurt, but in its weakened state, it only managed a gentle embrace. She stroked the manicured nails softly. It was actually kind of sad.

"I'll bring this one to Grimloch. I need to see him, and I think he'll be headed off soon to somewhere suitably far away." She looked at her mom. "When I get back, maybe you can show me how to teleport the rest of the pieces?" Her mom looked nervous, but she nodded.

"Not all the pieces, though." Willow picked up a small sliver and turned it over in the light. "I mean, I can't help but wonder what kind of potions could be brewed from bits of this. The sheer power in them . . . I'm going to keep some back and bring a few to the lab. You know, for science."

☽ ☽ ○ ☾ ☾

Grimloch was waiting inside the Succoro demon's old tent. She couldn't tell if he'd rested; she didn't even know if he slept. But he had changed his shirt.

"New shirt," she said, and pointed to it. "I like it."

It was gray, and he'd paired it with a brown scarf. "I found it here. The Succoro and I were the same size. I didn't think it would mind." Though it probably would have minded, since Grimloch was the one who killed it. He smoothed the buttons. "I wasn't sure about the color."

"I mostly like that you can't see the hole through your rib cage," Frankie said.

He smiled. "That will be healed in a week. The scar gone in a month."

"Brought you a souvenir," she said, and handed him the Countess's hand, wrapped in a dish towel and tied with a few of Frankie's shoelaces. "It's the same one that punched right through you."

"Very thoughtful. Thank you."

"We were hoping you could take it away for us. Hide it somewhere."

"I'll take it far away and bury it deep." He set the package aside and looked at her. It wasn't easy to hold still under the weight of those eyes, but for the first time, she didn't feel like she was lacking. "You did it, Frankie. You stopped her."

"Didn't kill her, though. You were right about that." She stepped closer and touched her fingers to his chest. It was solid, already healing. He had no reason to stay, no need of looking after. "So I guess you're going to go and look for her. Your slayer."

"I am," he said. But he didn't move away.

"How far?" she asked, voice light. "I mean, how far are you going?"

"I don't know. It's not really a question of how far. It's a question of how long."

"So how long?"

He looked down. He didn't seem to want to go, and that gave her hope. Though maybe he didn't want to go because he feared the answers that he would find. Even she feared the answers he might find. That Buffy and all the others were really gone.

"I'll go as far as I need to go, to know."

She nodded. "If she's alive. I get it. You must . . . really love her."

"I do."

She looked around the Succoro's tent. Already it looked less lived in and more abandoned. Pretty soon coming back would be depressing, unless she and Hailey fixed it up and kept on using it for things. Funny how fast a place turned sad and sour when it was empty.

"Then I hope you find her," she said brightly. "I guess I'll miss you; you've been kind of a good guy to have around." Not that they were friends or anything. Not that they could ever be more than that.

"I'll go for as far as I need, until I know," he said. "Or until you need me."

She looked up. "How will you know if I need you?"

He smiled. "I'm the Hunter of Thrace. I'll have one eye on the horizon. And one ear on you. Just don't get into any trouble, to try to lure me back."

"I would never!" She headed for the tent flap before he could see her exalted grin. He wouldn't be gone forever. She would see him again.

"Frankie," he said, and she paused. "You did well. You fought like one of them. Like a real slayer."

"Good," she said. "Because I am one."

ACKNOWLEDGMENTS

Holy crap, I got to write a Buffy book! This is ridiculous, and there are so many people to thank. First up: the fabulous editor Jocelyn Davies! Thank you for thinking of me for this project, and for geeking out on phone calls as we brainstormed our way through this first installment and mused on the high value of California real estate. I mean, sinkhole or no sinkhole, Sunnydale was going to be redeveloped.

Also a big thank-you to another excellent editor, Kieran Viola! Thank you for the amazing interim edit and for geeking out via email and all the moments of "Can you believe this is our job? EEEE!"

As always, big props to my eternally savvy agent, Adriann Ranta Zurhellen at Folio Literary Management. There is no better industry expert, and thank you for helping me find room in my schedule because one does not say no to Buffy.

Thank you to the entire team at Hyperion for keeping the Slayerverse going! And finally, thank you to the cast and crew of *Buffy the Vampire Slayer* for the show and the characters that I, and so many others in the world, never really got over. Buffy fans. For life.